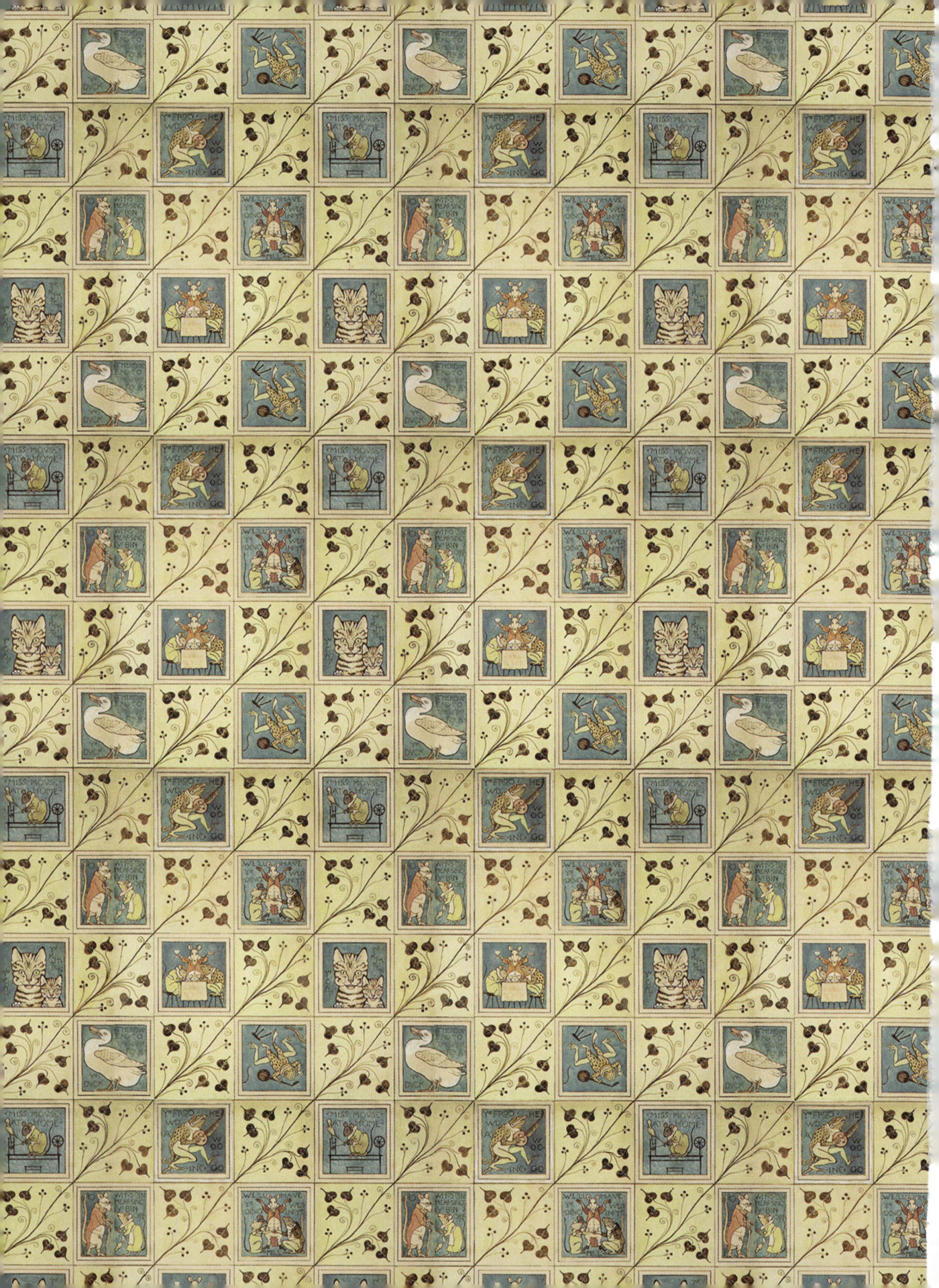

A
Treasury of Best-Loved
Fairy Tales

A Treasury of Best-Loved Fairy Tales

BARNES & NOBLE
NEW YORK

Compilation © 2018 Sterling Publishing Co., Inc.
Cover design and endpapers © 2018 Sterling Publishing Co., Inc.

All rights reserved. No part of this publication may be reproduced, stored in a retrieval system, or transmitted in any form or by any means (including electronic, mechanical, photocopying, recording, or otherwise) without prior written permission from the publisher.

This 2018 edition printed for Barnes & Noble Booksellers, Inc.
by Sterling Publishing Co., Inc.

ISBN 978-1-4351-6729-2

Manufactured in China

1 3 5 7 9 10 8 6 4 2

Cover illustration: Laurel Long
Cover design: Patrice Kaplan
Interior design: Kevin Ullrich
Endpapers: The Stapleton Collection/Bridgeman Images

Contents

CINDERELLA
    Illustrated by Arthur Rackham 1

THE TINDER-BOX
    Illustrated by Harry Clarke 10

HANSEL AND GRETEL
    Illustrated by Charles Robinson 18

THE UGLY DUCKLING
    Illustrated by Charles Robinson 28

RAPUNZEL
    Illustrated by Arthur Rackham 36

THE SEVEN VOYAGES OF SINBAD
    Illustrated by René Bull 42

THE GOLDEN GOOSE
    Illustrated by L. Leslie Brooke 76

LITTLE RED RIDING-HOOD
    Illustrated by Charles Robinson 88

TATTERCOATS
    Illustrated by Arthur Rackham 92

PUSS IN BOOTS
    Illustrated by Harry Clarke 98

THE EMPEROR'S NEW CLOTHES
    Illustrated by Harry Clarke 104

JACK THE GIANT-KILLER
    Illustrated by Arthur Rackham 110

Beauty and the Beast
    Illustrated by Eleanor Vere Boyle 128

The Three Little Pigs
    Illustrated by L. Leslie Brooke 156

Snow White and the Seven Dwarfs
    Illustrated by Charles Robinson........................ 164

Catskin
    Illustrated by Arthur Rackham 172

The Little Mermaid
    Illustrated by William Heath Robinson 178

The Steadfast Tin Soldier
    Illustrated by Harry Clarke.............................. 202

Mr. and Mrs. Vinegar
    Illustrated by Arthur Rackham 208

Aladdin and the Magic Lamp
    Illustrated by Thomas Mackenzie 216

Goldilocks and the Three Bears
    Illustrated by L. Leslie Brooke 260

The Three Heads of the Well
    Illustrated by Arthur Rackham 270

Mouseskin
    Illustrated by Charles Robinson........................ 278

The Storks
    Illustrated by Harry Clarke.............................. 284

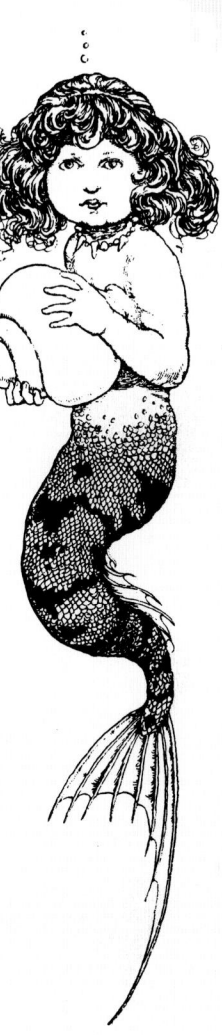

Dick Whittington and His Cat
    Illustrated by Arthur Rackham 290

Hop o' My Thumb
    Illustrated by Charles Robinson....................... 300

Jack and the Beanstalk
    Illustrated by Arthur Rackham 312

The Bogey-Beast
    Illustrated by Arthur Rackham 324

The Nightingale
    Illustrated by Harry Clarke............................... 328

The Fish and the Ring
    Illustrated by Arthur Rackham 338

Blue Beard
    Illustrated by Harry Clarke............................... 344

Tom Thumb
    Illustrated by L. Leslie Brooke 350

The Frog Prince
    Illustrated by Charles Robinson....................... 362

Ali Baba and the Forty Thieves
    Illustrated by René Bull.................................... 366

Sleeping Beauty
    Illustrated by Arthur Rackham 384

Cinderella

THE WIFE OF A RICH MAN FELL SICK, AND AS SHE FELT THAT HER END WAS drawing near, she called her only daughter to her bedside and said, "Dear child, be good and pious, and then the good God will always protect thee, and I will look down on thee from heaven and be near thee." Thereupon she closed her eyes and departed. Every day the maiden went out to her mother's grave, and wept, and she remained pious and good. When winter came the snow spread a white sheet over the grave, and when the spring sun had drawn it off again, the man had taken another wife.

The woman had brought two daughters into the house with her, who were beautiful and fair of face, but vile and black of heart. Now began a bad time for the poor step-child.

"Is the stupid goose to sit in the parlor with us?" said they. "He who wants to eat bread must earn it; out with the kitchen-wench."

They took her pretty clothes away from her, put an old gray bedgown on her, and gave her wooden shoes.

"Just look at the proud Princess, how decked out she is!" they cried, and laughed, and led her into the kitchen. There she had to do hard work from morning till night, get up before daybreak, carry water, light fires, cook and wash. Besides this, the sisters did her every imaginable injury—they mocked her and emptied her peas and lentils into the ashes, so that she was forced to sit and pick them out again. In the evening when she had worked till she was weary she had no bed to go to, but had to sleep by the fireside in the ashes. And as on that account she always looked dusty and dirty, they called her Cinderella.

It happened that the father was once going to the fair, and he asked his two step-daughters what he should bring back for them. "Beautiful dresses," said one, "Pearls and jewels," said the second. "And thou, Cinderella," said he, "what wilt thou have?" "Father, break off for me the first branch which knocks against your hat on your way home."

So he bought beautiful dresses, pearls and jewels for his two step-daughters, and on his way home, as he was riding through a green thicket, a hazel twig brushed against him and knocked off his hat. Then he broke off the branch and took it with him. When he reached home he gave his step-daughters the things which they had wished for, and to Cinderella he gave the branch from the hazel-bush. Cinderella thanked him, went to her mother's grave and planted the branch on it, and wept so much that the tears fell down on it and watered it. It grew, however, and became a handsome tree. Thrice a day Cinderella went and sat beneath it, and wept and prayed, and a little white bird always came on the tree, and if Cinderella expressed a wish, the bird threw down to her what she had wished for.

It happened, however, that the King appointed a festival which was to last three days, and to which all the beautiful young girls in the country were invited, in order that his son might choose himself a bride. When the two step-sisters heard that they too were to appear among the number, they were delighted, called Cinderella and said, "Comb our hair for us, brush our shoes and fasten our buckles, for we are going to the festival at the King's palace."

Cinderella obeyed, but wept, because she too would have liked to go with them to the dance, and begged her step-mother to allow her to do so. "Thou go, Cinderella!" said she; "Thou art dusty and dirty and wouldst go to the festival? Thou hast no clothes and shoes, and yet wouldst dance!"

As, however, Cinderella went on asking, the step-mother at last said, "I have emptied a dish of lentils into the ashes for thee, if thou hast picked them out again in two hours, thou shalt go with us."

The maiden went through the back-door into the garden, and called,

> "You tame pigeons, you turtle-doves,
> and all you birds beneath the sky,
> come and help me to pick
> The good into the pot,
> The bad into the crop."

Then two white pigeons came in by the kitchen-window, and afterward the turtle-doves, and at last all the birds beneath the sky, came whirring and crowding in, and alighted amongst the ashes. And the pigeons nodded with their heads and began pick, pick, pick, pick, and the rest began also pick, pick, pick, pick, and gathered all the good grains into the dish. Hardly had one hour passed before they had finished, and all flew out again.

Then the girl took the dish to her step-mother, and was glad, and believed that now she would be allowed to go with them to the festival. But the step-mother said, "No, Cinderella, thou hast no clothes and thou canst not dance; thou wouldst only be laughed at." And as Cinderella wept at this, the step-mother said, "If thou canst pick two dishes of lentils out of the ashes for me in one hour, thou shalt go with us." And she thought to herself, "That she most certainly cannot do." When the step-mother had emptied the two dishes of lentils amongst the ashes, the maiden went through the back-door into the garden and cried,

> "You tame pigeons, you turtle-doves,
> and all you birds beneath the sky,
> come and help me to pick
> The good into the pot,
> The bad into the crop."

Then two white pigeons came in by the kitchen-window, and afterward the turtle-doves, and at length all the birds beneath the sky, came whirring and crowding in, and alighted amongst the ashes. And the doves nodded with their heads and began pick, pick, pick, pick, and the others began also pick, pick, pick, pick, and gathered all the good seeds into the dishes, and before half an hour was over they had already finished, and all flew out again. Then the maiden carried the dishes to the step-mother and was delighted, and believed that she might now go with them to the festival. But the step-mother said, "All this will not help thee; thou goest not with us, for thou hast no clothes and canst not dance; we should be ashamed of thee!" On this she turned her back on Cinderella, and hurried away with her two proud daughters.

As no one was now at home, Cinderella went to her mother's grave beneath the hazel-tree, and cried,

"Shiver and quiver, little tree,
Silver and gold throw down over me."

Then the bird threw a gold and silver dress down to her, and slippers embroidered with silk and silver. She put on the dress with all speed, and went to the festival. Her step-sisters and the step-mother however did not know her, and thought she must be a foreign Princess, for she looked so beautiful in the golden dress. They never once thought of Cinderella, and believed that she was sitting at home in the dirt, picking lentils out of the ashes. The Prince went to meet her, took her by the hand and danced with her. He would dance with no other maiden, and never left loose of her hand, and if any one else came to invite her, he said, "This is my partner."

She danced till it was evening, and then she wanted to go home. But the King's son said, "I will go with thee and bear thee company," for he wished to see to whom the beautiful maiden belonged. She escaped from him, however, and sprang into the pigeon-house. The King's son waited until her father came, and then he told him that the stranger maiden had leapt into the pigeon-house. The old man thought, "Can it be Cinderella?" and they had to bring him an axe and a pickaxe that he might hew the pigeon-house to pieces, but no one was inside it. And when they got home Cinderella lay in her dirty clothes among the ashes, and a dim little oil-lamp was burning on the mantle-piece, for Cinderella had jumped quickly down from the back of the pigeon-house and had run to the little hazel-tree, and there she had taken off her beautiful clothes and laid them on the grave, and the bird had taken

them away again, and then she had placed herself in the kitchen amongst the ashes in her gray gown.

Next day when the festival began afresh, and her parents and the step-sisters had gone once more, Cinderella went to the hazel-tree and said—

"Shiver and quiver, little tree,
Silver and gold throw down over me."

Then the bird threw down a much more beautiful dress than on the preceding day. And when Cinderella appeared at the festival in this dress, every one was astonished at her beauty. The King's son had waited until she came, and instantly took her by the hand and danced with no one but her. When others came and invited her, he said, "She is my partner."

When evening came she wished to leave, and the King's son followed her and wanted to see into which house she went. But she sprang away from him, and into the garden behind the house. Therein stood a beautiful tall tree on which hung the most magnificent pears. She clambered so nimbly between the branches like a squirrel that the King's son did not know where she was gone. He waited until her father came, and said to him, "The stranger-maiden has escaped from me, and I believe she has climbed up the pear-tree." The father thought, "Can it be Cinderella?" and had an axe brought and cut the tree down, but no one was on it. And when they got into the kitchen, Cinderella lay there amongst the ashes, as usual, for she had jumped down on the other side of the tree, had taken the beautiful dress to the bird on the little hazel-tree, and put on her gray gown.

On the third day, when the parents and sisters had gone away, Cinderella went once more to her mother's grave and said to the little tree,—

"Shiver and quiver, little tree,
Silver and gold throw down over me."

And now the bird threw down to her a dress which was more splendid and magnificent than any she had yet had, and the slippers were golden.

And when she went to the festival in the dress, no one knew how to speak for astonishment. The King's son danced with her only, and if anyone invited her to dance, he said, "She is my partner."

When evening came, Cinderella wished to leave, and the King's son was anxious to go with her, but she escaped from him so quickly that he could not follow her. The King's son had, however, used a stratagem, and had caused the whole staircase to be smeared with pitch, and there, when she ran down, had the maiden's left slipper remained sticking. The King's son picked it up, and it was small and dainty, and all golden. Next morning, he went with it to the father, and said to him, "No one shall be my wife but she whose foot this golden slipper fits."

Then were the two sisters glad, for they had pretty feet. The eldest went with the shoe into her room and wanted to try it on, and her mother stood by. But she could not get her big toe into it, and the shoe was too small for her. Then her mother gave her a knife and said, "Cut the toe off; when thou art Queen thou wilt have no more need to go on foot." The maiden cut the toe off, forced the foot into the shoe, swallowed the pain, and went out to the King's son. Then he took her on his his horse as his bride and rode away with her. They were, however, obliged to pass the grave, and there, on the hazel-tree, sat the two pigeons and cried,

>"Turn and peep, turn and peep,
>There's blood within the shoe,
>The shoe it is too small for her,
>The true bride waits for you."

Then he looked at her foot and saw how the blood was streaming from it. He turned his horse round and took the false bride home again, and said she was not the true one, and that the other sister was to put the shoe on. Then this one went into her chamber and got her toes safely into the shoe, but her heel was too large. So her mother gave her a knife and said, "Cut a bit off thy heel; when thou art Queen thou wilt have no more need to go on foot." The maiden cut a bit off her heel, forced her foot into the shoe, swallowed the pain, and went out to the King's son. He took her on his horse as his bride, and rode away with her, but when they passed by the hazel-tree, two little pigeons sat on it and cried,

> "Turn and peep, turn and peep,
> There's blood within the shoe,
> The shoe it is too small for her,
> The true bride waits for you."

He looked down at her foot and saw how the blood was running out of her shoe, and how it had stained her white stocking. Then he turned his horse and took the false bride home again. "This also is not the right one," said he, "have you no other daughter?" "No," said the man, "There is still a little stunted kitchen-wench which my late wife left behind her, but she cannot possibly be the bride."

The King's son said he was to send her up to him; but the mother answered, "Oh, no, she is much too dirty, she cannot show herself!" He absolutely insisted on it, and Cinderella had to be called.

She first washed her hands and face clean, and then went and bowed down before the King's son, who gave her the golden shoe. Then she seated herself on a stool, drew her foot out of the heavy wooden shoe, and put it into the slipper, which fitted like a glove. And when she rose up and the King's son looked at her face he recognized the beautiful maiden who had danced with him and cried, "That is the true bride!" The step-mother and the two sisters were terrified and became pale with rage; he, however, took Cinderella on his horse and rode away with her. As they passed by the hazel-tree, the two white doves cried,

> "Turn and peep, turn and peep,
> No blood is in the shoe,
> The shoe is not too small for her,
> The true bride rides with you,"

and when they had cried that, the two came flying down and placed themselves on Cinderella's shoulders, one on the right, the other on the left, and remained sitting there.

When the wedding with the King's son had to be celebrated, the two false sisters came and wanted to get into favor with Cinderella and share her good fortune. When the betrothed couple went to church, the elder was at the right side and the younger at the left, and the pigeons pecked out one eye of each of them. Afterward as they came back, the elder was at the left, and the younger at the right, and then the pigeons pecked out the other eye of each. And thus, for their wickedness and falsehood, they were punished with blindness as long as they lived.

The Tinder-Box

There came a soldier marching along the high road—one, two! one, two! He had his knapsack on his back and a saber by his side, for he had been in the wars, and now he wanted to go home. And on the way he met with an old witch: she was very hideous, and her under-lip hung down upon her breast. She said, "Good evening, soldier. What a fine sword you have, and what a big knapsack! You're a proper soldier! Now you shall have as much money as you like to have."

"I thank you, you old witch!" said the soldier.

"Do you see that great tree?" quoth the witch; and she pointed to a tree which stood beside them. "It's quite hollow inside. You must climb to the top and then you'll see a hole, through which you can let yourself down and get deep into the tree. I'll tie a rope round your body, so that I can pull you up again when you call me."

"What am I to do down in the tree?" asked the soldier.

"Get money," replied the witch. "Listen to me. When you come down to the earth under the tree, you will find yourself in a great hall: it is quite light, for above three hundred lamps are burning there. Then you will see three doors; these you can open, for the keys are hanging there. If you go into the first chamber, you'll see a great chest in the middle of the floor; on this chest sits a dog, and he's got a pair of eyes as big as two teacups. But you need not care for that. I'll give you my blue-checked apron, and you can spread it out upon the floor; then go up quickly and take the dog, and set him on my apron; then open the chest, and take as many shillings as you like. They are of copper: if you prefer silver, you must go into the second chamber. But there sits a dog with a pair of eyes as big as mill-wheels. But do not care for that. Set him upon my apron, and take some of the money. And if you want gold, you can have that too—in fact, as much as you can carry—if you go into the third chamber. But the dog that sits on the money-chest there has two eyes as big as round towers. He is a fierce dog, you may be sure; but you needn't be afraid, for all that. Only set him on my apron, and he won't hurt you; and take out of the chest as much gold as you like."

"That's not so bad," said the soldier. "But what am I to give you, you old witch? for you will not do it for nothing, I fancy."

"No," replied the witch, "not a single shilling will I have. You shall only bring me an old tinder-box which my grandmother forgot when she was down there last."

"Then tie the rope round my body," cried the soldier.

"Here it is," said the witch, "and here's my blue-checked apron."

Then the soldier climbed up into the tree, let himself slip down into the hole, and stood, as the witch had said, in the great hall where the three hundred lamps were burning.

Now he opened the first door. Ugh! there sat the dog with eyes as big as teacups, staring at him. "You're a nice fellow!" exclaimed the soldier; and he set him on the witch's apron, and took as many copper shillings as his pockets would hold, and then locked the chest, set the dog on it again, and went into the second chamber. Aha! there sat the dog with eyes as big as mill-wheels.

"You should not stare so hard at me," said the soldier; "you might strain your eyes." And he set the dog upon the witch's apron. And when he saw the silver money in the chest, he threw away all the copper money he had, and filled his pockets and his knapsack with silver only. Then he went into the third chamber. O, but that was horrid! The dog there really had eyes as big as towers, and they turned round and round in his head like wheels.

"Good evening!" said the soldier; and he touched his cap, for he had never seen such a dog as that before. When he had looked at him a little more closely, he thought, "That will do," and lifted him down to the floor, and opened the chest. Mercy! what a quantity of gold was there! He could buy with it the whole town, and the sugar

The Tinder-Box

sucking-pigs of the cake-woman, and all the tin soldiers, whips, and rocking-horses in the whole world. Yes, that was a quantity of money! Now the soldier threw away all the silver coin with which he had filled his pockets and his knapsack, and took gold instead: yes, all his pockets, his knapsack, his boots, and his cap were filled, so that he could scarcely walk. Now indeed he had plenty of money. He put the dog on the chest, shut the door, and then called up through the tree, "Now pull me up, you old witch."

"Have you the tinder-box?" asked the Witch.

"Plague on it!" exclaimed the soldier, "I had clean forgotten that." And he went and brought it.

The witch drew him up, and he stood on the high road again, with pockets, boots, knapsack, and cap full of gold.

"What are you going to do with the tinder-box?" asked the soldier.

"That's nothing to you," retorted the witch. "You've had your money; just give me the tinder-box."

"Nonsense!" said the soldier. "Tell me directly what you're going to do with it or I'll draw my sword and cut off your head."

"No!" cried the witch.

So the soldier cut off her head. There she lay! But he tied up all his money in her apron, took it on his back like a bundle, put the tinder-box in his pocket, and went straight off toward the town.

That was a splendid town! And he put up at the very best inn, and asked for the finest rooms, and ordered his favorite dishes, for now he was rich, as he had so much money. The servant who had to clean his boots certainly thought them a remarkably old pair for such a rich gentleman; but he had not bought any new ones yet. The next day he procured proper boots and handsome clothes. Now our soldier had become a fine gentleman; and the people told him of all the splendid things which were in their city, and about the King, and what a pretty Princess the King's daughter was.

"Where can one get to see her?" asked the soldier.

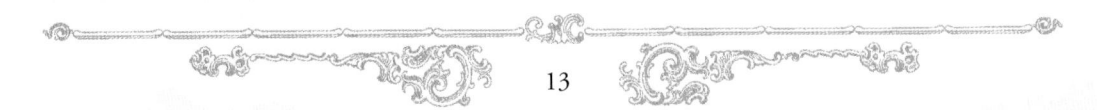

"She is not to be seen at all," said they all together; "she lives in a great copper castle, with a great many walls and towers round about it: no one but the King may go in and out there, for it has been prophesied that she shall marry a common soldier, and the King can't bear that."

"I should like to see her," thought the soldier; but he could not get leave to do so. Now he lived merrily, went to the theater, drove in the King's garden, and gave much money to the poor; and this was very kind of him, for he knew from old times how hard it is when one has not a shilling. Now he was rich, had fine clothes, and gained many friends, who all said he was a rare one, a true cavalier; and that pleased the soldier well. But as he spent money every day and never earned any, he had at last only two shillings left; and he was obliged to turn out of the fine rooms in which he had dwelt, and had to live in a little garret under the roof, and clean his boots for himself, and mend them with a darning needle. None of his friends came to see him, for there were too many stairs to climb.

It was quite dark one evening, and he could not even buy himself a candle, when it occurred to him that there was a candle-end in the tinder-box which he had taken out of the hollow tree into which the witch had helped him. He brought out the tinder-box and the candle-end; but as soon as he struck fire and the sparks rose up from the flint, the door flew open, and the dog who had eyes as big as a couple of tea-cups, and whom he had seen in the tree, stood before him, and said:

"What are my lord's commands?"

"What is this?" said the soldier. "That's a famous tinder-box, if I can get everything with it that I want! Bring me some money," said he to the dog; and whisk! the done was gone, and whisk! he was back again, with a great bag full of shillings in his mouth.

Now the soldier knew what a capital tinder-box this was. If he struck it once, the dog came who sat upon the chest of copper money; if he struck it twice, the dog who had the silver; and if he struck it three times, then appeared the dog who had the gold. Now the soldier moved back into the fine rooms, and appeared again in handsome clothes; and all his friends knew him again, and cared very much for him indeed.

Once he thought to himself, "It is a very strange thing that one cannot get to see the Princess. They all say she is very beautiful; but what is the use of that, if she has always to sit in the great copper castle with the many towers? Can I not get to see her at

The Tinder-Box

all? Where is my tinder-box?" And so he struck a light, and whisk! came the dog with eyes as big as teacups.

"It is midnight, certainly," said the soldier, "but I should very much like to see the Princess, only for one little moment."

And the dog was outside the door directly, and, before the soldier thought it, came back with the Princess. She sat upon the dog's back and slept; and every one could see she was a real Princess, for she was so lovely. The Soldier could not refrain from kissing her, for he was a thorough soldier. Then the dog ran back again with the Princess. But when morning came, and the King and Queen were drinking tea, the Princess said she had had a strange dream the night before, about a dog and a soldier—that she had ridden upon the dog, and the soldier had kissed her.

"That would be a fine history!" said the Queen.

So one of the old court ladies had to watch the next night by the Princess's bed, to see if this was really a dream, or what it might be.

The soldier had a great longing to see the lovely Princess again; so the dog came in the night, took her away, and ran as fast as he could. But the old lady put on water-boots, and ran just as fast after him. When she saw that they both entered a great house, she thought, "Now I know where it is"; and with a bit of chalk she drew a great cross on the door. Then she went home and lay down, and the dog came up with the Princess; but when he saw that there was a cross drawn on the door where the soldier lived, he took a piece of chalk too, and drew crosses on all the doors in the town. And that was cleverly done, for now the lady could not find the right door, because all the doors had crosses upon them.

In the morning early came the King and Queen, the old court lady and all the officers, to see where it was the Princess had been. "Here it is!" said the King, when he saw the first door with a cross upon it. "No, my dear husband, it is there!" said the Queen, who descried another door which also showed a cross. "But there is one, and there is one!" said all, for wherever they looked there were crosses on the doors. So they saw that it would avail them nothing if they searched on.

But the Queen was an exceedingly clever woman, who could do more than ride in a coach. She took her great good scissors, cut a piece of silk into pieces, and made a neat little bag; this bag she filled with fine wheat flour, and tied it on the Princess's back; and when that was done, she cut a little hole in the bag, so that the flour would be scattered along all the way which the Princess should take.

In the night the dog came again, took the Princess on his back, and ran with her to the soldier, who loved her very much, and would gladly have been a Prince, so that he might have her for his wife. The dog did not notice at all how the flour ran out in a stream from the castle to the windows of the soldier's house, where he ran up the wall with the Princess. In the morning the King and the Queen saw well enough where their daughter had been, and they took the soldier and put him in prison.

There he sat. Oh, but it was dark and disagreeable there! And they said to him, "To-morrow you shall be hanged." That was not amusing to hear, and he had left his tinder-box at the inn. In the morning he could see, through the iron grating of the window, how the people were hurrying out of the town to see him hanged. He heard the drums beat and saw the soldiers marching. All the people were running out, and among them was a shoemaker's boy with leather apron and slippers, and he galloped so fast that one of his slippers flew off, and came right against the wall where the soldier sat looking through the iron grating.

"Hallo, you shoemaker's boy! you needn't be in such a hurry," cried the soldier to him: "it will not begin till I come. But if you will run to where I lived, and bring me my tinder-box, you shall have four shillings: but you must put your best leg foremost."

The shoemaker's boy wanted to get the four shillings, so he went and brought the tinder-box, and—well, we shall hear now what happened.

Outside the town a great gallows had been built, and round it stood the soldiers and many hundred thousand people. The King and Queen sat on a splendid throne, opposite to the judges and the whole council. The soldier already stood upon the ladder; but as they were about to put the rope round his neck, he said that before a poor criminal suffered his punishment an innocent request was always granted to him. He wanted very much to smoke a pipe of tobacco, and it would be the last pipe he should smoke in the world. The King would not say "No" to this; so the soldier took his tinder-box, and struck fire. One—two—three!—and there suddenly stood all the

The Tinder-Box

dogs—the one with the eyes as big as teacups, the one with eyes as large as mill-wheels, and the one whose eyes were as big as round towers.

"Help me now, so that I may not be hanged," said the soldier.

And the dogs fell upon the judges and all the council, seized one by the leg and another by the nose, and tossed them all many feet into the air, so that they fell down and were all broken to pieces.

"I won't!" cried the King; but the biggest dog took him and the Queen, and threw them after the others. Then the soldiers were afraid, and the people cried, "Little soldier, you shall be our King, And marry the beautiful Princess!"

So they put the soldier into the King's coach, and all the three dogs darted on in front and cried "Hurrah!" and the boys whistled through their fingers, and the soldiers presented arms. The Princess came out of the copper castle, and became Queen, and she liked that well enough. The wedding lasted a week, and the three dogs sat at the table, too, and opened their eyes wider than ever at all they saw.

Hansel and Gretel

Once, as a poor woodman cut wood in the forest, he heard a little cry; so he followed the sound, till at last he looked up a high tree, and on one of the branches sat a very little child. Its mother had fallen asleep, and a vulture had taken it out of her lap and flown away with it, and left it on the tree. Then the woodcutter climbed up, took the little child down, and found it was a pretty little girl; and he said to himself, "I will take this poor child home, and bring her up with my own son Hansel." So he brought her to his cottage, and both grew up together: he called the little girl Gretel, and the two children were so very fond of each other that they were never happy but when they were together.

But the woodcutter became very poor, and had nothing in the world he could call his own; indeed he had scarcely bread enough for his wife and the two children to eat. At last the time came when even that was all gone, and he knew not where to seek for help in his need. At night, his wife said to him: "Husband, listen to me, and take the two children out early to-morrow morning; give each of them a piece of bread, and then lead them into the midst of the wood, where it is thickest, make a fire for them, and go away and leave them alone to shift for themselves, for we can no longer keep them here." "No, wife," said the husband, "I cannot find it in my heart to leave the children to the wild beasts of the forest; they would soon tear them to pieces." "Well, if you will not do as I say," answered the wife, "we must all starve together." And she would not let him have any peace until he came into her hard-hearted plan.

Meantime the poor children too were lying awake restless, and weak from hunger, so that they heard all that Hansel's mother said to her husband. "Now," thought Gretel to herself, "it is all up with us," and she began to weep. But Hansel crept to her bedside, and said, "Do not be afraid, Gretel, I will find out some help for us." Then he got up, put on his jacket, and opened the door and went out.

The moon shone bright upon the little court before the cottage, and the white pebbles glittered like daisies on the green meadows. So he stooped down, and put as many as he could into his pocket, and then went back to the house. "Now, Gretel," said he, "rest in peace!" and he went to bed and fell fast asleep.

Early in the morning, before the sun had risen, the woodman's wife came and awoke them. "Get up, children," said she, "we are going into the wood; there is a piece of bread for each of you, but take care of it, and keep some for the afternoon." Gretel took the bread, and carried it in her apron, because Hansel had his pocket full of stones; and they made their way into the wood.

After a time, Hansel stood still and looked toward home; and after a while he turned again, and so on several times. Then his father said, "Hansel, why do you keep turning and lagging about so?"

"Ah, Father," answered Hansel, "I am stopping to look at my white cat, that sits on the roof, and wants to say goodbye to me."

"You little fool!" said his mother, "that is not your cat; it is the morning sun shining on the chimney-top."

Now Hansel had not been looking at the cat, but had all the while been lingering behind, to drop from his pocket one white pebble after another along the road.

When they came into the midst of the wood the woodman said, "Run about, children, and pick up some wood, and I will make a fire to keep us all warm."

So they piled up a little heap of brushwood, and set it on fire; and as the flames burned bright, the mother said, "Now set yourselves by the fire, and go to sleep, while we go and cut wood in the forest; be sure you wait till we come again and fetch you." Hansel and Gretel sat by the fireside till the afternoon, and then ate their piece of bread. They fancied the woodman was still in the wood, because they thought they heard the blows of his axe; but it was a bough, which he had cunningly hung upon a tree in such a way that the wind blew it against the other boughs; and so it sounded as the axe does in cutting. Thus they waited till evening: but the woodman and his wife kept away, and no one came to fetch them.

When it was quite dark Gretel began to cry; but Hansel said: "Wait awhile till the moon rises." And when the moon rose he took her by the hand, and there lay the pebbles along the ground, glittering like new pieces of money, and marking out the way. Toward morning they came again to the woodman's house, and he was glad in his heart when he saw the children again, for he had grieved at leaving them alone.

Not long afterward there was again no bread in the house, and Hansel and Gretel heard the wife say to her husband: "The children found their way back once, and I took it in good part; but now there is only half a loaf of bread left for them in the house; to-morrow you must take them deeper into the wood, that they may not find their way out, or we shall all be starved."

It grieved the husband in his heart to do as his selfish wife wished, and he thought it would be better to share their last morsel with the children; but as he had done as she said once, he did not dare now to say no. When the children heard their plan, Hansel got up, and wanted to pick up pebbles as before. But when he came to the door, he found his mother had locked it. Still he comforted Gretel, and said, "Sleep in peace, dear Gretel! God is very kind, and will help us."

Early in the morning, a piece of bread was given to each of them, but still smaller than the one they had before. Upon the road Hansel crumbled his in his pocket and often stood still, and threw a crumb upon the ground. "Why do you lag so behind, Hansel?" said the woodman; "go your ways on before."

"I am looking at my little dove that is sitting upon the roof, and wants to say good-bye to me."

"You silly boy!" said the wife, "that is not your little dove; it is the morning sun, that shines on the chimney-top."

But Hansel still went on crumbling his bread, and throwing it on the ground. And thus they went on still further into the wood.

There they were again told to sit down by a large fire, and go to sleep; and the woodman and his wife said they would come in the evening and fetch them away. In the afternoon Hansel shared Gretel's bread, because he had strewed all his upon the road; but the day passed away, and evening passed away too, and no one came to the poor children. Still Hansel comforted Gretel, and said, "Wait till the moon rises; and then I shall be able to see the crumbs of bread which I have strewed, and they will show us the way home."

The moon rose; but when Hansel looked for the crumbs they were gone, for hundreds of little birds in the wood had found them and picked them up. Hansel, however, set out to try and find his way home; but they soon lost themselves, and went on through the night and all the next day, till at last they laid down and fell asleep for weariness. Another day they went on as before, but still did not come to the end of the wood; and they were as hungry as could be, for they had had nothing to eat.

In the afternoon of the third day they came to a strange little hut, made of bread, with a roof of cake, and windows of barley-sugar. "Now we will sit down and eat till we have had enough," said Hansel; "I will eat off the roof for my share; do you eat the windows, Gretel, they will be nice and sweet for you." While Gretel, however, was picking at the barley-sugar, a pretty voice called softly from within:

Hansel and Gretel

<blockquote>"Tip tap! who goes there?"</blockquote>

But the children answered,

<blockquote>"The wind, the wind,
That blows through the air!"</blockquote>

and went on eating. Now Gretel had broken out a round pane of the window for herself, and Hansel had torn off a large piece of cake from the roof, when the door opened, and a little old fairy came gliding out. At this Hansel and Gretel were so frightened, that they let fall what they had in their hands. But the old lady nodded to them, and said, "Dear children, come in with me; you shall have something good."

So she led them into her little hut, and brought out plenty to eat—milk and pancakes, with sugar, apples, and nuts; and then two beautiful little beds were got ready, and Gretel and Hansel laid themselves down, and thought they were in heaven. But the fairy was a spiteful one, and made her pretty sweatmeat house to entrap little children. Early in the morning, she went to their little beds; and though she saw the two sleeping and looking so sweetly, she had no pity on them, but was glad they were in her power. Then she took up Hansel, and fastened him up in a coop by himself, and when he awoke he found himself behind a grating, shut up safely, as chickens are; but she shook Gretel, and called out, "Get up, you lazy little thing, and fetch some water; and go into the kitchen, and cook something good to eat. Your brother is shut up yonder; I shall first fatten him, and when he is fat, I think I shall eat him."

When the fairy was gone, poor Gretel watched her time, and got up, and ran to Hansel, and told him what she had heard, and said, "We must run away quickly, for the old woman is a bad fairy, and will kill us." But Hansel said, "You must first steal away her fairy wand, that we may save ourselves if she should follow; and bring the pipe too that hangs up in her room."

Then the little maiden ran back, and fetched the magic wand and the pipe, and away they went together. So when the old fairy came back and could see no one at home, she sprang in a great rage to the window, and looked out into the wide world (which she could do far and near), and a long way off she spied Gretel, running away with her dear Hansel. "You are already a great way off," said she; "but you will still fall into my hands."

Then she put on her boots, which walked several miles at a step, and scarcely made two steps with them before she overtook the children; but Gretel saw that the fairy was coming after them, and, by the help of the wand, turned her friend Hansel into a lake of water, and herself into a swan, which swam about in the middle of it. So the fairy sat herself down on the shore, and took a great deal of trouble to decoy the swan, and threw crumbs of bread to it; but it would not come near her, and she was forced to go home in the evening without taking her revenge. Then Gretel changed herself and Hansel back into their own forms, and they journeyed on until dawn; and then the maiden turned herself into a beautiful rose, that grew in the midst of a quickset hedge; and Hansel sat by the side.

The fairy soon came striding along. "Good piper," said she, "may I pluck yon beautiful rose for myself?"

"Oh yes!" answered he. "And then," thought he to himself, "I will play you a tune meantime." So when she had crept into the hedge in a great hurry, to gather the flower—for she well knew what it was—he pulled out the pipe slyly, and began to play. Now the pipe was a fairy pipe, and, whether they liked it or not, whoever heard it was obliged to dance. So the old fairy was forced to dance a merry jig, on and on without any rest, and without being able to reach the rose. And as he did not cease playing a moment, the thorns at length tore the clothes from off her body, and pricked her sorely, and there she stuck quite fast.

Then Gretel set herself free once more, and on they went; but she grew very tired, and Hansel said: "Now I will hasten home for help."

And Gretel said, "I will stay here in the meantime, and wait for you." Then Hansel went away.

But when Gretel had stayed in the field a long time, and found he did not come back, she became quite sorrowful, and turned herself into a little daisy, and thought to herself: "Someone will come and tread me under foot, and so my sorrows will end." But it so happened that, as a shepherd was keeping watch in the field, he saw the daisy;

and thinking it very pretty, he took it home, placed it in a box in his room, and said: "I have never found so pretty a daisy before." From that time everything throve wonderfully at the shepherd's house. When he got up in the morning, all the household work was ready done; the room was swept and cleaned, the fire made, and the water fetched; and in the afternoon, when he came home, the cloth was laid, and a good dinner ready set for him. Although it pleased him, he was at length troubled to think how it could be, and went to a cunning woman who lived hard by, and asked what he should do. She said: "There must be witchcraft in it; look out to-morrow morning early, and see if anything stirs about in the room: if it does, throw a white cloth at once over it, and then the witchcraft will be stopped." The shepherd did as she said, and the next morning saw the box open, and the daisy come out; then he sprang up quickly, and threw a white cloth over it. In an instant the spell was broken, and Gretel stood before him, for it was she who had taken care of his house for him; and she was so beautiful, that he asked her if she would marry him. She said, "No," because she wished to be faithful to her dear Hansel; but she agreed to stay, and keep house for him till Hansel came back.

Time passed on, and Hansel came back at last; for the spiteful fairy had led him astray, and he had not been able for a long time to find his way, either home or back to Gretel. Then he and Gretel set out to go home; but after traveling a long way, Gretel became tired, and she and Hansel laid themselves down to sleep in a fine old hollow tree that grew in a meadow by the side of the wood. But as they slept the fairy—who had got out of the bush at last—came by; and finding her wand was glad to lay hold of it, and at once turned poor Hansel into a fawn.

Soon after Gretel awoke, and found what had happened. She wept bitterly over the poor creature; and the tears too rolled down his eyes, as he laid himself down beside her. Then she said: "Rest in peace, dear fawn; I will never, never leave thee." So she took off her golden necklace, and put it round his neck, and plucked some rushes, and plaited them into a soft string to fasten to it, and led the poor little thing by her side when she went to walk in the wood; and when they were tired they came back, and laid down to sleep by the side of the hollow tree, where they lodged at night: but nobody came near them except the little dwarfs that lived in the wood, and these watched over them.

At last one day they came to a little cottage; and Gretel having looked in, and seen that it was quite empty, thought to herself, "We can stay and live here." Then she went and gathered leaves and moss to make a soft bed for the fawn; and every morning she went out and plucked nuts, roots, and berries for herself, and sweet shrubs and tender grass for her friend. In the evening, when Gretel was tired, and had said her prayers, she laid her head upon the fawn for her pillow, and slept; and if poor Hansel could but have his right form again, she thought they should lead a very happy life.

They lived thus a long while in the wood by themselves, till it chanced that the King of that country came to hold a great hunt there. And when the fawn heard all around the echoing of the horns, and the baying of the dogs, and the merry shouts of the huntsmen, he wished very much to go and see what was going on. "Ah, sister," said he, "let me go out into the wood, I can stay no longer!" And he begged so long that she at last agreed to let him go. "But," said she, "be sure to come to me in the evening; I shall shut up the door, to keep out those wild huntsmen, and if you tap at it and say, 'Sister, let me in!' I shall know you; but if you don't speak, I shall keep the door fast." Then away sprang the fawn, and frisked and bounded along in the open air. The King and his huntsmen saw the beautiful creature, and followed, but could not overtake him; for when they thought they were sure of their prize, he sprang over the bushes, and was out of sight.

As it grew dark he came running home to the hut and tapped, and said, "Sister, let me in!" Then she opened the little door.

Next morning, when he heard the horn of the hunters, he said: "Sister, open the door for me, I must go again." Then she let him out, and said: "Come back in the evening, and remember what you are to say." When the King and the huntsmen saw the fawn with the golden collar again, they gave him chase; but he was too quick for them. The chase lasted the whole day; but at length the huntsmen nearly surrounded him, and one of them wounded him in the foot, so that he became sadly lame, and could hardly crawl home. The man who had wounded him followed close behind, and hid himself, and heard the little fawn say, "Sister, let me in!" upon which the door opened, and soon shut again. The huntsman went to the King and told him what he had seen and heard; then the King said, "To-morrow we will have another chase."

Gretel was very much frightened when she saw that her dear little fawn was wounded; but she washed the blood away, and put some healing herbs on it, and said: "Now go to bed, dear fawn, and you will soon be well again." The wound was so slight, that in the morning there was nothing to be seen of it; and when the horn blew, the little thing said: "I can't stay here, I must go and look on; I will take care that none of them shall catch me."

But Gretel said: "I am sure they will kill you this time: I will not let you go."

"I shall die of grief," said he, "if you keep me here; when I hear the horns, I feel as if I could fly."

Then Gretel was forced to let him go. So she opened the door with a heavy heart, and he bounded out.

When the King saw him, he said to his huntsmen: "Now chase him all day long, till you catch him; but let none of you do him any harm." The sun set, however, without their being able to overtake him, and the King called away the huntsmen, and said to the one who had watched: "Now come and show me the little hut." So they went to the door and tapped, and said, "Sister, let me in!" Then the door opened, and the King went in, and there stood a maiden more lovely than any he had ever seen. Gretel was frightened to see that it was not her fawn, but a King with a golden crown that was come into her hut; however, he spoke kindly to her, and took her hand, and said, "Will you come with me to my castle, and be my wife?"

"Yes," said the maiden, "I will go to your castle, but I cannot be your wife; and my fawn must go with me. I cannot part with that."

"Well," said the King, "he shall come and live with you all your life, and want for nothing." Just then in sprang the little fawn; and his sister tied the string to his neck, and they left the hut in the wood together.

Then the King took Gretel to his palace, and on the way she told him all her story. And then he sent for the fairy, and made her change the fawn into Hansel again; and he and Gretel loved one another, and were married, and lived happily together all their days in the good king's palace.

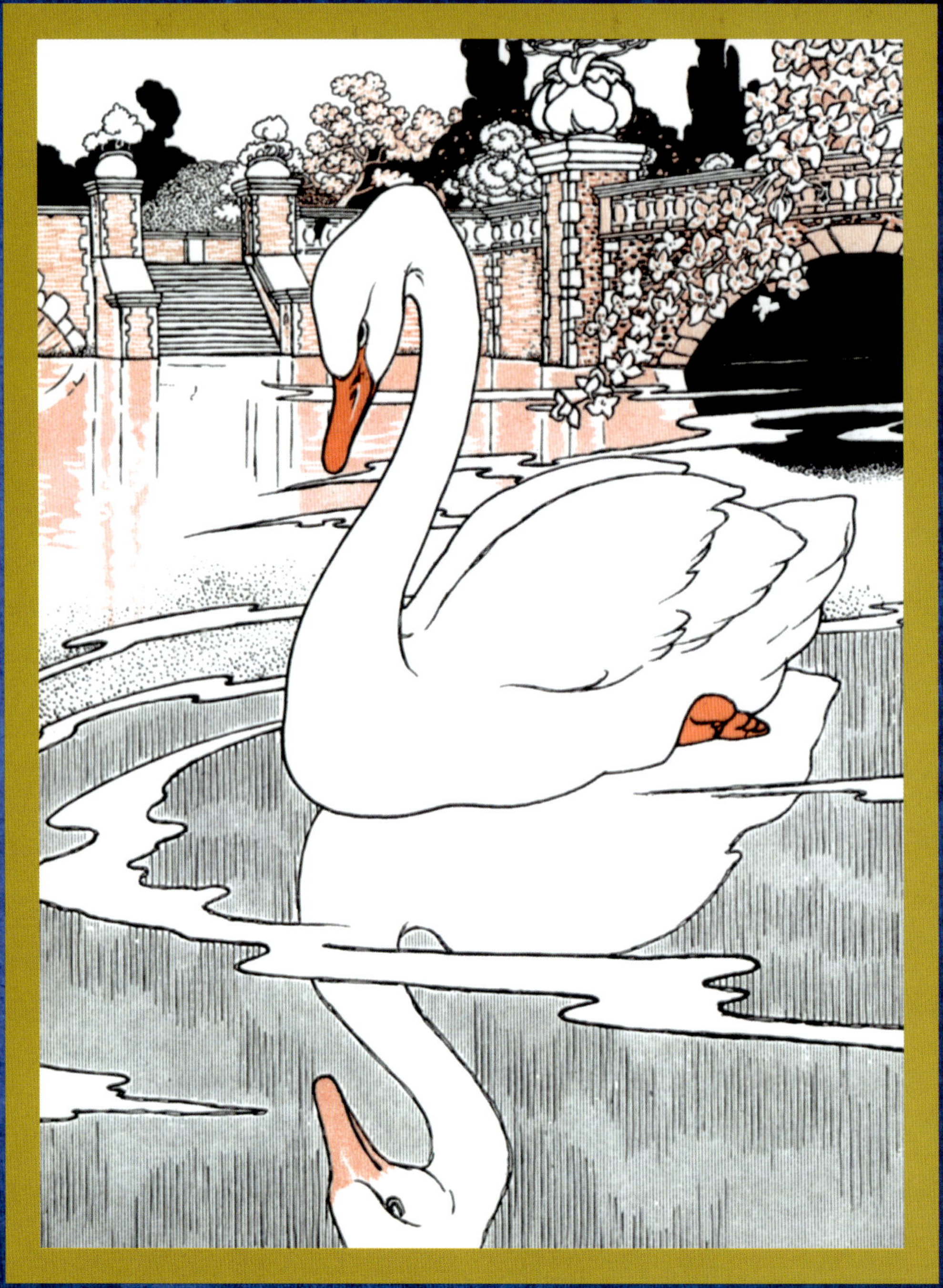

The Ugly Duckling

It was summertime, and it was beautiful in the country! The sunshine fell warmly on an old house, surrounded by deep canals, and from the walls down to the water's edge there grew large burdock leaves, so high that children could stand upright among them without being seen. This place was as wild and lonely as the thickest part of the wood, and on that account a duck had chosen to make her nest. She was sitting on her eggs; but the pleasure she had felt at first was now almost gone, because she had been there so long.

At last the eggs began to crack, and one little head after another appeared. "Quack, quack!" said the duck, and all the little ones got up as well as they could, and peeped about from under the green leaves.

"How large the world is!" said the little ones.

"Do you think this is the whole of the world?" asked the mother. "It stretches far away beyond the other side of the garden, down to the pastor's field; but I have never been there. Are you all here?" And then she got up. "No, I have not got you all; the largest egg is still here. How long, I wonder, will this last? I am so weary of it!" And she sat down again.

The great egg burst at last. "Peep, peep!" said the little one, and out it tumbled. But oh! how large and ugly it was! The duck looked at it. "That is a great, strong creature," said she; "none of the others is at all like it."

The next day was delightful weather, and the sun was shining warmly when the mother duck with her family went down to the canal. Splash! she went into the water. "Quack, quack!" cried she, and one duckling after another jumped in. The water closed over their heads, but all came up again and swam quite easily. All were there, even the ugly gray one was swimming about with the rest.

"Quack, quack!" said the mother duck. "Now come with me, I will take you into the world; but keep close to me, or someone may step on you; and beware of the cat."

When they came into the duckyard, two families were quarreling about the head of an eel, which in the end was carried off by the cat.

"See, my children, such is the way of the world," said the mother duck, sighing, for she too was fond of roasted eels. "Now use your legs," said she, "keep together, and bow to the old duck you see yonder. She is the noblest born of them all, and is of Spanish blood, which accounts for her dignified appearance and manners. And look, she has a red rag on her leg; that is considered a special mark of distinction and is the greatest honor a duck can have."

The other ducks who were in the yard looked at the little family and one of them said aloud: "Only see! now we have another brood, as if there were not enough of us already. And, fie! how ugly that one is; we will not endure it." And immediately one of the ducks flew at him and bit him on the neck.

"Leave him alone," said the mother; "he is doing no one any harm."

"Yes, but he is so large and ungainly."

"Those are fine children that our good mother has," said the old duck with the red rag on her leg. "All are pretty except that one, who certainly is not at all well favored. I wish his mother could improve him a little."

"Certainly he is not handsome," said the mother, "but he is very good and swims as well as the others, indeed rather better. I think in time he will grow like the others and perhaps will look smaller." And she stroked the duckling's neck and smoothed his ruffled feathers. "Besides," she added, "he is a drake; I think he will be very strong; so he will fight his way through."

"The other ducks are very pretty," said the old duck. "Pray make yourselves at home, and if you find an eel's head you can bring it to me."

And accordingly they made themselves at home.

But the poor duckling who had come last out of his egg-shell, and who was so ugly, was bitten, pecked, and teased by both ducks and hens. And the turkey-cock, who had come into the world with spurs on, and therefore fancied he was an emperor, puffed himself up like a ship in full sail, and marched up to the duckling quite red with passion. The poor thing scarcely knew what to do; he was quite distressed because he was so ugly.

So passed the first day, and afterward matters grew worse and worse. Even his brothers and sisters behaved unkindly, saying: "May the cat take you, you ugly thing!" The ducks bit him, the hens pecked him, and the girl who fed the poultry kicked him. He ran through the hedge and the little birds in the bushes were frightened and flew away. That is because I am so ugly, thought the duckling, and ran on. At last he came to a wide moor, where lived some wild ducks. There he lay the whole night, feeling very tired and sorrowful. In the morning the wild ducks flew up, and then they saw their new companion. "Pray who are you?" asked they; and the duckling greeted them as politely as possible.

"You are really very ugly," said one of the wild ducks; "but that does not matter to us if you do not wish to marry into our family."

Poor thing! he had never thought of marrying. He only wished to lie among the reeds and drink the water of the moor. There he stayed for two whole days. On the third day along came two wild geese, or rather goslings, for they had not been long out of their egg-shells, which accounts for their impertinence.

"Hark-ye," they said, "you are so ugly that we like you very well. Will you go with us and become a bird of passage? On another moor, not far from this, are some dear, sweet, wild geese, as lovely creatures as have ever said 'hiss, hiss.' It is a chance for you to get a wife. You may be lucky, ugly as you are."

Bang! a gun went off, and both goslings lay dead among the reeds. Bang! another gun went off and whole flocks of wild geese flew up from the rushes. Again and again the same alarming noise was heard.

There was a great shooting party. The sportsmen lay in ambush all around. The dogs splashed about in the mud, bending the reeds and rushes in all directions. How frightened the poor little duck was! He turned away his head, thinking to hide it under his wing, and at the same moment a fierce-looking dog passed close to him, his tongue hanging out of his mouth, his eyes sparkling fearfully. His jaws were wide open. He thrust his nose close to the duckling, showing his sharp white teeth, and then splash, splash! he was gone—gone without hurting him.

"Well! Let me be thankful," sighed the duckling. "I am so ugly that even a dog will not bite me."

And he lay still, though the shooting continued among the reeds. The noise did not cease until late in the day, and even then the poor little thing dared not stir. He waited several hours before he looked around him, and then hastened away from the moor as fast as he could.

Toward evening he reached a little hut, so wretched that it knew not on which side to fall, and therefore remained standing. He noticed that the door had lost one of its hinges and hung so much awry that there was a space between it and the wall wide enough to let him through. As the storm was becoming worse and worse, he crept into the room and hid in a corner.

In this room lived an old woman with her tom-cat and her hen. The cat, whom she called her little son, knew how to set up his back and purr. He could even throw out sparks when his fur was stroked the wrong way. The hen had very short legs, and was therefore called "Chickie Shortlegs"; she laid very good eggs, and the old woman loved her as her own child.

The next morning the cat began to mew and the hen to cackle when they saw the new guest.

"What is the matter?" asked the old woman, looking around. Her eyes were not good, so she took the duckling to be a fat duck who had lost her way. "This is a capital catch," she said. "I shall now have duck's eggs, if it be not a drake. We must wait and see." So the duckling was kept on trial for three weeks; but no eggs made their appearance.

The duckling sat in a corner feeling very sad, until finally the fresh air and bright sunshine that came into the room through the open door gave him such a strong desire to swim that he could not help telling the hen.

"What ails you?" said the hen. "You have nothing to do, and therefore you brood over these fancies; either lay eggs, or purr, then you will forget them."

"But it is so delicious to swim," said the duckling, "so delicious when the waters close over your head, and you plunge to the bottom."

"Well, that is a queer sort of pleasure," said the hen; "I think you must be crazy. Not to speak of myself, ask the cat—he is the wisest creature I know—whether he would like to swim, or to plunge to the bottom of the water. Ask your mistress. No one is cleverer than she. Do you think she would take pleasure in swimming, and in the waters closing over her head?"

"You do not understand me," said the duckling.

"What! we do not understand you! So you think yourself wiser than the cat and the old woman, not to speak of myself! Do not fancy any such thing, child, but be thankful for all the kindness that has been shown you. Are you not lodged in a warm room, and have you not the advantage of society from which you can learn something? Believe me, I wish you well. I tell you unpleasant truths, but it is thus that real friendship is shown. Come, for once give yourself the trouble either to learn to purr, or to lay eggs."

"I think I will take my chance and go out into the wide world again," said the duckling.

"Well, go then," said the hen.

So the duckling went away. He soon found water, and swam on the surface and plunged beneath it, but all the other creatures passed him by, because of his ugliness. The autumn came: the leaves turned yellow and brown; the wind caught them and danced them about; the air was cold; the clouds were heavy with hail or snow, and the raven sat on the hedge and croaked. The poor duckling was certainly not very comfortable!

One evening, just as the sun was setting, a flock of large birds rose from the brushwood. The duckling had never seen anything so beautiful before; their plumage was of a dazzling white, and they had long, slender necks. They were swans. They uttered a singular cry, spread out their long, splendid wings, and flew away from these cold regions to warmer countries, across the sea. They flew so high, so very high! and the ugly duckling's feelings were very strange. He turned round and round in the water like a wheel, strained his neck to look after them, and sent forth such a loud and strange cry that he almost frightened himself. Ah! he could not forget them, those noble birds! those happy birds! The duckling did not know what the birds were called, knew not whither they were flying, yet he loved them as he had never before loved anything. He envied them not. It would never have occurred to him to wish such beauty for himself. He would have been quite contented if the ducks in the duckyard had but endured his company.

And the winter was so cold! The duckling had to swim round and round in the water to keep it from freezing. But every night the opening in which he swam became smaller and the duckling had to make good use of his legs to prevent the water from freezing entirely. At last, exhausted, he lay stiff and cold in the ice.

Early in the morning a peasant passed by and saw him. He broke the ice in pieces with his wooden shoe and carried the duckling home to his wife.

The duckling soon revived. The children would have played with him, but he thought they wished to tease him, and in his terror jumped into the milk-pail, so that the milk was splashed about the room. The good woman screamed and clapped her hands. He flew first into the tub where the butter was kept, and thence into the meal-barrel, and out again.

The woman screamed, and struck at him with the tongs; the children ran races with each other trying to catch him, and laughed and screamed likewise. It was well for him that the door stood open; he jumped out among the bushes, into the new-fallen snow, and lay there as in a dream.

But it would be too sad to relate all the trouble and misery he had to suffer during that winter. He was lying on a moor among the reeds when the sun began to shine warmly again. The larks were singing, and beautiful spring had returned.

Once more he shook his wings. They were stronger than formerly, and bore him forward quickly; and, before he was well aware of it, he was in a large garden where the apple trees stood in full bloom, where the syringas sent forth their fragrance, and hung their long green branches down into the winding canal. Oh! everything was so lovely, so full of the freshness of spring!

Out of the thicket came three beautiful white swans. They displayed their feathers so proudly, and swam so lightly! The duckling knew the glorious creatures and was seized with a strange sadness.

"I will fly to them, those kingly birds!" he said. "They will kill me, because I, ugly as I am, have presumed to approach them; but it matters not. Better be killed by them than be bitten by the ducks, pecked by the hens, kicked by the girl who feeds the poultry, and have so much to suffer during the winter!" He flew into the water and swam toward the beautiful creatures. They saw him and shot forward to meet him. "Only kill me," said the poor duckling and he bowed his head low, expecting death. But what did he see in the water? He saw beneath him his own form, no longer that of a plump, ugly, gray bird. It was the reflection of a swan!

It matters not to have been born in a duckyard if one has been hatched from a swan's egg.

The larger swans swam around him and stroked him with their beaks. He was very happy.

Some little children were running about in the garden. They threw grain and bread into the water, and the youngest exclaimed: "There is a new one!" The others also cried out: "Yes, a new swan has come!" and they clapped their hands, and ran and told their father and mother. Bread and cake were thrown into the water, and everyone said: "The new one is the best, so young and so beautiful!" and the old swans bowed before him. The young swan felt quite ashamed and hid his head under his wing. He was all too happy, but still not proud, for a good heart is never proud.

He remembered how he had been laughed at and cruelly treated, and he now heard everyone say he was the most beautiful of all beautiful birds. The syringas bent down their branches toward him, and the sun shone warmly and brightly. He shook his feathers, stretched his slender neck, and in the joy of his heart said, "How little did I dream of so much happiness when I was the ugly, despised duckling!"

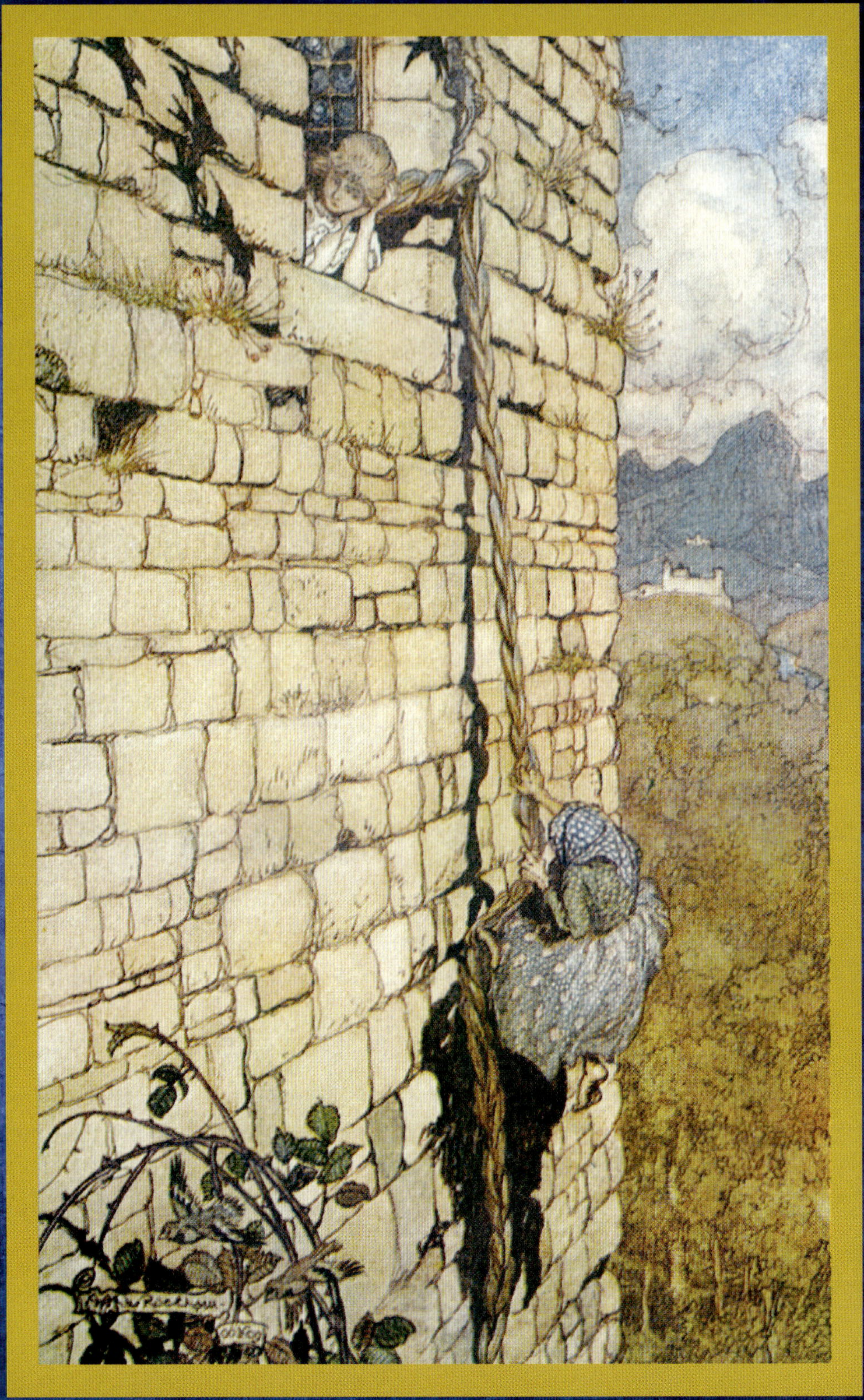

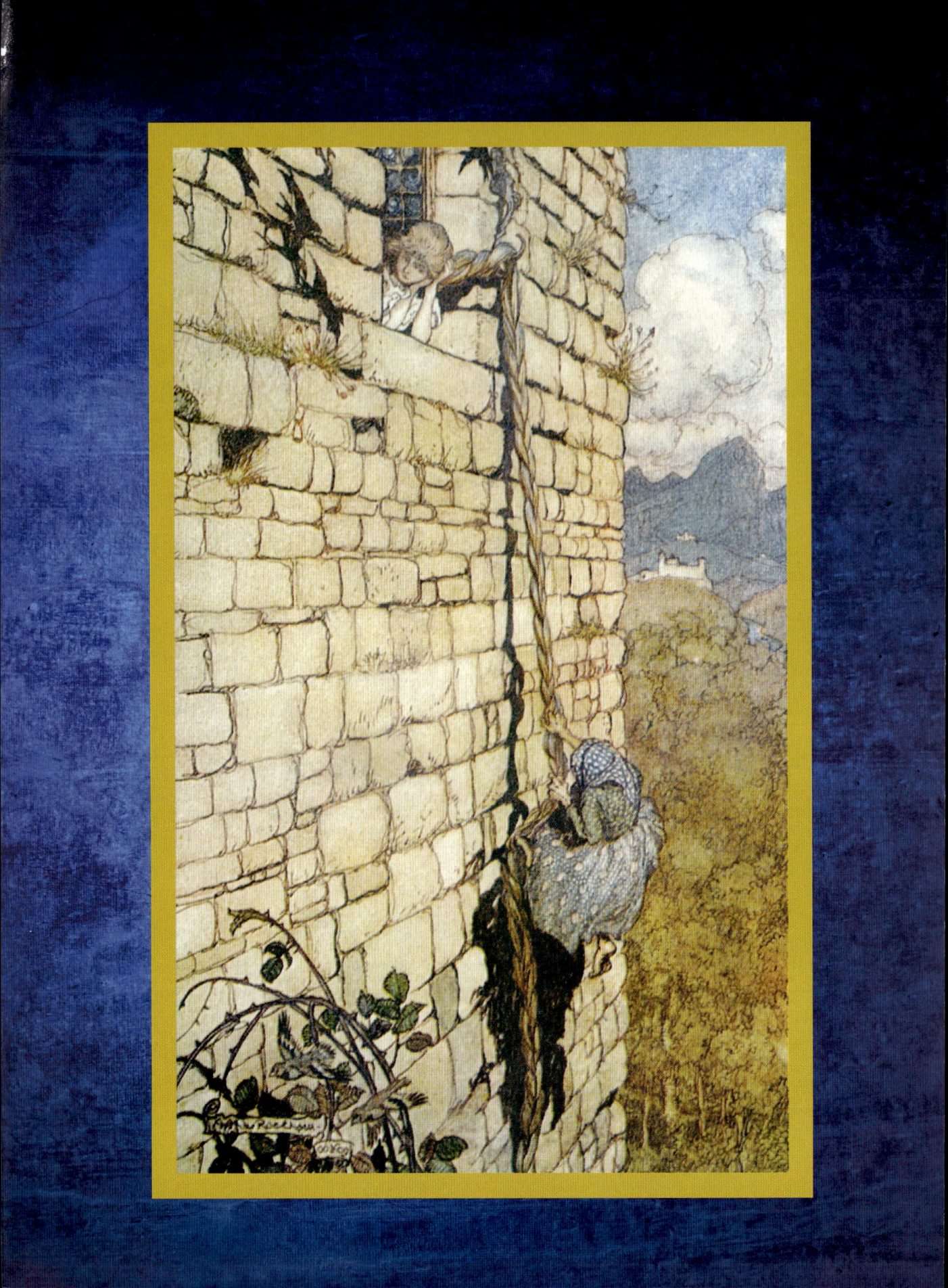

Rapunzel

There were once a man and a woman who had long in vain wished for a child. At length the woman hoped that God was about to grant her desire. These people had a little window at the back of their house from which a splendid garden could be seen, which was full of the most beautiful flowers and herbs. It was, however, surrounded by a high wall, and no one dared to go into it because it belonged to an enchantress, who had great power and was dreaded by all the world. One day the woman was standing by this window and looking down into the garden, when she saw a bed which was planted with the most beautiful rampion (rapunzel), and it looked so fresh and green that she longed for it, and had the greatest desire to eat some. This desire increased every day, and as she knew that she could not get any of it, she quite pined away, and looked pale and miserable.

Then her husband was alarmed, and asked, "What aileth thee, dear wife?" "Ah," she replied, "if I can't get some of the rampion, which is in the garden behind our house, to eat, I shall die." The man, who loved her, thought, "Sooner than let thy wife die, bring her some of the rampion thyself, let it cost thee what it will."

In the twilight of the evening, he clambered down over the wall into the garden of the enchantress, hastily clutched a handful of rampion, and took it to his wife. She at once made herself a salad of it, and ate it with much relish. She, however, liked it so much—so very much, that the next day she longed for it three times as much as before. If he was to have any rest, her husband must once more descend into the garden. In the gloom of evening, therefore, he let himself down again; but when he had clambered down the wall he was terribly afraid, for he saw the enchantress standing before him. "How canst thou dare," said she with angry look, "to descend into my garden and steal my rampion like a thief? Thou shalt suffer for it!"

"Ah," answered he, "let mercy take the place of justice, I only made up my mind to do it out of necessity. My wife saw your rampion from the window, and felt such a longing for it that she would have died if she had not got some to eat."

Then the enchantress allowed her anger to be softened, and said to him, "If the case be as thou sayest, I will allow thee to take away with thee as much rampion as thou wilt, only I make one condition, thou must give me the child which thy wife will bring into the world; it shall be well treated, and I will care for it like a mother."

The man in his terror consented to everything, and when the woman was brought to bed, the enchantress appeared at once, gave the child the name of Rapunzel, and took it away with her.

Rapunzel grew into the most beautiful child beneath the sun. When she was twelve years old, the enchantress shut her into a tower, which lay in a forest, and had neither stairs nor door, but quite at the top was a little window. When the enchantress wanted to go in, she placed herself beneath it and cried,

> "Rapunzel, Rapunzel,
> Let down thy hair to me."

Rapunzel had magnificent long hair, fine as spun gold, and when she heard the voice of the enchantress she unfastened her braided tresses, wound them round one of the hooks of the window above, and then the hair fell twenty ells down, and the enchantress climbed up by it.

After a year or two, it came to pass that the King's son rode through the forest and went by the tower. Then he heard a song, which was so charming that he stood still and listened. This was Rapunzel, who in her solitude passed her time in letting her sweet voice resound. The King's son wanted to climb up to her, and looked for the door of the tower, but none was to be found. He rode home, but the singing had so deeply touched his heart, that every day he went out into the forest and listened to it. Once when he was thus standing behind a tree, he saw that an enchantress came there, and he heard how she cried,

> "Rapunzel, Rapunzel,
> Let down thy hair."

Then Rapunzel let down the braids of her hair, and the enchantress climbed up to her. "If that is the ladder by which one mounts, I will for once try my fortune," said he, and the next day when it began to grow dark, he went to the tower and cried,

"Rapunzel, Rapunzel,
Let down thy hair."

Immediately the hair fell down and the King's son climbed up.

At first Rapunzel was terribly frightened when a man such as her eyes had never yet beheld, came to her; but the King's son began to talk to her quite like a friend, and told her that his heart had been so stirred that it had let him have no rest, and he had been forced to see her. Then Rapunzel lost her fear, and when he asked her if she would take him for her husband, and she saw that he was young and handsome, she thought, "He will love me more than old Dame Gothel does"; and she said yes, and laid her hand in his. She said, "I will willingly go away with thee, but I do not know how to get down. Bring with thee a skein of silk every time that thou comest, and I will weave a ladder with it, and when that is ready I will descend, and thou wilt take me on thy horse."

They agreed that until that time he should come to her every evening, for the old woman came by day. The enchantress remarked nothing of this, until once Rapunzel said to her, "Tell me, Dame Gothel, how it happens that you are so much heavier for me to draw up than the young King's son—he is with me in a moment."

"Ah! thou wicked child," cried the enchantress "What do I hear thee say! I thought I had separated thee from all the world, and yet thou hast deceived me!"

In her anger she clutched Rapunzel's beautiful tresses, wrapped them twice round her left hand, seized a pair of scissors with the right, and snip, snap, they were cut off, and the lovely braids lay on the ground. And she was so pitiless that she took poor Rapunzel into a desert where she had to live in great grief and misery.

On the same day, however, that she cast out Rapunzel, the enchantress in the evening fastened the braids of hair which she had cut off, to the hook of the window, and when the King's son came and cried,

"Rapunzel, Rapunzel,
Let down thy hair,"

she let the hair down. The King's son ascended, but he did not find his dearest Rapunzel above, but the enchantress, who gazed at him with wicked and venomous looks.

"Aha!" she cried mockingly, "Thou wouldst fetch thy dearest, but the beautiful bird sits no longer singing in the nest; the cat has got it, and will scratch out thy eyes as well. Rapunzel is lost to thee; thou wilt never see her more."

The King's son was beside himself with pain, and in his despair he leapt down from the tower. He escaped with his life, but the thorns into which he fell, pierced his eyes. Then he wandered quite blind about the forest, ate nothing but roots and berries, and did nothing but lament and weep over the loss of his dearest wife.

Thus he roamed about in misery for some years, and at length came to the desert where Rapunzel, with the twins to which she had given birth, a boy and a girl, lived in wretchedness. He heard a voice, and it seemed so familiar to him that he went toward it, and when he approached, Rapunzel knew him and fell on his neck and wept. Two of her tears wetted his eyes and they grew clear again, and he could see with them as before.

He led her to his kingdom where he was joyfully received, and they lived for a long time afterward, happy and contented.

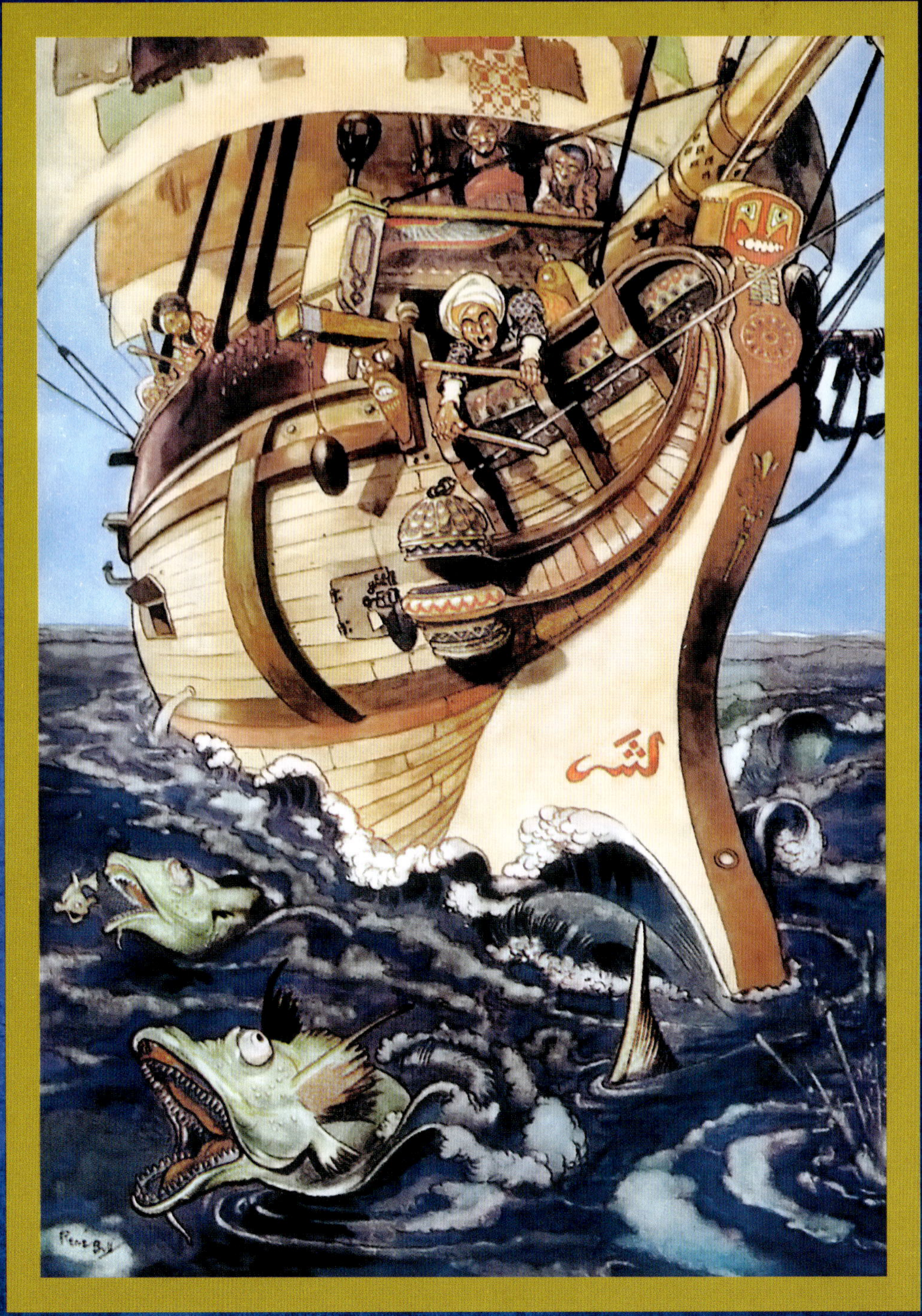

The Seven Voyages of Sinbad

In the reign of the Caliph Haroun al Raschid there dwelt, in Bagdad, a poor porter named Hindbad, who often had to carry heavy burdens, which he could scarcely support. One very hot day he was laboring along a strange street, and overcome by fatigue he sat down near a great house to rest. The porter complimented himself upon his good fortune in finding such a pleasant place, for while he sat there reached his ear sweet sounds of music, and his senses were also soothed by sweet smells. Wondering who lived in so fine a house, he inquired of one of the servants. What, said the man, do you not know that Sinbad the Sailor, the famous circumnavigator of the world, lives here? Alas, replied Hindbad, what a difference there is between Sinbad's lot and mine. Yet what greater merits does he possess that he should prosper and I starve? Now Sinbad happened to overhear this remark, and anxious to see a man who expressed such strange views he sent for Hindbad. Accordingly Hindbad was led into the great hall, where there was a sumptuous repast spread, and a goodly company assembled. The poor porter felt very uncomfortable, until Sinbad bade him draw near, and seating him at his right hand, served him himself, and gave him excellent wine, of which there was abundance upon the sideboard.

When the repast was over, Sinbad asked him why he complained of his condition. My lord, replied Hindbad, I confess that my fatigue put me out of humor, and occasioned me to utter some indiscreet words, which I beg you to pardon. Do not think I am so unjust, resumed Sinbad, as to resent such a complaint. But that you may know that my wealth has not been acquired without labor, I recite the history of travels for your benefit; and I think that, when you have heard it, you will acknowledge how wonderful have been my adventures. Sinbad then related his story as follows:—

THE FIRST VOYAGE

When still a very young man I inherited a large fortune from my father, and at once set about amusing myself. I lived luxuriously, and soon found that money was decreasing, while nothing was added to replace the expenditure. Quickly seeing the folly of my ways, I invested the remainder of my fortune with some merchants of Bussorah, and joined them in their voyage, which was toward the Indies by way of the Persian Gulf.

In our voyage we touched at several islands, where we sold or exchanged our goods. One day, whilst under sail, we were becalmed near a small island, but little elevated above the level of the water, and resembling a green meadow. The captain ordered his sails to be furled, and permitted such persons as were so inclined to land; of this number I was one.

But while we were enjoying ourselves in eating and drinking, and recovering ourselves from the fatigue of the sea, the island on a sudden trembled, and shook us terribly.

The trembling of the island was perceived on board the ship, and we were called upon to re-embark speedily, or we should all be lost; for what we took for an island proved to be the back of a sea monster. The nimblest got into the sloop, others betook themselves to swimming; but for myself I was still upon the back of the creature, when he dived into the sea, and I had time only to catch hold of a piece of wood that we had brought out of the ship to make a fire. Meanwhile, the captain, having received those on board who were in the sloop, and taken up some of those that swam, resolved to improve the favorable gale that had just risen, and hoisting his sails pursued his voyage, so that it was impossible for me to recover the ship.

Thus was I exposed to the mercy of the waves. I struggled for my life all the rest of the day and the following night. By this time I found my strength gone, and despaired of saving my life, when happily a wave threw me against an island. I struggled up the steep bank by aid of some roots, and lay down upon the ground half dead, until the sun appeared. Then, though I was very feeble, both from hard labor and want of food, I crept along to find some herbs fit to eat, and had the good luck not only to procure some, but likewise to discover a spring of excellent water, which contributed much to recover me. As I advanced farther into the island, I was not a little surprised and startled to hear a voice and see a man, who asked me who I was. I related to him my adventure, after which, taking me by the hand, he led me into a cave, where there were several other people, no less amazed to see me than I was to see them.

I partook of some provisions which they offered me. I then asked them what they did in such a desert place, to which they answered, that they were grooms belonging to Maha-râjah, sovereign of the island, and that they were about to lead the King's horses back to the palace. They added, that they were to return home on the morrow, and, had I been one day later, I must have perished, because the inhabited part of the island was at a great distance, and it would have been impossible for me to have got thither without a guide.

When the grooms set out I accompanied them, and was duly presented to the Maha-râjah, who was much interested in my adventure, and bade me stay with him as long as I desired.

Being a merchant, I met with men of my own profession, and particularly inquired for those who were strangers, that perchance I might hear news from Bagdad, or find an opportunity to return. For the Maha-râjah's capital is situated on the seacoast, and has a fine harbor, where ships arrive daily from the different quarters of the world. I frequented also the society of the learned Indians, and took delight to hear them converse; but withal, I took care to make my court regularly to the Maha-râjah, and conversed with the governors and petty Kings, his tributaries, that were about him. They put a thousand questions respecting my country; and I, being willing to inform myself as to their laws and customs, asked them concerning everything which I thought worth knowing.

There belongs to this King an island named Cassel. They assured me that every night a noise of drums was heard there, whence the mariners fancied that it was the residence of Degial. I determined to visit this wonderful place, and in my way thither saw fishes of one hundred and two hundred cubits long, that occasion more fear than hurt; for they are so timorous, that they will fly upon the rattling of two sticks or boards. I saw likewise other fish, that had heads like owls.

As I was one day at the port after my return, the ship in which I had set sail arrived, and the crew began to unload the goods. I saw my own bales with my name upon them, and going up to the captain said, I am that Sinbad whom you thought to be dead, and those bales are mine.

When the captain heard me speak thus, Heavens, he exclaimed, whom can we trust in these times? There is no faith left among men. I saw Sinbad perish with my own eyes, as did also the passengers on board, and yet you tell me you are that Sinbad. What impudence is this? To look on you, one would take you to be a man of probity, and yet you tell a horrible falsehood, in order to possess yourself of what does not belong to you. After much discussion, the captain was convinced of the truth of my words, and, having seen me identified by members of the crew, he handed me over my goods, congratulating me upon my escape.

I took out what was most valuable in my bales, and presented them to the Maha-râjah, who, knowing my misfortune, asked me how I came by such rarities. I acquainted him with the circumstance of their recovery. He was pleased at my good luck, accepted my present, and in return gave me one much more considerable. Upon this, I took leave of him, and went aboard the same ship, after I had exchanged my goods for the commodities of that country. We passed by several islands, and at last arrived at Bussorah, from whence I came to this city, with the value of one hundred thousand sequins.

Sinbad stopped here, and ordered the musicians to proceed with their concert, which the story had interrupted. The company continued enjoying themselves till the evening, and it was time to retire, when Sinbad sent for a purse of one hundred sequins, and giving it to the porter said, Take this, Hindbad, return to your home, and come back to-morrow to hear more of my adventures. The porter went away, astonished at the honor done, and the present made him, and arrayed in his best apparel returned to Sinbad's house next day. After he had graciously received and feasted his guest, Sinbad continued his narrative:—

THE SECOND VOYAGE

I designed, after my first voyage, to spend the rest of my days at Bagdad; but it was not long ere I grew weary of an indolent life, and, therefore, I set out a second time upon a voyage. We embarked on board a good ship, and, after recommending ourselves to God, set sail. We traded from island to island, and exchanged commodities with great profit. One day we landed at an island covered with several sorts of fruit-trees, but we could see neither man nor animal. We went to take a little fresh air in the meadows, along the streams that watered them. Whilst some diverted themselves with gathering flowers, and other fruits, I took my wine and provisions, and sat down near a stream betwixt two high trees, which formed a thick shade. I made a good meal, and afterward fell asleep. I cannot tell how long I slept, but when I awoke the ship was gone.

I was much alarmed, said Sinbad, at finding the ship gone. I got up and looked around me, but could not see one of the merchants who landed with me. I perceived the ship under sail, but at such a distance, that I lost sight of her in a short time. I upbraided myself a hundred times for not being content with the produce of my first voyage, that might have sufficed me all my life. But all this was in vain, and my repentance too late. Not knowing what to do, I climbed up to the top of a lofty tree, whence I looked about on all sides, to see if I could discover anything that could give me hopes. When I gazed over the land I beheld something white; and coming down, I took what provision I had left, and went toward it, the distance being so great, that I could not distinguish what it was.

As I approached, I thought it to be a white dome of a prodigious height and extent; and when I came up to it, I touched it, and found it to be very smooth. I went round to see if it was open on any side, but saw it was not, and that there was no climbing up to the top as it was so smooth. It was at least fifty paces round.

By this time the sun was about to set, and all of a sudden the sky became as dark as if it had been covered with a thick cloud. I was much astonished at this sudden darkness, but much more when I found it occasioned by a bird of monstrous size, that came flying toward me. I remembered that I had often heard mariners speak of a miraculous bird called a roc, and conceived that the great dome which I so much admired must be its egg. In a short time, the bird alighted, and sat over the egg. As I perceived her coming, I crept close to the egg, so that I had before me one of the legs of the bird, which was as big as the trunk of a tree. I tied myself strongly to it with my turban, in hopes that the roc next morning would carry me with her out of this desert island. After having passed the night in this condition, the bird flew away as soon as it was daylight, and carried me so high, that I could not discern the earth; she afterward descended with so much rapidity that I lost my senses. But when I found myself on the ground, I speedily untied the knot, and had scarcely done so, when the roc, having taken up a serpent of a great length in her bill, flew away.

The spot where it left me was encompassed on all sides by mountains, that seemed to reach above the clouds, and so steep that there was no possibility of getting out of the valley. This was a new perplexity; so that when I compared this place with the desert island from which the roc had brought me, I found that I had gained nothing by the change.

As I walked through this valley, I perceived it was strewn with diamonds, some of which were of a surprising size. I took pleasure in looking upon them; but shortly saw at a distance such objects as greatly diminished my satisfaction, and which I could not view without terror, namely, a great number of serpents, so monstrous, that the least of them was capable of swallowing an elephant. They retired in the day-time to their dens, where they hid themselves from the roc, their enemy, and came out only in the night.

I spent the day in walking about in the valley, resting myself at times in such places as I thought most convenient. When night came on, I went into a cave, where I thought I might repose in safety. I secured the entrance, which was low and narrow, with a great stone to preserve me from the serpents; but not so far as to exclude the light. I supped on part of my provisions, but the serpents, which began hissing round me, put me into such extreme fear, that you may easily imagine I did not sleep. When day appeared, the serpents retired, and I came out of the cave trembling. I can justly say that I walked upon diamonds, without feeling any inclination to touch them. At last I sat down, and notwithstanding my apprehensions, not having closed my eyes during the night, fell asleep, after having eaten a little more of my provision. But I had scarcely shut my eyes, when something that fell by me with a great noise awaked me. This was a large piece of raw meat; and at the same time I saw several others fall down from the rocks in different places.

I had always regarded as fabulous what I had heard sailors and others relate of the valley of diamonds, and of the stratagems employed by merchants to obtain jewels from thence; but now I found that they had stated nothing but the truth. For as a fact, the merchants come to the neighborhood of this valley, when the eagles have young ones, and throwing great joints of meat into the valley, the diamonds, upon whose points they fall, stick to them; the eagles, which are stronger in this country than anywhere else, pounce with great force upon those pieces of meat, and carry them to their nests on the precipices of the rocks to feed their young; the merchants at this time run to their nests, disturb and drive off the eagles by their shouts, and take away the diamonds that stick to the meat.

The happy idea struck me that here was a means of escape from my living tomb; so I collected a number of the largest diamonds, with which I filled my wallet, which I tied to my girdle. Then I fastened one of the joints of meat to the middle of my back by means of my turban cloth, and lay down with my face to the ground.

I had scarcely placed myself in this posture when the eagles came. Each of them seized a piece of meat, and one of the strongest having taken me up, with the piece of meat to which I was fastened, carried me to his nest on the top of the mountain. The merchants began their shouting to frighten the eagles; and when they had obliged them to quit their prey, one of them came to the nest where I was. He was much alarmed when he saw me; but recovering himself, instead of inquiring how I came thither, began to quarrel with me, and asked why I stole his goods. You will treat me, replied I, with more civility, when you know me better. Do not be uneasy; I have diamonds enough for you and myself, more than all the other merchants together. Whatever they have they owe to chance, but I selected for myself in the bottom of the valley those which you see in this bag. I had scarcely done speaking, when the other merchants came crowding about us, much astonished to see me; but they were much more surprised when I told them my story. Yet they did not so much admire my stratagem to effect my deliverance, as my courage in putting it into execution.

They conducted me to their encampment, and there, having opened my bag, they were surprised at the largeness of my diamonds, and confessed that in all the courts which they had visited they had never seen any of such size and perfection. I prayed the merchant, who owned the nest to which I had been carried (for every merchant had his own), to take as many for his share as he pleased. He contented himself with one, and that too the least of them; and when I pressed him to take more, without fear of doing me any injury, No, said he, I am very well satisfied with this which is valuable enough to save me the trouble of making any more voyages, and will raise as great a fortune as I desire.

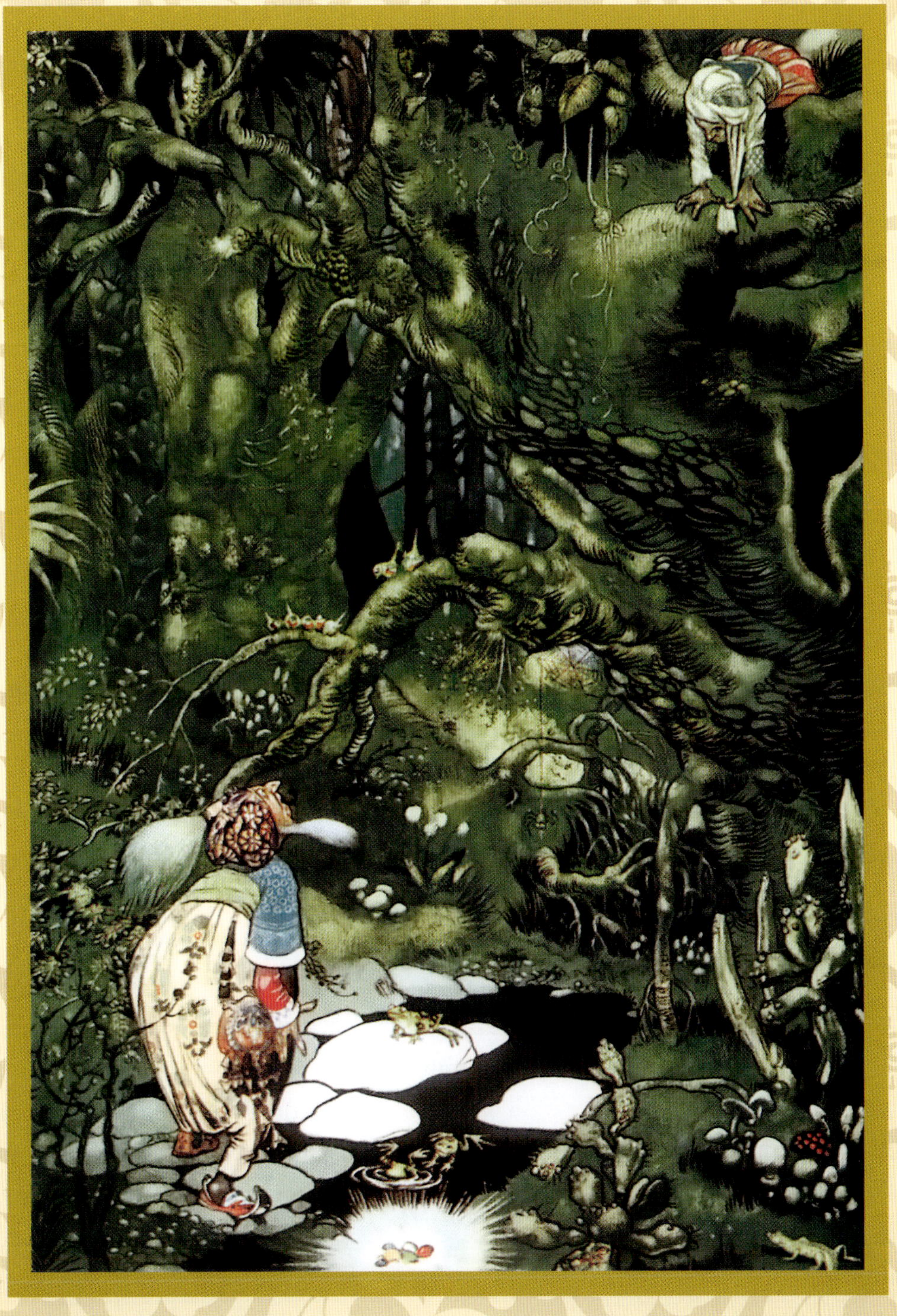

I spent the night with the merchants, to whom I related my story a second time, for the satisfaction of those who had not heard it. I could not moderate my joy when I found myself delivered from the danger I have mentioned. I thought myself in a dream, and could scarcely believe myself out of danger. When at length I reached home I gave large presents to the poor, and lived luxuriously upon my hard-earned wealth.

Then Sinbad ended the account of his second voyage, and, having given Hindbad another hundred sequins, asked him to come on the next day to hear his further adventures.

THE THIRD VOYAGE

I soon wearied of the idle, luxurious life I led, and therefore I undertook another voyage. Overtaken by a dreadful tempest in the main ocean, we were driven upon an island which, the captain told us, was inhabited by hairy savages, who would speedily attack us; and, though they were but dwarfs, yet our misfortune was such, that we must make no resistance, for they were more in number than the locusts; and if we happened to kill one of them, they would all fall upon us and destroy us.

It was not long before the captain's words were proved, for an innumerable multitude of frightful savages, about two feet high, covered all over with red hair, came swimming toward us, and encompassed our ship. We advanced into the island on which we were, and came to a palace, elegantly built, and very lofty, with a gate of ebony of two leaves, which we forced open. We entered the court, where we saw before us a large apartment, with a porch, having on one side a heap of human bones, and on the other a vast number of roasting spits. Our fears were not diminished when the gate of the apartment opened with a loud crash, and there came out the horrible figure of a black man, as tall as a lofty palm-tree. He had but one eye, and that in the middle of his forehead, where it looked as red as a burning coal. His foreteeth were very long and sharp, and stood out of his mouth, which was as deep as that of a horse. His upper lip hung down upon his breast. His ears resembled those of an elephant, and covered his shoulders; and his nails were as long and crooked as the talons of the greatest birds. At the sight of so frightful a giant, we became insensible, and lay like dead men. When he had considered us well, he advanced toward us, and laying his hand upon me, took me up by the nape of my neck, and turned me round as a butcher would do a sheep's head. After having examined me, and perceiving me to be so lean that I had nothing but skin and bone, he let me go. He took up all the rest one by one, and viewed them in the same manner. The captain being the fattest, he held him with one hand, as I would do a sparrow, and thrust a spit through him; he then kindled a great fire, roasted, and ate him in his apartment for his supper. Having finished his repast, he returned to his porch, where he lay and fell asleep, snoring louder than thunder.

We all sat numbed by fear, but the next day, after the giant had gone out, we devised a means of vengeance. And so, when he had again made a supper off one of our number, and lay down to sleep, we prepared to execute the daring design. Therefore nine of us and myself, when we heard him snore, each armed with a spit, the points of which we had made red hot, approached the monster and thrust the spits into his eye at the same time, so that he was blind. The giant made wild efforts to seize us, but finding that we had hidden he went out roaring in his agony.

We lost no time in fleeing from the palace, and soon reached the shore, where we contrived to construct some rafts upon which to sail away in case of need. But, knowing the danger that such a voyage would entail, we waited in the hope that the giant might be dead, since he had ceased to howl. Day had scarcely dawned, however, when we saw our enemy coming toward us, led by two others, nearly as big as himself, and accompanied by a host of others.

We immediately took to our rafts; whereupon the giants, enraged at being thus balked, took up great stones, and, running to the shore, entered the water up to the middle, and threw so exactly that they sunk all the rafts but that I was upon; and all my companions, except the two with me, were drowned. We rowed with all our might, and got out of the reach of the giants, and tossed about for a day and night until at last we reached an island, whereon grew much excellent fruit.

At night we went to sleep on the seashore; but were awakened by the noise of a serpent of surprising length and thickness, whose scales made a rustling noise as he wound himself along. It swallowed up one of my comrades, notwithstanding his loud cries, and the efforts he made to extricate himself from it. Dashing him several times against the ground, it crushed him, and we could hear it gnaw and tear the poor wretch's bones, though we had fled to a considerable distance. Seeing the danger to which we were exposed, we climbed a tall tree the next night to escape the serpent. But, to our horror, the monster raised himself against the trunk of the tree, and, perceiving my companion, who was lower down than I, swallowed him and withdrew.

I remained upon the tree till it was day, and then came down, and collected together a great quantity of small wood, brambles, and dry thorns, and making them up into faggots, made a wide circle with them round the tree, and also tied some of them to the branches over my head. Having done this, when the evening came, I shut myself up within this circle, with the melancholy satisfaction, that I had neglected nothing which could preserve me from the cruel destiny with which I was threatened. The serpent failed not to come at the usual hour, and went round the tree, seeking for an opportunity to devour me, but was prevented by the rampart I had made; so that he lay till day, like a cat watching in vain for a mouse that has fortunately reached a place of safety. When day appeared he retired, but I dared not to leave my fort until the sun arose.

As I ran toward the sea, determined no longer to prolong my miserable existence, I perceived a ship at a considerable distance. I called as loud as I could, and taking the linen from my turban, displayed it, that they might observe me. This had the desired effect; the crew perceived me, and the captain sent his boat for me. As soon as I came on board, the merchants and seamen flocked about me, to know how I came into that desert island; and after I had related to them all that had befallen me, the oldest among them said to me, They had several times heard of the giants that dwelt in that island, that they were cannibals, and ate men raw as well as roasted; and as to the serpents, they added, that there were abundance in the island, that hid themselves by day, and came abroad by night. After having testified their joy at my escaping so many dangers, they brought me the best of their provisions; and the captain, as being the man who had deserted me upon my second voyage, seeing that I was in rags, was so generous as to give me one of his own suits. I soon made myself known to him, whereupon he exclaimed, God be praised. I rejoice that fortune has rectified my fault. There are your goods, which I always took care to preserve. I took them from him, thanked him warmly for his honesty, and contrived to deal so well on the voyage that I arrived at Bussorah with another vast fortune. From Bussorah I returned to Bagdad, where I gave a great deal to the poor, and bought another considerable estate in addition to what I had already.

Having thus finished the account of his third voyage, Sinbad sent Hindbad on his way, after he had given him another hundred sequins, and invited him to dinner the next day to hear the continuation of his adventures.

THE FOURTH VOYAGE

It was not long before I again started on a journey. This time I traveled through Persia and arrived at a port, where I took ship. We had not been long at sea when a great storm overtook us, which was so violent that the sails were split into a thousand pieces, and the ship was stranded; several of the merchants and seamen were drowned, and the cargo was lost.

I had the good fortune, with several of the merchants and mariners, to get upon some planks, and we were carried by the current to an island which lay before us. There we found fruit and spring water, which preserved our lives; and we lay down almost where we had landed and slept.

Next morning, as soon as the sun was up, we walked from the shore, and advancing into the island saw some houses, which we approached. As soon as we drew near, we were encompassed by a great number of natives, who seized us, shared us among them, and carried us to their respective habitations.

I and five of my comrades were carried to one place; here they made us sit down, and gave us a certain herb, which they made signs to us to eat. My comrades not taking notice that the natives ate none of it themselves, thought only of satisfying their hunger, and ate with greediness. But I, suspecting some trick, would not so much as taste it, which happened well for me; for in a little time after, I perceived my companions had lost their senses, and that when they spoke to me, they knew not what they said.

The natives fed us afterward with rice, prepared with oil of cocoa-nuts; and my comrades, who had lost their reason, ate of it greedily. I also partook of it, but very sparingly. They gave us that herb at first on purpose to deprive us of our senses, that we might not be aware of the sad destiny prepared for us; and they supplied us with rice to fatten us; for, being cannibals, their design was to eat us as soon as we grew fat. This accordingly happened, for they devoured my comrades, who were not sensible of their condition; but my senses being entire, you may easily guess that instead of growing fat, as the rest did, I grew leaner every day. The fear of death under which I labored turned all my food into poison. I fell into a languishing distemper, which proved my safety; for the natives, having killed and eaten my companions, seeing me to be withered, lean, and sick, deferred my death.

Meanwhile I had much liberty, so that scarcely any notice was taken of what I did, and this gave me an opportunity one day to get at a distance from the houses and to make my escape. An old man, who saw me, and suspected my design, called to me as loud as he could to return; but instead of obeying him, I redoubled my speed, and quickly got out of sight. I traveled as fast as I could, and chose those places which seemed most deserted, living for seven days on the fruit I gathered.

On the eighth day I came near the sea, and saw some white people like myself, gathering pepper, of which there was great plenty in that place. As soon as they saw me they came to meet me, and asked me in Arabic, who I was, and whence I came. I was overjoyed to hear them speak in my own language, and satisfied their curiosity by giving them an account of my shipwreck, and how I fell into the hands of the natives. Those natives, replied they, eat men, and by what miracle did you escape their cruelty? I related to them the circumstances I have just mentioned, at which they were wonderfully surprised.

I stayed with them till they had gathered their quantity of pepper, and then sailed with them to the island from whence they had come. They presented me to their King, who was a good Prince. He listened to my story, bade me welcome, and soon had conceived a great friendship for me, which fact made me a person of importance in the capital.

None of these people ride with either saddle or bridle, and so, wishing to honor the King, I went to a workman, and gave him a model for making the stock of a saddle. When that was done, I covered it myself with velvet and leather, and embroidered it with gold. I afterward went to a smith, who made me a bit, according to the pattern I showed him, and also some stirrups. When I had all the trappings completed, I presented them to the King, and put them upon one of his horses. His Majesty mounted immediately, and was so pleased with them, that he testified his satisfaction by large presents, and said: I wish you to marry and think no more of your own land, but stay here as long as you live. I durst not resist the Prince's will, and he gave me one of the ladies of his court, noble, beautiful, and rich. The ceremonies of marriage being over, I went and dwelt with my wife, and for some time we lived together in perfect harmony. I was not, however, satisfied with my banishment, therefore designed to make my escape upon the first opportunity, and to return to Bagdad, which my present settlement, howsoever advantageous, could not make me forget.

At this time the wife of one of my neighbors, with whom I had contracted a very strict friendship, fell sick, and died. I went to see and comfort him in his affliction, and finding him absorbed in sorrow, I said to him as soon as I saw him, God preserve you and grant you a long life. Alas! replied he, your good wishes are vain, for I must be buried this day with my wife. This is a law which our ancestors established in this island, and it is always observed inviolably. The living husband is interred with the dead wife, and the living wife with the dead husband. Nothing can save me; every one must submit to this law.

While he was giving me an account of this barbarous custom, the very relation of which chilled my blood, his kindred, friends, and neighbors, came in a body to assist at the funeral. They dressed the body of the woman in her richest apparel, and all her jewels, as if it had been her wedding-day; then they placed her on an open coffin, and began their march to the place of burial. The husband walked at the head of the company, and followed the corpse. They proceeded to a high mountain, and when they had reached the place of their destination, they took up a large stone, which covered the mouth of a deep pit, and let down the corpse with all its apparel and jewels. Then the husband, embracing his kindred and friends, suffered himself to be put into another open coffin without resistance, with a pot of water, and seven small loaves, and was let down in the same manner. The mountain was of considerable length, and extended along the seashore, and the pit was very deep. The ceremony being over, the aperture was again covered with the stone, and the company returned.

Not long after this I was destined to share a like fate, for my wife, of whose health I took particular care, fell sick and died. In spite of every effort on my part, the law of the land had to be fulfilled; and so, accompanied by the King and the chief nobles, who had come to honor me at the grave, I was lowered into the tomb with my wife's body and the usual supply of bread and water. I had come to the end of my provisions, and was expecting death, when I heard a puffing noise as of something breathing. I moved toward the place whence the sound came, and heard a skurrying of feet as the creature ran away. I pursued it, and at last perceived what seemed to be a star in the distance. The speck of light grew larger as I approached, and I soon found that it was a hole in the side of the mountain, above the seashore. I cast myself upon the sand overcome with joy, and as I raised my eyes to heaven, I perceived a ship at no great distance. I waved my turban linen, which attracted the attention of those on board; whereupon they sent a boat which carried me safely on board. I told the captain that I was a shipwrecked merchant, and he believed my story, and without asking any questions took me with him.

After a long voyage, during which we called at several ports, whereat I made much money, I arrived happily at Bagdad with infinite riches, of which it is needless to trouble you with the detail. Out of gratitude to God for his mercies, I contributed liberally toward the support of several mosques, and the subsistence of the poor, gave myself up to the society of my kindred and friends, enjoying myself with them in festivities and amusements.

Sinbad then presented another hundred sequins to the porter, and bade him honor him with his presence again next day.

THE FIFTH VOYAGE

The pleasures I enjoyed had again charms enough to make me forget all the troubles and calamities I had undergone, but could not cure me of my inclination to make new voyages. I therefore bought goods, departed with them for the best seaport; and there, that I might not be obliged to depend upon a captain, but have a ship at my own command, I remained till one was built on purpose, at my own charge. When the ship was ready, I went on board with my goods; but not having enough to load her, I agreed to take with me several merchants of different nations with their merchandise.

We sailed with the first fair wind, and after a long navigation, the first place we touched at was a desert island, where we found an egg of a roc, equal in size to that I formerly mentioned. There was a young roc in it just ready to be hatched, and its bill had begun to appear.

The merchants who landed with me broke the egg with hatchets, and pulled out the young roc piecemeal, and roasted it. I had earnestly entreated them not to meddle with the egg, but they would not listen to me.

Scarcely had they finished their repast, when there appeared in the air at a considerable distance from us two great clouds. The captain whom I had hired to navigate my ship, knowing by experience what they meant, said they were the male and female roc that belonged to the young one, and pressed us to re-embark with all speed, to prevent the misfortune which he saw would otherwise befall us. We hastened on board, and set sail with all possible expedition.

In the meantime, the two rocs approached with a frightful noise, which they redoubled when they saw the egg broken and their young one gone. They flew back in the direction they had come, and disappeared for some time, while we made all the sail we could to endeavor to prevent that which unhappily befell us.

They soon returned, and we observed that each of them carried between its talons stones of a monstrous size. When they came directly over my ship, they hovered, and one of them let fall a stone, but by the dexterity of the steersman it missed us, and falling into the sea, divided the water so that we could almost see the bottom. The other roc, to our misfortune, threw his massive burden so exactly upon the middle of the ship as to split it into a thousand pieces. The mariners and passengers were all crushed to death, or sunk. I myself was of the number of the latter; but as I came up again, I fortunately caught hold of a piece of the wreck, and swimming sometimes with one hand, and sometimes with the other, but always holding fast my board, the wind and the tide favoring me, I came to an island, whose shore was very steep. I overcame that difficulty, however, and got ashore.

I sat down upon the grass, to recover myself from my fatigue, after which I went into the island to explore it. It seemed to be a delicious garden. I found trees everywhere, some of them bearing green, and others ripe fruits, and streams of fresh pure water running in pleasant meanders. I ate of the fruits, which I found excellent; and drank of the water, which was very sweet and good.

When night closed in, I lay down upon the grass in a convenient spot, but could not sleep an hour at a time, my mind being apprehensive of danger. I spent the best part of the night in alarm, and reproached myself for my imprudence in not remaining at home, rather than undertaking this last voyage. These reflections carried me so far, that I began to form a design against my life; but daylight dispersed these melancholy thoughts. I got up, and walked among the trees, but not without some fears.

As I advanced into the island, I saw an old man who appeared very weak and infirm. He was sitting on the bank of a stream, and at first I took him to be one who had been shipwrecked like myself. I went toward him and saluted him, but he only slightly bowed his head. I asked him why he sat so still, but instead of answering me, he made a sign for me to take him upon my back, and carry him over the brook, signifying that it was to gather fruit.

I believed him really to stand in need of my assistance, took him upon my back, and having carried him over, bade him get down, and for that end stooped, that he might get off with ease; but instead of doing so the old man, who to me appeared quite decrepit, clasped his legs nimbly about my neck, so tightly that I swooned.

Notwithstanding my fainting, the ill-natured old fellow kept fast about my neck, but opened his legs a little to give me time to recover my breath. When I had done so, he thrust one of his feet against my stomach, and struck me so rude on the side with the other, that he forced me to rise up against my will. Having arisen, he made me walk under the trees, and forced me now and then to stop, to gather and eat fruit such as we found. He never left me all day, and when I lay down to rest at night, laid himself down with me, holding always fast about my neck. Every morning he pushed me to make me awake, and afterward obliged me to get up and walk, and pressed me with his feet. You may judge then, gentlemen, what trouble I was in, to be loaded with such a burden of which I could not get rid.

One day I found in my way several dry calabashes that had fallen from a tree. I took a large one, and after cleaning it, pressed into it some juice of grapes, which abounded in the island; having filled the calabash, I put it by in a convenient place, and going thither again some days after, I tasted it, and found the wine so good that it soon made me forget my sorrow, gave me new vigor, and so exhilarated my spirits that I began to sing and dance as I walked along.

The old man perceiving the effect which this liquor had upon me, and that I carried him with more ease than before, made me a sign to give him some of it. I handed him the calabash, and the liquor pleasing his palate, he drank it all off, and was soon so intoxicated that his grip released. Seizing this opportunity, I threw him upon the ground, where he lay without motion; I then took up a great stone, and crushed his head to pieces.

I was extremely glad to be thus freed for ever from this troublesome fellow. I now walked toward the beach, where I met the crew of a ship that had cast anchor to take in water. They were surprised to see me, but more so at hearing the particulars of my adventures. You fell, said they, into the hands of the Old Man of the Sea, and are the first who ever escaped strangling by his malicious tricks. He never quitted those he had once made himself master of, till he had destroyed them, and he has made this island notorious by the number of men he has slain; so that the merchants and mariners who landed upon it, durst not advance into the island but in numbers at a time. After saying this, they carried me with them to the ship. The captain received me with great kindness when they told him what had befallen me. He put out again to sea, and after some days' sail, we arrived at the harbor of a great city, the houses of which were built with hewn stone.

One of the merchants who had taken me into his friendship invited me to go along with him, and gave me a large bag, and having recommended me to some people of the town, who used to gather cocoa-nuts, desired them to take me with them. Go, said he, follow them, and act as you see them do, but do not separate from them, otherwise you may endanger your life. Having thus spoken, he gave me provisions for the journey, and I went with them.

We came to a thick forest of cocoa palms, very lofty, with trunks so smooth that it was not possible to climb to the branches that bore the fruit. When we entered the forest we saw a great number of apes of several sizes, who fled as soon as they perceived us, and climbed up to the top of the trees with surprising swiftness.

The merchants with whom I was gathered stones and threw them at the apes on the trees. I did the same, and the apes out of revenge threw cocoa-nuts at us so fast, and with such gestures, as sufficiently testified their anger and resentment. We gathered up the cocoa-nuts, and from time to time threw stones to provoke the apes; so that by this stratagem we filled our bags with cocoa-nuts. I soon sold mine, and returned several times to the forest, so that I made a considerable sum.

The vessel in which I had come sailed with some merchants, who loaded her with cocoa-nuts. I expected the arrival of another, which anchored soon after for the like loading. I embarked in her all the cocoa-nuts I had, and when she was ready to sail, took leave of the merchant who had been so kind to me; but he could not embark with me, because he had not finished his business at the port. We sailed toward the islands, where pepper grows in great plenty. From thence we went to the Isle of Comari, where the best species of wood of aloes grows, and whose inhabitants have made it an inviolable law to themselves to drink no wine. I exchanged my cocoa-nuts in those islands for pepper and wood of aloes, and went with other merchants pearl-fishing. I hired divers, who brought me up some that were very large and pure. I embarked in a vessel that happily arrived at Bussorah; from thence I returned to Bagdad, where I made vast sums of my pepper, wood of aloes, and pearls. I gave the tenth of my gains in alms, as I had done upon my return from my other voyages, and endeavored to dissipate my fatigues by amusements of different kinds.

When he had thus finished his story Sinbad presented Hindbad with a hundred sequins, as before, and entreated him to present himself at the usual hour the next day.

The Seven Voyages of Sinbad

THE SIXTH VOYAGE

The roving spirit being in me, I could not stay long idle; and so, after a year's rest, I made ready for my sixth voyage, in spite of the entreaties of my friends and kinsfolk. This time I traveled through Persia and the Indies before taking ship, and at last embarked, at a distant port, in a vessel that was bound for a long voyage. We had sailed far when one day the captain quitted his post in great grief, and casting away his turban, cried, in a voice of agony, A rapid current carries the ship along with it, and we shall all perish in less than a quarter of an hour. Pray to God to deliver us from this peril; we cannot escape if He does not take pity on us. At these words he ordered the sails to be lowered; but all the ropes broke, and the ship was carried by the current to the foot of an inaccessible mountain, where she struck and went to pieces, yet in such a manner that we saved our lives, our provisions, and the best of our goods.

This being over, the captain said to us, God has done what pleased Him. Each of us may dog his grave, and bid the world adieu; for we are all in so fatal a place that none shipwrecked here ever returned to their homes. His discourse afflicted us sensibly, and we embraced each other, bewailing our deplorable lot.

The mountain at the foot of which we were wrecked formed part of the coast of a very large island. It is also incredible what a quantity of goods and riches we found cast ashore. All these objects served only to augment our despair. In all other places, rivers run from their channels into the sea, but here a river of fresh water runs out of the sea into a dark cavern, whose entrance is very high and spacious. What is most remarkable in this place is, that the stones of the mountain are of crystal, rubies, or other precious stones. Trees also grow here, most of which are wood of aloes, equal in goodness to those of Comari.

To finish the description of this place, which may well be called a gulf, since nothing ever returns from it, it is not possible for ships to get off when once they approach within a certain distance. If they be driven thither by a wind from the sea, the wind and the current impel them; and if they come into it when a land-wind blows, which might seem to favor their getting out again, the height of the mountain stops the wind, and occasions a calm, so that the force of the current carries them ashore: and what completes the misfortune is, that there is no possibility of ascending the mountain, or of escaping by sea.

We were, indeed, in a sorry plight; and the number of wrecks and skeletons which were upon the coast confirmed the captain's statement that our chance of escape was very small, and although the spot was fair enough to see, we mourned our lot, and awaited death with such patience as we could command.

At last our provisions began to run short, and one by one the members of the company died, until I was left alone out of the whole number. Those who died first, continued Sinbad, were interred by the survivors, and I paid the last duty to all my companions: nor are you to wonder at this; for besides that I husbanded the provisions that fell to my share better than they, I had some of my own, which I did not share with my comrades; yet when I buried the last, I had so little remaining, that I thought I could not long survive: I dug a grave, resolving to lie down in it, because there was no one left to inter me. I must confess to you at the same time, that while I was thus employed, I could not but reproach myself as the cause of my own ruin, and repented that I had ever undertaken this last voyage. Nor did I stop at reflections only, but had well nigh hastened my own death, and began to tear my hands with my teeth.

But it pleased God once more to take compassion on me, and put it in my mind to go to the bank of the river which ran into the great cavern. Considering its probable course with great attention, I said to myself: This river, which runs thus underground, must somewhere have an issue. If I make a raft, and leave myself to the current, it will convey me to some inhabited country, or I shall perish. If I be drowned, I lose nothing, but only change one kind of death for another; and if I get out of this fatal place, I shall not only avoid the sad fate of my comrades, but perhaps find some new occasion of enriching myself. Who knows but fortune waits, upon my getting off this dangerous shelf to, to compensate my shipwreck with usury.

I immediately went to work upon large pieces of timber and cables, for I had choice of them, and tied them together so strongly, that I soon made a very solid raft. When I had finished, I loaded it with some bulses of rubies, emeralds, ambergris, rock-crystal, and bales of rich stuffs, and leaving it to the course of the river, resigned myself to the will of God, comforting myself with the reflection that in any case it little mattered how death came, whether in the form of drowning or starvation.

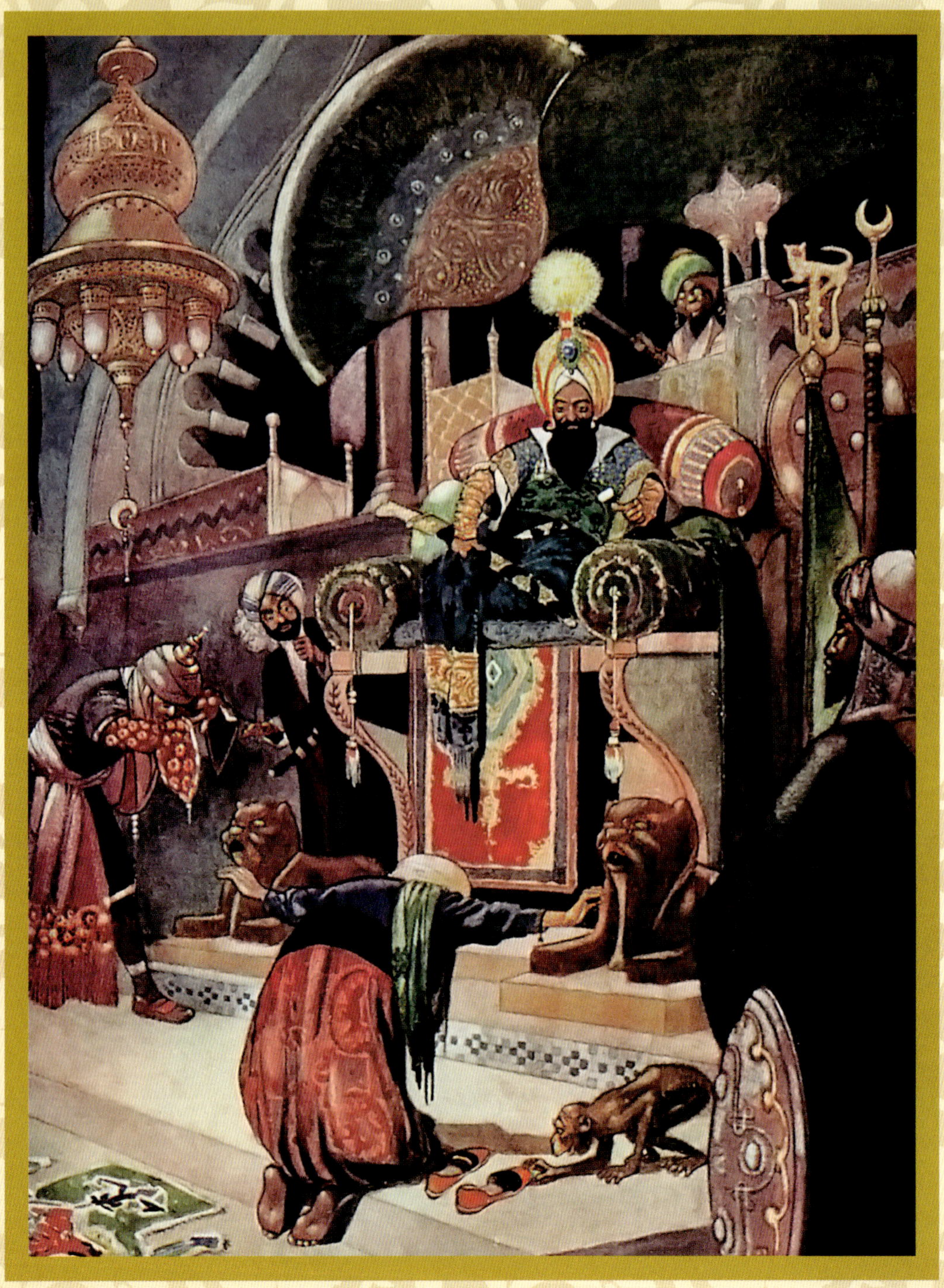

As soon as I entered the cavern, I lost all light, and the stream carried me I knew not whither. Thus I floated some days in perfect darkness, and once found the arch so low that it very nearly touched my head, which made me cautious afterward to avoid the like danger. All this while I ate nothing but what was just necessary to support nature; yet, notwithstanding my frugality, all my provisions were spent, and I lost consciousness. I cannot tell how long I remained insensible; but when I revived, I was surprised to find myself in an extensive plain on the brink of a river, where my raft was tied, amidst a great number of natives. I got up as soon as I saw them, and saluted them. They spoke to me, but I did not understand their language. I was so transported with joy that I cried aloud in Arabic, expressing my gratitude to God.

One of the natives, who understood Arabic, hearing me speak thus, came toward me, and said, Brother, pray tell us your history, for it must be extraordinary; how did you venture yourself upon this river, and whence did you come? I begged of them first to give me something to eat, and assured them I would then satisfy their curiosity. They gave me several sorts of food, and when I had I related all that had befallen me, which they listened to with attentive surprise, and, having brought a gorse they conducted me to their King, that he might hear so remarkable a story.

We marched till we came to the capital of Serendib, for it was in that island I had landed. The natives presented me to their King; I approached his throne, and saluted him as I used to do the Kings of the Indies; that is to say, I prostrated myself at his feet. The Prince ordered me to rise, received me with an obliging air, and made me sit down near him. He first asked me my name, and I answered, People call me Sinbad the voyager, because of the many voyages I have undertaken, and I am a citizen of Bagdad. I then narrated all my adventures without reserve, and observing that he looked on my jewels with pleasure, and viewed the most remarkable among them one after another, I fell prostrate at his feet, and took the liberty to say to him, Sir, not only my person is at Your Majesty's service, but the cargo of the raft, and I would beg of you to dispose of it as your own. He answered me with a smile, Sinbad, instead of taking from you, I intend to add presents worthy of your acceptance.

All the answer I returned was a prayer for the prosperity of that nobly-minded Prince and commendations of his generosity and bounty. He charged one of his officers to take care of me, and ordered people to serve me at his own expense. The officer was very faithful in the execution of his commission, and caused all the goods to be carried to the lodgings provided for me.

The isle of Serendib is situated just under the equinoctial line; so that the days and nights there are always of twelve hours each, and the island is eighty parasangs in length, and as many in breadth.

The capital stands at the end of a fine valley, in the middle of the island, encompassed by mountains the highest in the world. They are seen three days' sail off at sea. Rubies and several sorts of minerals abound, and the rocks are for the most part composed of a metalline stone made use of to cut and polish other precious stones. All kinds of rare plants and trees grow there, especially cedars and cocoa-nut. There is also a pearl-fishery in the mouth of its principal river; and in some of its valleys are found diamonds.

Having spent some time in the capital, and visited all the places of interest around, among which is the place where Adam dwelt after his banishment from Paradise, I prayed the King to allow me to return to my own country, and he granted me permission in the most obliging and most honorable manner. He forced a rich present upon me; and when I went to take my leave of him, he gave me one much more considerable, and at the same time charged me with a letter for the Commander of the Faithful, our sovereign, saying to me, I pray you give this present from me, and this letter to the caliph, and assure him of my friendship.

The letter from the King of Serendib was written on the skin of a certain animal of great value, because of its being so scarce, and of a yellowish color. The characters of this letter were of azure, and the contents as follows:—

"The King of the Indies, before whom march one hundred elephants, who lives in a palace that shines with one hundred thousand rubies, and who has in his treasury twenty thousand crowns enriched with diamonds, to Caliph Haroun al Raschid.

"Though the present we send you be inconsiderable, receive it however as a brother and a friend, in consideration of the hearty friendship which we bear for you, and of which we are willing to give you proof. We desire the same part in your friendship, considering that we believe it to be our merit, being of the same dignity with yourself. We conjure you this in quality of a brother. Adieu."

The present consisted firstly of one single ruby made into a cup, about half a foot high, an inch thick, and filled with round pearls of half a drachm each. Secondly, the skin of a serpent, whose scales were as large as an ordinary piece of gold, and had the virtue to preserve from sickness those who lay upon it. Thirdly, fifty thousand drachms of the best wood of aloes, with thirty grains of camphire as big as pistachios. And, fourthly, a female of exceeding beauty, whose apparel was all covered over with jewels.

The ship set sail, and after a very successful navigation we landed at Bussorah, and from thence I went to Bagdad, where I immediately went to deliver the King's letter to the caliph. And after I had presented myself, the caliph listened with attention to my description of the Indies, which showed that the King had in no way exaggerated his wealth. And I likewise described the manners and customs of the people, which also interested the Commander of the Faithful.

Having spoken thus, Sinbad notified that the account of his sixth voyage was at an end, and presented Hindbad with another hundred sequins, urging him to return next day to hear the history of his seventh and last voyage.

THE SEVENTH AND FINAL VOYAGE

After my sixth voyage I had made up my mind to stay at home. I absolutely laid aside all thoughts of traveling; for, besides that my age now required rest, I was resolved no more to expose myself to such risks as I had encountered; so that I thought of nothing but to pass the rest of my days in tranquility. But one day a messenger came from the caliph summoning me to the palace, and when I came into the presence chamber the caliph said, Sinbad, I stand in need of your service; you must carry my answer and present to the King of Serendib. It is but just I should return his civility.

I tried to escape from this new trial, and narrated all my adventures to the caliph. As soon as I had finished, I confess, said he, that the things you tell me are very extraordinary, yet you must for my sake undertake this voyage which I propose to you. You will only have to go to the Isle of Serendib, and deliver the commission which I give you. After that you are at liberty to return. But you must go; for you know it would not comport with my dignity, to be indebted to the King of that island. Perceiving that the caliph insisted upon my compliance, I submitted, and told him that I was willing to obey. He was very well pleased, and ordered me one thousand sequins for the expenses of my journey. I therefore prepared for my departure in a few days; and as soon as the caliph's letter and present were delivered to me, I went to Bussorah, where I embarked, and had a very happy voyage. Having arrived at the Isle of Serendib, I was at once led, with great ceremony, to the palace, where the King, seeing me, exclaimed, Sinbad, you are welcome; I have many times thought of you since you departed; I bless the day on which we see one another once more. I made my compliment to him, and after having thanked him for his kindness, delivered the caliph's letter and present, which he received with all imaginable satisfaction.

The caliph's present was a complete suit of cloth of gold, valued at one thousand sequins; fifty robes of rich stuff; a hundred of white cloth, the finest of Cairo, Suez, and Alexandria; a vessel of agate broader than deep, an inch thick, and half a foot wide, the bottom of which represented in bas-relief a man with one knee on the ground, who held a bow and an arrow ready to discharge at a lion. He sent him also a rich tablet, which, according to tradition, belonged to the great Solomon.

The caliph's letter was as follows:—

"Greeting, in the name of the sovereign guide of the right way, from the dependent on God, Haroun al Raschid, whom God hath set in the place of viceregent to His Prophet, after his ancestors of happy memory, to the potent and esteemed Rajah of Serendib.

"We received your letter with joy, and send you this from our imperial residence, the garden of superior wits. We hope, when you look upon it, you will perceive our good intention and be pleased with it. Adieu."

The King of Serendib was highly gratified that the caliph answered his friendship. A little time after this audience, I, with great difficulty, obtained permission to return, and with a very handsome present I embarked to return to Bagdad, but had not the good fortune to arrive there so speedily as I had hoped. God ordered it otherwise.

Three or four days after my departure, we were attacked by corsairs, who easily seized upon our ship, and took those of the crew who did not fall in the fight into a far country, and sold us as slaves.

I, being one of the number, fell into the hands of a rich merchant, who, as soon as he bought me, carried me to his house, treated me well, and clad me handsomely for a slave. Some days after, not knowing who I was, he asked me if I understood any trade. I answered that I was no mechanic, but a merchant, and that the corsairs, who sold me, had robbed me of all I possessed. But tell me, replied he, can you shoot with a bow? I answered that the bow was one of my exercises in my youth. He gave me a bow and arrows, and, taking me behind him upon an elephant, carried me to a thick forest some leagues from the town. We penetrated a great way into the wood, and when he thought fit to stop, he bade me alight; then showing me a great tree, Climb up that, said he, and shoot at the elephants as you see them pass by, for there is a prodigious number of them in this forest; and if any of them fall, come and give me notice. Having spoken thus, he left me victuals, and returned to the town, and I continued upon the tree all night.

I saw no elephant during that time, but next morning, as soon as the sun was up, I perceived a great number. I shot several arrows among them, and at last one of the elephants fell, when the rest retired immediately, and left me at liberty to go and acquaint my patron with my booty. When I had informed him, he gave me a good meal, commended my dexterity, and caressed me highly. We went afterward together to the forest, where we dug a hole for the elephant, my patron designing to return when it was rotten and take his teeth to trade with.

I continued this employment for two months, and killed an elephant every day, getting sometimes upon one tree and sometimes upon another. One morning, as I looked for the elephants, I perceived with extreme amazement that, instead of passing by me across the forest as usual, they stopped, and came to me with a horrible noise, in such number that the plain was covered and shook under them. They encompassed the tree in which I was concealed, with their trunks extended, and all fixed their eyes upon me. At this alarming spectacle I continued immovable, and was so much terrified that my bow and arrows fell out of my hand.

My fears were not without cause; for after the elephants had stared upon me some time, one of the largest of them put his trunk round the foot of the tree, plucked it up, and threw it on the ground. I fell with the tree, and the elephant, taking me up with his trunk, laid me on his back, and, followed by all the others, carried me to a hill, where he deposited me and withdrew with the herd. Imagine my surprise when I got up and saw that the hill was covered with elephants' bones and teeth. I at once guessed that this was the burial-ground of the elephants, and admired the instinct of the animals; for I doubted not but that they carried me thither on purpose to tell me that I should forbear to persecute them, since I did it only for their teeth. I did not stay on the hill, but turned toward the city, and, after having traveled a day and a night, I came to my patron. I met no elephant in my way, which made me think they had retired farther into the forest, to leave me at liberty to come back to the hill without any obstacle.

My master was overjoyed to see me. Ah, poor Sinbad, exclaimed he, I was in great trouble to know what was become of you. I have been at the forest, where I found a tree newly pulled up, and a bow and arrows on the ground, and after having sought for you in vain, I despaired of ever seeing you more. Pray tell me what befell you, and by what good chance thou art still alive. I satisfied his curiosity, and going both of us next morning to the hill, he found to his great joy that what I had told him was true. We loaded the elephant which had carried us with as many teeth as he could bear; and when I told him what I had found he hastened to reach the hill, and we carried away as much ivory as we could. After we reached home, he said, Sinbad, not only are we made rich, but you have also saved many lives, for hitherto a large number of slaves perished in the task of obtaining ivory. Consider yourself no longer a slave, and ask whatever you will from me, for you are evidently chosen by God for some great work.

To this obliging declaration I replied, Your giving me my liberty is enough to discharge what you owe me, and I desire no other reward for the service I had the good fortune to do to you but leave to return to my own country. Very well, said he, the monsoon will in a little time bring ships for ivory. I will then send you home, and give you wherewith to bear your charges. I thanked him again for my liberty and his good intentions toward me. I stayed with him expecting the monsoon, and during that time we made so many journeys to the hill that we filled all our warehouses with ivory. The other merchants who traded in it did the same, for it could not be long concealed from them.

The ships arrived at last, and my patron, himself having made choice of the ship wherein I was to embark, loaded half of it with ivory on my account, laid in provisions in abundance for my passage, and besides obliged me to accept a present of some curiosities of the country of great value, for which I returned him a thousand thanks, and then departed, after a sad leave-taking.

We stopped at some islands to take in fresh provisions. Our vessel being come to a port on the mainland in the Indies, we touched there, and not being willing to venture by sea to Bussorah, I landed my proportion of the ivory, resolving to proceed on my journey by land. I made vast sums of my ivory, bought several rarities, which I intended for presents, and when my equipage was ready, set out in company with a large caravan of merchants. I was a long time on the way, and suffered much, but endured all with patience, when I considered that I had nothing to fear from the seas, from pirates, from serpents, or from the other perils to which I had been exposed.

All these fatigues ended at last, and I arrived safe at Bagdad. I went immediately to wait upon the caliph, and gave him an account of my embassy. That Prince said he had been uneasy, as I was so long in returning, but that he always hoped God would preserve me. When I told him the adventure of the elephants he seemed much surprised, and would never have given any credit to it had he not known my veracity. He deemed this story, and the other relations I had given him, to be so curious that he ordered one of his secretaries to write them in characters of gold and lay them up in his treasury. I retired well satisfied with the honors I received and the presents which he gave me, and ever since I have devoted myself wholly to my family, kindred, and friends.

Sinbad here finished the relation of his seventh and last voyage, and then addressing himself to Hindbad, Well, friend said he, did you ever hear of any person that suffered so much as I have done, or of any mortal that has gone through so many vicissitudes? Is it not reasonable that, after all this, I should enjoy a quiet and pleasant life? Hindbad drew near and kissed his hand in token of his respect, and said how insignificant were his own troubles compared with those he had heard related. Sinbad gave him another hundred sequins, and told him that every day there would be a place laid for him at his table, and that he could always rely upon the friendship of Sinbad the Sailor.

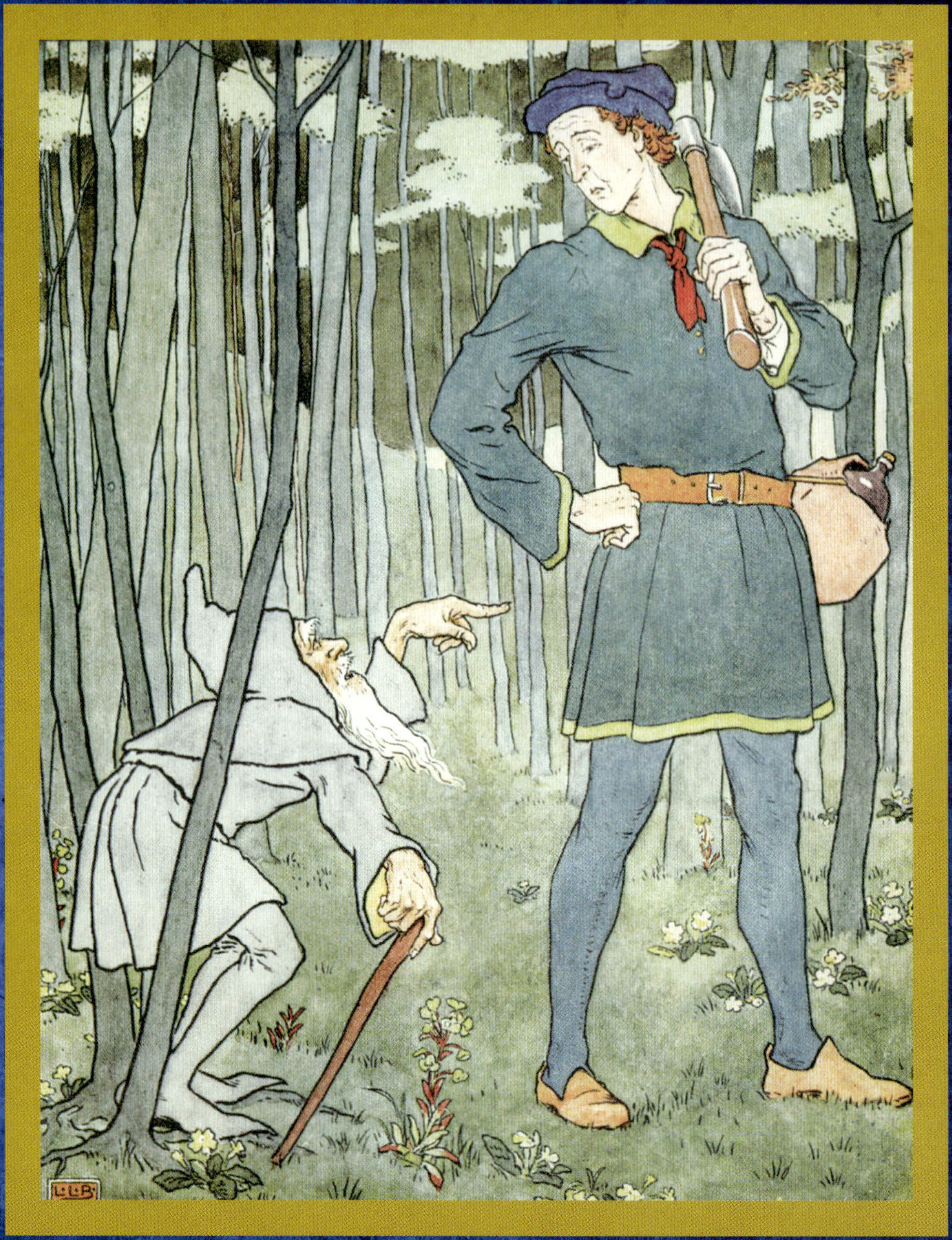

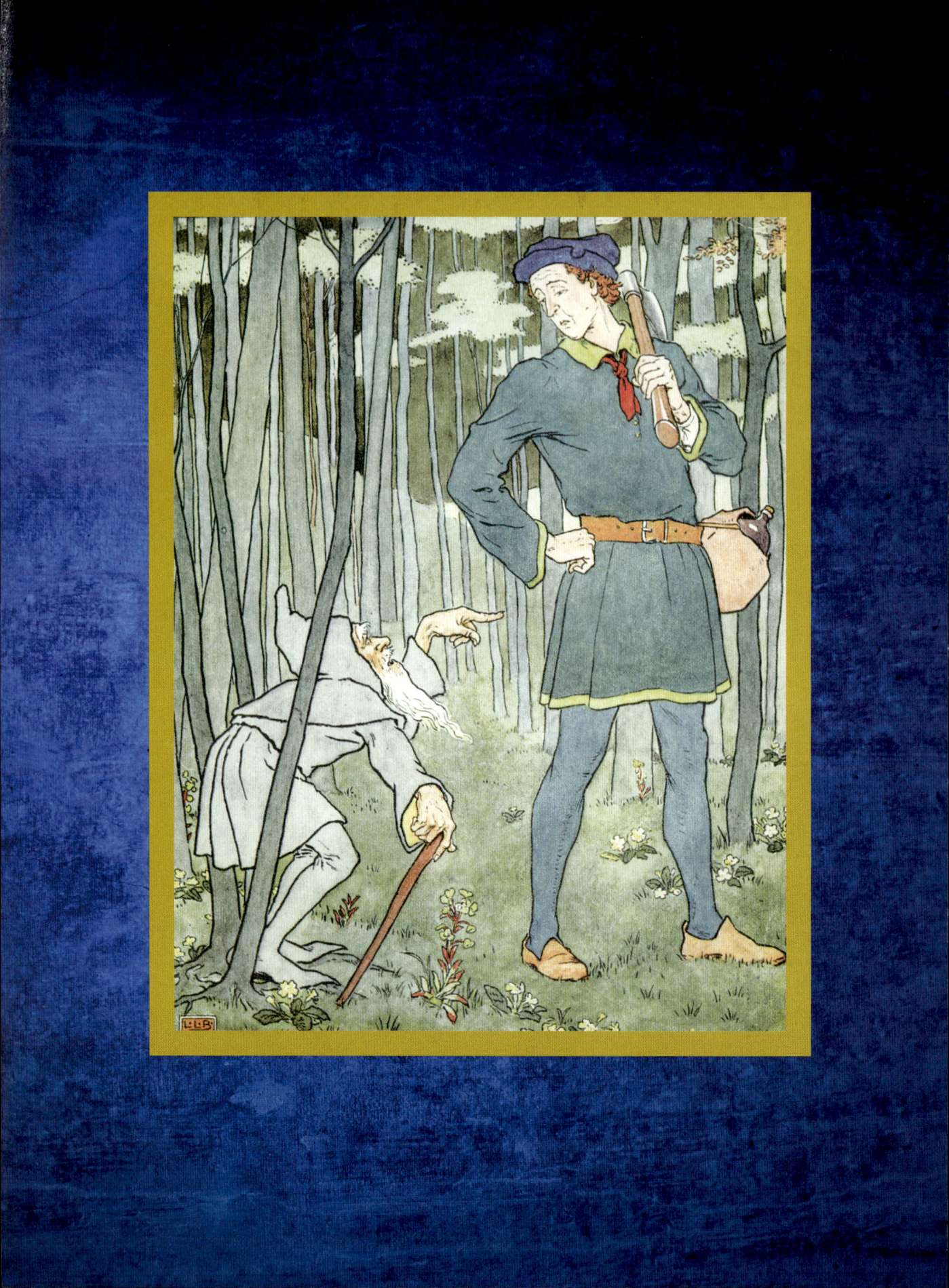

The Golden Goose

There was once a man who had three sons, the youngest of whom was called the Simpleton. He was laughed at and despised and neglected on all occasions. Now it happened one day that the eldest son wanted to go into the forest, to hew wood, and his Mother gave him a beautiful cake and a bottle of wine to take with him, so that he might not suffer from hunger or thirst. When he came to the wood he met a little old gray man, who, bidding him good-day, said: "Give me a small piece of the cake in your wallet, and let me drink a mouthful of your wine; I am so hungry and thirsty." But the clever son answered: "If I were to give you my cake and wine, I should have none for myself, so be off with you," and he left the little man standing there, and walked away. Hardly had he begun to hew down a tree, when his axe slipped and cut his arm, so that he had to go home at once and have the wound bound up. This was the work of the little gray man.

Thereupon the second son went into the wood, and the Mother gave him, as she had given to the eldest, a sweet cake and a bottle of wine. The little old man met him also, and begged for a small slice of cake and a drink of wine. But the second son spoke out quite plainly. "What I give to you I lose myself—be off with you," and he left the little man standing there, and walked on. Punishment was not long in coming to him, for he had given but two strokes at a tree when he cut his leg so badly that he had to be carried home.

Then said the Simpleton: "Father, let me go into the forest and hew wood." But his Father answered him: "Your brothers have done themselves much harm, so as you understand nothing about wood-cutting you had better not try." But the Simpleton begged for so long that at last the Father said: "Well, go if you like; experience will soon make you wiser." To him the Mother gave a cake, but it was made with water and had been baked in the ashes, and with it she gave him a bottle of sour beer. When he came to the wood the little gray man met him also, and greeted him, and said: "Give me a slice of your cake and a drink from your bottle; I am so hungry and thirsty." The Simpleton replied: "I have only a cake that has been baked in the ashes, and some sour beer, but if that will satisfy you, let us sit down and eat together." So they sat themselves down, and as the Simpleton held out his food it became a rich cake, and the sour beer became good wine.

So they ate and drank together, and when the meal was finished, the little man said: "As you have a good heart and give so willingly a share of your own, I will grant you good luck. Yonder stands an old tree; hew it down, and in its roots you will find something." Saying this the old man took his departure, and off went the Simpleton and cut down the tree. When it fell, there among its roots sat a goose, with feathers of pure gold. He lifted her out, and carried her with him to an inn where he intended to stay the night.

Now the innkeeper had three daughters, who on seeing the goose were curious to know what wonderful kind of a bird it could be, and longed to have one of its golden feathers. The eldest daughter thought to herself, "Surely a chance will come for me to pull out one of those feathers"; and so when the Simpleton had gone out, she caught the goose by the wing. But there her hand stuck fast! Shortly afterward the second daughter came, as she too was longing for a golden feather. She had hardly touched her sister, however, when she also stuck fast. And lastly came the third daughter with the same object. At this the others cried out, "Keep off, for goodness' sake, keep off!" But she, not understanding why they told her to keep away, thought to herself, "If they go to the goose, why should not I?" She sprang forward, but as she touched her sister she too stuck fast, and pull as she might she could not get away; and thus they had all to pass the night beside the goose.

The next morning the Simpleton took the goose under his arm and went on his way, without troubling himself at all about the three girls who were hanging to the

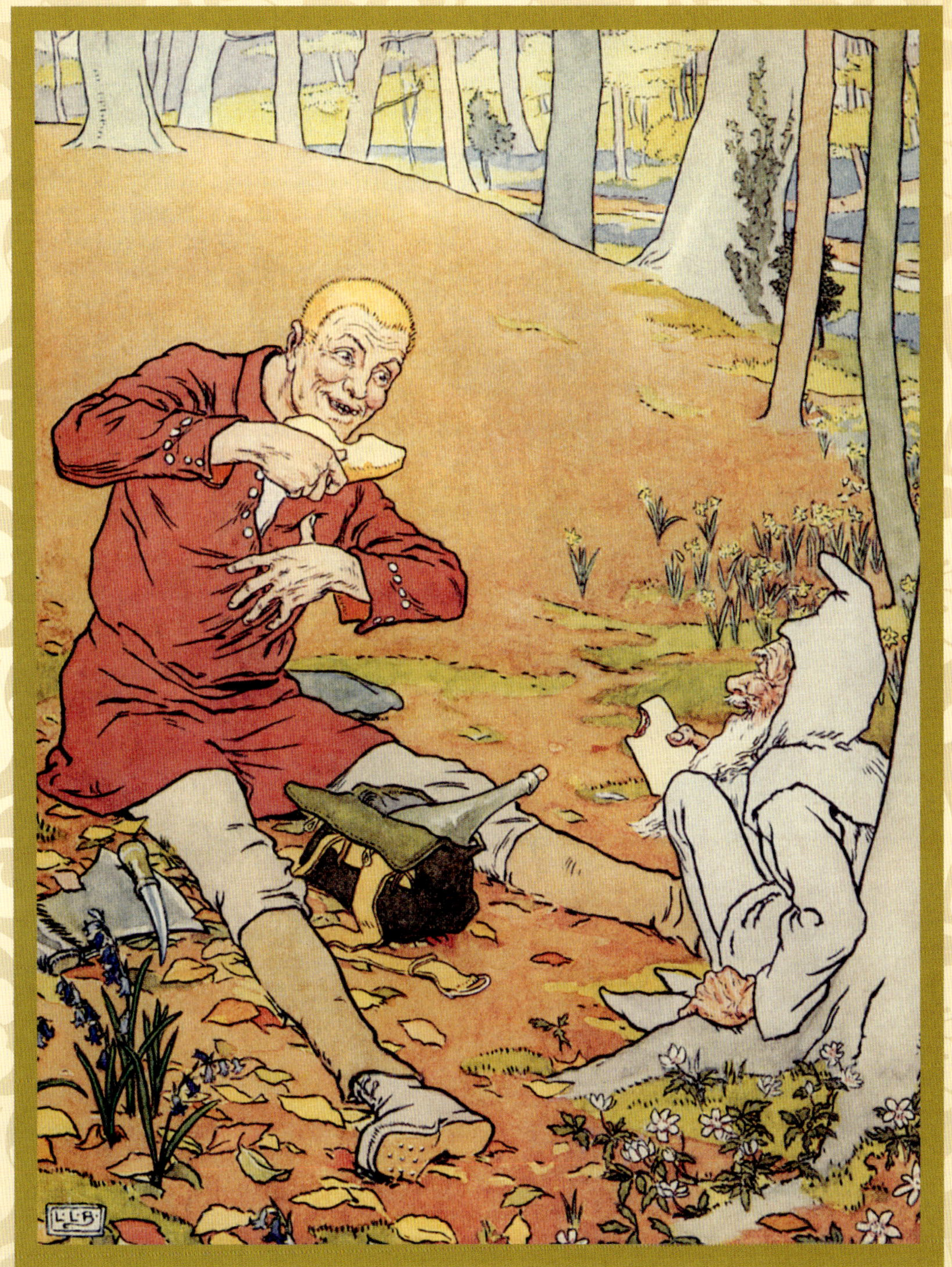

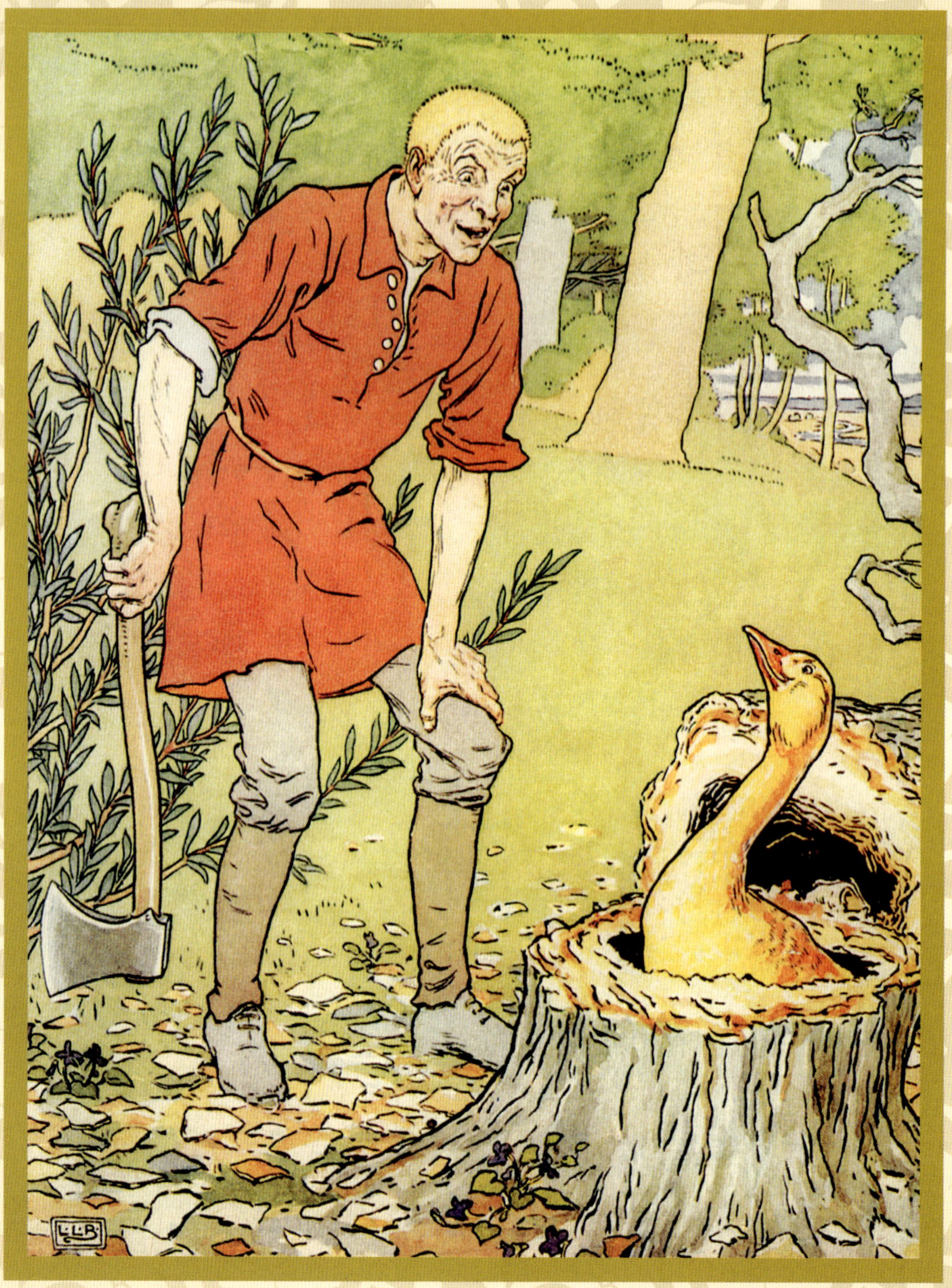

bird. There they went, always running behind him, now to the right, now to the left, whichever way he chose to go. In the middle of the fields they met the parson, and when he saw the procession he called out, "Shame on you, you naughty girls, why do you run after a young fellow in this way? Come, leave go!" With this he caught the youngest by the hand, and tried to pull her back, but when he touched her he found he could not get away, and he too must needs run behind. Then the sexton came along, and saw the parson following on the heels of the three girls. This so astonished him that he called out, "Hi! Sir Parson, whither away so fast? Do you forget that to-day we have a christening?" and ran after him, and caught him by the coat, but he too remained sticking fast.

As the five now ran on, one behind the other, two laborers who were returning from the field with their tools, came along. The parson called out to them and begged that they would set him and the sexton free. No sooner had they touched the sexton, than they too had to hang on, and now there were seven running after the Simpleton and the goose.

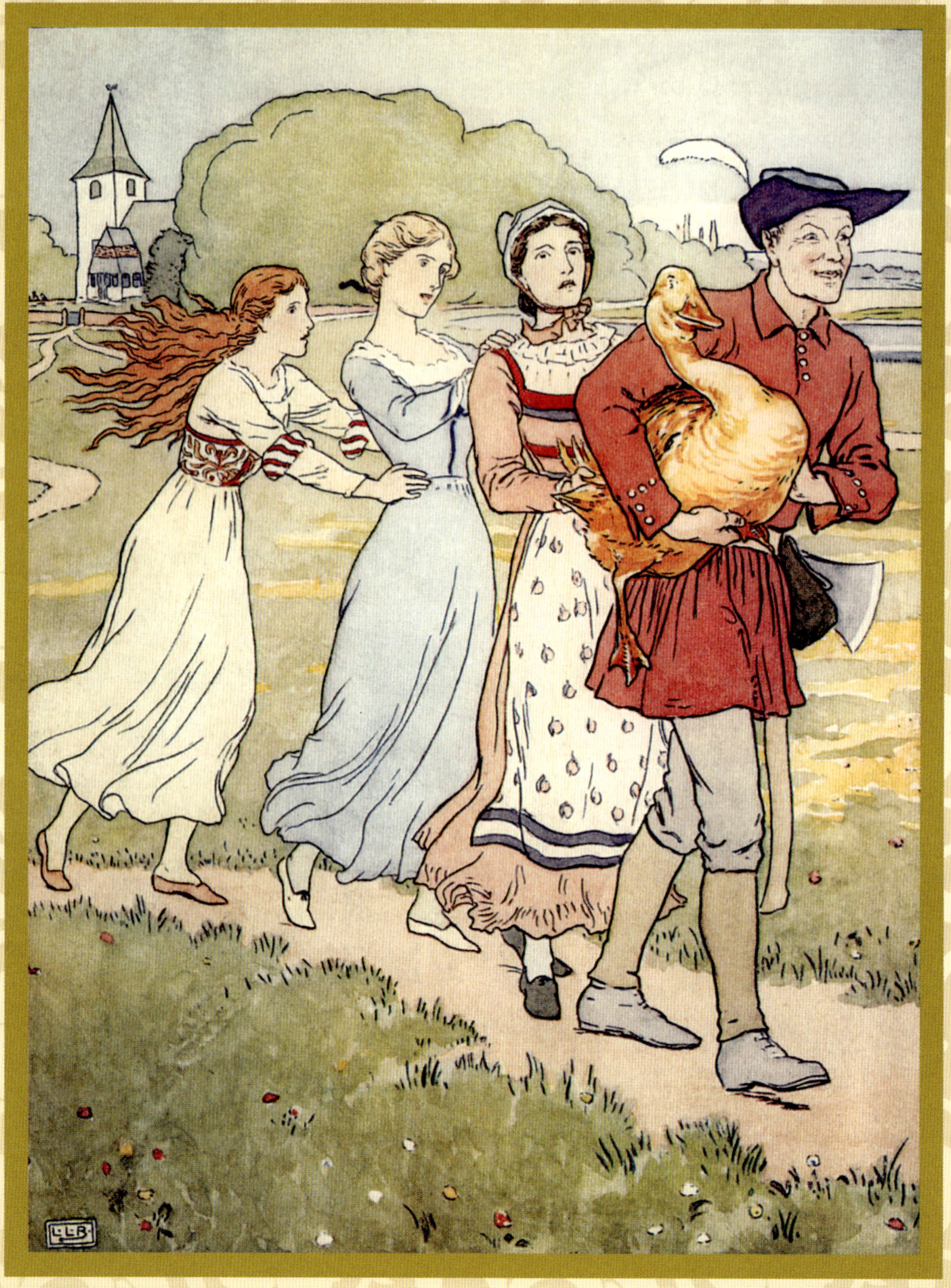

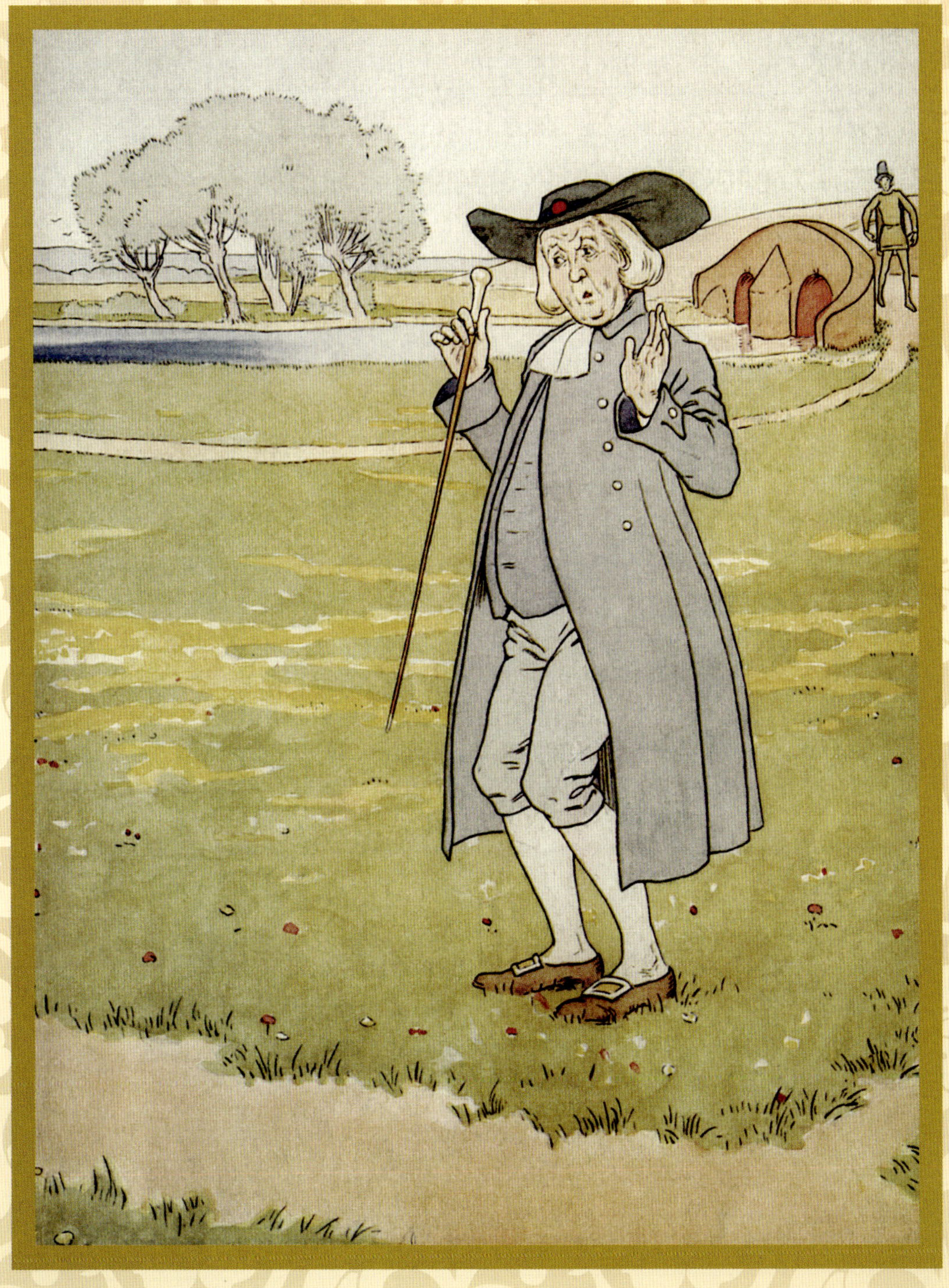

In this way they came to a city where a King reigned who had an only daughter, who was so serious that no one could make her laugh. Therefore he had announced that whoever should make her laugh should have her for his wife. When the Simpleton heard this he went with his goose and his train before the Princess, and when she saw the seven people all running behind each other, she began to laugh, and she laughed and laughed till it seemed as though she could never stop. Thereupon the Simpleton demanded her for his wife, but the King was not pleased at the thought of such a son-in-law, and he made all kinds of objections. He told the Simpleton that he must first bring him a man who could drink off a whole cellarful of wine. At once the Simpleton thought of the little gray man, who would be sure to help him, so off he went into the wood, and in the place where he had cut down the tree he saw a man sitting who looked most miserable. The Simpleton asked him what was the cause of his trouble.

"I have such a thirst," the man answered, "and I cannot quench it. I cannot bear cold water. I have indeed emptied a cask of wine, but what is a drop like that to a thirsty man?"

"In that case I can help you," said the Simpleton. "Just come with me and you shall be satisfied."

He led him to the King's cellar, and the man at once sat down in front of the great cask, and drank and drank till before a day was over he had drunk the whole cellarful of wine. Then the Simpleton demanded his bride again, but the King was angry that a mean fellow everyone called a Simpleton should win his daughter, and he made new conditions. Before giving him his daughter to wife he said that the Simpleton must find a man who would eat a whole mountain of bread. The Simpleton did not stop long to consider, but went off straight to the wood. There in

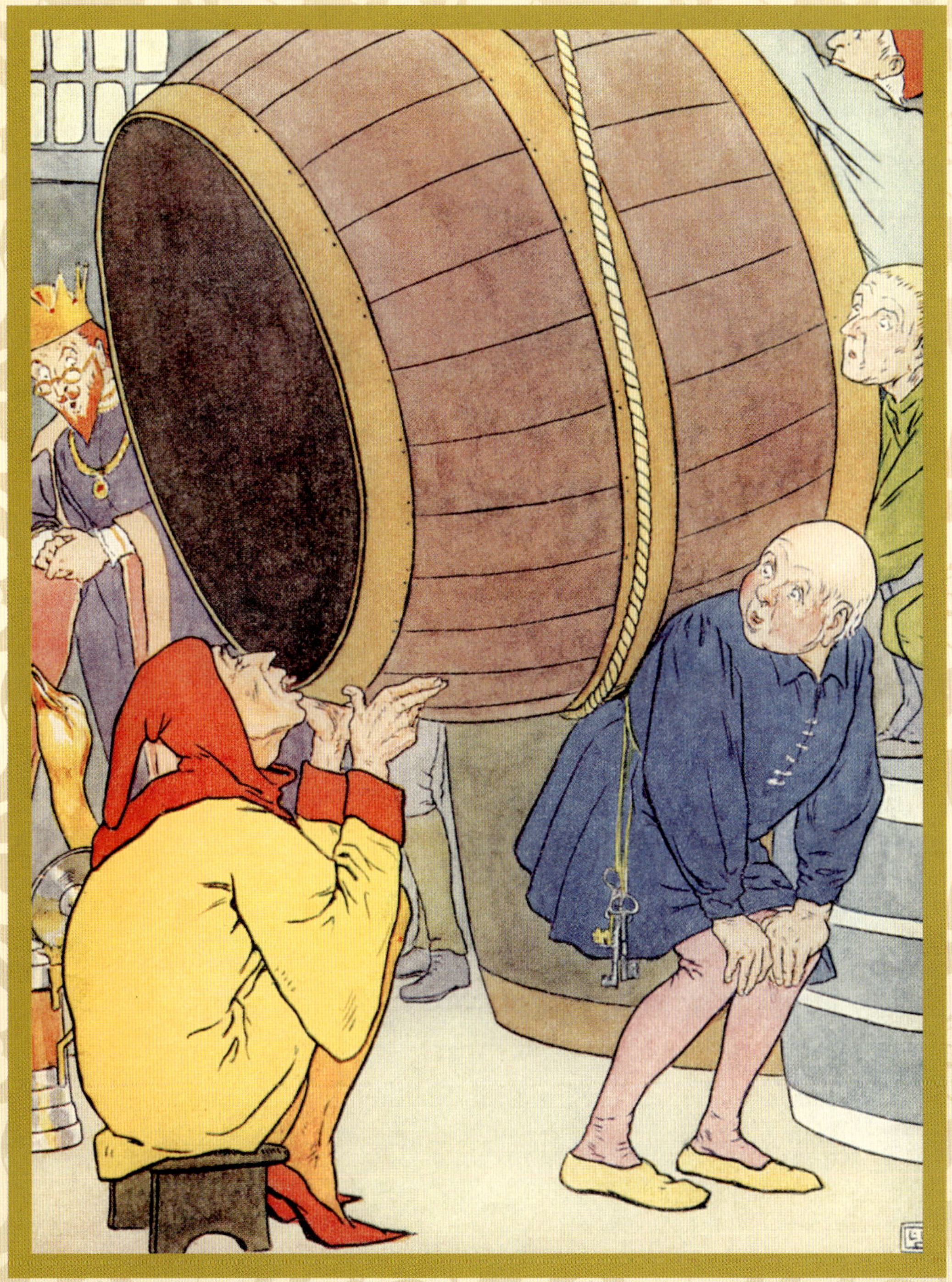

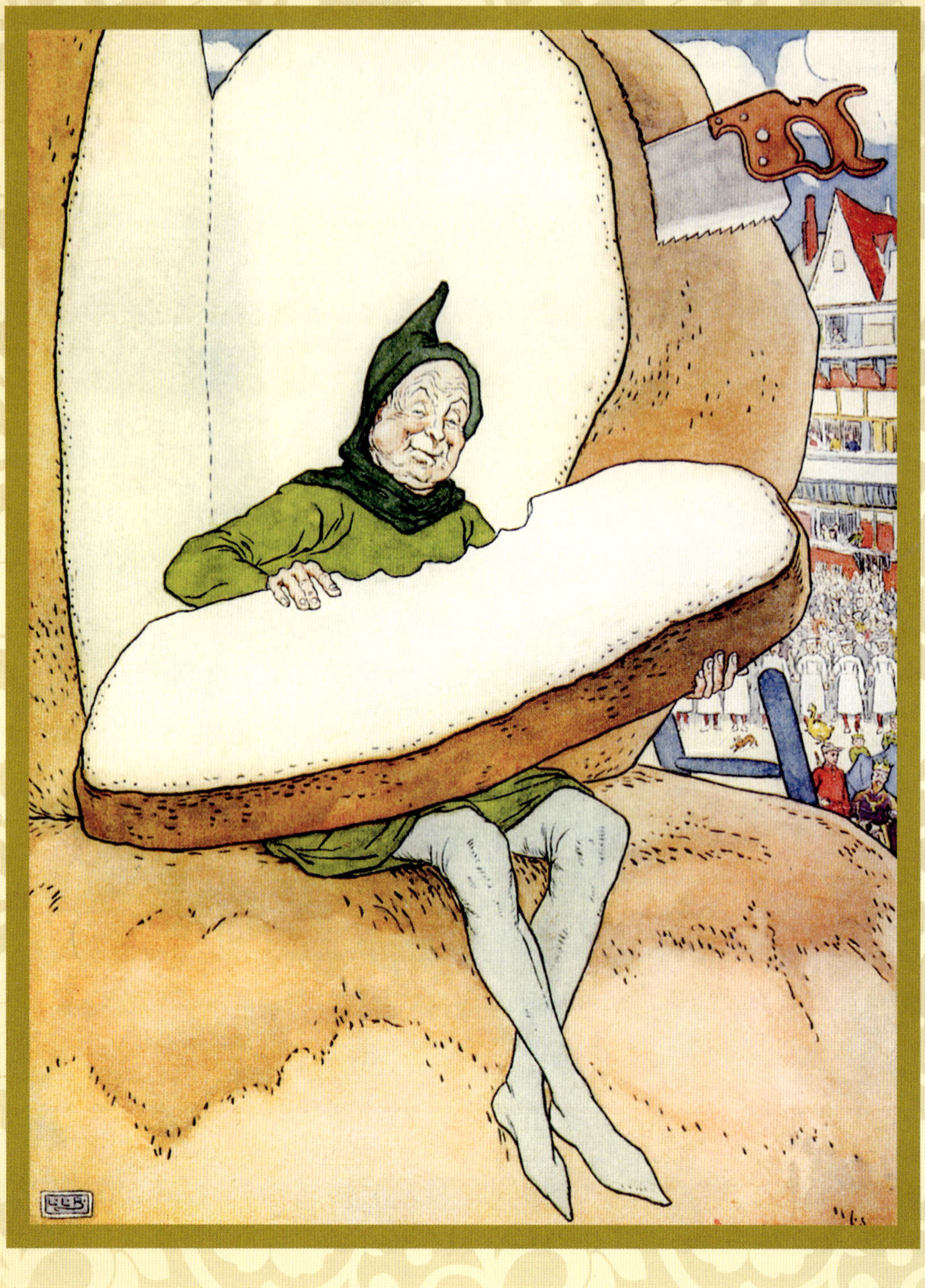

The Golden Goose

the same place as before sat a man who was buckling a strap tightly around him, and looking very depressed. He said:

"I have eaten a whole ovenful of loaves, but what help is that when a man is as hungry as I am? I feel quite empty, and I must strap myself together if I am not to die of hunger."

The Simpleton was delighted on hearing this, and said: "Get up at once and come with me. I will give you enough to eat to satisfy your hunger."

He led him to the King, who meanwhile had ordered all the meal in the kingdom to be brought together, and an immense mountain of bread baked from it. The man from the wood set to work on it, and in one day the whole mountain had disappeared.

For the third time the Simpleton demanded his bride, but yet again the King tried to put him off, and said that he must bring him a ship that would go both on land and water.

"If you are really able to sail such a ship," said he, "you shall at once have my daughter for your wife."

The Simpleton went into the wood, and there sat the little old gray man to whom he had given his cake.

"I have drunk for you, and I have eaten for you," said the little man, "and I will also give you the ship; all this I do for you because you were kind to me."

Then he gave the Simpleton a ship that went both on land and water, and when the King saw it he knew he could no longer keep back his daughter. The wedding was celebrated, and after the King's death, the Simpleton inherited the kingdom, and lived very happily ever after with his wife.

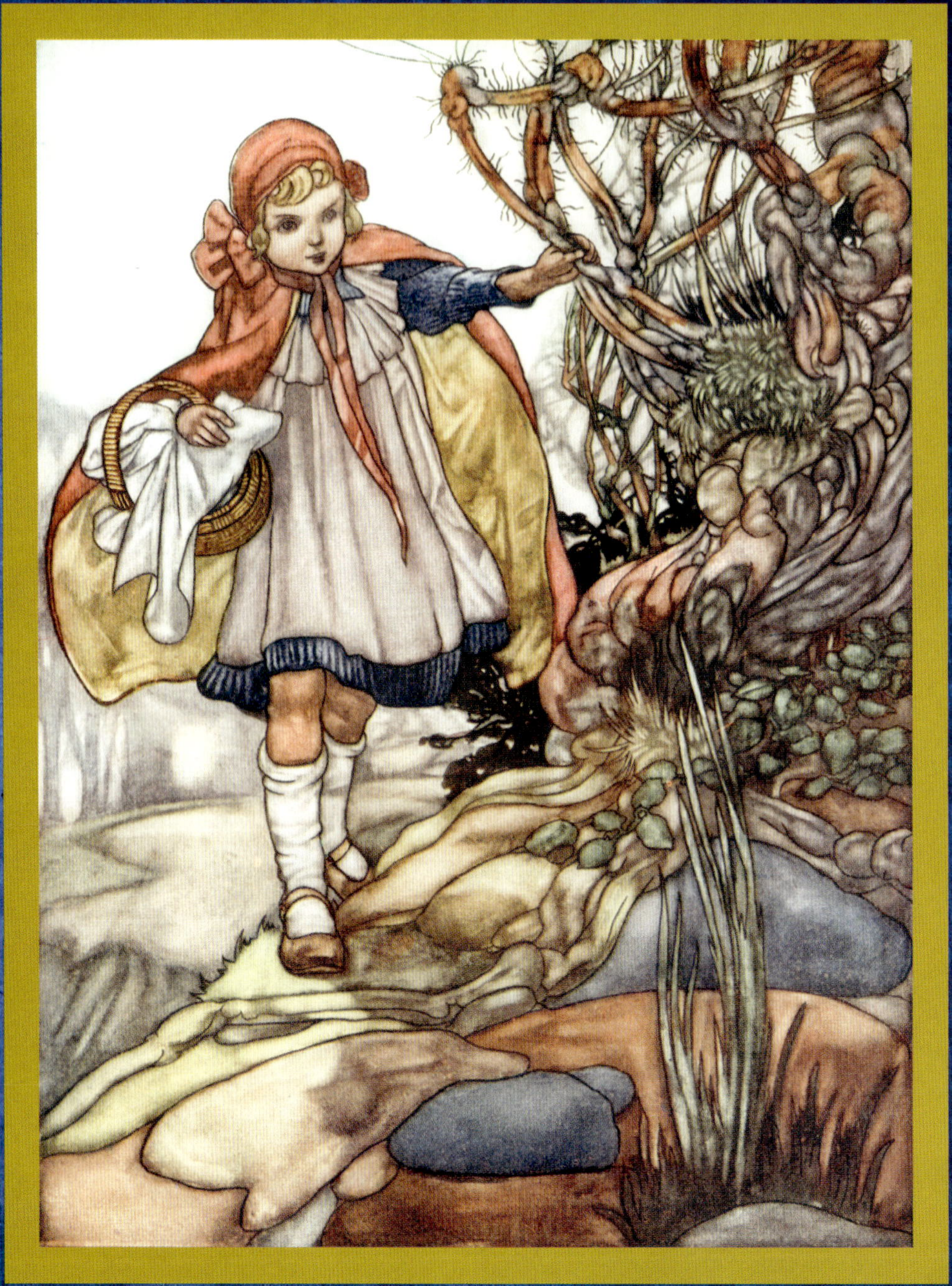

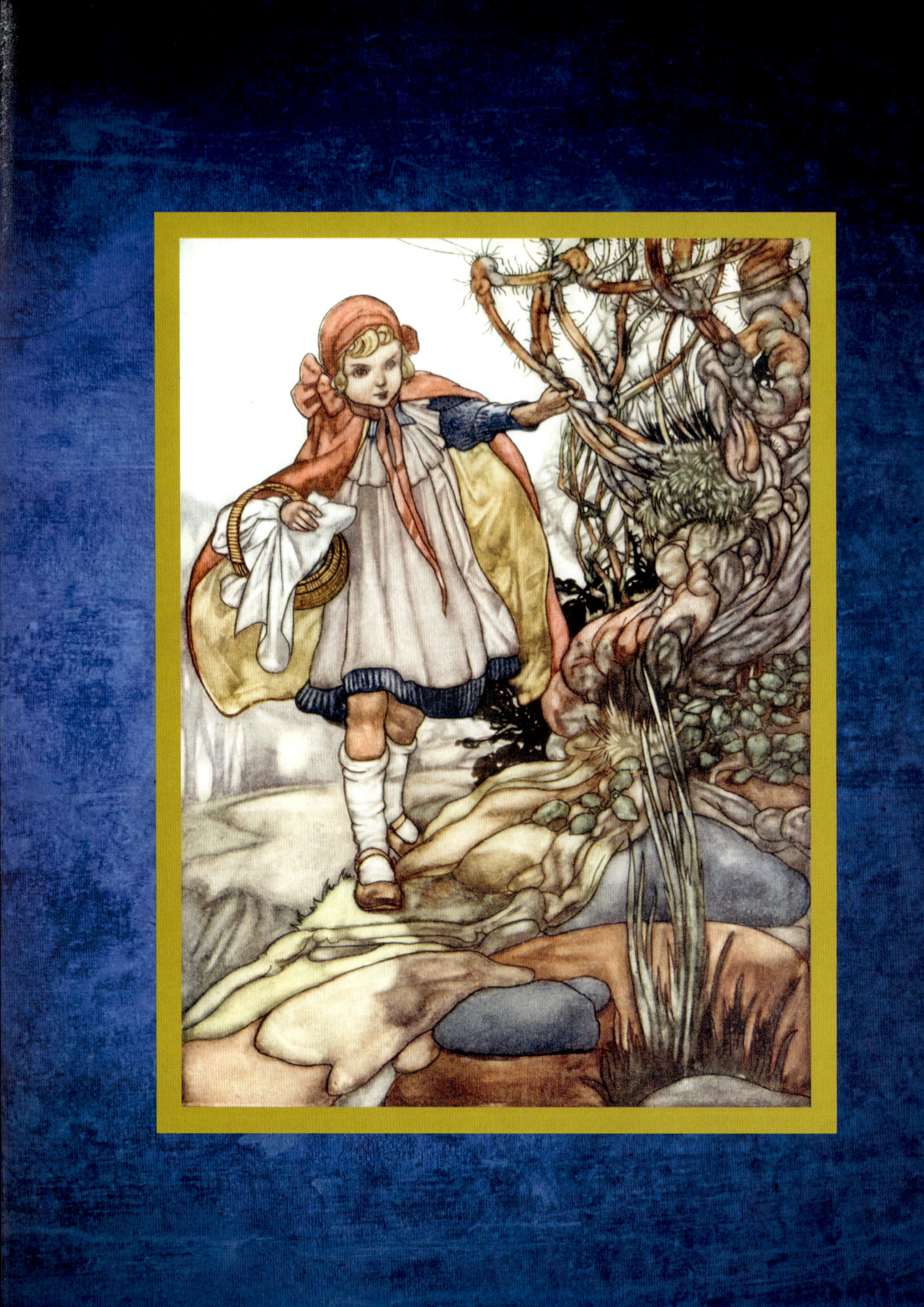

Little Red Riding-Hood

Once upon a time there lived a country girl, who was the sweetest creature ever seen. Her grandmother had made for her a pretty red hood, which so became the child that every one called her Little Red Riding-Hood. One day her mother, having made some cakes, said to her:

"Go, my child, and see how your grandmother does, for I hear she is ill; carry her some of these cakes, and a little pot of butter."

Little Red Riding-Hood, with a basket filled with the cakes and the pot of butter, immediately set out for her grandmother's house, which was in a village a little distance away.

As she was crossing a wood she met a wolf, who had a mind to eat her up, but dared not do so because of some woodcutters at work near them in the forest. He ventured, however, to ask her whither she was going.

The little girl, not knowing how dangerous it was to talk to a wolf, replied:

"I am going to see my grandmother, and carry her these cakes and a pot of butter."

"Does she live far off?" said the wolf.

"Oh, yes," answered Little Red Riding-Hood, "beyond the mill you see yonder, at the first house in the village."

"Well," said the wolf, "I will go and see her too; I will take this way, and you take that, and see which will be there soonest."

The wolf set out, running as fast as he could, and taking the nearest way, while the little girl took the longest, and amused herself as she went with gathering nuts, running after butterflies, and making nosegays of such flowers as she found within her reach.

The wolf soon arrived at the dwelling of the grandmother, and knocked at the door.

"Who is there?" said the old woman.

"It is your grandchild, Little Red Riding-Hood," replied the wolf, counterfeiting her voice; "I have brought you some cakes, and a little pot of butter, which Mother has sent you."

The good old woman, who was ill in bed, called out:

"Pull the bobbin, and the latch will go up."

The wolf pulled the bobbin, and the door opened. He sprang upon the poor old grandmother and ate her up in a moment.

The wolf then shut the door and laid himself down in the bed, and waited for Little Red Riding-Hood, who arrived soon after. Tap, tap!

"Who is there?"

She was at first a little frightened at the hoarse voice of the wolf, but supposing that her grandmother had got a cold, she answered:

"It is your grandchild, Little Red Riding-Hood. Mother has sent you some cakes, and a little pot of butter."

The wolf called out, softening his voice,

"Pull the bobbin, and the latch will go up."

Little Red Riding-Hood pulled the bobbin, and the door opened.

When she came into the room, the wolf, hiding himself under the bedclothes, said, trying all he could to speak in a feeble voice:

"Put the basket, my child, on the stool; take off your clothes, and come into bed with me."

Little Red Riding-Hood accordingly undressed herself and stepped into bed; where, wondering to see how her grandmother looked in her nightclothes, she said:

"Grandmother, what great arms you have got."

"The better to hug thee, my child."

"Grandmother, what great ears you have got."

"The better to hear thee, my child."

"Grandmother, what great eyes you have got."

"The better to see thee, my child."

"Grandmother, what great teeth you have got."

"The better to eat thee up"; and, saying these words, the wicked wolf fell upon Little Red Riding-Hood, and ate her up in a few mouthfuls.

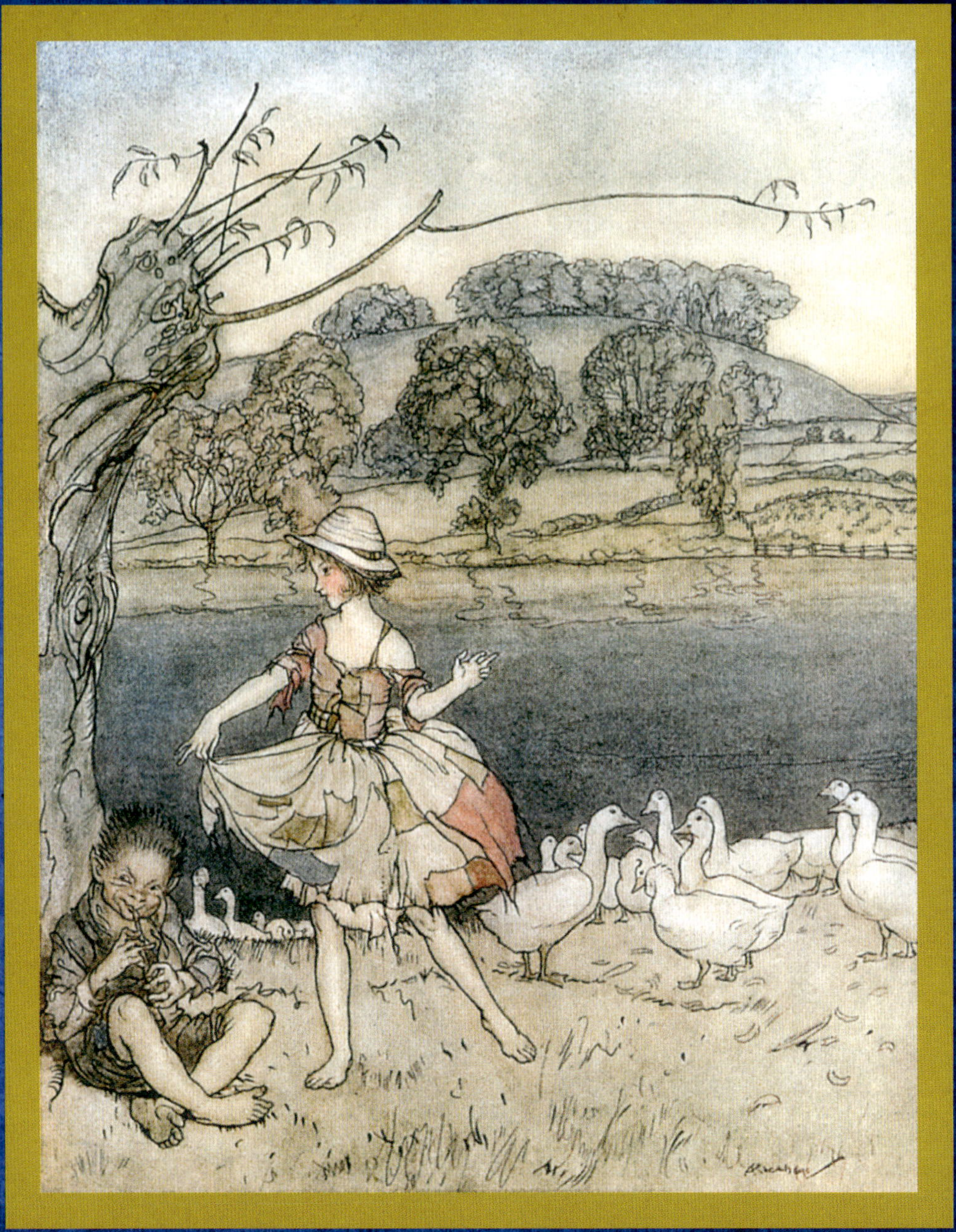

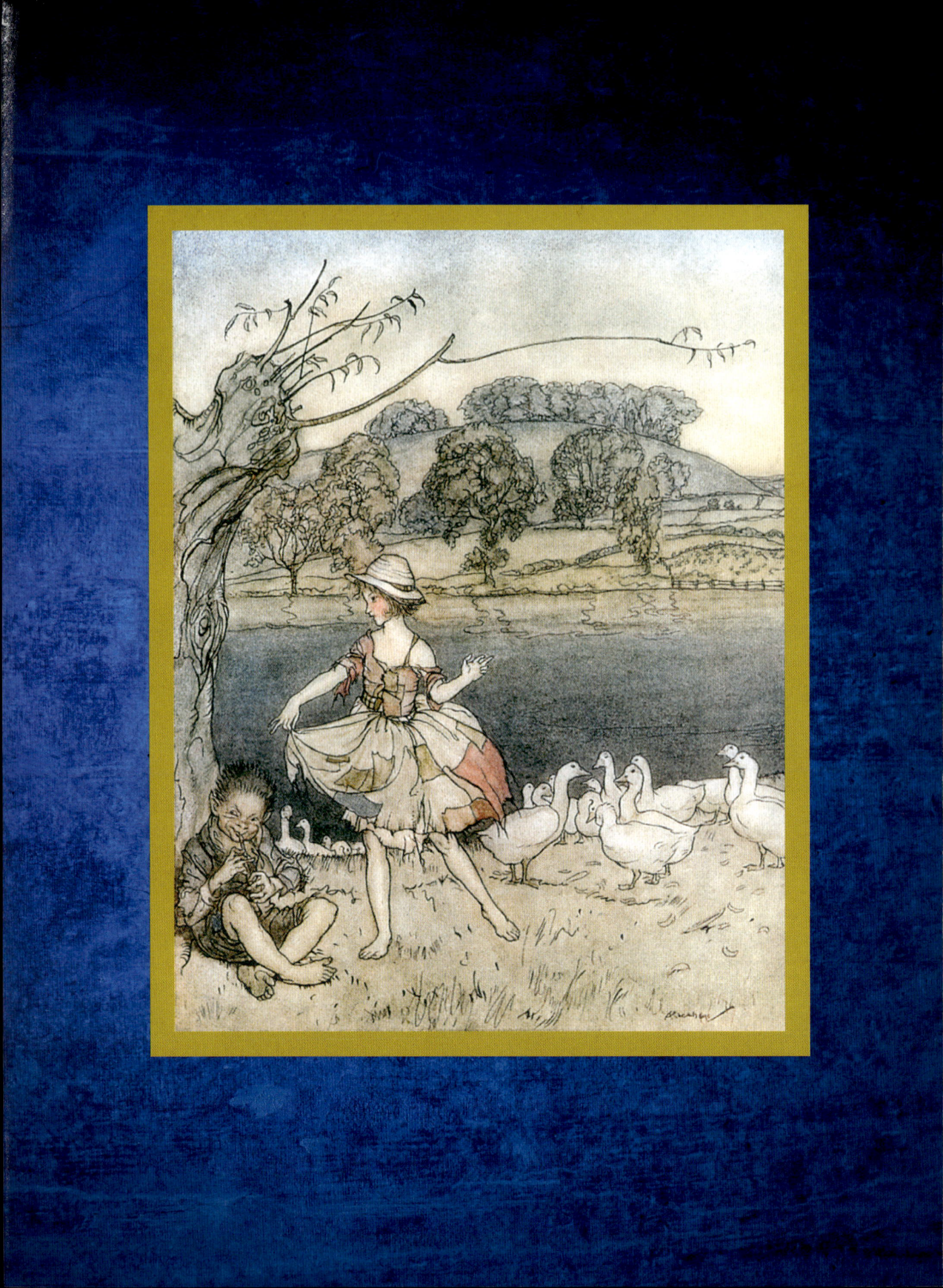

Tattercoats

In a great palace by the sea there once dwelt a very rich old lord, who had neither wife nor children living, only one little granddaughter, whose face he had never seen in all her life. He hated her bitterly, because at her birth his favorite daughter died; and when the old nurse brought him the baby he swore that it might live or die as it liked, but he would never look on its face as long as it lived.

So he turned his back, and sat by his window looking out over the sea, and weeping great tears for his lost daughter, till his white hair and beard grew down over his shoulders and twined round his chair and crept into the chinks of the floor, and his tears, dropping on to the window-ledge, wore a channel through the stone, and ran away in a little river to the great sea. Meanwhile, his granddaughter grew up with no one to care for her, or clothe her; only the old nurse, when no one was by, would sometimes give her a dish of scraps from the kitchen, or a torn petticoat from the rag-bag; while the other servants of the palace would drive her from the house with blows and mocking words, calling her "Tattercoats," and pointing to her bare feet and shoulders, till she ran away, crying, to hide among the bushes.

So she grew up, with little to eat or to wear, spending her days out of doors, her only companion a crippled gooseherd, who fed his flock of geese on the common. And this gooseherd was a queer, merry, little chap and, when she was hungry, or cold, or tired, he would play to her so gaily on his little pipe, that she forgot all her troubles, and would fall to dancing with his flock of noisy geese for partners.

Now one day people told each other that the King was traveling through the land, and was to give a great ball to all the lords and ladies of the country in the town near by, and that the Prince, his only son, was to choose a wife from amongst the maidens in the company. In due time one of the royal invitations to the ball was brought to the Palace by the sea, and the servants carried it up to the old lord, who still sat by his window, wrapped in his long white hair and weeping into the little river that was fed by his tears.

But when he heard the King's command, he dried his eyes and bade them bring shears to cut him loose, for his hair had bound him a fast prisoner, and he could not move. And then he sent them for rich clothes, and jewels, which he put on; and he ordered them to saddle the white horse, with gold and silk, that he might ride to meet the King; but he quite forgot he had a granddaughter to take to the ball.

Meanwhile Tattercoats sat by the kitchen-door weeping, because she could not go to see the grand doings. And when the old nurse heard her crying she went to the Lord of the Palace, and begged him to take his granddaughter with him to the King's ball.

But he only frowned and told her to be silent; while the servants laughed and said, "Tattercoats is happy in her rags, playing with the gooseherd! Let her be—it is all she is fit for."

A second, and then a third time, the old nurse begged him to let the girl go with him, but she was answered only by black looks and fierce words, till she was driven from the room by the jeering servants, with blows and mocking words.

Weeping over her ill-success, the old nurse went to look for Tattercoats; but the girl had been turned from the door by the cook, and had run away to tell her friend the gooseherd how unhappy she was because she could not go to the King's ball.

Now when the gooseherd had listened to her story, he bade her cheer up, and proposed that they should go together into the town to see the King, and all the fine things; and when she looked sorrowfully down at her rags and bare feet he played a note or two upon his pipe, so gay and merry, that she forgot all about her tears and her troubles, and before she well knew, the gooseherd had taken her by the hand, and she, and he, and the geese before them, were dancing down the road toward the town.

"Even cripples can dance when they choose," said the gooseherd.

Before they had gone very far a handsome young man, splendidly dressed, riding up, stopped to ask the way to the castle where the King was staying, and when he found that they too were going thither, he got off his horse and walked beside them along the road.

"You seem merry folk," he said, "and will be good company."

"Good company, indeed," said the gooseherd, and played a new tune that was not a dance.

It was a curious tune, and it made the strange young man stare and stare and stare at Tattercoats till he couldn't see her rags—till he couldn't, to tell the truth, see anything but her beautiful face.

Then he said, "You are the most beautiful maiden in the world. Will you marry me?"

Then the gooseherd smiled to himself, and played sweeter than ever.

But Tattercoats laughed. "Not I," said she; "you would be finely put to shame, and so would I be, if you took a goose-girl for your wife! Go and ask one of the great ladies you will see to-night at the King's ball and do not flout poor Tattercoats."

But the more she refused him the sweeter the pipe played, and the deeper the young man fell in love; till at last he begged her to come that night at twelve to the King's ball, just as she was, with the gooseherd and his geese, in her torn petticoat and bare feet, and see if he wouldn't dance with her before the King, and the lords and ladies, and present her to them all, as his dear and honored bride.

Now at first Tattercoats said she would not; but the gooseherd said, "Take fortune when it comes, little one."

So when night came, and the hall in the castle was full of light and music, and the lords and ladies were dancing before the King, just as the clock struck twelve, Tattercoats and the gooseherd, followed by his flock of noisy geese, hissing and swaying their heads, entered at the great doors, and walked straight up the ball-room, while on either side the ladies whispered, the lords laughed, and the King seated at the far end stared in amazement.

But as they came in front of the throne Tattercoats' lover rose from beside the King, and came to meet her. Taking her by the hand, he kissed her thrice before them all, and turned to the King.

"Father!" he said—for it was the Prince himself—"I have made my choice, and here is my bride, the loveliest girl in all the land, and the sweetest as well!"

Before he had finished speaking, the gooseherd had put his pipe to his lips and played a few notes that sounded like a bird singing far off in the woods; and as he played Tattercoats' rags were changed to shining robes sewn with glittering jewels, a golden crown lay upon her golden hair, and the flock of geese behind her became a crowd of dainty pages, bearing her long train.

And as the King rose to greet her as his daughter the trumpets sounded loudly in honor of the new Princess, and the people outside in the street said to each other:

"Ah! now the Prince has chosen for his wife the loveliest girl in all the land!"

But the gooseherd was never seen again, and no one knew what became of him; while the old lord went home once more to his palace by the sea, for he could not stay at court, when he had sworn never to look on his granddaughter's face.

So there he still sits by his window—if you could only see him, as you may some day—weeping more bitterly than ever. And his white hair has bound him to the stones, and the river of his tears runs away to the great sea.

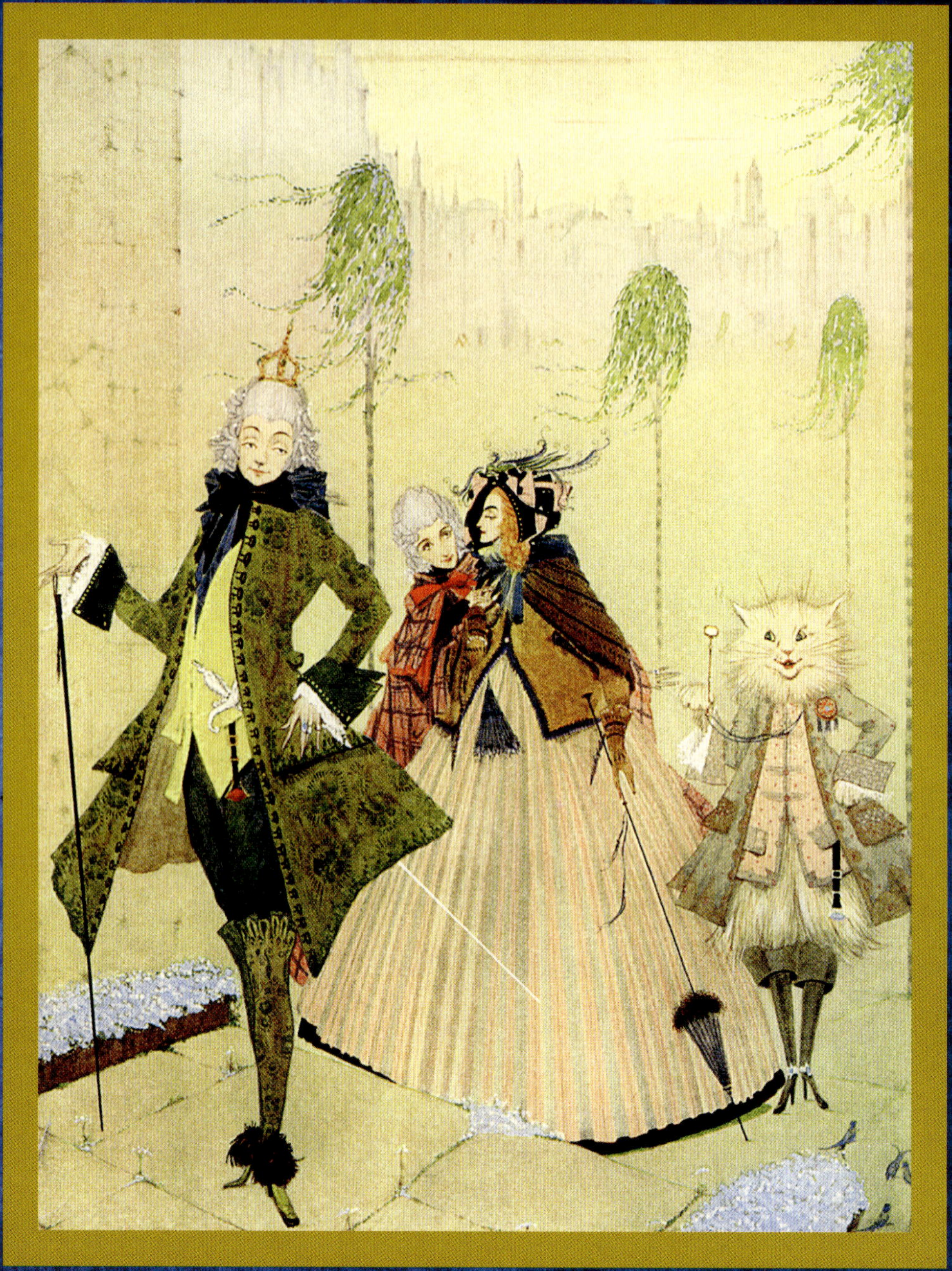

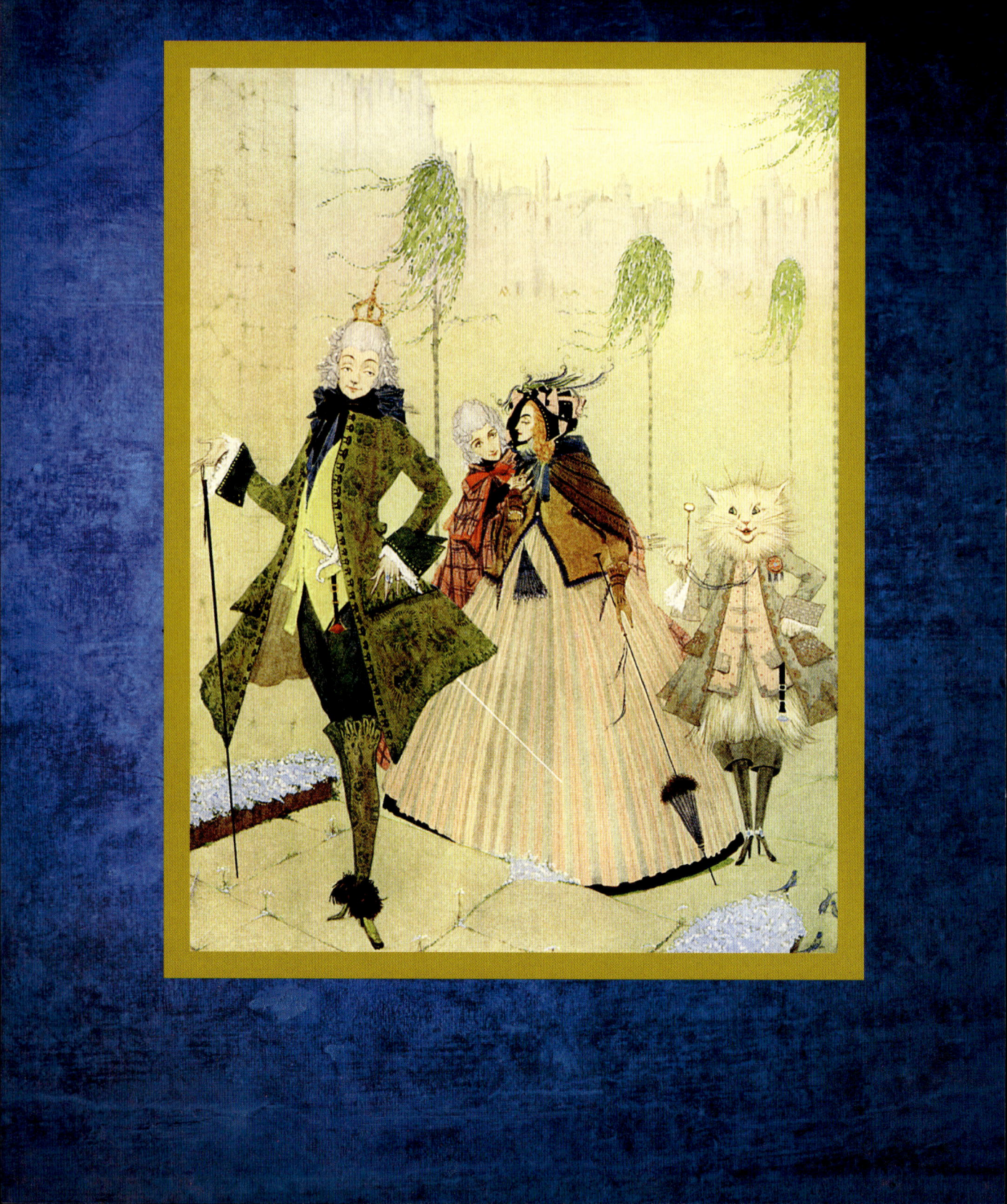

Puss in Boots

There was a miller who left no more estate to the three sons he had than his mill, his ass, and his cat. The partition was soon made. Neither scrivener nor attorney was sent for. They would soon have eaten up all the poor patrimony. The eldest had the mill, the second the ass, and the youngest nothing but the cat. The poor young fellow was quite comfortless at having so poor a lot.

"My brothers," said he, "may get their living handsomely enough by joining their stocks together; but for my part, when I have eaten up my cat, and made me a muff of his skin, I must die of hunger."

The Cat, who heard all this, but made as if he did not, said to him with a grave and serious air:

"Do not thus afflict yourself, my good master. You have nothing else to do but to give me a bag and get a pair of boots made for me that I may scamper through the dirt and the brambles, and you shall see that you have not so bad a portion in me as you imagine."

The Cat's master did not build very much upon what he said. He had often seen him play a great many cunning tricks to catch rats and mice, as when he used to hang by the heels, or hide himself in the meal, and make as if he were dead; so that he did not altogether despair of his affording him some help in his miserable condition. When the Cat had what he asked for he booted himself very gallantly, and putting his bag about his neck, he held the strings of it in his two forepaws and went into a warren where was great abundance of rabbits. He put bran and sow-thistle into his bag, and stretching out at length, as if he had been dead, he waited for some young rabbits, not yet acquainted with the deceits of the world, to come and rummage his bag for what he had put into it.

Scarce was he lain down but he had what he wanted. A rash and foolish young rabbit jumped into his bag, and Monsieur Puss, immediately drawing close the strings, took and killed him without pity. Proud of his prey, he went with it to the palace and asked to speak with his majesty. He was shown upstairs into the King's apartment, and, making a low reverence, said to him:

"I have brought you, sir, a rabbit of the warren, which my noble lord the Marquis of Carabas" (for that was the title which puss was pleased to give his master) "has commanded me to present to your majesty from him."

"Tell thy master," said the King, "that I thank him and that he does me a great deal of pleasure."

Another time he went and hid himself among some standing corn, holding still his bag open, and when a brace of partridges ran into it he drew the strings and so caught them both. He went and made a present of these to the King, as he had done before of the rabbit which he took in the warren. The King, in like manner, received the partridges with great pleasure, and ordered him some money for drink.

The Cat continued for two or three months thus to carry his Majesty, from time to time, game of his master's taking. One day in particular, when he knew for certain that he was to take the air along the river-side, with his daughter, the most beautiful Princess in the world, he said to his master:

"If you will follow my advice your fortune is made. You have nothing else to do but go and wash yourself in the river, in that part I shall show you, and leave the rest to me."

The Marquis of Carabas did what the Cat advised him to, without knowing why or wherefore. While he was washing the King passed by, and the Cat began to cry out:

"Help! help! My Lord Marquis of Carabas is going to be drowned."

At this noise the King put his head out of the coach-window, and, finding it was the Cat who had so often brought him such good game, he commanded his guards to run immediately to the assistance of his Lordship the Marquis of Carabas. While they were drawing the poor Marquis out of the river, the Cat came up to the coach and told the King that, while his master was washing, there came by some rogues, who went off with his clothes, though he had cried out: "Thieves! thieves!" several times, as loud as he could.

This cunning Cat had hidden them under a great stone. The King immediately commanded the officers of his wardrobe to run and fetch one of his best suits for the Lord Marquis of Carabas.

The King caressed him after a very extraordinary manner, and as the fine clothes he had given him extremely set off his good mien (for he was well made and very handsome in his person), the King's daughter took a secret inclination to him, and the Marquis of Carabas had no sooner cast two or three respectful and somewhat tender glances but she fell in love with him to distraction. The King would needs have him come into the coach and take part of the airing. The Cat, quite overjoyed to see his project begin to succeed, marched on before, and, meeting with some countrymen, who were mowing a meadow, he said to them:

"Good people, you who are mowing, if you do not tell the King that the meadow you mow belongs to my Lord Marquis of Carabas, you shall be chopped as small as herbs for the pot."

The King did not fail asking of the mowers to whom the meadow they were mowing belonged.

"To my Lord Marquis of Carabas," answered they altogether, for the Cat's threats had made them terribly afraid.

"You see, sir," said the Marquis, "this is a meadow which never fails to yield a plentiful harvest every year."

The Master Cat, who went still on before, met with some reapers, and said to them:

"Good people, you who are reaping, if you do not tell the King that all this corn belongs to the Marquis of Carabas, you shall be chopped as small as herbs for the pot."

The King, who passed by a moment after, would needs know to whom all that corn, which he then saw, did belong.

"To my Lord Marquis of Carabas," replied the reapers, and the King was very well pleased with it, as well as the Marquis, whom he congratulated thereupon. The Master Cat, who went always before, said the same words to all he met, and the King was astonished at the vast estates of my Lord Marquis of Carabas.

Monsieur Puss came at last to a stately castle, the master of which was an ogre, the richest had ever been known; for all the lands which the King had then gone over belonged to this castle. The Cat, who had taken care to inform himself who this ogre was and what he could do, asked to speak with him, saying he could not pass so near his castle without having the honor of paying his respects to him.

The ogre received him as civilly as an ogre could do, and made him sit down.

"I have been assured," said the Cat, "that you have the gift of being able to change yourself into all sorts of creatures you have a mind to; you can, for example, transform yourself into a lion, or elephant, and the like."

"That is true," answered the ogre very briskly; "and to convince you, you shall see me now become a lion."

Puss was so sadly terrified at the sight of a lion so near him that he immediately got into the gutter, not without abundance of trouble and danger, because of his boots, which were of no use at all to him in walking upon the tiles. A little while after, when Puss saw that the ogre had resumed his natural form, he came down, and owned he had been very much frightened.

"I have been, moreover, informed," said the Cat, "but I know not how to believe it, that you have also the power to take on you the shape of the smallest animals; for example, to change yourself into a rat or a mouse; but I must own to you I take this to be impossible."

"Impossible!" cried the ogre; "you shall see that presently."

And at the same time he changed himself into a mouse, and began to run about the floor. Puss no sooner perceived this but he fell upon him and ate him up.

Meanwhile the King, who saw, as he passed, this fine castle of the ogre's, had a mind to go into it. Puss, who heard the noise of his Majesty's coach running over the draw-bridge, ran out, and said to the King:

"Your Majesty is welcome to this castle of my Lord Marquis of Carabas."

"What! my Lord Marquis," cried the King, "and does this castle also belong to you? There can be nothing finer than this court and all the stately buildings which surround it; let us go into it, if you please."

The Marquis gave his hand to the Princess, and followed the King, who went first. They passed into a spacious hall, where they found a magnificent collation, which the ogre had prepared for his friends, who were that very day to visit him, but dared not to enter, knowing the King was there. His Majesty was perfectly charmed with the good qualities of my Lord Marquis of Carabas, as was his daughter, who had fallen violently in love with him, and, seeing the vast estate he possessed, said to him, after having drunk five or six glasses:

"It will be owing to yourself only, my Lord Marquis, if you are not my son-in-law."

The Marquis, making several low bows, accepted the honor which his Majesty conferred upon him, and forthwith, that very same day, married the Princess.

Puss became a great lord, and never ran after mice any more but only for his diversion.

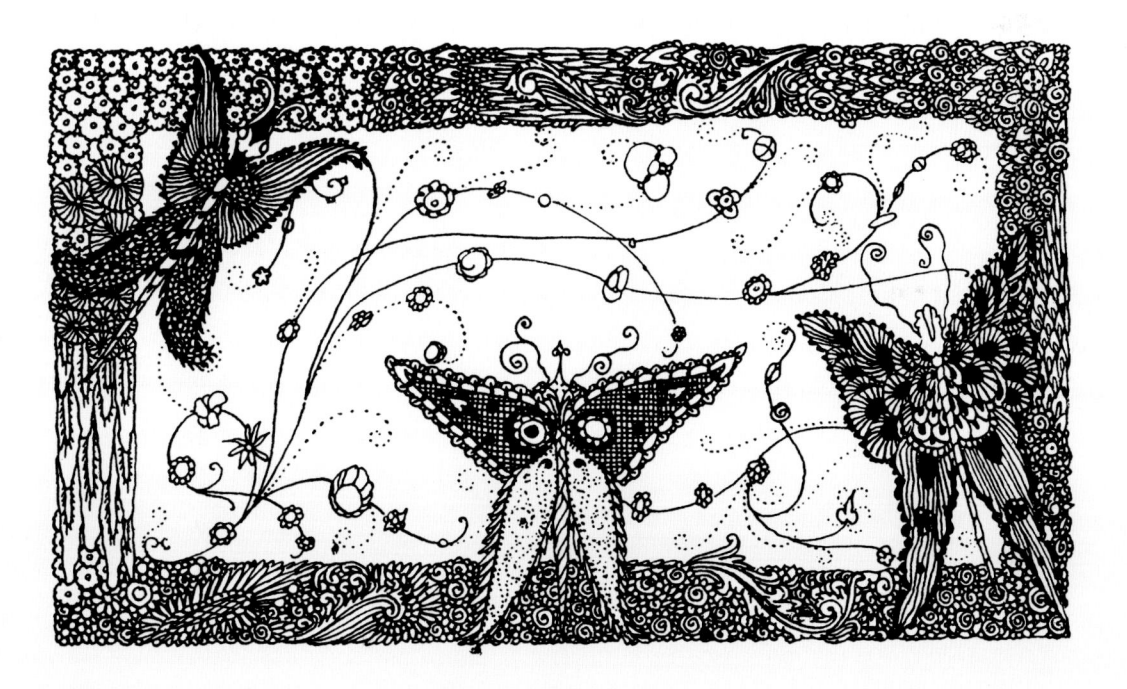

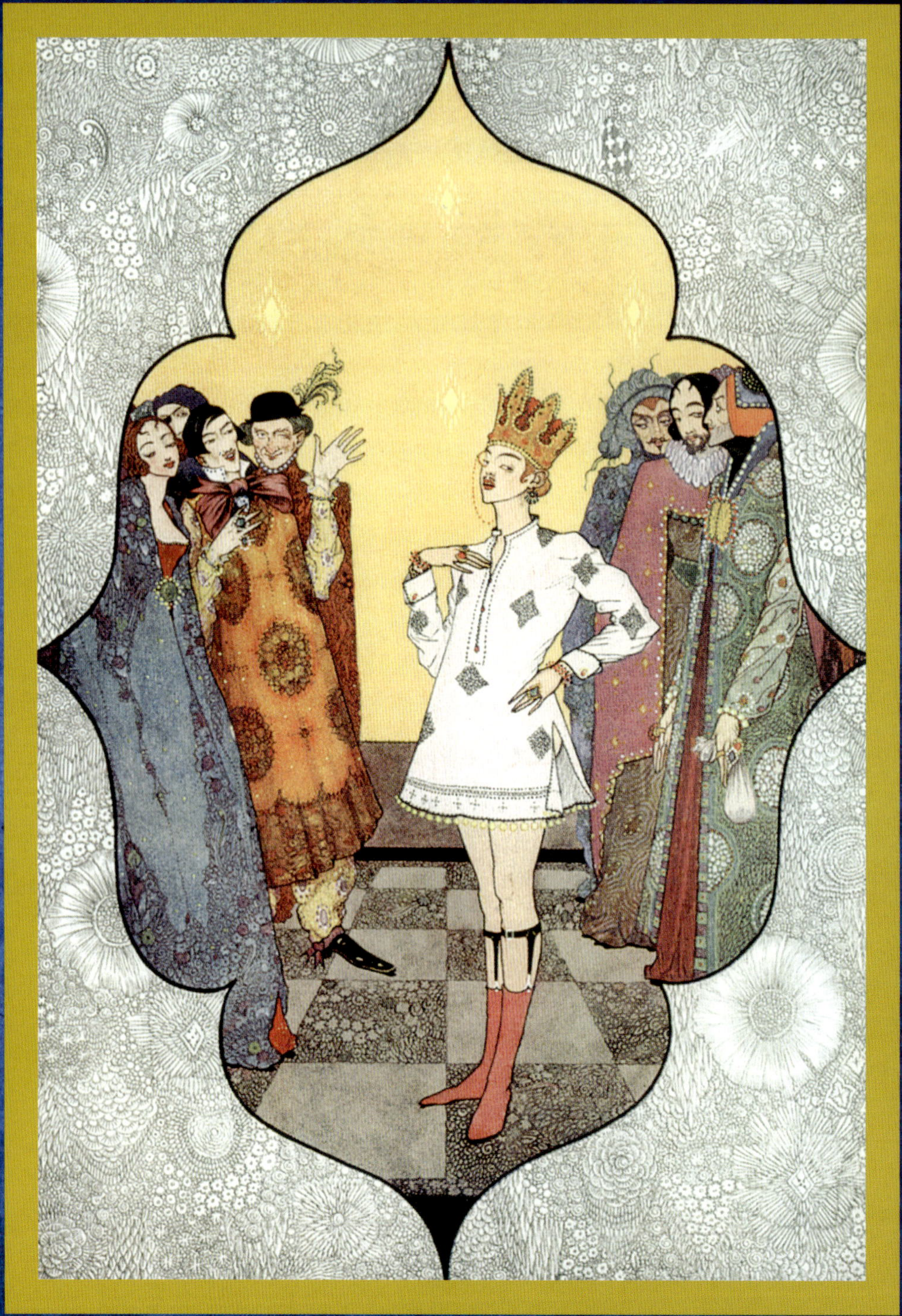

The Emperor's New Clothes

MANY YEARS AGO THERE LIVED AN EMPEROR, WHO CARED SO enormously for new clothes that he spent all his money upon them, that he might be very fine. He did not care about his soldiers, nor about the theater, and only liked to drive out and show his new clothes. He had a coat for every hour of the day; and just as they say of a King, "He is in council," one always said of him, "The Emperor is in the wardrobe."

In the great city in which he lived it was always very merry; every day a number of strangers arrived there. One day two cheats came: they gave themselves out as weavers, and declared that they could weave the finest stuff any one could imagine. Not only were their colors and patterns, they said, uncommonly beautiful, but the clothes made of the stuff possessed the wonderful quality that they became invisible to any one who was unfit for the office he held, or was incorrigibly stupid.

"Those would be capital clothes!" thought the Emperor. "If I wore those, I should be able to find out what men in my empire are not fit for the places they have; I could distinguish the clever from the stupid. Yes, the stuff must be woven for me directly!"

And he gave the two cheats a great deal of cash in hand, that they might begin their work at once.

As for them, they put up two looms, and pretended to be working; but they had nothing at all on their looms. They at once demanded the finest silk and the costliest gold; this they put into their own pockets, and worked at the empty looms till late into the night.

"I should like to know how far they have got on with the stuff," thought the Emperor. But he felt quite uncomfortable when he thought that those who were not fit for their offices could not see it. He believed, indeed, that he had nothing to fear for himself, but yet he preferred first to send some one else to see how matters stood. All the people in the whole city knew what peculiar power the stuff possessed, and all were anxious to see how bad or how stupid their neighbors were.

"I will send my honest old Minister to the weavers," thought the Emperor. "He can judge best how the stuff looks, for he has sense, and no one understands his office better than he."

Now the good old Minister went out into the hall where the two cheats sat working at the empty looms.

"Mercy preserve us!" thought the old Minister, and he opened his eyes wide. "I cannot see anything at all!" But he did not say this.

Both the cheats begged him to be kind enough to come nearer, and asked if he did not approve of the colors and the pattern. Then they pointed to the empty loom, and the poor old Minister went on opening his eyes; but he could see nothing, for there was nothing to see.

"Mercy!" thought he, "can I indeed be so stupid? I never thought that, and not a soul must know it. Am I not fit for my office?—No, it will never do for me to tell that I could not see the stuff."

"Do you say nothing to it?" said one of the weavers.

"Oh, it is charming—quite enchanting!" answered the old Minister, as he peered through his spectacles. "What a fine pattern, and what colors! Yes, I shall tell the Emperor that I am very much pleased with it."

"Well, we are glad of that," said both the weavers; and then they named the colors, and explained the strange pattern. The old Minister listened attentively, that he might be able to repeat it to the Emperor. And he did so.

The Emperor's New Clothes

Now the cheats asked for more money, and more silk and gold, which they declared they wanted for weaving. They put all into their own pockets, and not a thread was put upon the loom; but they continued to work at the empty frames as before.

The Emperor soon sent again, dispatching another honest statesman, to see how the weaving was going on, and if the stuff would soon be ready. He fared just like the first: he looked and looked, but, as there was nothing to be seen but the empty looms, he could see nothing.

"Is not that a pretty piece of stuff?" asked the two cheats; and they displayed and explained the handsome pattern which was not there at all.

"I am not stupid!" thought the man; "it must be my good office, for which I am not fit. It is odd enough, but I must not let it be noticed." And so he praised the stuff which he did not see, and expressed his pleasure at the beautiful colors and the charming pattern. "Yes, it is enchanting," he said to the Emperor.

All the people in the town were talking of the gorgeous stuff. The Emperor wished to see it himself while it was still upon the loom. With a whole crowd of chosen men, among whom were also the two honest statesmen who had already been there, he went to the two cunning cheats, who were now weaving with might and main without fiber or thread.

"Is that not splendid?" said the two old statesmen, who had already been there once. "Does not your Majesty remark the pattern and the colors?" And then they pointed to the empty loom, for they thought that the others could see the stuff.

"What's this?" thought the Emperor. "I can see nothing at all! That is terrible. Am I stupid? Am I not fit to be Emperor? That would be the most dreadful thing that could happen to me.—Oh, it is very pretty!" he said aloud. "It has our exalted approbation." And he nodded in a contented way, and gazed at the empty loom, for he would not say that he saw nothing. The whole suite whom he had with him looked and looked, and saw nothing, any more than the rest; but, like the Emperor, they said, "That is pretty!" and counseled him to wear these splendid new clothes for the first time at the great procession that was presently to take place. "It is splendid, tasteful, excellent!" went from mouth to mouth. On all sides there seemed to be general rejoicing, and the Emperor gave the cheats the title of Imperial Court Weavers.

The Emperor's New Clothes

The whole night before the morning on which the procession was to take place the cheats were up, and had lighted more than sixteen candles. The people could see that they were hard at work, completing the Emperor's new clothes. They pretended to take the stuff from the loom; they made cuts in the air with scissors; they sewed with needles without thread; and at last they said, "Now the clothes are ready!"

The Emperor came himself with his noblest cavaliers; and the two cheats lifted up one arm as if they were holding something, and said, "See, here are the trousers! here is the coat! here is the cloak!" and so on. "It is as light as a spider's web: one would think one had nothing on; but that is just the beauty of it."

"Yes," said all the cavaliers; but they could not see anything, for nothing was there.

The Emperor took off his clothes, and the cheats pretended to put on him each new garment as it was ready; and the Emperor turned round and round before the mirror.

"Oh, how well they look! how capitally they fit!" said all. "What a pattern! what colors! That is a splendid dress!"

"Well, I am ready," replied the Emperor. "Does it not suit me well?" And then he turned again to the mirror, for he wanted it to appear as if he contemplated his adornment with great interest.

The chamberlains, who were to carry the train, stooped down with their hands toward the floor, just as if they were picking up the mantle; then they pretended to be holding something up in the air. They did not dare to let it be noticed that they saw nothing.

So the Emperor went in procession under the rich canopy, and every one in the streets said, "How incomparable are the Emperor's new clothes! what a train he has to his mantle! how it fits him!" No one would let it be perceived that he could see nothing, for that would have shown that he was not fit for his office, or was very stupid.

"But he has nothing on!" a little child cried out at last.

"Just hear what that innocent says!" said the father; and one whispered to another what the child had said.

"But he has nothing on!" said the whole people at length. That touched the Emperor, for it seemed to him that they were right; but he thought within himself, "I must go through with the procession." And the chamberlains held on tighter than ever, and carried the train which did not exist at all.

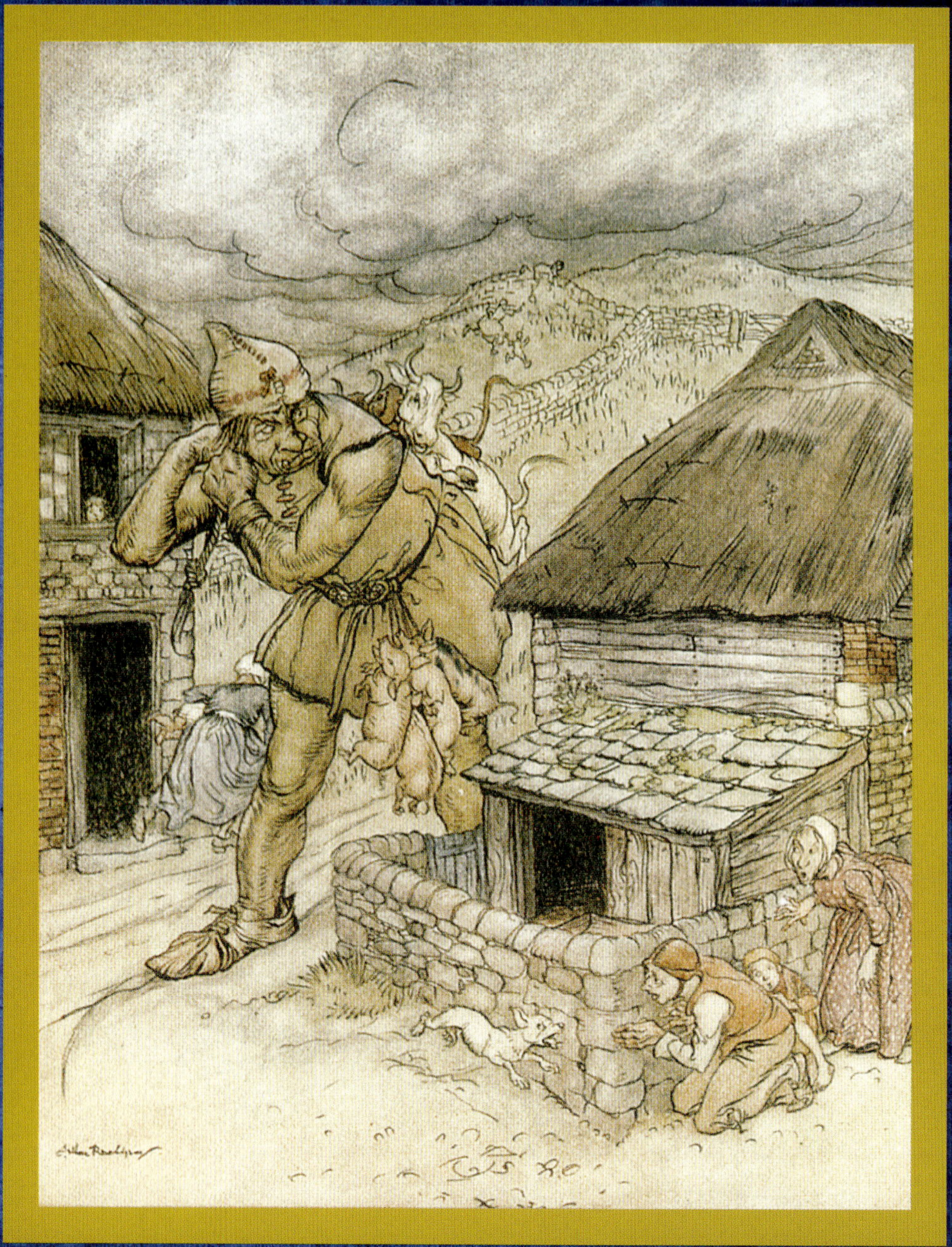

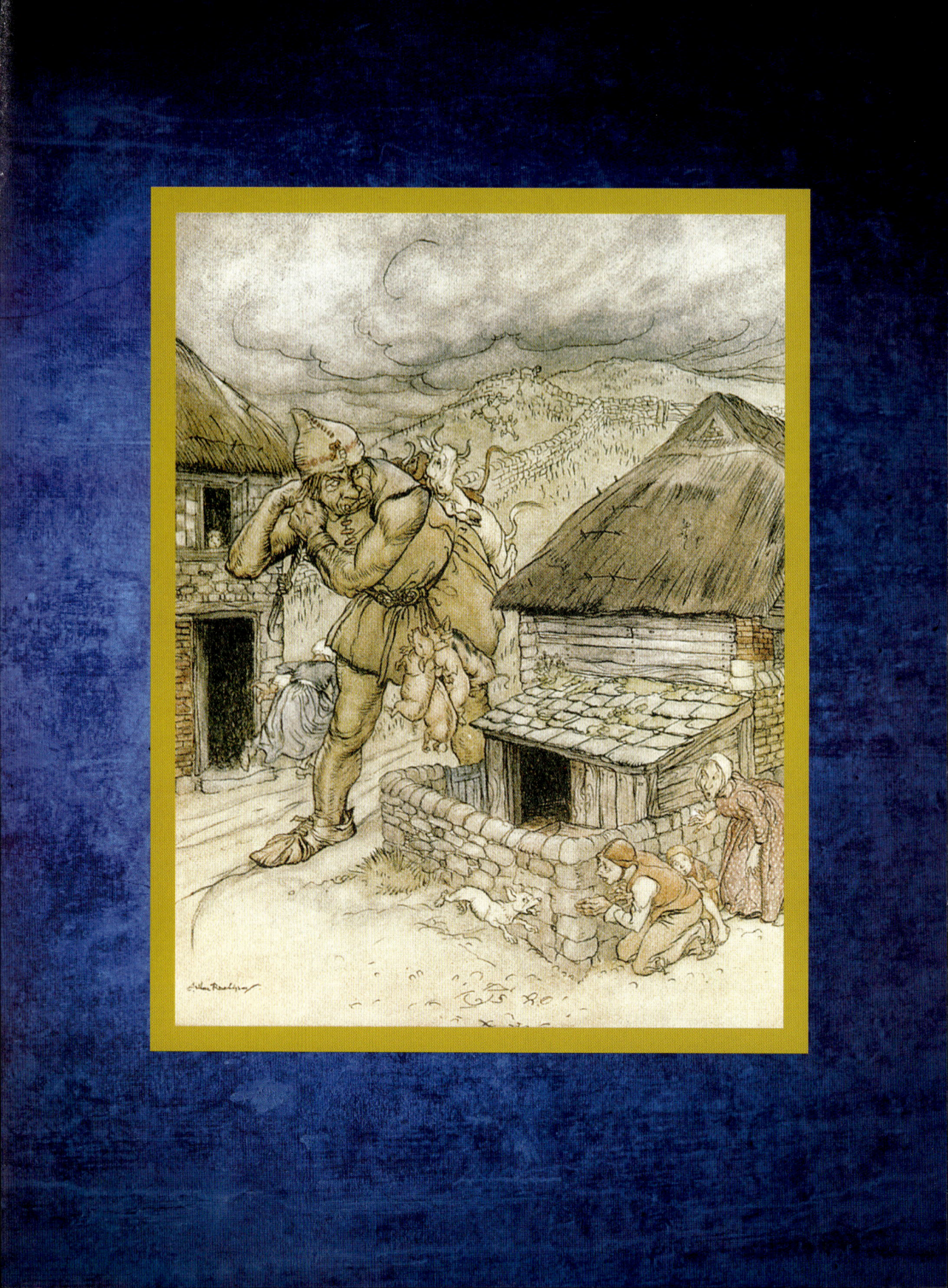

Jack the Giant-Killer

I

When good King Arthur reigned with Guinevere his Queen, there lived, near the Land's End in Cornwall, a farmer who had one only son called Jack. Now Jack was brisk and ready; of such a lively wit that none nor nothing could worst him.

In those days, the Mount of St. Michael in Cornwall was the fastness of a hugeous giant whose name was Cormoran.

He was full eighteen feet in height, some three yards about his middle, of a grim fierce face, and he was the terror of all the country-side. He lived in a cave amidst the rocky Mount, and when he desired victuals he would wade across the tides to the mainland and furnish himself forth with all that came in his way. The poor folk and the rich folk alike ran out of their houses and hid themselves when they heard the swish-swash of his big feet in the water; for if he saw them, he would think nothing of broiling half-a-dozen or so of them for breakfast. As it was, he seized their cattle by the score, carrying off half-a-dozen fat oxen on his back at a time, and hanging sheep and pigs to his waistbelt like bunches of dip-candles. Now this had gone on for long years, and the poor folk of Cornwall were in despair, for none could put an end to the Giant Cormoran.

It so happened that one market day Jack, then quite a young lad, found the town upside down over some new exploit of the giant's. Women were weeping, men were cursing, and the magistrates were sitting in Council over what was to be done. But none could suggest a plan. Then Jack, blithe and gay, went up to the magistrates, and with a fine courtesy—for he was ever polite—asked them what reward would be given to him who killed the giant Cormoran.

"The treasures of the Giant's Cave," quoth they.

"Every whit of it?" quoth Jack, who was never to be done.

"To the last farthing," quoth they.

"Then will I undertake the task," said Jack, and forthwith set about the business.

It was winter-time, and having got himself a horn, a pickaxe, and a shovel, he went over to the Mount in the dark evening, set to work, and before dawn he had dug a pit, no less than twenty-two feet deep and nigh as big across. This he covered with long thin sticks and straw, sprinkling a little loose mold over all to make it look like solid ground. So, just as dawn was breaking, he planted himself fair and square on the side of the pit that was farthest from the giant's cave, raised the horn to his lips, and with full blast sounded:

Tantivy! Tantivy! Tantivy!

just as he would have done had he been hunting a fox.

Of course this woke the giant, who rushed in a rage out of his cave, and seeing little Jack, fair and square blowing away at his horn, as calm and cool as may be, he became still more angry, and made for the disturber of his rest bawling out, "I'll teach you to wake a giant, you little whippersnapper. You shall pay dearly for your tantivys, I'll take you and broil you whole for break—"

He had only got as far as this when crash—he fell into the pit! So there was a break indeed; such a one that it caused the very foundations of the Mount to shake.

But Jack shook with laughter. "Ho, ho!" he cried, "how about breakfast now, Sir Giant? Will you have me broiled or baked? And will no diet serve you but poor little Jack? Faith! I've got you in Lob's pound now! You're in the stocks for bad behavior, and

I'll plague you as I like. Would I had rotten eggs; but this will do as well." And with that he up with his pickaxe and dealt the Giant Cormoran such a most weighty knock on the very crown of his head, that he killed him on the spot.

Whereupon Jack calmly filled up the pit with earth again and went to search the cave, where he found much treasure.

Now when the magistrates heard of Jack's great exploit, they proclaimed that henceforth he should be known as—

JACK THE GIANT-KILLER.

And they presented him with a sword and belt, on which these words were embroidered in gold:

> Here's the valiant Cornishman,
> Who slew the giant Cormoran.

II

Of course the news of Jack's victory soon spread over all England, so that another giant named Blunderbore, who lived to the north, hearing of it, vowed if ever he came across Jack he would be revenged upon him. Now this giant Blunderbore was lord of an enchanted castle that stood in the middle of a lonesome forest.

It so happened that Jack, about four months after he had killed Cormoran, had occasion to journey into Wales, and on the road he passed this forest. Weary with walking, and finding a pleasant fountain by the wayside, he lay down to rest and was soon fast asleep.

Now the giant Blunderbore, coming to the well for water, found Jack sleeping, and knew by the lines embroidered on his belt that here was the far-famed giant-killer. Rejoiced at his luck, the giant, without more ado, lifted Jack to his shoulder and began to carry him through the wood to the enchanted castle.

But the rustling of the boughs awakened Jack, who, finding himself already in the clutches of the giant, was terrified; nor was his alarm decreased by seeing the courtyard of the castle all strewn with men's bones.

"Yours will be with them ere long," said Blunderbore as he locked poor Jack into an immense chamber above the castle gateway. It had a high-pitched, beamed roof, and one window that looked down the road. Here poor Jack was to stay while Blunderbore went to fetch his brother-giant who lived in the same wood, that he might share in the feast.

Now, after a time, Jack, watching through the window, saw the two giants tramping hastily down the road, eager for their dinner.

"Now," quoth Jack to himself, "my death or my deliverance is at hand." For he had thought out a plan. In one corner of the room he had seen two strong cords. These he took, and making a cunning noose at the end of each, he hung them out of the window, and as the giants were unlocking the iron door of the gate managed to slip them over their heads without their noticing it. Then, quick as thought, he tied the other ends to a beam, so that as the giants moved on the nooses tightened and throttled them until they grew black in the face. Seeing this, Jack slid down the ropes, and drawing his sword, slew them both.

So, taking the keys of the castle, he unlocked all the doors and set free three beauteous ladies who, tied by the hair of their heads, he found almost starved to death.

"Sweet ladies," quoth Jack kneeling on one knee—for he was ever polite—"here are the keys of this enchanted castle. I have destroyed the giant Blunderbore and his brutish brother, and thus have restored to you your liberty. These keys should bring you all else you require."

So saying he proceeded on his journey to Wales.

III

He traveled as fast as he could; perhaps too fast, for, losing his way he found himself benighted and far from any habitation. He wandered on always in hopes, until on entering a narrow valley he came on a very large, dreary-looking house standing alone.

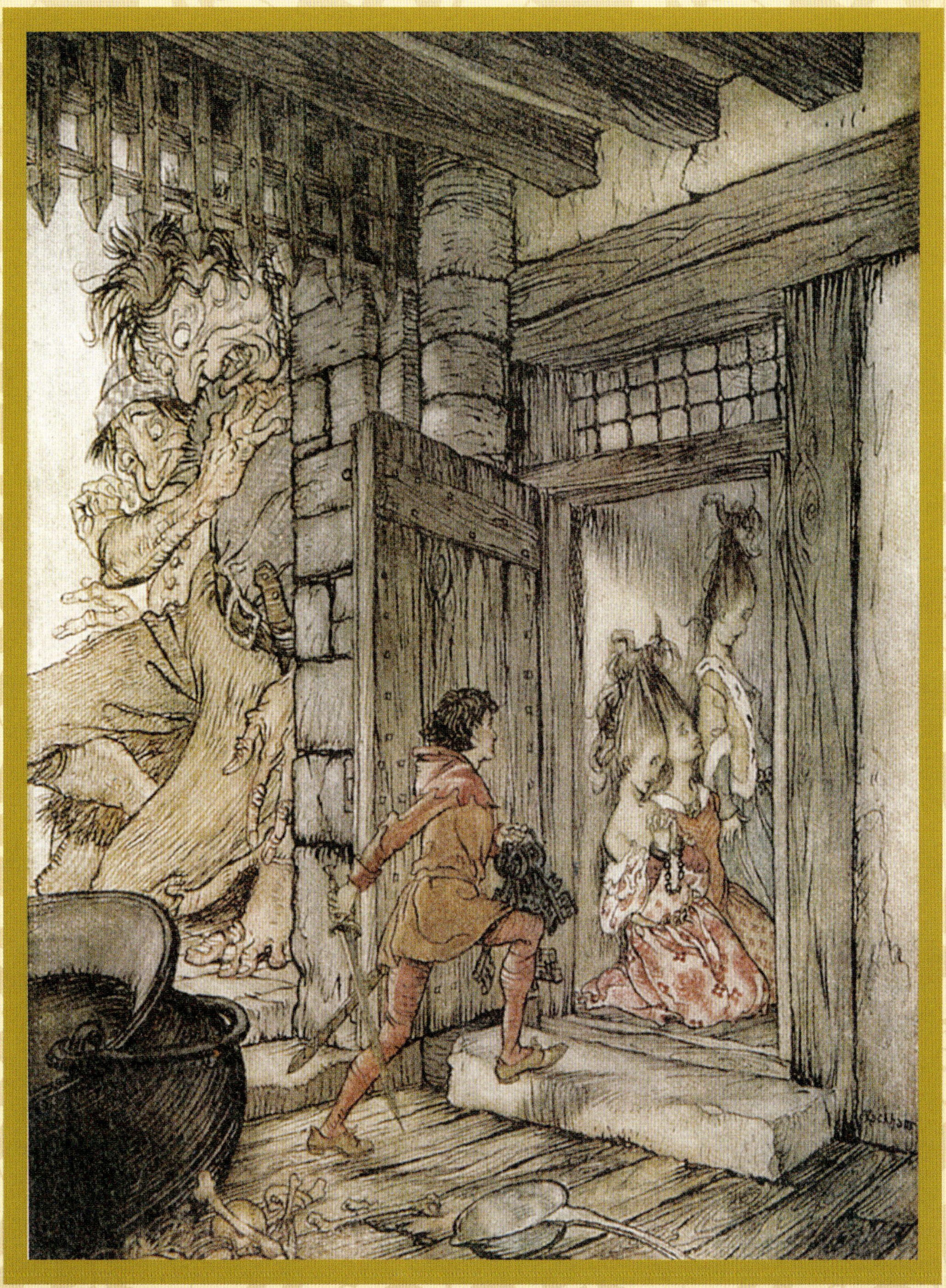

Being anxious for shelter he went up to the door and knocked. You may imagine his surprise and alarm when the summons was answered by a giant with two heads. But though this monster's look was exceedingly fierce, his manners were quite polite. The truth being that he was a Welsh giant, and as such double-faced and smooth, given to gaining his malicious ends by a show of false friendship.

So he welcomed Jack heartily in a strong Welsh accent, and prepared a bedroom for him, where he was left with kind wishes for a good rest. Jack, however, was too tired to sleep well, and as he lay awake, he overheard his host muttering to himself in the next room. Having very keen ears he was able to make out these words or something like them:

> "Though here you lodge with me this night,
> You shall not see the morning light.
> My club shall dash your brains outright."

"Say'st thou so!" quoth Jack to himself, starting up at once. "So that is your Welsh trick, is it? But I will be even with you." Then, leaving his bed, he laid a big billet of wood among the blankets and, taking one of these to keep himself warm, made himself snug in a corner of the room, pretending to snore, so as to make Mr. Giant think he was asleep.

And sure enough, after a little time in came the monster on tiptoe as if treading on eggs, and carrying a big club. Then—

Whack! Whack! Whack!

Jack could hear the bed being belabored until the Giant, thinking every bone of his guest's skin must be broken, stole out of the room again; whereupon Jack went calmly to bed once more and slept soundly! Next morning the giant couldn't believe his eyes when he saw Jack coming down the stairs fresh and hearty.

"Odds splutter hur nails!" he cried astonished. "Did she sleep well? Was there not nothing felt in the night?"

"Oh," replied Jack, laughing in his sleeve, "I think a rat did come and give me two or three flaps of his tail."

On this the giant was dumbfounded, and led Jack to breakfast, bringing him a bowl which held at least four gallons of hasty-pudding, and bidding him, as a man of such mettle, eat the lot. Now Jack when traveling wore under his cloak a leathern bag to carry his things withal; so, quick as thought he hitched this round in front with the opening just un'der his chin; thus, as he ate, he could slip the best part of the pudding into it without the giant's being any the wiser. So they sat down to breakfast, the giant gobbling down his own measure of hasty-pudding, while Jack made away with his.

"See," says crafty Jack when he had finished. "I'll show you a trick worth two of yours," and with that he up with a carving-knife and ripping up the leathern bag out fell all the hasty-pudding on the floor!

"Odds splutter hur nails!" cried the giant, not to be undone. "Hur can do that hurself!" Whereupon he seized the carving-knife, and ripping open his own belly fell down dead.

Thus was Jack quit of the Welsh giant.

IV

Now it so happened that in those days when gallant knights were always seeking adventures. King Arthur's only son, a very valiant Prince, begged of his father a large sum of money to enable him to journey to Wales, and there strive to set free a certain beautiful lady who was possessed by seven evil spirits. In vain the King denied him; so at last he gave way and the Prince set out with two horses, one of which he rode, the other laden with gold pieces. Now after some days' journey the Prince came to a market-town in Wales where there was a great commotion. On asking the reason for it he was told that, according to law, the corpse of a very generous man had been arrested on its way to the grave, because, in life, it had owed large sums to the money-lenders.

"That is a cruel law," said the young Prince. "Go, bury the dead in peace, and let the creditors come to my lodgings; I will pay the debts of the dead."

So the creditors came, but they were so numerous that by evening the Prince had but twopence left for himself, and could not go further on his journey.

Now it so happened that Jack the Giant-Killer on his way to Wales passed through the town, and, hearing of the Prince's plight, was so taken with his kindness and generosity that he determined to be the Prince's servant. So this was agreed upon, and next morning, after Jack had paid the reckoning with his last farthing, the two set out together. But as they were leaving the town, an old woman ran after the Prince and called out, "Justice! Justice! The dead man owed me twopence these seven years. Pay me as well as the others."

And the Prince, kind and generous, put his hand to his pocket and gave the old woman the twopence that was left to him. So now they had not a penny between them, and when the sun grew low the Prince said:

"Jack! Since we have no money, how are we to get a night's lodging?"

Then Jack replied, "We shall do well enough, Master; for within two or three miles of this place there lives a huge and monstrous giant with three heads who can fight four hundred men in armor and make them fly from him like chaff before the wind."

"And what good will that be to us?" quoth the Prince. "He will for sure chop us up in a mouthful."

"Nay," said Jack, laughing. "Let me go and prepare the way for you. By all accounts this giant is a dolt. Mayhap I may manage better than that."

So the Prince remained where he was, and Jack pricked his steed at full speed till he came to the giant's castle, at the gate of which he knocked so loud that he made the neighboring hills resound.

On this the giant roared from within in a voice like thunder:

"Who's there?"

Then said Jack as bold as brass, "None but your poor cousin Jack."

"Cousin Jack!" quoth the giant astounded. "And what news with my poor cousin Jack?" For, see you, he was quite taken aback; so Jack made haste to reassure him.

"Dear coz, heavy news, God wot!"

"Heavy news," echoed the giant, half afraid. "God wot no heavy news can come to me. Have I not three heads? Can I not fight five hundred men in armor? Can I not make them fly like chaff before the wind?"

"True," replied crafty Jack, "but I came to warn you because the great King Arthur's son with a thousand men in armor is on his way to kill you."

At this the giant began to shiver and to shake. "Ah! Cousin Jack! Kind cousin Jack! This is heavy news indeed," quoth he. "Tell me, what am I to do?"

"Hide yourself in the vault," says crafty Jack, "and I will lock and bolt and bar you in, and keep the key till the Prince has gone. So you will be safe."

Then the giant made haste and ran down into the vault and Jack locked, and bolted, and barred him in. Then being thus secure, he went and fetched his master, and the two made themselves heartily merry over what the giant was to have had for supper, while the miserable monster shivered and shook with fright in the underground vault.

Well, after a good night's rest Jack woke his master in early morn, and having furnished him well with gold and silver from the giant's treasure, bade him ride three miles forward on his journey. So when Jack judged that the Prince was pretty well out of the smell of the giant, he took the key and let his prisoner out. He was half dead with cold and damp, but very grateful; and he begged Jack to let him know what he would be given as a reward for saving the giant's life and castle from destruction, and he should have it.

"You're very welcome," said Jack, who always had his eyes about him. "All I want is the old coat and cap, together with the rusty old sword and slippers which are at your bed-head."

When the giant heard this he sighed, and shook his head. "You don't know what you are asking," quoth he. "They are the most precious things I possess, but as I have promised, you must have them. The coat will make you invisible, the cap will tell you all you want to know, the sword will cut asunder whatever you strike, and the slippers will take you wherever you want to go in the twinkling of an eye!"

So Jack, overjoyed, rode away with the coat and cap, the sword and the slippers, and soon overtook his master; and they rode on together until they reached the castle where the beautiful lady lived whom the Prince sought.

Now she was very beautiful, for all she was possessed of seven devils, and when she heard the Prince sought her as a suitor, she smiled and ordered a splendid banquet to be prepared for his reception. And she sat on his right hand, and plied him with food and drink.

And when the repast was over she took out her own handkerchief and wiped his lips gently, and said with a smile:

"I have a task for you, my lord! You must show me that kerchief to-morrow morning or lose your head."

And with that she put the handkerchief in her bosom and said, "Good-night!"

The Prince was in despair, but Jack said nothing till his master was in bed. Then he put on the old cap he had got from the giant, and lo! in a minute he knew all that he wanted to know. So, in the dead of the night, when the beautiful lady called on one of her familiar spirits to carry her to Lucifer himself. Jack was beforehand with her, and putting on his coat of darkness and his slippers of swiftness, was there as soon as she was. And when she gave the handkerchief to the Devil, bidding him keep it safe, and he put it away on a high shelf, Jack just up and nipped it away in a trice!

So the next morning when the beauteous enchanted lady looked to see the Prince crestfallen, he just made a fine bow and presented her with the handkerchief.

At first she was terribly disappointed, but as the day drew on, she ordered another and still more splendid repast to be got ready. And this time when the repast was over, she kissed the Prince full on the lips and said:

"I have a task for you, my lover. Show me to-morrow morning the last lips I kiss to-night or you lose your head."

Then the Prince, who by this time was head over ears in love, said tenderly, "If you will kiss none but mine, I will."

Now the beauteous lady for all she was possessed by seven devils could not but see that the Prince was a very handsome young man; so she blushed a little, and said:

"That is neither here nor there: you must show me them, or death is your portion."

So the Prince went to his bed, sorrowful as before; but Jack put on the cap of knowledge and knew in a moment all he wanted to know.

Thus when, in the dead of the night, the beauteous lady called on her familiar spirit to take her to Lucifer himself, Jack in his coat of darkness and his shoes of swiftness was there before her.

"Thou hast betrayed me once," said the beauteous lady to Lucifer, frowning, "by letting go my handkerchief. Now will I give thee something none can steal, and so best the Prince, King's son though he be."

With that she kissed the loathly demon full on the lips, and left him. Whereupon Jack with one blow of the rusty sword of strength, cut off Lucifer's head and, hiding it under his coat of darkness, brought it back to his master.

Thus next morning when the beauteous lady, with malice in her beautiful eyes, asked the Prince to show her the lips she had last kissed, he pulled out the demon's head by the horns. On that the seven devils, which possessed the poor lady, gave seven dreadful shrieks and left her. Thus the enchantment being broken, she appeared in all her perfect beauty and goodness.

So she and the Prince were married the very next morning. After which they journeyed back to the court of King Arthur, where Jack the Giant-Killer, for his many exploits, was made one of the Knights of the Round Table.

V

This, however, did not satisfy our hero, who was soon on the road again searching for giants. Now he had not gone far when he came upon one, seated on a huge block of timber near the entrance to a dark cave. He was a most terrific giant. His goggle eyes were as coals of fire, his countenance was grim and gruesome; his cheeks, like huge flitches of bacon, were covered with a stubbly beard, the bristles of which resembled rods of iron wire, while the locks of hair that fell on his brawny shoulders showed like curled snakes or hissing adders. He held a knotted iron club, and breathed so heavily you could hear him a mile away. Nothing daunted by this fearsome sight, Jack alighted from his horse and putting on his coat of darkness went close up to the giant and; said softly: "Hullo! is that you? It will not be long before I have you fast by your beard."

So saying he made a cut with the sword of strength at the giant's head, but, somehow, missing his aim, cut off the I nose instead, clean as a whistle! My goodness! How the giant roared! It was like claps of thunder, and he began to lay about him with the knotted iron club, like one possessed. But Jack in his coat of darkness easily dodged the blows, and running in behind, drove the sword up to the hilt into the giant's back, so that he fell stone dead.

Jack then cut off the head and sent it to King Arthur by a wagoner whom he hired for the purpose. After which he began to search the giant's cave to find his treasure. He passed through many windings and turnings until he came to a huge hall paved and roofed with freestone. At the upper end of this was an immense fireplace where hung an iron cauldron, the like of which, for size, Jack had never seen before. It was boiling and gave out a savory steam; while beside it, on the right hand, stood a big massive table set out with huge platters and mugs. Here it was that the giants used to dine. Going a little further he came upon a sort of window barred with iron, and looking within beheld a vast number of miserable captives.

"Alas! Alack!" they cried on seeing him. Art come, young man, to join us in this dreadful prison?"

"That depends," quoth Jack; "but first tell me wherefore you are thus held imprisoned?"

"Through no fault," they cried at once. "We are captives of the cruel giants and are kept here and well nourished until such time as the monsters desire a feast. Then they choose the fattest and sup off them."

On hearing this Jack straightway unlocked the door of the prison and set the poor fellows free. Then, searching the giants' coffers he divided the gold and silver equally amongst the captives as some redress for their sufferings, and taking them to a neighboring castle gave them a right good feast.

VI

Now as they were all making merry over their deliverance, and praising Jack's prowess, a messenger arrived to say that one Thunderdell, a huge giant with two heads, having heard of the death of his kinsman, was on his way from the northern dales to be revenged, and was already within a mile or two of the castle, the country folk with their flocks and herds flying before him like chaff before the wind.

Now the castle with its gardens stood on a small island that was surrounded by a moat twenty feet wide and thirty feet deep, having very steep sides. And this moat was spanned by a drawbridge. This, without a moment's delay, Jack ordered should be sawn on both sides at the middle, so as to leave only one plank uncut over which he in his invisible coat of darkness passed swiftly to meet his enemy, bearing in his hand the wonderful sword of strength.

Now though the giant could not, of course, see Jack, he could smell him, for giants have keen noses. Therefore Thunderdell cried out in a voice like his name:

> "Fee, fi, fo, fum!
> I smell the blood of an Englishman.
> Be he alive, or be he dead,
> I'll grind his bones to make my bread!"

"Is that so?" quoth Jack, cheerful as ever. "Then art thou a monstrous miller for sure!"

On this the giant peering round everywhere for a glimpse of his foe, shouted out:

"Art thou, indeed, the villain who hath killed so many of my kinsmen? Then, indeed, will I tear thee to pieces with my teeth, suck thy blood, and grind thy bones to powder."

"Thou'lt have to catch me first," quoth Jack, laughing, and throwing off his coat of darkness and putting on his slippers of swiftness he began nimbly to lead the giant a pretty dance, he leaping and doubling light as a feather, the monster following heavily like a walking tower, so that the very foundations of the earth seemed to shake at every step. At this game the onlookers nearly split their sides with laughter, until Jack, judging there had been enough of it, made for the drawbridge, ran neatly over the single plank, and reaching the other side waited in teasing fashion for his adversary.

On came the giant at full speed, foaming at the mouth with rage, and flourishing his club. But when he came to the middle of the bridge his great weight, of course, broke the plank, and there he was fallen headlong into the moat, rolling and wallowing like a whale, plunging from place to place yet unable to get out and be revenged.

The spectators greeted his efforts with roars of laughter, and Jack himself was at first too overcome with merriment to do more than scoff. At last, however, he went for a rope, cast it over the giant's two heads, so with the help of a team of horses drew them shoreward, where two blows from the sword of strength settled the matter.

VII

After some time spent in mirth and pastimes, Jack began once more to grow restless, and taking leave of his companions set out for fresh adventures.

He traveled far and fast, through woods, and vales, and hills, till at last he came, late at night, on a lonesome house set at the foot of a high mountain.

Knocking at the door, it was opened by an old man whose head was white as snow.

"Father," said Jack, ever courteous, "can you lodge a benighted traveler?"

"Ay, that will I, and welcome to my poor cottage," replied the old man.

Whereupon Jack came in, and after supper they sate together chatting in friendly fashion. Then it was that the old man, seeing by Jack's belt that he was the famous Giant-Killer, spoke in this wise:

"My son! You are the great conqueror of evil monsters. Now close by there lives one well worthy of your prowess. On the top of yonder high hill is an enchanted castle kept by a giant named Galligantua, who, by the help of a wicked old magician, inveigles many beautiful ladies and valiant knights into the castle, where they are transformed into all sorts of birds and beasts, yea, even into fishes and insects. There they live pitiably in confinement; but most of all do I grieve for a duke's daughter whom they kidnapped in her father's garden, bringing her hither in a burning chariot drawn by fiery dragons. Her form is that of a white hind; and though many valiant knights have tried their utmost to break the spell and work her deliverance, none have succeeded; for, see you, at the entrance to the castle are two dreadful griffins who destroy every one who attempts to pass them by."

Now Jack bethought him of the coat of darkness which had served him so well before, and he put on the cap of knowledge, and in an instant he knew what had to be done. Then the very next morning, at dawn-time. Jack arose and put on his invisible coat and his slippers of swiftness. And in the twinkling of an eye there he was on the top of the mountain! And there were the two griffins guarding the castle gates—horrible creatures with forked tails and tongues. But they could not see him because of the coat of darkness, so he passed them by unharmed.

And hung to the doors of the gateway he found a golden trumpet on a silver chain, and beneath it was engraved in red lettering:

> Whoever shall this trumpet blow
> Will cause the giant's overthrow.
> The black enchantment he will break,
> And gladness out of sadness make.

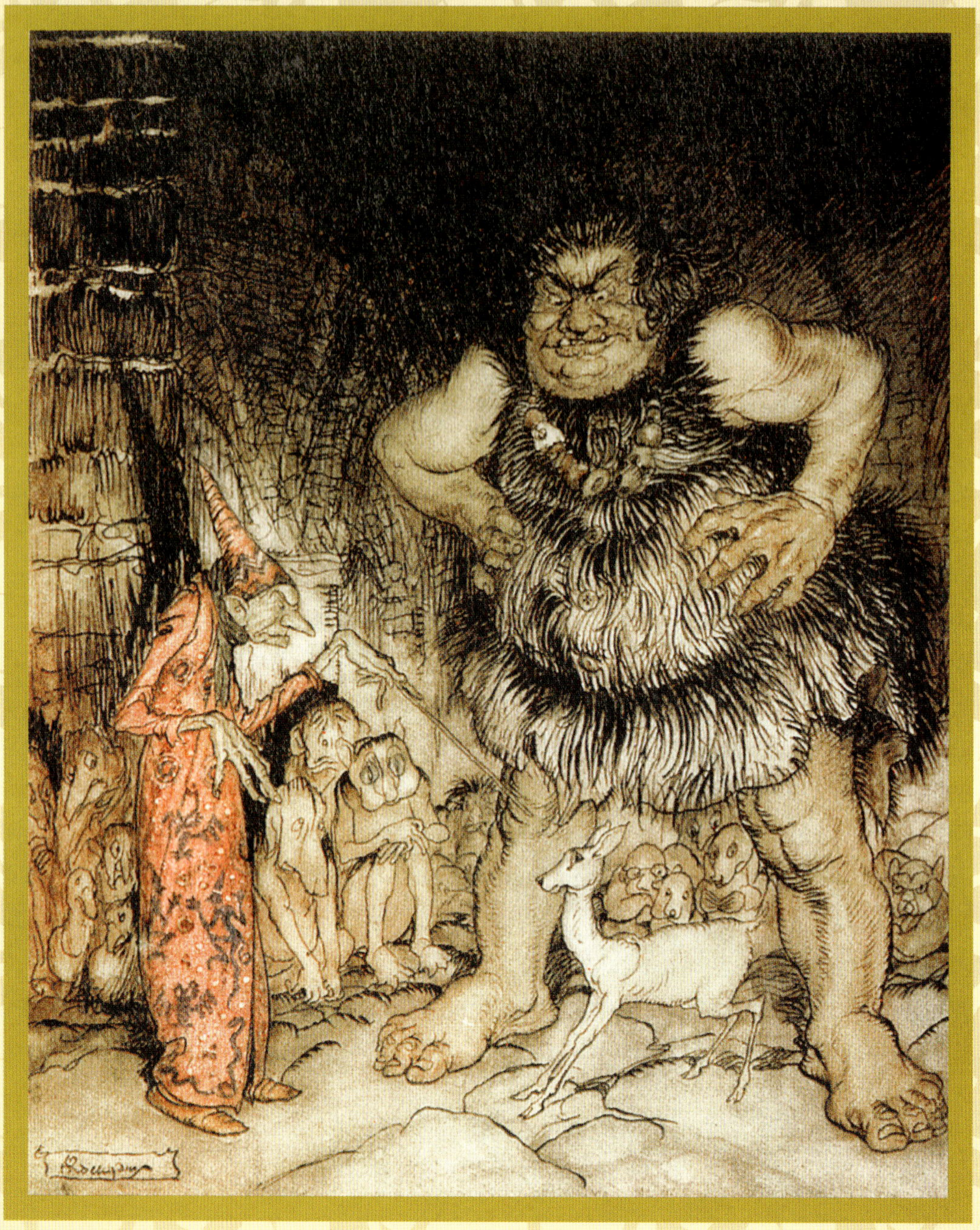

No sooner had Jack read these words than he put the horn to his lips and blew a loud

Tantivy! Tantivy! Tantivy!

Now at the very first note the castle trembled to its vast foundations, and before he had finished the measure, both the giant and the magician were biting their thumbs and tearing their hair, knowing that their wickedness must now come to an end. But the giant showed fight and took up his club to defend himself; whereupon Jack, with one clean cut of the sword of strength, severed his head from his body, and would doubtless have done the same to the magician, but that the latter was a coward, and, calling up a whirlwind, was swept away by it into the air, nor has he ever been seen or heard of since. The enchantments being thus broken, all the valiant knights and beautiful ladies who had been transformed into birds and beasts and fishes and reptiles and insects, returned to their proper shapes, including the duke's daughter, who, from being a white hind, showed as the most beauteous maiden upon whom the sun ever shone. Now, no sooner had this occurred than the whole castle vanished away in a cloud of smoke, and from that moment giants vanished also from the land.

So Jack, when he had presented the head of Galligantua to King Arthur, together with all the lords and ladies he had delivered from enchantment, found he had nothing more to do. As a reward for past services, however, King Arthur bestowed the hand of the duke's daughter upon honest Jack the Giant-Killer. So married they were, and the whole Kingdom was filled with joy at their wedding. Furthermore, the King bestowed on Jack a noble castle with a magnificent estate belonging thereto, whereon he, his lady, and their children lived in great joy and content for the rest of their days.

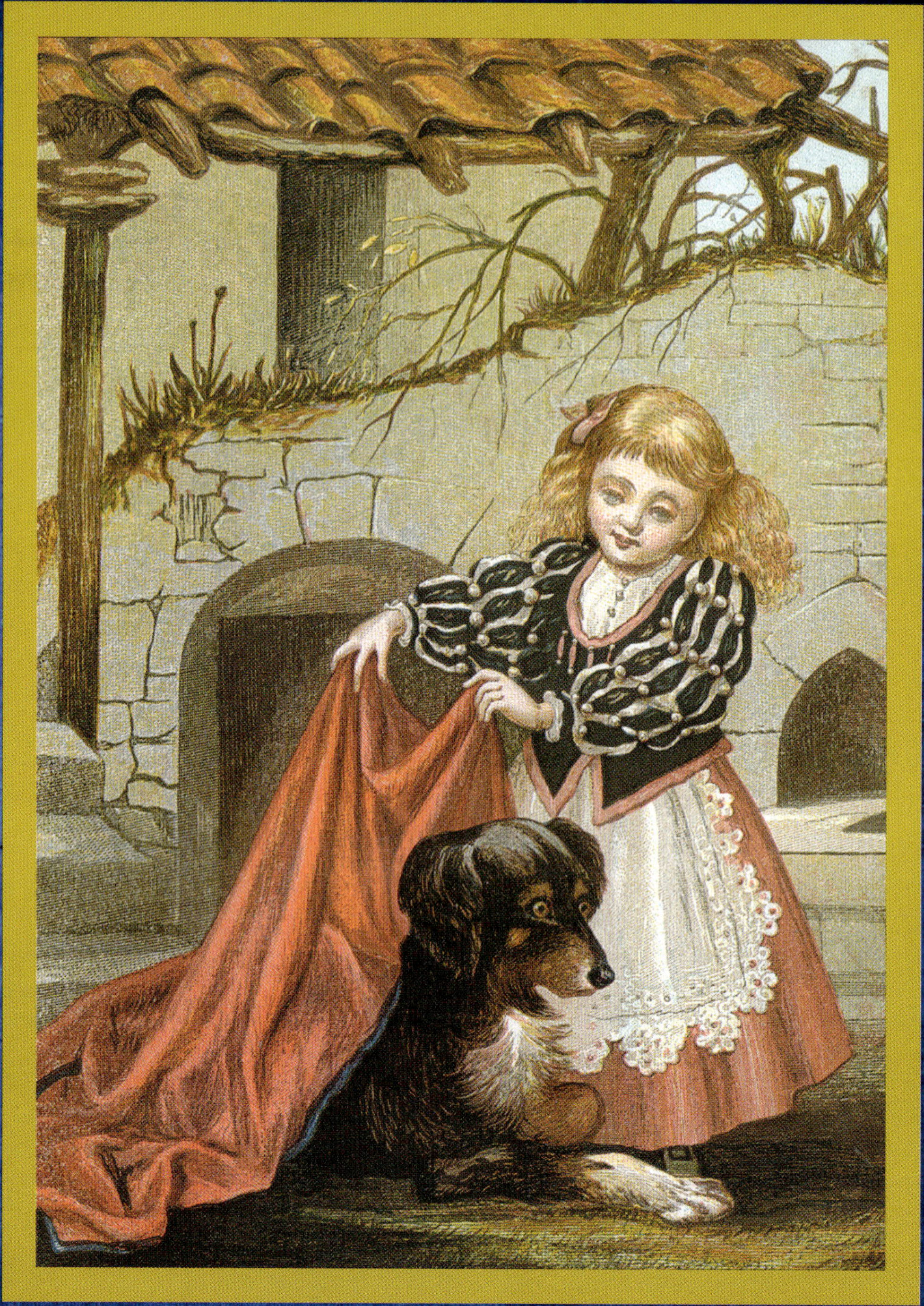

Beauty and the Beast

Once, long ago, in a certain city whose name is forgotten, there lived a merchant-master. He had three sons and three daughters, but his wife was dead. The man was happy in his children; for the sons were well-grown and brave, and the daughters beautiful. Men called both elder maidens passing fair. One, like dusky night, black-haired and brown-eyed—the other, bright as the morning, with long tresses of red gold. But the third daughter, born years later, outshone both in her perfect loveliness. Such a lovely maid was never seen—so they named her simply, Beauty. No fairy godmother came with gifts to call her so; but she grew so sweet and lovely, that in the city where she dwelt they knew her by no other name. Howbeit, many a one said, it was but her happy, innocent soul that gave the sunshine to her face. Sometimes it would happen, that one of the great masters in painting or sculpture of those old times, journeying through that place, and beholding her pass down the street, would beseech her to stay a while, that with pencil or with chisel, he might do some image of that gracious, lovesome mien, to make him glad in after days. And thus, it may be, Beauty lives still under the dimness of some old canvas—the St. Catherine or the Virgin Mother of some Holy Family—or smiles may be, in the carven face of an angel, in the niche beside some old cathedral door. Even from the time when she was a little child, Beauty possessed the gift of a loving heart. And the love she so freely gave, was paid back to her again in

full measure. They who were despised and ugly, in their wretchedness wanted never a kind word or look from her, nor were unholpen by her in their need. Most tenderly she loved all God's suffering creatures, whether of bird or beast; she took them to her heart, and made joy to soothe and comfort them. And she withheld not her small hand from succoring the most ill-favored of earth's children. Self-forgetful, in her large charity, she tended even herbs, and such unlovely, blossomless, and scentless plants, as might call for her tender care. And the child would oftentimes fetch water for some poor neglected weed, fainting in the hot sun, or stay to prop some weak climbing plant torn down by the rough wind. And Beauty was greatly beloved; and notwithstanding that she never knew a mother's love, her child days went lightly by, and the rose-light of her own sweet joyous spirit shone back to her from all things round. But as the maiden grew from infancy into youth, her meek heart was pained by her sisters' pride and arrogance. Many were the sharp cruel words she heard; many a hard rebuke must she endure from that ungentle pair. Their pride and hardness knew no end. Vain were they of their many lovers, of their gold-embroidered gowns, of their goodly persons; for well they wist that of all fair women thereabout—but for their young sister—they were held peerless. So they envied Beauty the lovely face that God gave her, and the love her kindness won for her. Noble youths sought many a time to gain in marriage one or another of them; but none seemed great enough, or rich enough. Yet they would not let them go, but with half smiles and double words, kept the young men following in their train.

Time sped quickly in the rich city where the merchant dwelt. Day and night the hours danced on to the sound of music and feasting. Beauty's sisters reigned like queens amid their young companions—damsels nigh as fair as they—but of whom they made not much account, for the splendor of the merchant's daughters cast a cold shadow all around.

On great feast days, when the house was set in order, and the sisters in their rich apparel, and gold crowns upon their heads, sat under silken canopies, with all their lovers at their feet, right glad were they when Beauty sat not with them. At such times the girl, in the glory of her lustrous loveliness, would call the children, to come forth into the fields and woods, and gather flowers with her; or perchance she might steal away to succor in their distress, poor miserable ones, who lay sick and forlorn of hope, in rude dwellings beyond the city walls. Then were the sisters left to reign alone; and no prayer did they ever make to Beauty, for her to share the joyance of such festal days.

But that sweet maiden gave no heed at all to such unkindness. She would seek flowers of rare bloom, and therewith weave garlands and set them in her sisters' hair, all unaware that meanwhile sharp stings of envious hatred stung them, when they marked how men's faces lit up with gladness whenever Beauty passed by, clad only in her simple gown. And so neglect and unkindness did not touch her gentle life. And home was beyond all things dear to her, for the great love and reverence she bore her father. Dearer moreover than aught else beside, save only his gold (which was indeed no hoarded wealth), was the youngest born to him. Yet the Prince-Merchant took most delight withal, in his many-oared galleys and full-sailed ships, which ever and anon went out across the harbor bar, and in due course came back into port gold-laden, and heavy with precious merchandise from lands beyond the sunrise.

But Fortune is not always kind, and there be many winds both fair and foul; and black days there be, when the Fates send forth a wind, which blows no good to any living soul. So fared it with the merchant. For on a day, watchers upon the high watchtower, out-worn with long waiting, and with gazing seaward in vain, heard the clatter of iron shoes upon the beaten way below. And anon came messengers on swift coursers from some outland place, who did their message, and cried out to the men to cease their watch, for that the ships would return no more. They told how fierce storms had arisen, and had so buffeted the ships that they drove right upon the rocks; the heavy cargo sank down, and all had perished in the sea. Thus sorrow and a great heaviness fell upon the merchant and all his house. The elder daughters slept not, nor ate, for two days and two nights. No more dreams of pride for them. No more days of idle joy. Fortune hid her face, and the world hid hers, for it had come to pass that the rich man, was on a sudden, poor. The suitors melted away, every one, like ghosts at cockcrow. And not one had said, "Stay with us; my home is thine." Beauty, it is true, might abide in that city, a well-loved, honored wife; but ruin and unhappiness had crept up to the door, and, like a deadly snake, enfolded all her father's house; and she cared not to live at ease, when they who were dear to her, might scarce have bread to eat. Her brothers knit their brows, and spake no word good or bad; only, they laid by in the great painted chest, their swords, and gay clothing of furred mantles and plumed caps, and went to toil in the fields.

Leagues away, on a barren sandy ridge above the sea, in long-past years, the sea-kings had built them a stronghold. Little of it now had fire and war and time's long decay left whole, save one tempest-shaken tower. And under the tower a village, where dwelt rude fisher folk. A poor place withal for he who was once a rich lord! A possession that no man might take much pride in. But thither the ruined merchant now must wend, to make his abode there, and strive to win some daily bread, in rough toil with the fishing-boats. So the man with his children departed, and came to dwell in the tower on the gray hill, amidst of wretched huts. And what scanty gear they had, was carried on the backs of one or two hired mules. It was a dark and windy night, the night when they came there, in the season of the year that leaves first turn from green to gold, and barley sheaves stand in the fields, and the vintage is done. The sun had arisen in the morning when Beauty opened the old brown door and looked out from under its low-browed arch. Far down, beyond the curving yellow sands, lay a great sea-plain, silver bright, glittering in changeful lights and color. Up to the roots of the far-off white mountains, olive woods clothed all the land with mists of shimmering gray. Corn-fields lay anear, between long stretches of purple-shadowed forest. And the girl laughed for gladness of heart, calling aloud to her sisters to come and behold with her this glorious new wonderland where Fate had led them. But they, so soon as they came and stood beside the open door, did but cast one glance down upon those poverty-stricken huts, below the steep hard by, then muttering one to the other, "Better in our graves than here!" they turned away their faces from God's earth and sea: and therewith, through sore repining and complaint, they both fell sick: and on their hard beds made what cheer they might with empty dreams, and lamentation for the goodly days that had been.

 In the old homestead on the hill, the year wore on merrily, for Beauty made great sunshine in that place. Her light step and the music of her happy voice seemed everywhere—all about the house, in the low dark rooms and up and down the creaking stair. A glory seemed to shine round her lovely face when you saw it at the door. Like the wild birds, she was for ever flitting here and there, and singing as she went. She lent the young strength of her white arms to the ancient crone who kept the house. She came wherever she was called. It was Beauty who drew the water and kneaded the cakes, and led the cows to pasture in the dewy grass-lands in the morning. It was Beauty who set the table, and made ready for father and hungry brothers against their return at evening, from the long day's work. Right glad and willing was she, to labor from red dawn to dark, for the love she bore them. And whatever work she set her hand to, wheresoever she did any service, all things she touched seemed nobler, since that she had to do with them. But greater joy she had otherwhile, on the days when she was sent to keep goats upon the hill. Strong and light of foot herself as a young kid, she climbed the rugged paths among the rocks, following after her wayward herd. Many a day would she wander with them through the great woods till the sun was low. But ever as she went, on the hills under the blue sky, or through the forest amid the green darkness of noonday, sea and sky, and sun and shadow, taught the maiden marvelous things. Many a secret did the wind whisper; many a strange tale her eyes read in the flowery grass; many a song, for her alone, sang the mountain stream, hurrying over the stones. And when Beauty led home her flock at sun-down, after such sweet days as these they noted how, when she crossed the threshold and came into the dark house-room, her eyes would shine with a diviner light, than the full health of youth only might give.

Days and months went by; till in the second winter, one morning a weary horseman drew rein at the door. He told that the merchant's heaviest-laden ship, one of those long since given up for lost, had on a sudden sailed into a distant sea-port, and now lay safely anchored in the bay. Loud were the rejoicings that day within the gray old tower on the hill. Joy and laughter filled all hearts. The elder sisters straightway lost themselves in happy day-dreams of a golden coming time; of a joyous life to be lived once more, when they should return to the great rich city. They hastened their father's quick departure for the ship; but as needs must, their farewells were long, for they prayed him to bring back to them many a rich thing that their hearts desired—jeweled coifs, and silken gowns and gold-embroidered stuffs; stores of perfumed gloves and precious stones; and golden chains, and strings of pearls. Each sister longed after something better, and of higher price than the other. So the merchant promised all, and made ready to be gone. Then Beauty put up her sweet face to bid farewell, as she stood beside the horse, and held his stirrup for the beloved father. And he stooped down to kiss her, saying, "And wilt thou nought, thou best-loved child? Choose only what thing is most rare and longed for, it is granted."

But Beauty whispered, "Bring me a white rose, my father—a little white rose!"

And seeing that no words could move her in this, but that she would have a rose, a white rose, he promised that and rode away.

So in this changing world the evil days for them seemed passed away for evermore. It was now winter, and when that tide drew near that the merchant should come home, Beauty's sisters sat all day in the little turret window watching; or they went pacing up and down the bare gray ridge, waiting to behold from afar the long train of laden mules. From early morning, through the glaring noon-tide, oftentimes till after moon-rise, when long shadows lengthened, still would they keep untiring watch. Small care indeed had they to see again their father's face; but their souls yearned for the gold and the silver and the treasure he should bring with him.

Alas! the longed-for hour, when at last it came, was in no wise like the picture that eager greed, had held up before their minds' eye. Bad luck still clave fast to the ill-starred merchant; or so it seemed; for when he came anear the wished-for harbor, he saw indeed amidst crowded masts a little smoldering smoke and flame, and folks running to and fro upon the quay; but his own good ship with her bales of costly merchandise, he never saw. That very night, by misadventure, some spark from the shipmen's fire had fallen unheeded, and the ship had burned down to the edge of the cold water. Thus sore smitten, and in great heaviness, the merchant must wend home again. Poor had he left it, and poor must he return. Full well might cruel fancy now paint for him—as wearily, with down-bent head, he turned to fare back the way that he had come—the grief of such an empty home-coming. "Alas!" he sighed, as he looked round across the wide wintry plain, "unhappy that I am! I cannot even take home with me the one little white rose for Beauty." And so, very sorrowfully, did he ride on for many a weary mile, in the rain and the wind. Lost in troubled thought, he forgot to mark which way his horse might go. On a sudden the creaking sound of thick branches overhead, with storms of dry dead leaves whirled past his face, and many a wild sound, as of the great north wind in winter battling with the strong-limbed forest-trees, aroused him and recalled him to himself. All around seemed strange, and unlike the road he knew. Painfully for a time the merchant and his tired beast made head against the driving blast. The forest path seemed as though it would never end; the wind blew as though it would never cease. But at sundown there fell a calm. The dark clouds broke, and in the clear evening light, the man turned into a way he deemed that he had gone, once in older times, under shelter of a gray stone wall. On the right hand, between straight red bolls of tall fir-trees, shone the far-off open country. The wall closed in upon the left; and above the moldering weed-grown coping, from within, rose dark cypress spires against the sky. Arbutus trees, all a-flame with rich ripe fruit amidst gold-green leaves, tossed down their scarlet balls upon the wet stony way below. And withal, from the other side came a great sweetness as of summer roses upon the air; but a few paces farther on, white roses, like floods of surging foam, overtopped the high wall. Between the whiteness of uncounted roses scarce any green at all might show. Now as the merchant beheld these foam-white flowers, he thought on Beauty's simple wish. Then he cast about in his mind how to reach up to them; and anon he spied a quaintly-painted gateway in the wall, and a little door set therein. Without more ado he dismounted, and pushing open the little door, passed through into a fairy garden. Within the greenness of that enchanted space there was not any more winter. Green paths overhung by pale-blossomed acacias, led to grassy lawns closed in by well-clipt hedges of box and rosemary, and broidered all over with little flowers, blue, pink, and lilac, mixt with the short thick grass. Long narrow terraces rising in green steps one above the other, set with fruit-trees in full bloom, made lines of lovely color. Wild violets crept fragrantly about their roots, or hung in purple draperies from step to step. Under the shadowy dark-stemmed trees blood-red lilies burnt with a sultry glow. Here and there, in the blackness of some deeper gloom, pure star-like flowers, poised on tall slender stalks, gleamed white and ghostly. But everywhere about that garden, roses grew and bloomed, scattering their delicate petals upon the grass. Through the silence came a low murmuring of unseen waters; the thrush sang hidden amid thick leaves. The man scarce could tell if all the sweetness of that place were truth, or but woven magic. How this might be seemed nought to him, so he might pluck a living rose or two for Beauty. Yet he trod lightly, lest a spell should snap, and the dream melt away, leaving him alone in some drear bleak waste.

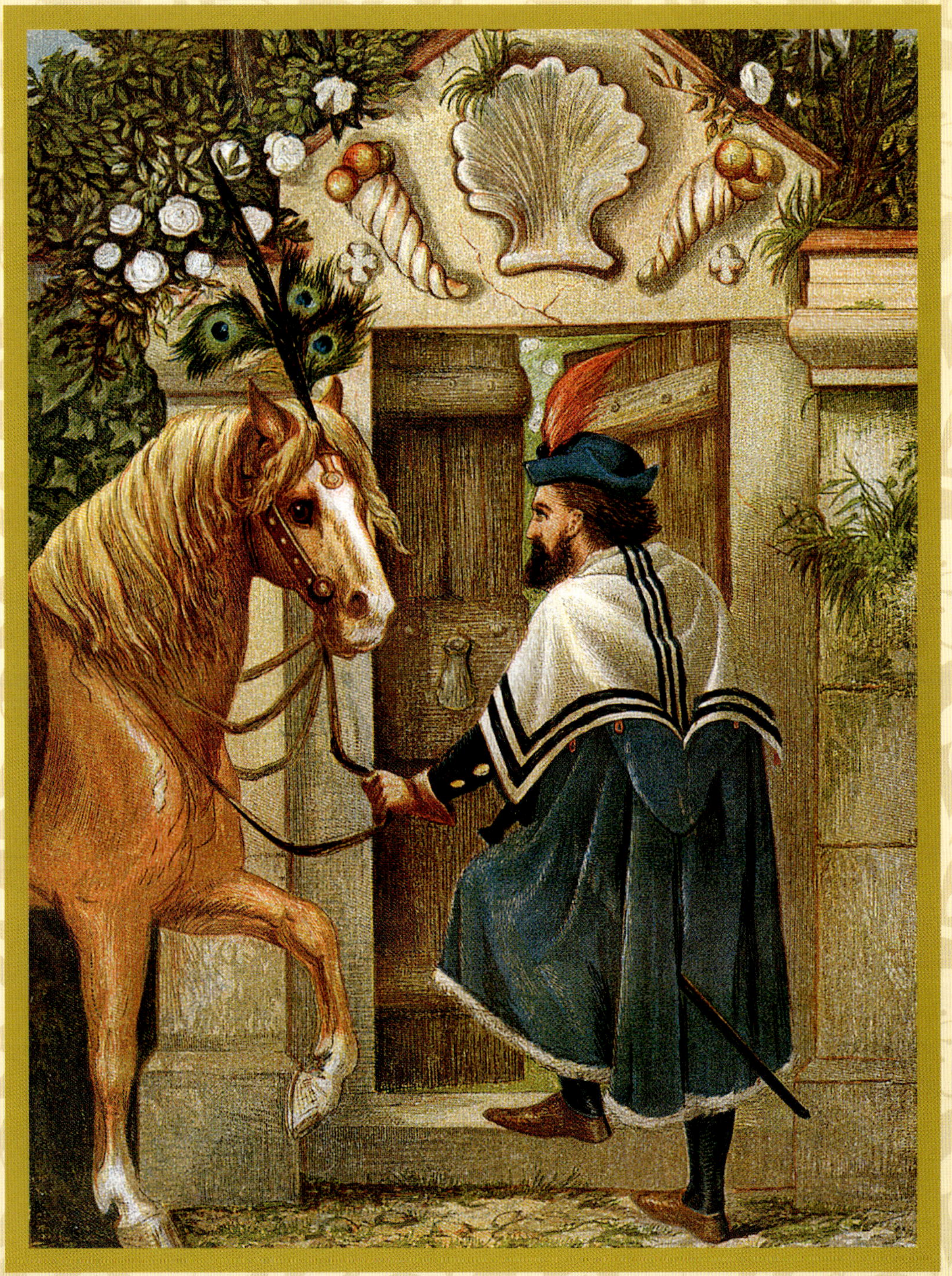

But as he held the plucked flowers in his hand, a dread of some nameless unknown thing began to chill the man's heart. Night seemed gathering round. The loud birds ceased their music; the merry-voiced fountains ran dully; and a shuddering dreadful sound, creeping up a-nigh him, turned all his blood to ice. The heavy dragging rustle as of some huge beast beneath the trees, became at length a grizzly shape, on the open green. The man was 'ware of great blackness and the grating of teeth. What more he could never tell, for betwixt the strange darkness and his mortal fear, standing there unarmed—nought in his right hand but some stolen roses—sight failed him. Then the Beast stayed still, and the roses dropt from the man's grasp; and that Beast spake in a voice which was terrible to hearken to, so shaken was it by despair and rage.

"Who, wretched man art thou, that darest enter here and steal my roses? Meet were it did I slay thee there where thou standest!"

But now the merchant, in whose breast there beat no woman's heart, gat together all his strength and wit. So he turned and faced the Beast.

"That were poorly done, fair sir," said he, "to slay an unarmed man—one, too, less mighty than thyself. The child shall yet win sweeter flowers than these; take back thy roses and let me be gone." And he cast down the flowers, and spurned them with his foot.

But the Beast's wrath on a sudden changed, as with a grievous voice he groaned, "For whom, then, art thou thus lost?"

Then the man told him all; of his bootless journey to the distant seaport—of how his eldest daughters had desired jewels and gold raiment, and of Beauty's wish for one white rose.

Silently the Beast heard; then, drawing a deep breath, like a human sigh, he spake again very softly. "Merchant," he said, "death is the price they pay who steal that without which life to me were one long death. But if life still to thee is sweet, thou must bring hither that young maid of whom thou spakest. Half a year will I await her coming: but if she come not then, in thine own house will I seek her, and little more joy will life hold then for thee or her. So get thee gone, and take this rose for Beauty." With that the Beast brake off a rose, and thrust it into the merchant's hand, who, for a moment stood still, and heard in the glimmering twilight that huge creature depart,

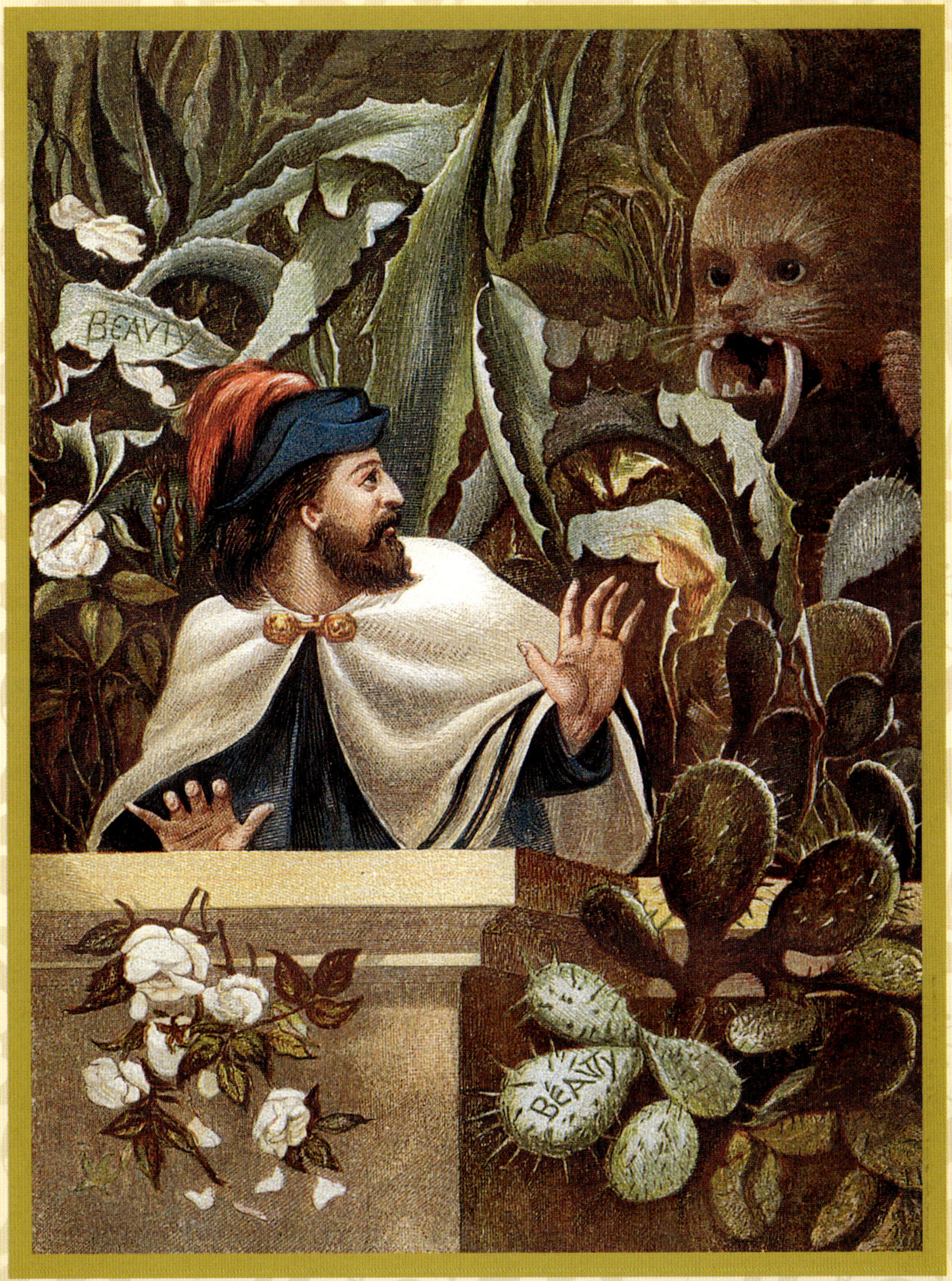
BEAVTY

crashing and sliding backward amid the trees. Then the man, dazed and bewildered, hasted back to the little door in the wall. Hard by stood the chestnut horse, tied to a tree, watchful and impatient. On the earth lay a white thin covering of snow, and on the snow the morning sun shone fair. The horse and his rider made good speed along the echoing white road, till at the border of the wood the merchant slacked rein, and there, a little way down the hill before him, he saw the well-known homestead. The gray ridge and the ancient tower, the curving shore, and blue sea beyond. And now, slowly pacing down the steep way, he fell on meditation. Almost he thought within himself, last night's strange chance to be a fearsome dream. But the rose in his hand shot back a terror that no vision, but indeed a dismal fate, had overtaken him; and that now, joyless and unholpen must he abide. Wild thoughts beset him: thoughts of the deep broad water and safe haven on that other side; deadly thoughts to make an end of life and misery for him and for the child he loved. Yet, as day drew on, Care and Fear fled. Hope once more danced lightly in the man's soul, for neither age nor misfortune had yet quite dulled his cheer; and now, upon the level road, he joyously spurred on to meet his children waiting at the door. You may well believe how with bitter and hard words Beauty's sisters bemoaned themselves to see their father's poor return. No long train of sumpter mules and servants! Only Beauty was glad. She laughed gently, and made him joy and sweet welcome as he kissed her, putting the dear-bought rose into her hand. But soon must the bitter tale be told. So with set white face, amid choking sobs, the father must confess how with that hateful vow he had sold his child's life. But she embraced him in her arms, and with loving smiles bade him take heart, and put fear from him; for that although half a year was but a little space to live, there yet was time for a few happy days, and for hope, within a mile to light upon some escape from misery. As for the three brothers, they made light of the matter; but when they knew all the truth, swore great oaths that their sister should not go.

Days and weeks went quickly by in cloud and sunshine. Each night the little load of trouble, or it might be peace, that the day had gathered slipped away into the Great Storehouse, and was forgotten. One wretched thought only remained in the darkness and silence to perplex the hapless merchant with a dull surprise and bewildered dread of what soon or late must come. As for Beauty, since her father hid within himself the secret terror that after the busy day was done, laid wait and beset for him the dark hours, she wasted small care on aught, but how best to make cheer in their poor house. But ofttimes would a sharp pain strike athwart the father's heart, when at evening he wended home from the fishing or the field. Then, perchance, after the cliff was climbed, he would look toward Beauty's casement in the tower—there, amid bud and blossom, a face would smile down upon him, fairer than any rose. For in some old earthen pot, that dear-bought briar had been set, and it had taken root and grown into a goodly plant. And Beauty tended it well, and loved her blooming rose-tree, and never a doubt nor fear of any deadly Beast beclouded her strong heart.

But now, when summer-tide was full, on a blue June day, when his sons were all away in the fields, the man looked wanly in his young daughter's face; and she, well knowing what that was he would say to her, went and wrapped a gray mantle round her, and set forth with him to the outward gate. And there she bade farewell to her sisters, who followed, making some hollow show of false sorrow. Tenderly her father lifted up the maid and set her upon a lean rough-coated farm horse, which awaited them, tied to the gate. And then, leading the horse by the bridle-rein, as in a dream, they fared forth together on their fateful way. Soon the steep path that had wound through barren rocks, began to cross the sandy plain, and before the sun was high, they had passed on into a beautiful green world of young corn, all bedashed with jeweled blooms of blue and scarlet and gold, between the thin-eared ranks. Loud sang under the white clouds, whole heavenward companies of the quivering, gray-winged bird. White cottage walls gleamed under deep thatch, each one in its little close of orchard or of fragrant walnut-trees. And upon the upland slopes lay many a fair homestead, half seen amid the crowding of rich corn-stacks. And so the narrowing way led on to the storm blown pines and thickets of dwarf oak, which crowned a dark line of hill above. Slowly they toiled up the height, for the noonday sun shone hotly down; and there under the shade the twain stayed a while, and undid the little store of food they had to eat by the way, and let their wearied beast go, in the scanty grass near by. When long shadows stretched over the land, they were afoot once more. And now the merchant followed, dumb with a despair that had no words, while Beauty on her horse went shining through the wood. Sorrowfully the winds made dole in the leafy boughs above their heads. And ever as they went the trees grew more thick together, with black night down within the forest depths. Twisted roots crawled serpent-wise across the path, and needs must the travelers go carefully and slow. Night drew on, and the man began to mark the way with care, and sought through the darkness for the old stone wall, he thought to be not far from that place. Right so there came to them some glimmer of moon-litten stone between the trees, anigh the dimness of their path. And now the long garden wall echoed back the sound of the iron-shod hoofs. But smooth and without break seemed that length of ordered stones. And though the man sought painfully, feeling with his hands where the shadows fell thickest, yet it seemed he might never find the little door. Many an odorous wave of delicious fragrance came over from the other side. And in the uncertain light, Beauty perceived an overhanging of white roses amidst tangled weeds. And therewithal, as in a dream strange things do happen with great ease and likelihood, so whilst yet they sought the entrance, on a sudden they were within the garden of the Beast. Light seemed to shine from the far end of a wide grassy way, and onward to that light, must they go. After a few paces the travelers came anear the lighted windows and open gates of a large fair manor. Gently her father lifted down Beauty from the horse, and leaving him to go whither he would, they entered, dazzled with a great silvery blaze of light. These twain were utterly alone. No sound, no living creature greeted them there.

So in shivering silence, treading lightly in that marble-pillared place, where the lightest footstep echoed and rang again, they came to a marvelous painted hall. Beauty gazed with wonder on the red rose-leaves that strewed the floor, on the golden hangings and the festal garlands on the walls, and the banquet spread with care awaiting them. And because their bodies were faint from weariness and hunger, they sat them down on the gold-wrought chairs to make what cheer they might, notwithstanding that their very souls were chilled with dread of the yet unseen presence. So they ate and drank; and afterward, as they still sat there, there seemed to grow upon the air, drawing from distant corners of the house, and along the corridors, a dreadful sound, which made them tremble with affright; and the man knew that the Beast came nigh. So they began to bid each other farewell. Vainly did the maiden strive to hide her trouble when that perilous shape came anear. And first the creature gazed at Beauty, as she shrank back, clinging to her father, to whom he spake with a man's voice, but in slow and halting speech: "Good friend, ye be welcome, for well and truly ye have holden your promise." And then to her—"Beauty, come you here of your will?"

And she answered quickly, "Yea, in good sooth."

The Beast seemed well pleased at that. Nevertheless, in gruesome tones, he required of the merchant to be gone on the morrow, and that he might never behold him any more. Then, with a strange, wistful look at the girl, of mingled ruth and kindness, from under the shaggy beast-like brows, he turned from the lighted chamber, and gat him away to the darkness of his unknown den.

So that night, long after moonset, Beauty and her father still sat together, hand laid to hand, speaking of past things, and loth to part—these two, for whom all the joy of life seemed done—while the lights burned low and the summer night waned fast. Overmuch sorrow had made their eyes heavy, and they longed for some short rest before the coming of the day that was to bring such bitter parting. Two fair sleeping rooms they found prepared. And at dawn, in the gray light, a pale woman, clad in long white raiment, stood beside Beauty's bed. She called very softly to the girl, bidding her have no fear of aught in that place, but to keep her heart strong and true. Beauty was fain to tell this dream to her father, that their parting might not be all too dark and hopeless.

When the sun was risen, the merchant looked out, and saw his horse waiting, saddled, by the door. So with white set face he made him ready; and as though constrained by some dreadful fate, he slowly departed, nor once looked back to the gate, where Beauty stood in the dewy morning light. There was no red in her cheek, and her gray eyes were bright with unshed tears, as from the threshold she watched him go. And so to her the world became desolate; and yesterday seemed far away; and full far away and strange, already seemed to her the familiar faces and sounds of home, as ever, fainter and fainter came back the ring of horse-hoofs along the road, and died at last in the distance.

Therewithal Beauty went back into the silent house. She made no sorrow out of measure, for she was great of heart; and the young are strong, and slow to cast hope away. And within her soul also lay a little hidden hope, most like to prophecy, that even in this place—where some grizzly death might steal out and seize her unawares from the dim corners of her prison—she might light soon upon the golden treasure key, whereby a door should open on the secret way leading back to old happier days, or perchance to some undreamed-of, goodlier world, and her heart should win its scarce-known, unpronounced desire.

Day followed day, and the girl forgot to call the Beast's house her prison. No troublous season of fear and doubt had she, but only long summer days of peaceful sweetness, and nights of dreamless sleep. Daily when the sun went down, and Beauty sat in the golden hall at supper, the Beast came and sat there with her; and his dreadful noise had grown less fearsome in her ears, and even was as it were, an unheard terror. She ate and drank, conversing kindly, and heeding little the ugliness of the presence that sat anear. Each night after supper, that ill-favored Beast did ask the lady, "Would she have him to her husband?" And every time she made answer, "No—that might she never do." And there with the Beast would hang down his head, and sigh so dolorously that it were marvel to hear. And then Beauty grieved very sorely for him, and full fain was she to pray him to come back, whereas he shuffled from out of the sight of her. But yet her lips could never shape fair words which her true heart forbade.

Days went by, until the added sum of them at last made three long years: and still Beauty's life passed on dreamfully, in the palace of the Beast. But for the sweet-voiced thrushes and nightingales, which made melody in the rose-garden without, all day long and after sun-down—the silence of that solitude might have made the girl's heart sad. Within the dusky pine-branches, wild doves had their nests, and to her ear their note had human tones. Often as she listened would their never-ending love-plaint seem to bring anigh old home-scenes in that other world, she used, she thought, to know full well.

After the three twelvemonths—which in that spellbound place seemed but one summer long—there came a day when the lonely maid wandered further in the garden than had been her wont. The gold hem of her gown slid shining over the daisies and pink petals drifted down from thorny brakes upon the grass, as she passed along green paths, to where the flowers and the broad sunshine ceased. Under the beeches, in the sun-flecked shade, her feet pressed last year's crisp brown leaves; hard by, under a knot of firs, a little thread of clear water, fell sparkling into a marble basin. And Beauty

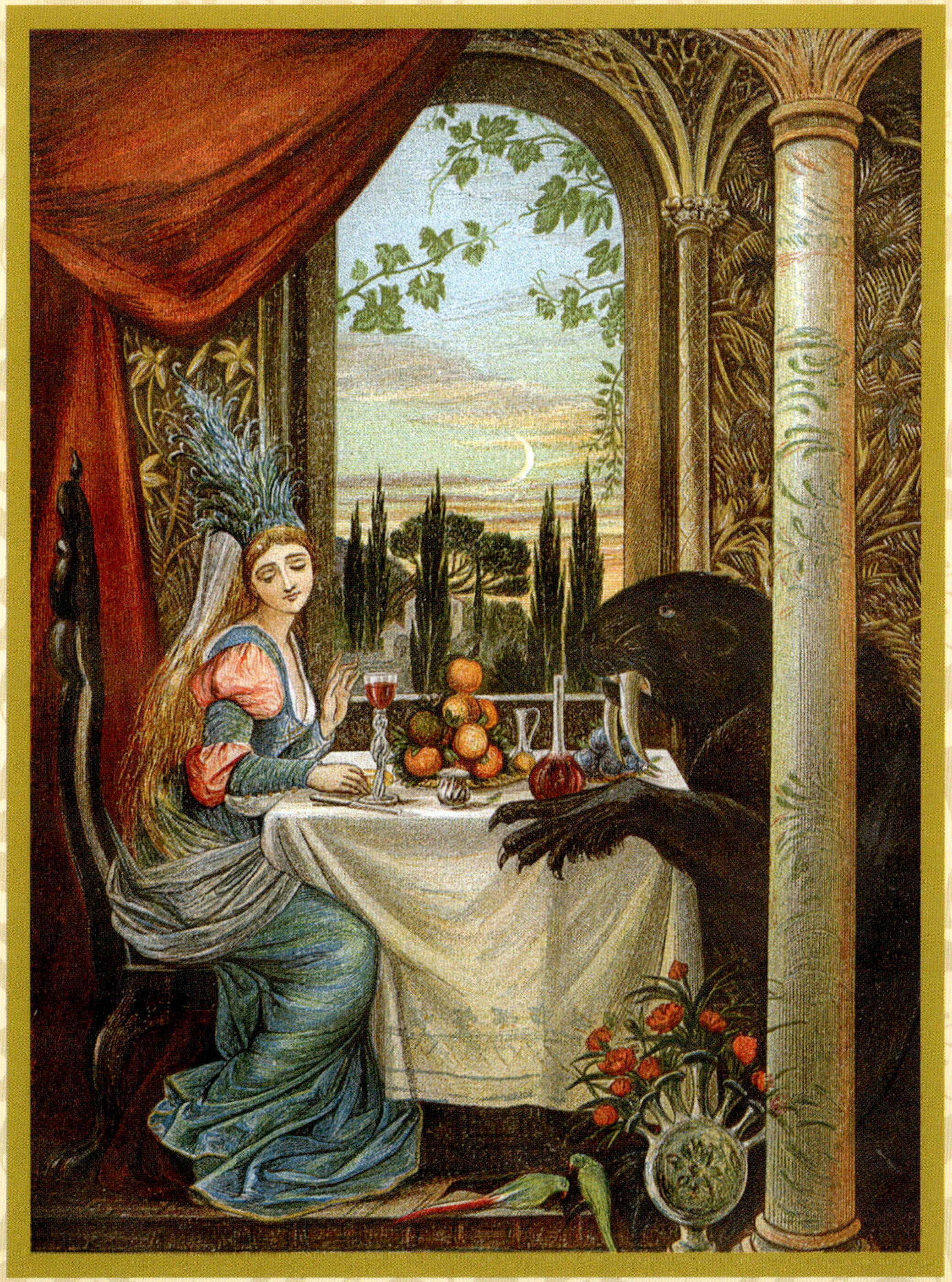

leaned over the sculptured edge, while many thoughts both sweet and bitter, went to and fro across her brain. Down in the clear pool wavered gleams of some other blue—shadows of other, not familiar, branching trees; till, as she gazed into that little shallow, she deemed some picture lay there. Through the leaves she dimly beheld, as in a very far distance, an old gray tower, on a sandy ridge, beside the rippling sea. Coldly shone the distant sunlight on the tower. The heavy iron-studded door stood wide open; and there in the weed-grown court browsed the white goats, or climbed the ruined wall, to reach down wandering tendrils of wild vine rooted in the stones. Very solitary did that old gray tower seem, as, dimmed with gathering tears, her eyes sought, but all in vain, one whom she might nowhere find; then, as she gazed steadfastly, a dead leaf fell and blurred the image, erewhile distinct and living.

Beauty was passing heavy when she rose and left the beechen grove. And when, as she moved again along the fresh grassy pleasance, gray clouds had dulled the sunshine, and a new fear oppressed her joyous spirit.

That evening-tide, at supper, the Beast might well discover how the lady strove, but could not, to hide some sharp grief. Yet so daffish was he withal, that no manner of cheer could he make her, nor yet require her to say what had gone amiss; but only might he sit before her in troubled thought and look askance with down-hung head.

Then at last spake Beauty, in naught misdoubting the Beast (for he had ever shown himself kind and courteous to her, like a knight of old time)—

"Sir, I fain would go to see my father for a space. In the little fountain under the fir-tree, I saw an image of the tower; but my father, nor none else, I could nowhere see, and therefore I greatly fear for him."

Thereupon the Beast made great dole; yet he could in no wise refuse so sweet a one anything she would ask, were it much or little.

"Full woe am I of your departing," he said, "for I fear me sore that you will not come again."

But Beauty answered again, "I promise you of my faith; for and I be not sick, that in seven days' time will I return."

Then was the Beast comforted; and he gave her a golden ring of quaint device, whereon was graven an unknown word in antique letters. And this ring she was to lay under her pillow, on the night before the day set for her return. Then was Beauty cut to the heart when she heard the Beast groan, as he turned and went his way.

On the morrow that place was empty of her sweet presence. For when the maiden awoke, all things were strange about her, and yet remembered well; for she lay in the low poor sleeping room of old days, in her father's tower by the sea. Beside the bed hung great store of silken gowns, very rich, and well beseen with gold and silver embroideries, and sewn with pearls and many stones of price. Ill might such royal weed beseem that poor dark place, which still she called her home; but since there was no other, she did on in haste, the meanest of all that rich appareling. Then lightly ran down the tottering stair to greet the beloved father. The merchant, sitting idle and alone in the house-place, did certainly hear that which he thought to be a well-known step. Yet so smitten was he with grief and long solitude, that scarce he could find will to look up with dull eyes, when Beauty came anear, and stood in the low arched doorway. There, for a moment, she made sunlight in the dark with her lovely face and the sheen of her gold-wrought gown. And when she was kneeling at his feet, scarce indeed might Beauty persuade her father but that she were some hollow shape, sent of enchantment to mock his wretchedness; no, scarcely, even when she held him close, embracing him with loving arms, and had kissed him a hundred times could he believe it was herself. And as at last he let yield to joyful welcome, and with hand clasping hand they sat together, they each told other all that had befell since that bitter day they parted; she, her bootless fears, her days of unhoped peace; and he, of the elder sisters' marriages, of the three brothers gone away with many of that land to fight for the Holy Sepulchre. And while they made great joy together, and the aged crone began to set the board, right so the trampling of horse-hoofs sounded upon the stones without. Beauty looked out, and beheld her sisters with their husbands, at the door. Unbidden guests were they that morn; and with their coming all the new gladness seemed to die away within the house; for the hearts of those sisters were evil, and in their hands they brought no blessing. Yet did Beauty strive to give them such kindly welcoming as she might. Some pity, indeed, must she give them; for no happy life was theirs. The elder had espoused a very proud and learned man, but poor; and by him she was greatly despised. And the younger had for husband a rich man, of very seemly person, who cared nought for other goodliness than his own; and had scorn for his wife, withal she was so fair. So when they were lighted down from their horses, and had come into the house, and had begun to consider their young sister, how she was well beseen like a Princess, in her shining gown, though serving them with such kindly grace, they were passing envious; and hatred, like a sharp thorn, pierced through their jealous hearts. Sore grieved were they when they knew that to her the Beast was in no wise perilous. But to her sisters Beauty made but short the tale of how she fared in that place. So within a while the two sisters departed secretly into the green close behind the old tower, and came to a little hazel-brake anigh the wild; and there they sat them down and made complaint, bewailing them with tears and moans.

"Now are we in most evil plight," said they, "that our sister, younger than we, should go thus appareled in silken stuffs, and live in a King's palace" (for so they called the house of the Beast). And then they took secret council one with the other; for they said, "so we may but prevail to keep her here yet another seven nights over and above the time she appointed with the Beast he will surely be avenged of her falsehood; and then shall no gold save her life!"

And none heard save only the raven who abode in the trees. So these two women came softly back into the house; and they showed unwonted love for their sister, making much of her, and praying her to forget their mauger, and the wrong they had done her in the old days before time past.

And the maid, in her guilelessness, heard with joy their false words. And when the day was almost come that she should depart they made show of grief, and besought her to abide with them but one seven nights longer. Beauty looked to her father; but he covered his face, and dared say nought, for he was sore afeared of the Beast's wrath.

And so for that while Beauty forgot her promise, and let herself be forsworn, and yielded her will to those two women, nought witting of their most felon device. Thus it came to pass that she was well-nigh lost for the bitter malice of them that wished her death.

Yet in all these days the maid was not glad; but greatly troubled when she thought on the Beast. Very pitiful waxed Beauty's heart, as she remembered of all her friend's goodness, and his sorrow of her departing. And so it happened, that on the tenth night after,

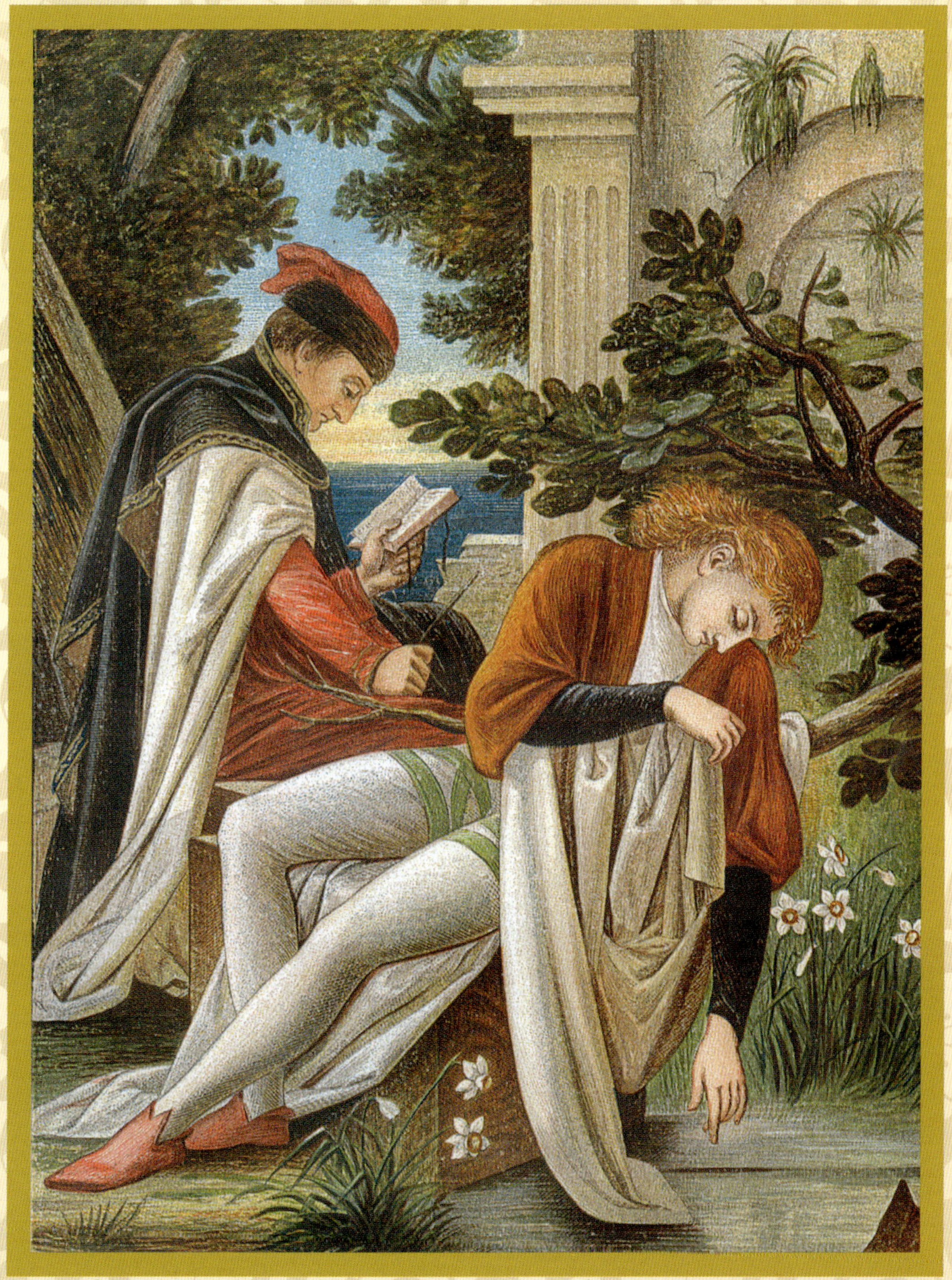

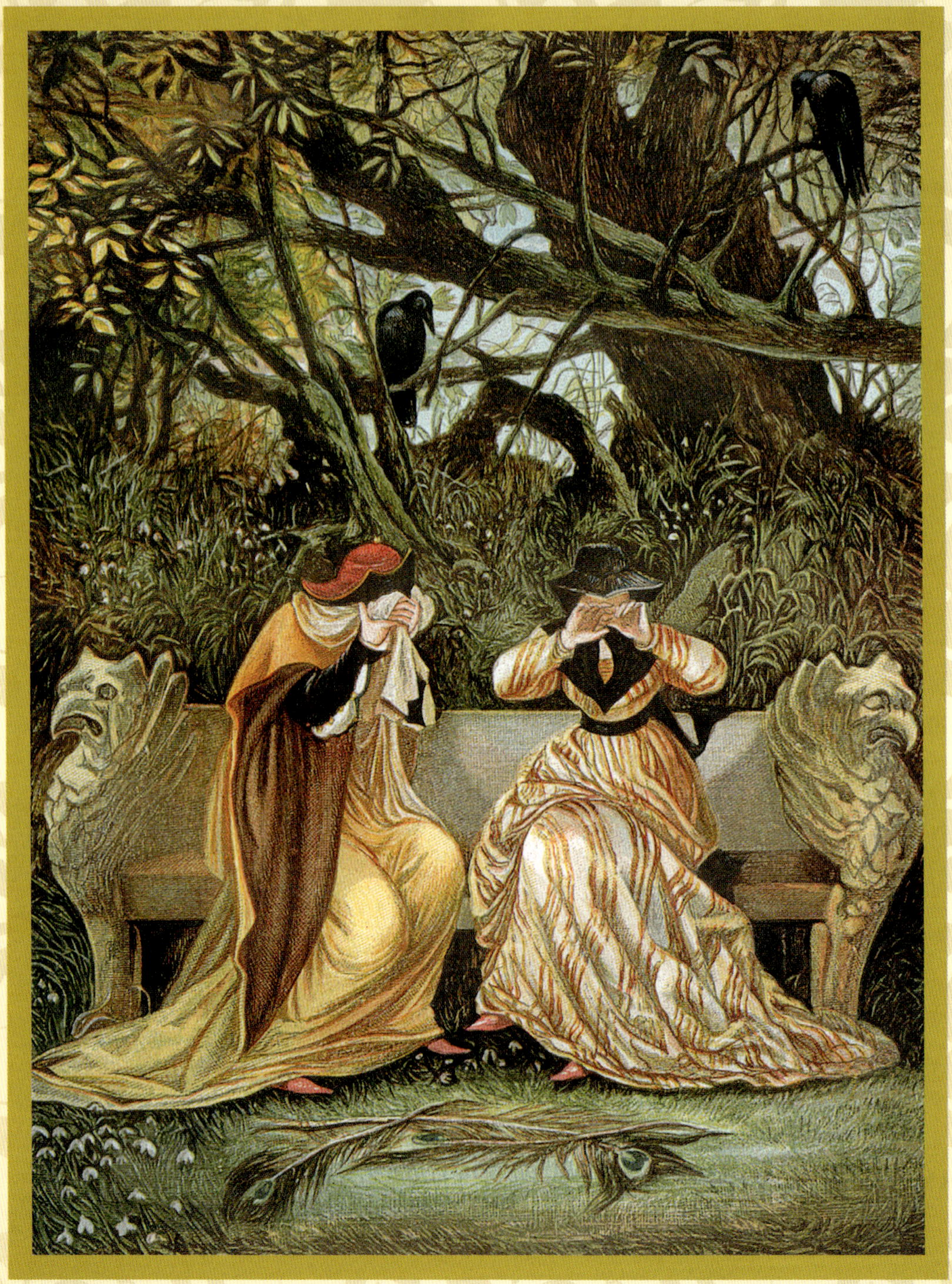

she dreamed a dream. She beheld the Beast as he lay a-dying under a great tree in the garden. And the garden was a very great way off, and she so far away, she might not help him in his sore need; nor call to him, nor with tender words hold him back from death. With that great horror she awoke in the darkness, and weeping, gave herself the blame.

"Alas!" she said, "my broken faith; alas! that ever I should have thus forsook my friend; and if he die, now must I grieve to my life's end." Then she hastily laid her magic ring under the pillow, which was all wetted with her weeping. And soon for heaviness she fell on sleep. In the springing of the day Beauty opened her eyes, and, behold, she lay in the green-hung chamber wherein she had so greatly longed to be.

The golden autumn day rose fair and still on the silent manor and the garden of the Beast. All the long hours until evensong, must the maiden wait; then he would show himself, and she would comfort him, and tell him of sweet coming days, wherein she never more would leave him.

The golden hours sped slowly. Slowly and softly fell the rose-leaves upon the grass. The song-birds that day hid in hushed silence, anear the garden bowers where Beauty sat alone, weaving flowers and fruits and birds unknown to earth, upon the silken loom. And evermore the longed-for evening hour drew on. Anon she heard the clock smite, and she gat her with haste into the house.

In the hall the table was covered, and Beauty, arrayed in a broidered gown of red samite, sat in her place and waited. No fresh garlands behanged the walls, but only brown and withered leaves. And she wist not anything of the Beast; and she had no mind to eat and drink, for a cold dread overcame her that some misadventure had befallen him, whiles she listened for the least sound whereby she might know that he approached. But when he came not within a while, she must needs go seek him throughout the manor. But the chambers were empty, and the garden void, and whenas she called none answer came. Then she bethought her of the little fountain in the wood, and she ran thither. There, indeed, under a pine-tree upon the grass, lay that hapless Beast in a deadly swoon. And Beauty sank down upon her knees beside him, and raised his head in her arms; and it dread her sore but that he were in great peril of death. And then she grieved, and gave herself reproach and upbraiding. And, "Oh, dear Beast! what aileth thee?" she cried. "Alas! that ever he saw me to have such sorrow."

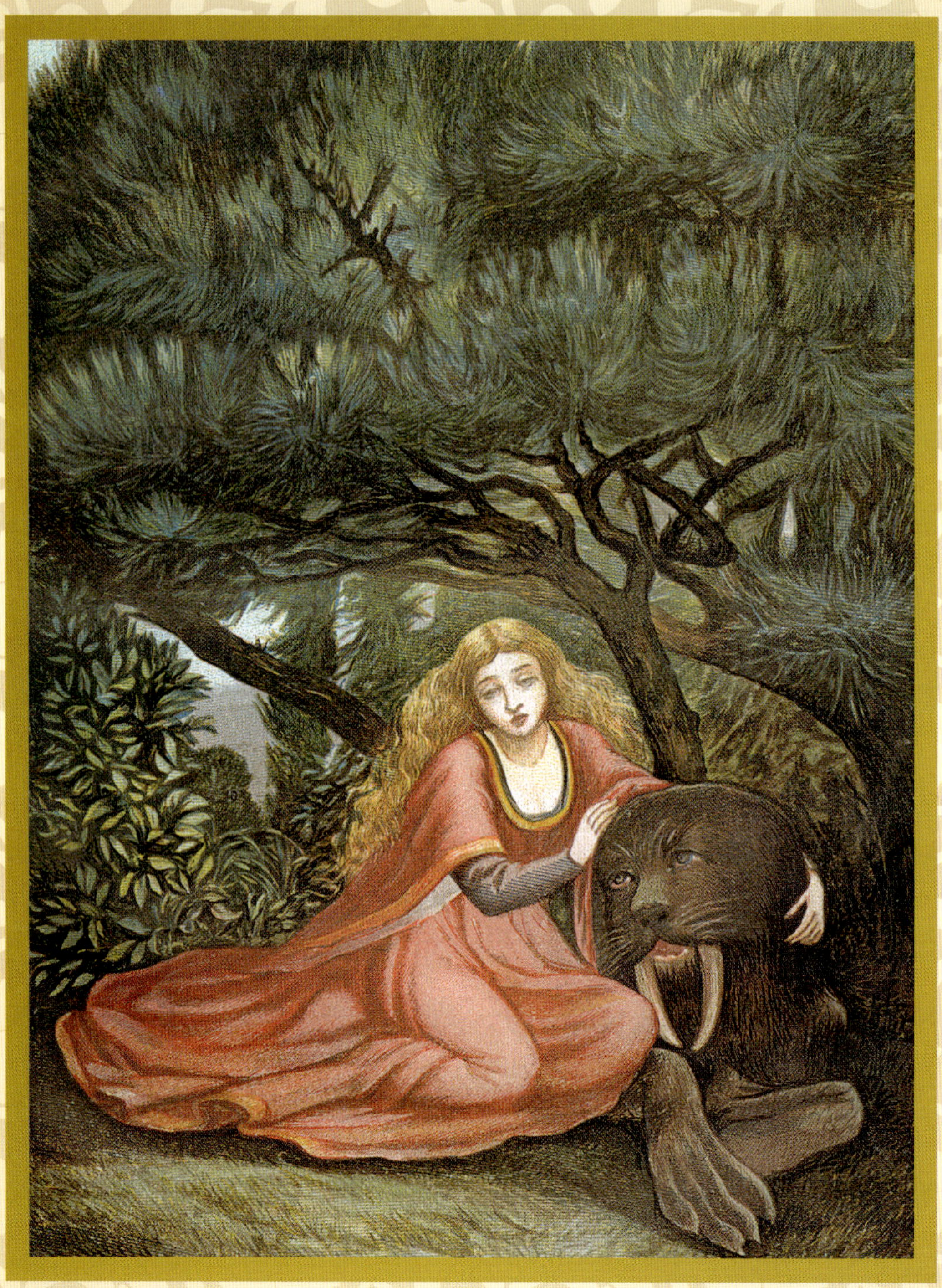

But when she had fetched a little water, and had put it in his mouth, the Beast came to himself. So he opened his eyes and looked upon the girl full sadly. And therewithal he said, in a full weak voice, "Alas! fair maid, why hast thou so long delayed? for now I fear me I shall die: for I feel well, the deep draughts of death draw to my heart."

Then did she make great moan, and besought the Beast of his love for her not to die and forsake her. But he seemed as though he heard not; and ever his breath came slower, and more faint. And then Beauty fell to weeping as though her heart would break; and remembering her of all his gentleness and kindness, and that now he was like to die through her unkindness, in her anguish she called the Beast her love, her only love.

With that word there befell a strange adventure. But one moment agone, the maid had holden in her arms the Beast's grim, hairy head; and in her grief she knew not how it slid away from her embrace. For when she looked, there was nought but crushed leaves and grass where the dying Beast had lain. Also a dreamlike brightness seemed to mingle silverly about the dusk of evening, as though the moon had risen, or that starlight trembled upon the gloom. Then all bewildered and amazed, she deemed that some young Prince, clad in rich clothes, with jeweled mantle and scarlet plume, stood anear. So, forgetting fear in her trouble, she prayed him without more ado to tell her, "Had he seen the Beast? For," she said, "mine own dear Beast lay here but now, and like to die, and he is gone, and I know not where he is become."

But the strange Prince held his peace, and none answer gave he to her most piteous cry; only he kneeled down beside the maid, and then full gently did he kiss her golden hair, that spread all wide adown her neck, and then he kissed her red lips; and whenas, wondering and angered, she drew from him, and would have started away, he took her in his arms and said, "Oh lovely one, do you not then know me? Look at me, and see; for indeed I am that Beast, and he was me!"

But Beauty trembled, nor durst she look; for well she knew there had been some enchantment; and, sithence, it was a man and no Beast that spake, yet in his voice, and in the words he said, she seemed to hearken to the friend that she had lost erewhile. Then quick tears, but not of sorrow, filled her eyes, for an unwonted thing had happened; yet was it to her but as the fulfillment of some dear dream in old, forgotten, long-past days.

And so, alone together there, amid the brown dusk of coming night, for a little space, were they silent for very joy. And then did Beauty, in all maiden trust, give him, that had been the Beast, her true word, and promised that she would be his wedded wife. Then he lifted her to her feet, and led her home along those same sweet grassy paths. And as they went, he told her all the tale of the cruel spell which had bound him since these many woeful years, in that unhappy shape, and how nought but a dear maiden's love might set him free, and of how great had been his hopeless love for her.

Silently the white moths floated by. The gentle winds of summer sighed odorously, and stirred the broad hazel-leaves on either hand the close green alley, as they went; while loose-petaled roses bloomed and fell in aisles of overarching sweetness.

Therewith a great clearness shone around them; and as they came nigh the house, burning lights shone from the windows; and there was music, and the noise of merry voices mingling in songs and laughter. Strange sounds, long unheard in that still house! Then from the door the Beast's mother, a sweet and noble lady, came forth to meet them; and great joy made she, as she beheld her son, coming in his own likeness, as he was or that strange magic was laid on him. And then she embraced Beauty, and with her heart she made her right welcome.

Now the lady was a Queen. She was the same that came afore to Beauty in a dream to comfort her.

Here then endeth the tale; sith it were over-long to tell of the revels and the dances, and of how the golden Hall was engarlanded with roses, and of the great feast held there, on the day that Beauty and the Beast were wedded together; nor need we tell, of how the merchant-master was called from his lonely tower, and came thither on his fair child's marriage morn; whenas his sorrowful days had end for evermore; and of how his three brave sons became most noble knights, and greatly renowned for the destroying of many pagan knights and giants, and of divers fell beasts and griffins of that time.

But Beauty's sisters, came never near that happy house. For wit you well, the winter rasure of such-like cankers, may not approach the green summer, wherein the flower of true love flourisheth.

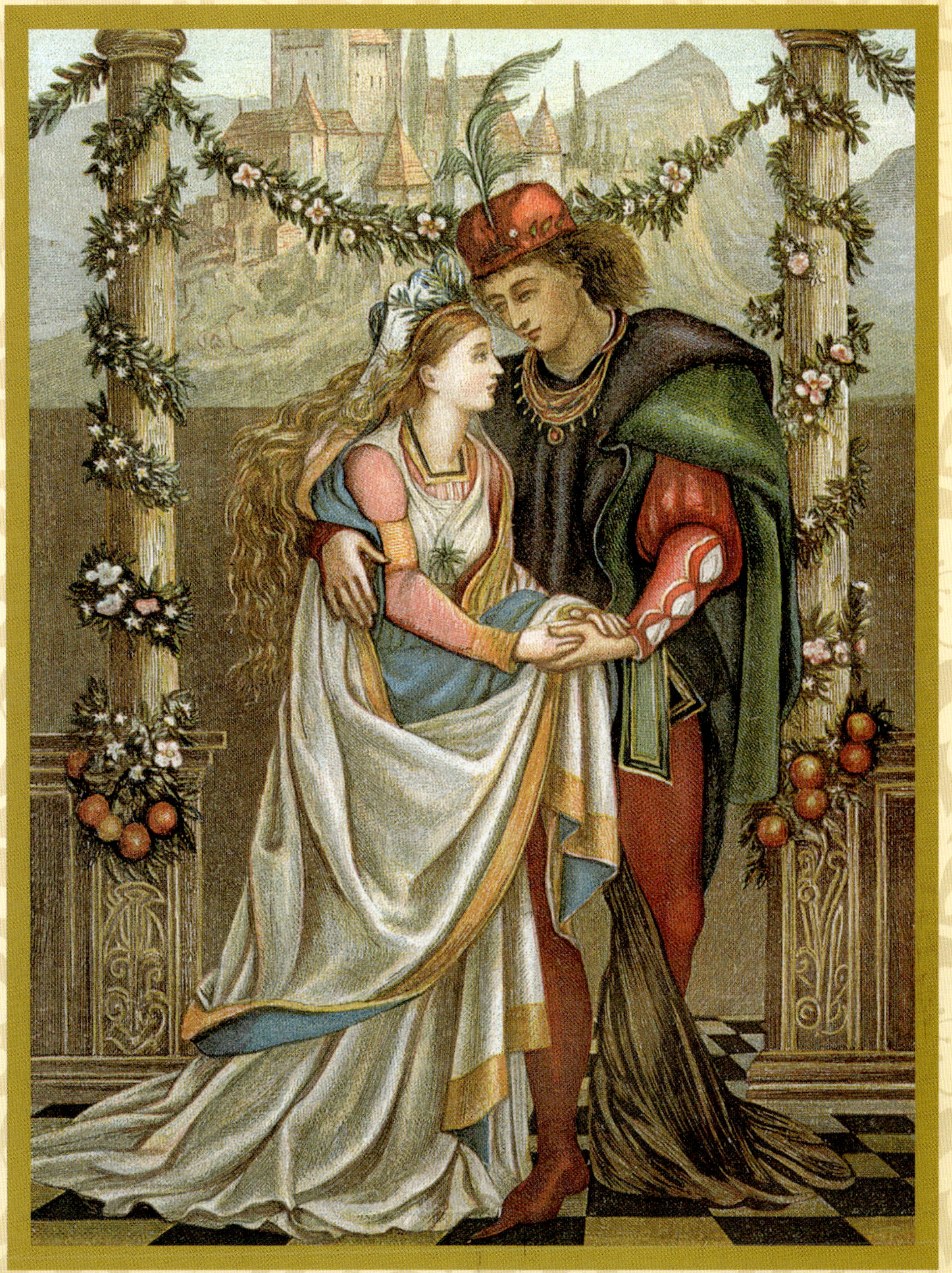

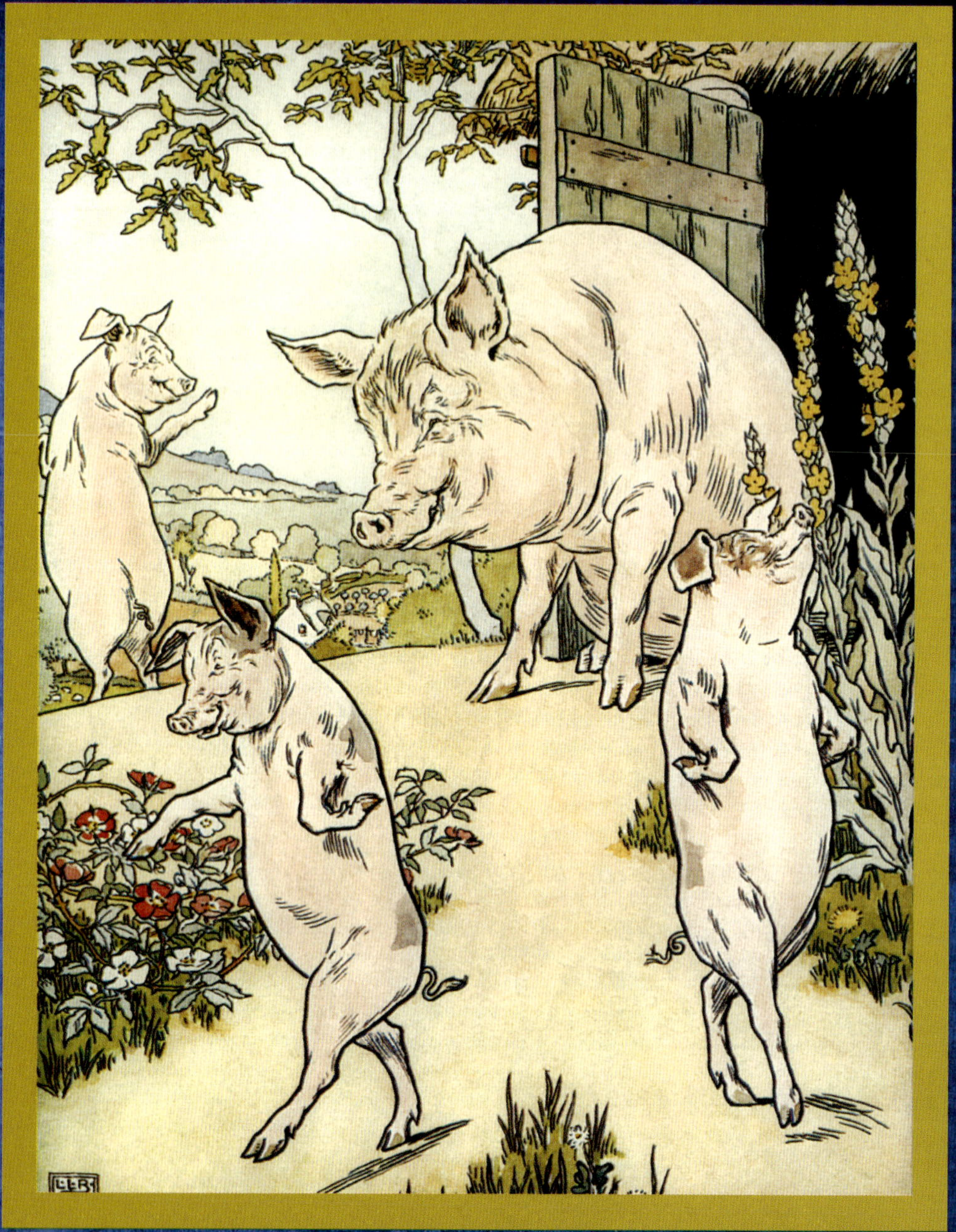

The third little Pig met a Man with a load of bricks, and said, "Please, Man, give me those bricks to build a house with"; so the Man gave him the bricks, and he built his house with them. So the Wolf came, as he did to the other little Pigs, and said, "Little Pig, little Pig, let me come in."

"No, no, by the hair of my chinny chin chin."

"Then I'll huff and I'll puff, and I'll blow your house in." Well, he huffed and he puffed, and he huffed and he puffed, and he puffed and he huffed; but he could not get the house down. When he found that he could not, with all his huffing and puffing, blow the house down, he said, "Little Pig, I know where there is a nice field of turnips."

"Where?" said the little Pig.

"Oh, in Mr. Smith's home-field; and if you will be ready to-morrow morning, I will call for you, and we will go together and get some for dinner."

"Very well," said the little Pig, "I will be ready. What time do you mean to go?"

The Three Little Pigs

Once upon a time there was an old Sow with three little Pigs, and as she had not enough to keep them, she sent them out to seek their fortune.

The first that went off met a Man with a bundle of straw, and said to him, "Please, Man, give me that straw to build me a house"; which the Man did, and the little Pig built a house with it. Presently came along a Wolf, and knocked at the door, and said, "Little Pig, little Pig, let me come in."

To which the Pig answered, "No, no, by the hair of my chinny chin chin."

"Then I'll huff and I'll puff, and I'll blow your house in!" said the Wolf. So he huffed, and he puffed, and he blew his house in, and ate up the little Pig.

The second Pig met a Man with a bundle of furze, and said, "Please, Man, give me that furze to build a house"; which the Man did, and the Pig built his house. Then along came the Wolf and said, "Little Pig, little Pig, let me come in."

"No, no, by the hair of my chinny chin chin."

"Then I'll puff and I'll huff, and I'll blow your house in!" So he huffed and he puffed, and he puffed and he huffed, and at last he blew the house down, and ate up the second little Pig.

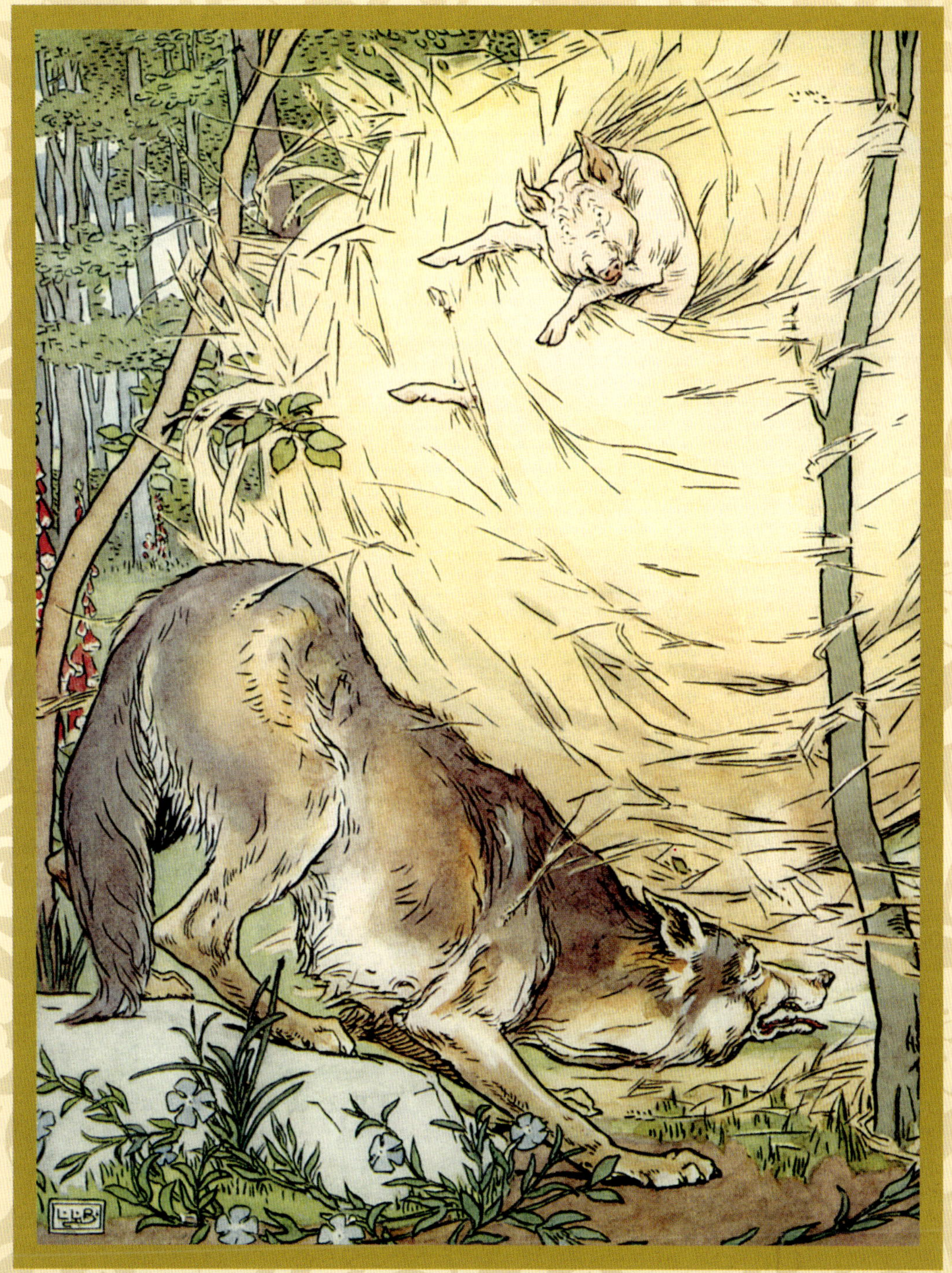

"Oh, at six o'clock."

Well, the little Pig got up at five, and got the turnips and was home again before six.

When the Wolf came he said, "Little Pig, are you ready?"

"Ready!" said the little Pig, "I have been and come back again, and got a nice pot-full for dinner."

The Wolf felt very angry at this, but thought that he would be up to the little Pig somehow or other; so he said, "Little Pig, I know where there is a nice apple-tree."

"Where?" said the Pig.

"Down at Merry-garden," replied the Wolf; "and if you will not deceive me I will come for you, at five o'clock to-morrow, and we will go together and get some apples."

Well, the little Pig woke at four the next morning, and bustled up, and went off for the apples, hoping to get back before the Wolf came; but he had farther to go, and had to climb the tree, so that just as he was coming down from it, he saw the Wolf coming, which, as you may suppose, frightened him very much. When the Wolf came up he said, "Little Pig, what! are you here before me? Are they nice apples?"

"Yes, very," said the little Pig; "I will throw you down one." And he threw it so far that, while the Wolf was gone to pick it up, the little Pig jumped down and ran home.

The next day the Wolf came again, and said to the little Pig, "Little Pig, there is a Fair in the Town this afternoon: will you go?"

"Oh, yes," said the Pig, "I will go; what time shall you be ready?"

"At three," said the Wolf.

So the little Pig went off before the time, as usual, and got to the Fair, and bought a butter churn, and was on his way home with it when he saw the Wolf coming. Then he could not tell what to do. So he got into the churn to hide, and in doing so turned it round, and it began to roll, and rolled down the hill with the Pig inside it, which frightened the Wolf so much that he ran home without going to the Fair.

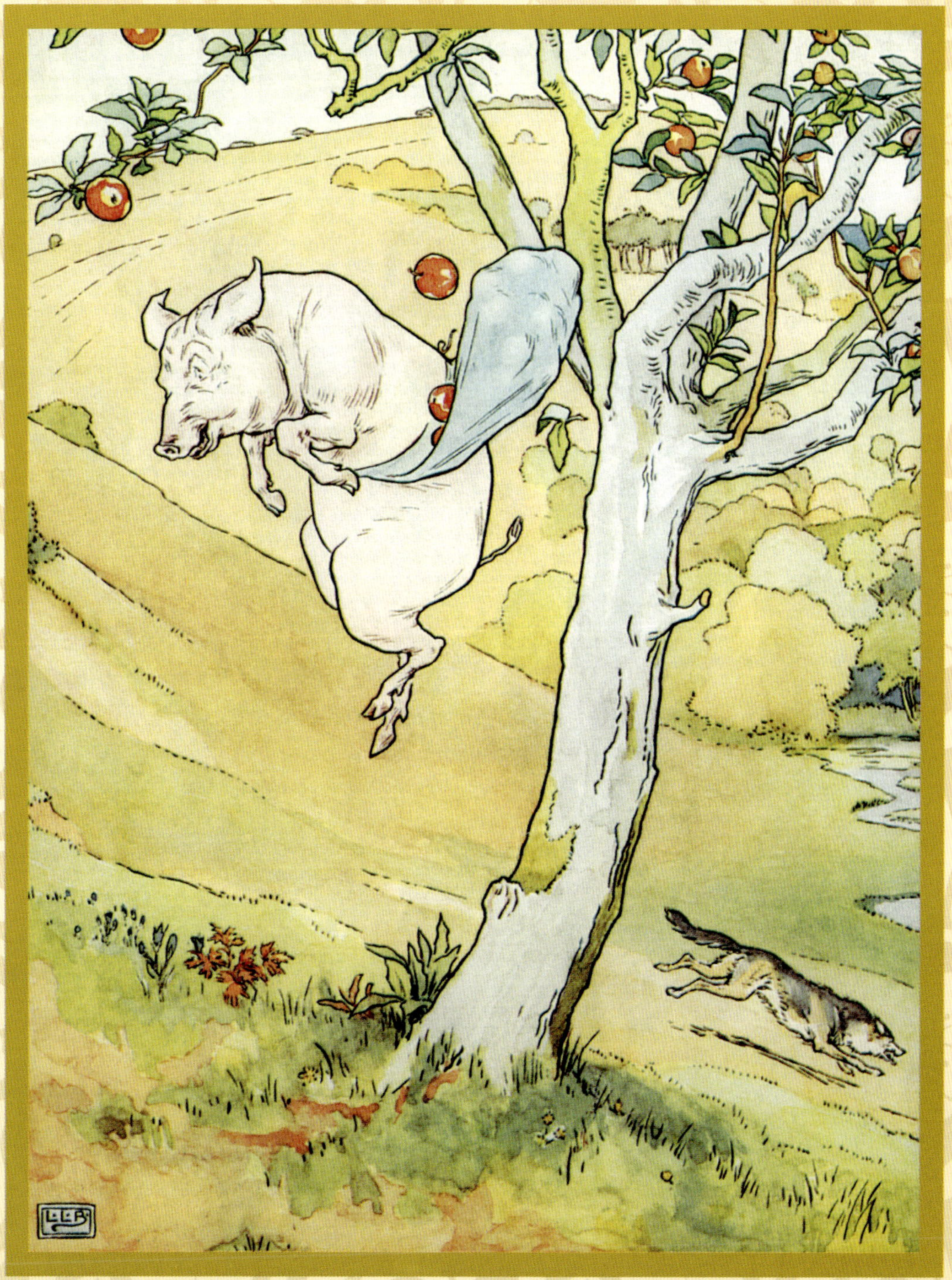

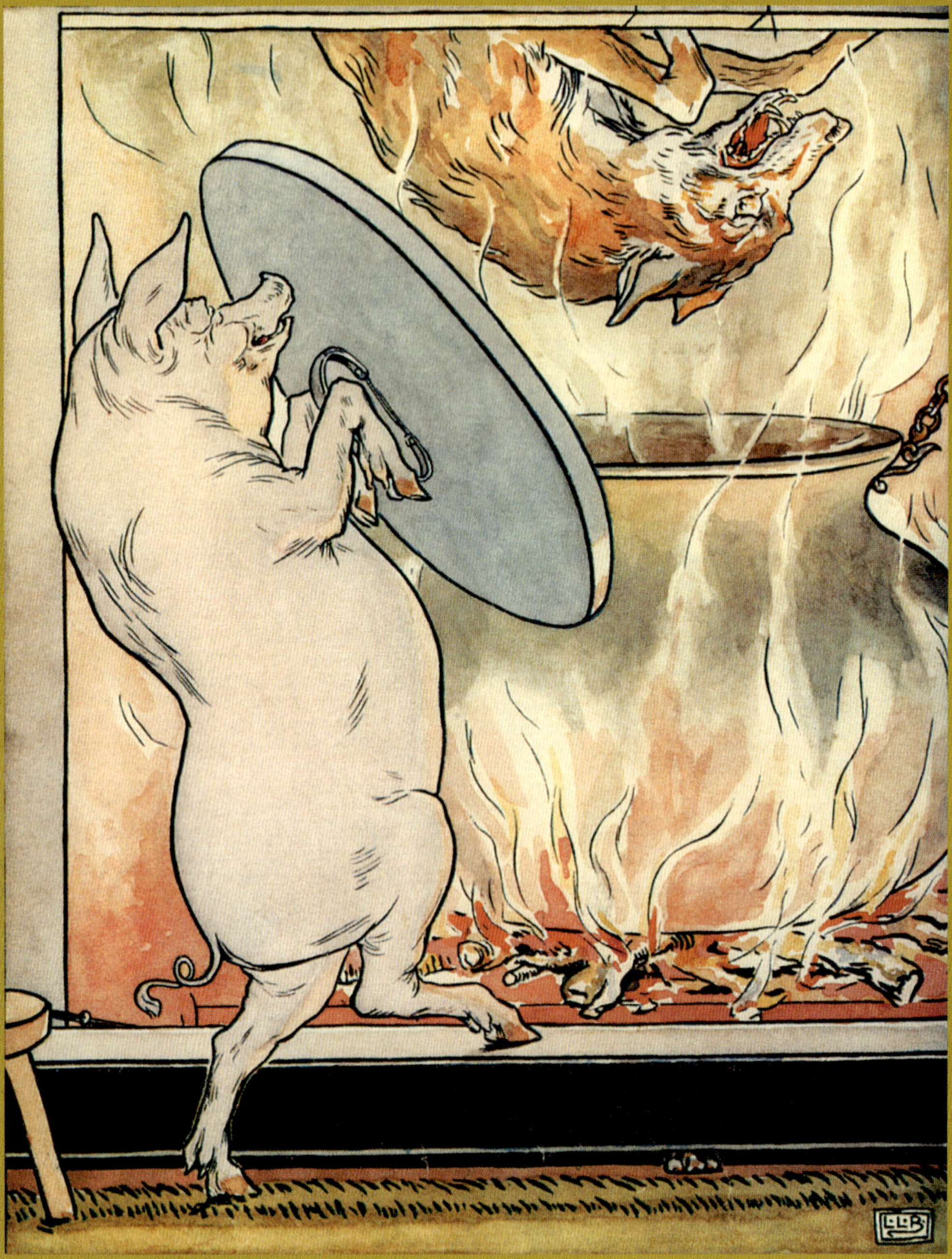

The Three Little Pigs

He went to the little Pig's house, and told him how frightened he had been by a great round thing which came down the hill past him.

Then the little Pig said, "Hah! I frightened you, did I? I had been to the Fair and bought a butter churn, and when I saw you I got into it, and rolled down the hill."

Then the Wolf was very angry indeed, and declared he eat up the little Pig, and that he would get down the chimney after him.

When the little Pig saw what he was about, he hung on the pot full of water, and made up a blazing fire, and, just as the Wolf was coming down, took off the cover of the pot, and in fell the Wolf. And the little Pig put on the cover again in an instant, boiled him up, and ate him for supper, and lived happy ever after.

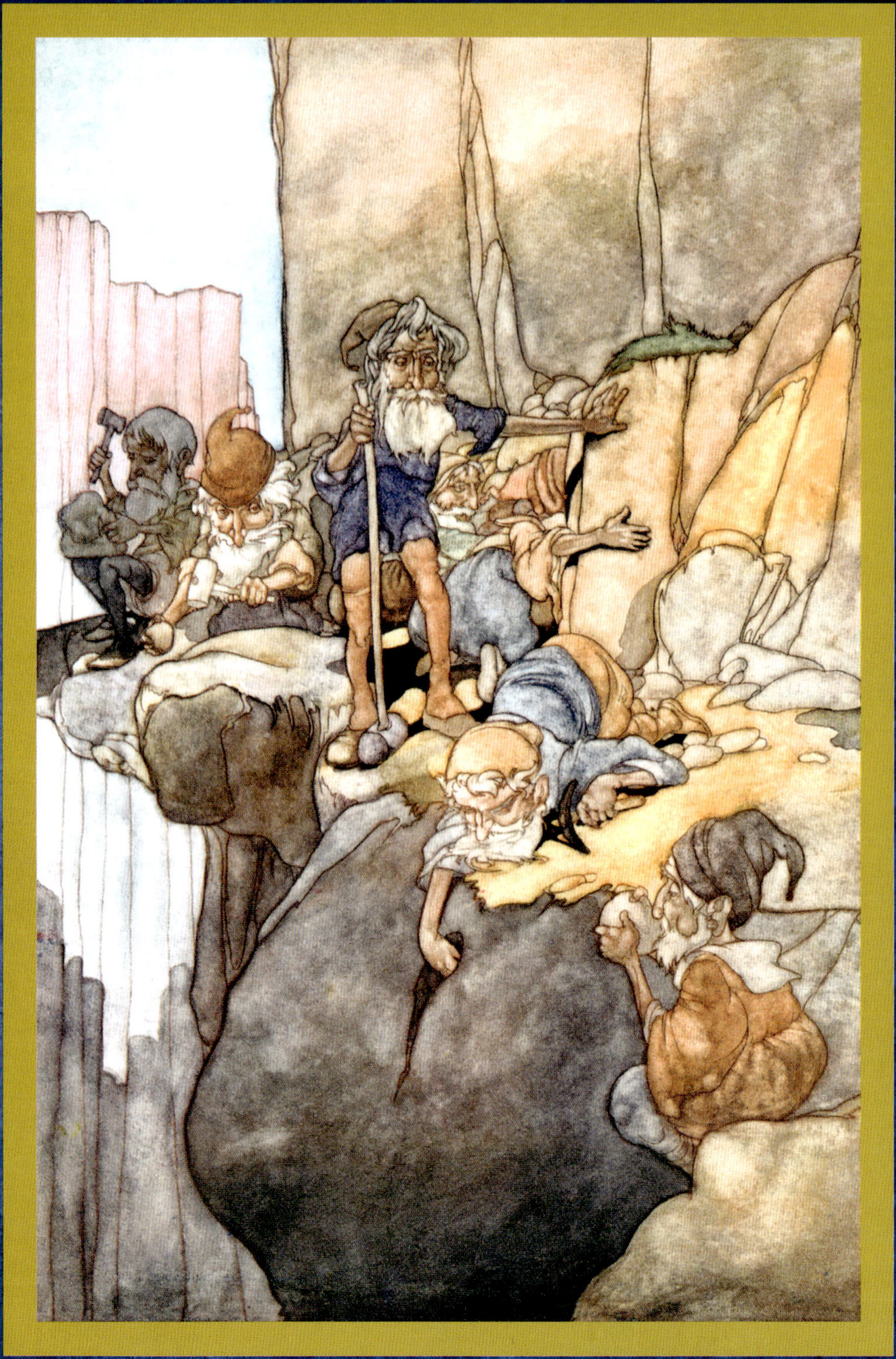

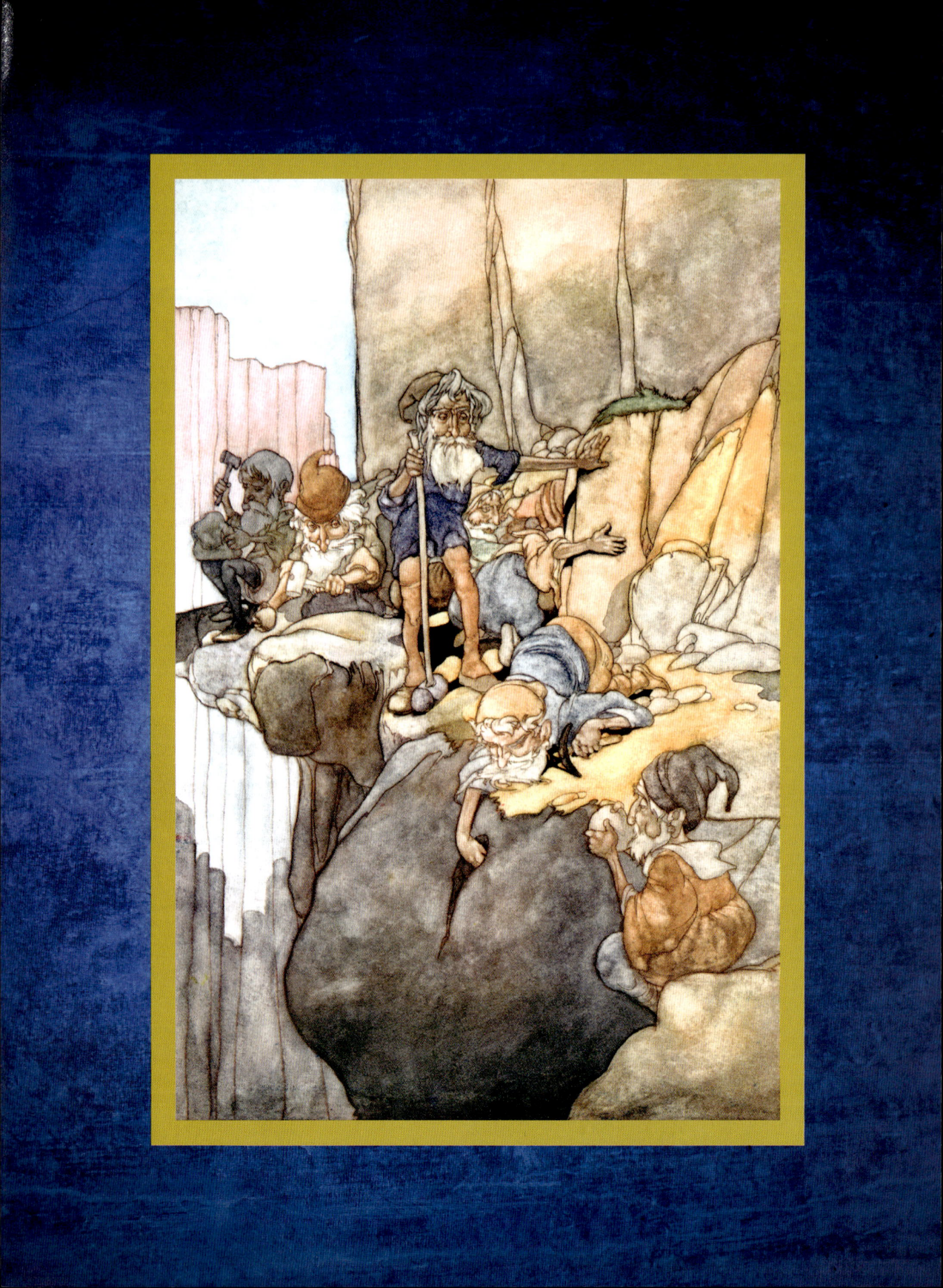

Snow White and the Seven Dwarfs

It was the middle of winter when a certain Queen sat working at her window the frame of which was made of fine black ebony; and as she was looking out upon the snow, she pricked her finger, and three drops of blood fell upon it. Then she gazed upon the red drops which sprinkled the white snow, and said: "Would that my little daughter may be as white as snow, as red as blood, and as black as ebony!" And so the little girl grew up: her skin was as white as snow, her cheeks as rosy as the blood, and her hair as black as ebony; and she was called Snow White.

But this Queen died; and the King soon married another wife, who had a magical looking-glass, to which she used to go and gaze upon herself, and say:

> "Tell me, glass, tell me true!
> Of all the ladies in the land,
> Who is fairest, tell me who?"

And the glass answered:

> "Thou, Queen, art the fairest in all the land."

But when Snow White she was seven years old, the glass one day answered the Queen:

"Thou, Queen, art fair, and beauteous to see,
But Snow White is lovelier far than thee!"

When she heard this she turned pale with rage and envy; and called to one of her servants, and said:

"Take Snow White away into the wide wood, that I may never see her any more."

Then the servant led her away; but his heart melted when she begged him to spare her life, and he said:

"I will not hurt thee, thou pretty child."

So he left her by herself; and he felt as if a great weight were taken off his heart when he had made up his mind not to kill her.

Then poor Snow White wandered along through the wood in great fear. In the evening she came to a cottage, and went in to rest herself, for her little feet would carry her no farther. Everything was neat: on the table was spread a white cloth, and there were seven little plates with seven little loaves, and seven little glasses with wine in them; and knives and forks laid in order; and by the wall stood seven little beds. Then, as she was very hungry, she picked a little piece off each loaf, and drank a very little wine out of each glass; and after that she thought she would lie down and rest. So she tried all the little beds; but one was too long, another was too short, till at last the seventh suited her; and there she laid herself down and went to sleep. Presently, in came the masters of the cottage, seven little dwarfs who lived among the mountains, and dug and searched for gold. They lighted up their seven lamps, and saw directly that all was not right.

The first said: "Who has been sitting on my stool?"

The second: "Who has been eating off my plate?"

The third: "Who has been picking my bread?"

The fourth: "Who has been meddling with my spoon?"

The fifth: "Who has been handling my fork?"

The sixth: "Who has been cutting with my knife?"

The seventh: "Who has been drinking my wine?"

Then the first looked round and said: "Who has been lying on my bed?"

And the rest came running to him, and everyone cried out that somebody had been upon his bed. But the seventh saw Snow White, and called all his brethren to come and see her; and they cried out with wonder and astonishment and brought their lamps to look at her, and said:

"Good heavens! what a lovely child she is!"

And they were very glad to see her, and took care not to wake her; and the seventh dwarf slept an hour with each of the other dwarfs in turn, till the night was gone.

In the morning Snow White told them her story; and they pitied her, and said if she would keep all things in order, and cook and wash, and knit and spin for them, she might stay where she was, and they would take good care of her. Then they went out all day long to their work, seeking for gold and silver in the mountains; and Snow White remained at home.

The Queen, now that she thought Snow White was dead, believed that she was certainly the handsomest lady in the land; and she went to the glass and said:

> "Tell me, glass, tell me true!
> Of all the ladies in the land,
> Who is fairest, tell me who?"

And the glass answered:

> "Thou, Queen, art the fairest in all this land:
> But over the hills, in the greenwood shade,
> Where the seven dwarfs their dwelling have made,
> There Snow White is hiding her head; and she
> Is lovelier far, O Queen! than thee."

Then the Queen was alarmed; for she knew that the glass always spoke the truth, and was sure that the servant had betrayed her. She could not bear to think that anyone lived more beautiful than she was; so she disguised herself up as an old peddler, and went her way over the hills, to the place where the dwarfs dwelt. Then she knocked at the door, and cried:

"Fine wares to sell!"

Snow White looked out at the window, and said:

"Good day, good-woman; what have you to sell?"

"Good wares, fine wares," said she; "laces and bobbins of all colors."

"I will let the old lady in; she seems to be a very good sort of body," thought Snow White, so she ran down, and unbolted the door.

"Bless me!" said the old woman, "how badly your stays are laced! Let me lace them up with one of my nice new laces."

Snow White did not dream of any mischief; so she stood before the old woman; but she set to work so nimbly, and pulled the lace so tight, that Snow White lost her breath and fell down as if dead.

"There's an end to all thy beauty," said the spiteful Queen, and went away home.

In the evening the seven dwarfs returned, and were grieved to see their faithful Snow White stretched upon the ground motionless, as if dead. However, they lifted her up, and when they found what was the matter, they cut the lace; and in a little time she began to breathe, and soon came to life again. Then they said:

"The old woman was the Queen herself; take care another time, and let no one in when we are away."

When the Queen got home, she went straight to her glass, and spoke to it as usual; but it still said:

> "Thou, Queen, art the fairest in all this land;
> But over the hills, in the greenwood shade,
> Where the seven dwarfs their dwelling have made,
> There Snow White is hiding her head; and she
> Is lovelier far, O Queen! than thee."

Then the blood ran cold in her heart with spite and malice to see that Snow White still lived; and she dressed herself again in a very different disguise, and took with her a poisoned comb. When she reached the dwarfs' cottage, she knocked at the door, and cried:

"Fine wares to sell!"

But Snow White said: "I dare not let anyone in."

Then the Queen said, "Only look at my beautiful combs," and gave her the poisoned one. And it looked so pretty that she took it up and put it into her hair to try it, but the moment it touched her head, the poison was so powerful that she fell down senseless.

"There you may lie," said the Queen, and went her way. By good luck the dwarfs returned early that evening, and when they saw Snow White lying on the ground, they thought what had happened, and soon found the poisoned comb. And when they took it away, she recovered; and they warned her once more not to open the door to anyone.

Meantime the Queen went home to her glass, and trembled with rage when she received the same answer as before. She went secretly into a chamber, and prepared a poisoned apple: the outside looked rosy and tempting, but whoever tasted it was sure to die. Then she dressed herself up as a peasant's wife, and traveled over the hills to the dwarfs' cottage, and knocked at the door; but Snow White put her head out of the window, and said:

"I dare not let anyone in."

"Do as you please," said the old woman, "but at any rate take this pretty apple; I will make you a present of it."

"No," said Snow White, "I dare not take it."

"You silly girl!" answered the other, "what are you afraid of? do you think it is poisoned? Come! do you eat one part, and I will eat the other."

Now the apple was so prepared that one side was good, though the other side was poisoned. Then Snow White was much tempted to taste, for the apple looked so exceedingly nice; and when she saw the old woman eat, she could refrain no longer. But she had scarcely put the piece into her mouth, when she fell down dead upon the ground.

"This time nothing will save thee," said the Queen; and she went home to her glass, and at last it said:

"Thou, Queen, art the fairest of all the fair."

And then her wicked heart was glad, and as happy as such a heart could be.

When evening came, and the dwarfs returned, they found Snow White lying on the ground: no breath came from her lips, and they were afraid that she was dead. They lifted her up, and combed her hair, and washed her face with wine and water; but all was in vain, the little girl seemed quite dead. So they laid her upon a bier, and watched and bewailed her three whole days; then they proposed to bury her: but her cheeks were still rosy; and her face looked as it did while she was alive; so they made a coffin of glass that they might still look at her, and wrote her name upon it in golden letters, and that she was a King's daughter. And the coffin was placed upon the hill, and one of the dwarfs always sat by it and watched.

And thus Snow White lay for a long time, and still only looked as though she were asleep; for she was even now as white as snow, and as red as blood, and as black as ebony. At last a Prince came and called at the dwarfs' house; and he saw Snow White, and read what was written in golden letters. Then he offered the dwarfs money, and earnestly prayed them to let him take her away; but they said:

"We will not part with her for all the gold in the world."

At last, however, they had pity on him, and gave him the coffin: but the moment he lifted it up to carry it home with him, the piece of apple fell from between her lips, and Snow White awoke, and said:

"Where am I?"

And the Prince answered, "Thou art safe with me."

Then he told her all that had happened, and said: "I love you far better than all the world: come with me to my father's palace, and you shall be my wife."

And Snow White consented, and went home with the Prince: and everything was prepared with pomp and splendor for their wedding.

To the feast was invited, among the rest, Snow White's old enemy, the Queen; and as she was dressing herself in fine rich clothes, she looked in the glass and said:

> "Tell me, glass, tell me true!
> Of all the ladies in the land,
> Who is fairest, tell me who?"

And the glass answered:

> "Thou, lady, art loveliest here, I ween;
> But lovelier far is the new-made Queen."

When she heard this she started with rage; but her envy and curiosity were so great, that she could not help setting out to see the bride. And when she got there, and saw that it was no other than Snow White, who, as she thought, had been dead a long while, she choked with passion, and fell ill and died; but Snow White and the Prince lived and reigned happily over that land many years.

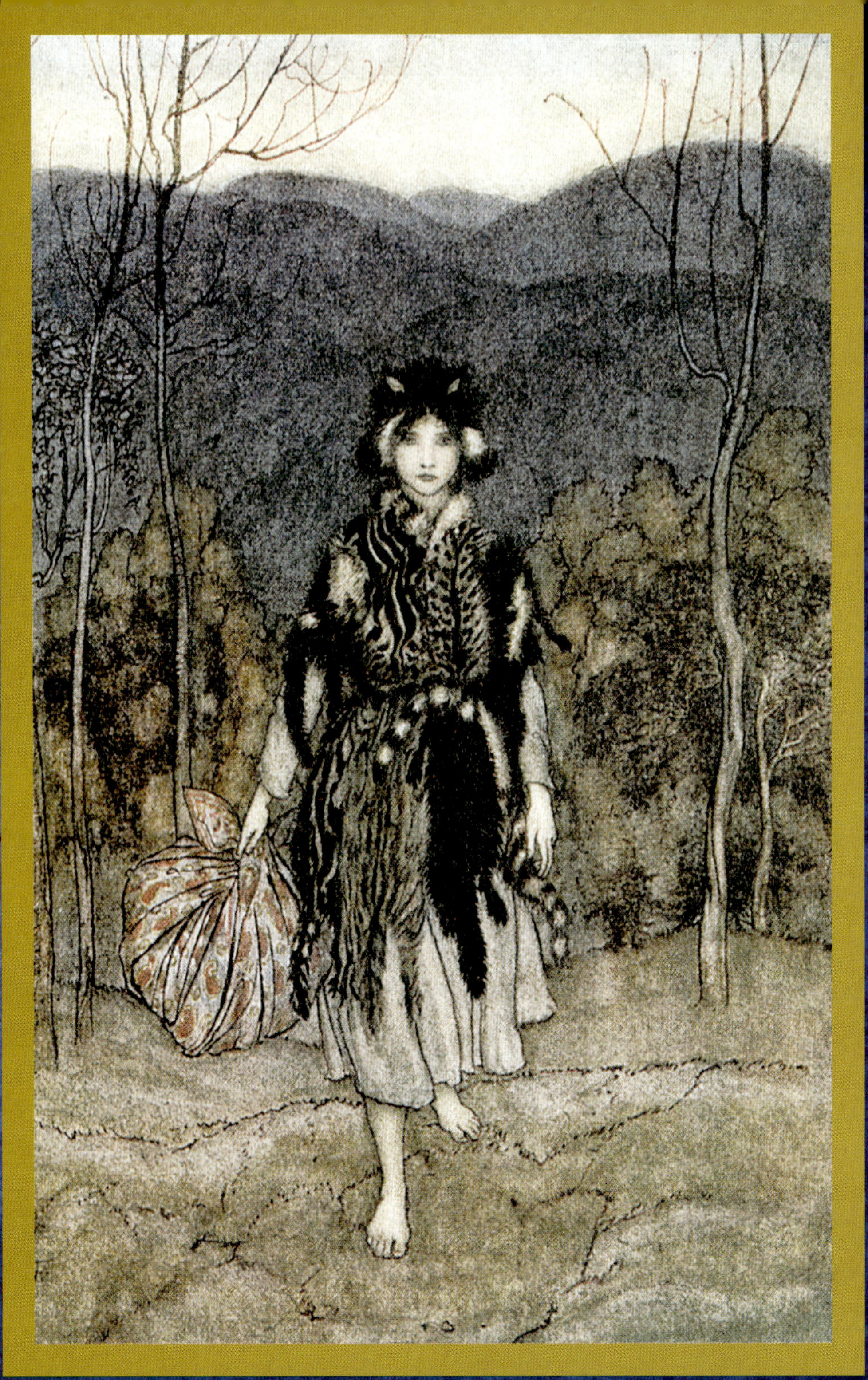

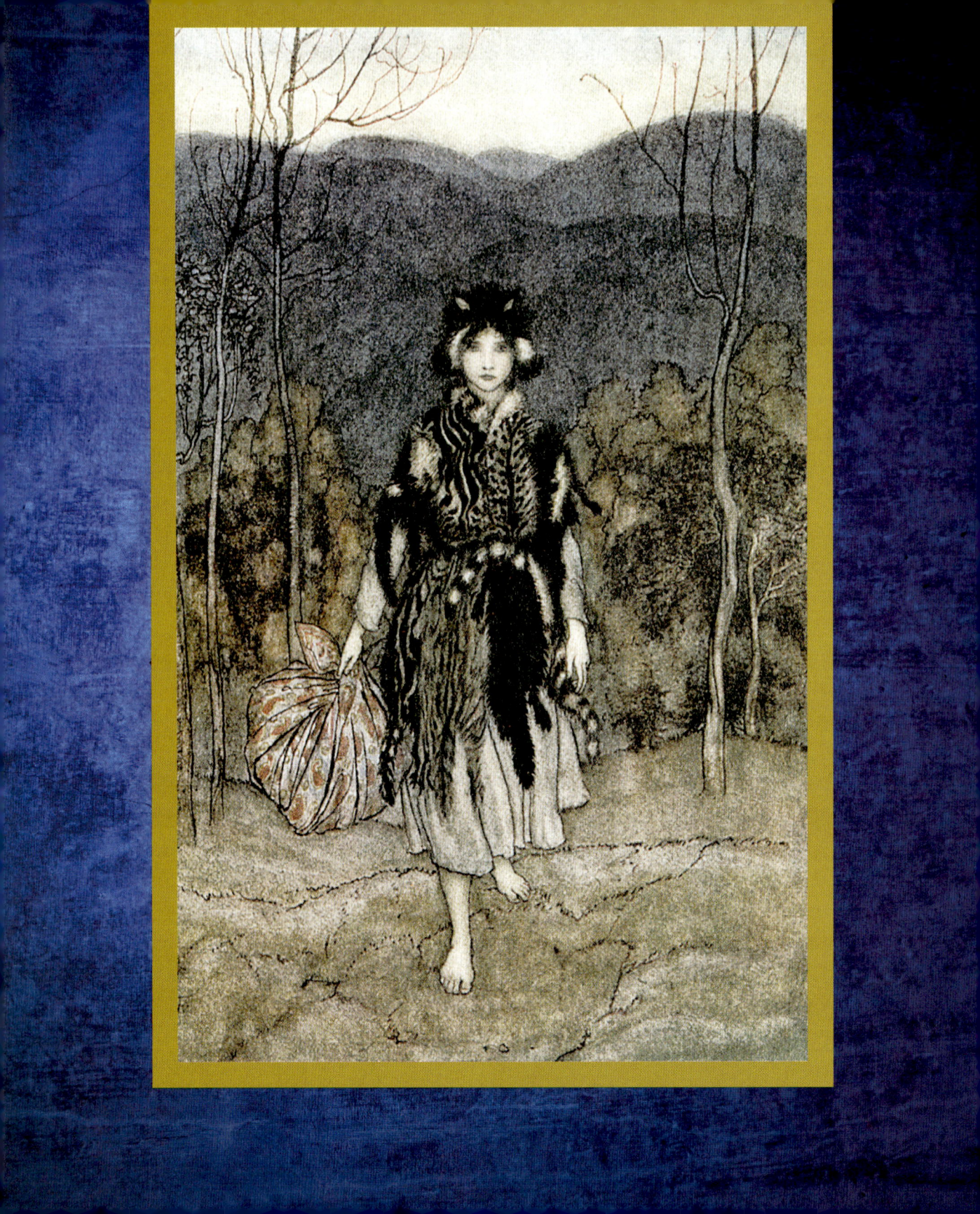

Catskin

Once upon a time there lived a gentleman who owned fine lands and houses, and he very much wanted to have a son to be heir to them. So when his wife brought him a daughter, though she was bonny as bonny could be, he cared nought for her, and said:

"Let me never see her face."

So she grew up to be a beautiful maiden, though her father never set eyes on her till she was fifteen years old and was ready to be married.

Then her father said roughly, "She shall marry the first that comes for her." Now when this became known, who should come along and be first but a nasty, horrid, old man! So she didn't know what to do, and went to the hen-wife and asked her advice. And the hen-wife said, "Say you will not take him unless they give you a coat of silver cloth." Well, they gave her a coat of silver cloth, but she wouldn't take him for all that, but went again to the hen-wife, who said, "Say you will not take him unless they give you a coat of beaten gold." Well, they gave her a coat of beaten gold, but still she would not take the old man, but went again to the hen-wife, who said, "Say you will not take him unless they give you a coat made of the feathers of all the birds of the air." So they sent out a man with a great heap of peas; and the man cried to all the birds of the air, "Each bird take a pea and put down a feather." So each bird took a pea and put down one of its feathers: and they took all the feathers and made a coat of them and gave it to her; but still she would not take the nasty, horrid, old man, but asked the hen-wife once again what she was to do, and the hen-wife said, "Say they must first make you a coat of catskin." Then they made her a coat of catskin; and she put it on, and tied up her other coats into a bundle, and when it was night-time ran away with it into the woods.

Now she went along, and went along, and went along, till at the end of the wood she saw a fine castle. Then she hid her fine dresses by a crystal waterfall and went up to the castle gates and asked for work. The lady of the castle saw her, and told her, "I'm sorry I have no better place, but if you like you may be our scullion." So down she went into the kitchen, and they called her Catskin, because of her dress. But the cook was very cruel to her, and led her a sad life.

Well, soon after that it happened that the young lord of the castle came home, and there was to be a grand ball in honor of the occasion. And when they were speaking about it among the servants, "Dear me, Mrs. Cook," said Catskin, "how much I should like to go!"

"What! You dirty impudent slut," said the cook, "you go among all the fine lords and ladies with your filthy catskin? A fine figure you'd cut!" and with that she took a basin of water and dashed it into Catskin's face. But Catskin only shook her ears and said nothing.

Now when the day of the ball arrived, Catskin slipped out of the house and went to the edge of the forest where she had hidden her dresses. Then she bathed herself in a crystal waterfall, and put on her coat of silver cloth, and hastened away to the ball. As soon as she entered all were overcome by her beauty and grace, while the young lord at once lost his heart to her. He asked her to be his partner for the first dance; and he would dance with none other the livelong night.

When it came to parting time, the young lord said, "Pray tell me, fair maid, where you live?"

But Catskin curtsied and said:

> "Kind sir, if the truth I must tell,
> At the sign of the 'Basin of Water' I dwell."

Then she flew from the castle and donned her catskin robe again, and slipped into the scullery, unbeknown to the cook.

The young lord went the very next day and searched for the sign of the "Basin of Water"; but he could not find it. So he went to his mother, the lady of the castle, and declared he would wed none other but the lady of the silver dress, and would never rest till he had found her. So another ball was soon arranged in hopes that the beautiful maid would appear again.

So Catskin said to the cook, "Oh, how I should like to go!" Whereupon the cook screamed out in a rage, "What, you, you dirty, impudent slut! You would cut a fine figure among all the fine lords and ladies." And with that she up with a ladle and broke it across Catskin's back. But Catskin only shook her ears, and ran off to the forest, where, first of all, she bathed, and then she put on her coat of beaten gold, and off she went to the ball-room.

As soon as she entered all eyes were upon her; and the young lord at once recognized her as the lady of the "Basin of Water," claimed her hand for the first dance, and did not leave her till the last. When that came, he again asked her where she lived. But all that she would say was:

> "Kind sir, if the truth I must tell,
> At the sign of the 'Broken Ladle' I dwell";

and with that she curtsied and flew from the ball, off with her golden robe, on with her catskin, and into the scullery without the cook's knowing.

Next day, when the young lord could not find where the sign of the "Broken Ladle" was, he begged his mother to have another grand ball, so that he might meet the beautiful maid once more.

Then Catskin said to the cook, "Oh, how I wish I could go to the ball!" Whereupon the cook called out: "A fine figure you'd cut!" and broke the skimmer across her head. But Catskin only shook her ears, and went off to the forest, where she first bathed in the crystal spring, and then donned her coat of feathers, and so off to the ball-room.

When she entered every one was surprised at so beautiful a face and form dressed in so rich and rare a dress; but the young lord at once recognized his beautiful sweetheart, and would dance with none but her the whole evening. When the ball came to an end he pressed her to tell him where she lived, but all she would answer was:

> "Kind sir, if the truth I must tell,
> At the sign of the 'Broken Skimmer' I dwell";

and with that she curtsied, and was off to the forest. But this time the young lord followed her, and watched her change her fine dress of feathers for her catskin dress, and then he knew her for his own scullery-maid.

Next day he went to his mother, and told her that he wished to marry the scullery-maid, Catskin.

"Never," said the lady of the Castle, "never so long as I live."

Well, the young lord was so grieved, that he took to his bed and was very ill indeed. The doctor tried to cure him, but he would not take any medicine unless from the hands of Catskin. At last the doctor went to the mother, and said that her son would die if she did not consent to his marriage with Catskin; so she had to give way. Then she summoned Catskin to her, and Catskin put on her coat of beaten gold before she went to see the lady; and she, of course, was overcome at once, and was only too glad to wed her son to so beautiful a maid.

So they were married, and after a time a little son was born to them, and grew up a fine little lad. Now one day, when he was about four years old, a beggar woman came to the door, and Lady Catskin gave some money to the little lord and told him to go and give it to the beggar woman. So he went and gave it, putting it into the hand of the woman's baby child; and the child leant forward and kissed the little lord.

Now the wicked old cook (who had never been sent away, because Catskin was too kind-hearted) was looking on, and she said, "See how beggars' brats take to one another!"

This insult hurt Catskin dreadfully: and she went to her husband, the young lord, and told him all about her father, and begged he would go and find out what had become of her parents. So they set out in the lord's grand coach, and traveled through the forest till they came to the house of Catskin's father. Then they put up at an inn near, and Catskin stopped there, while her husband went to see if her father would own she was his daughter.

Now her father had never had any other child, and his wife had died; so he was all alone in the world, and sate moping and miserable. When the young lord came in he hardly looked up, he was so miserable. Then Catskin's husband drew a chair close up to him, and asked him, "Pray, sir, had you not once a young daughter whom you would never see or own?"

And the miserable man said with tears, "It is true; I am a hardened sinner. But I would give all my worldly goods if I could but see her once before I die."

Then the young lord told him what had happened to Catskin, and took him to the inn, and afterward brought his father-in-law to his own castle, where they lived happy ever afterward.

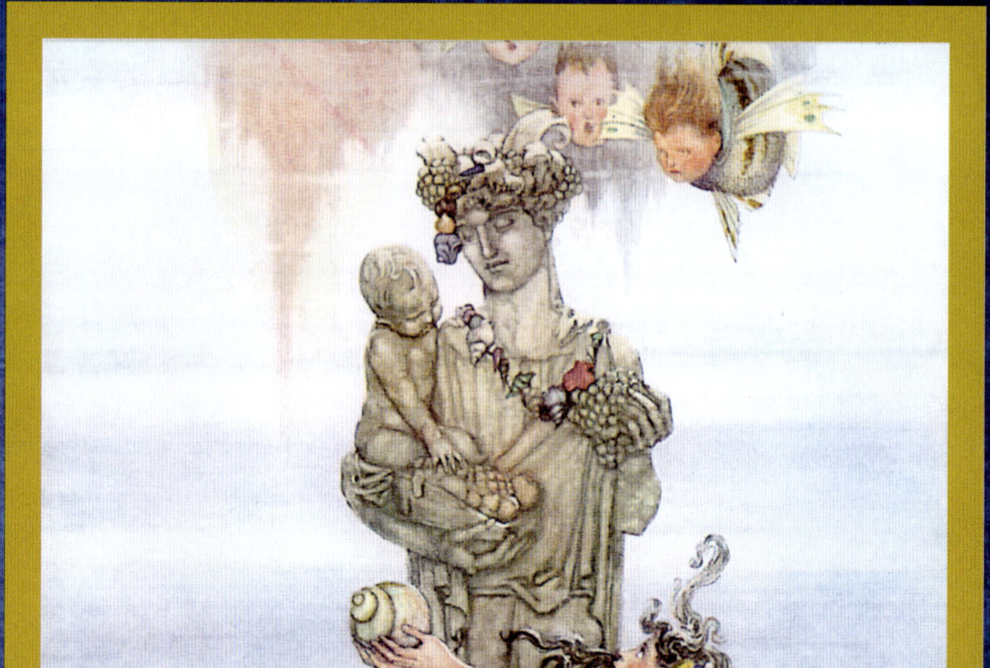

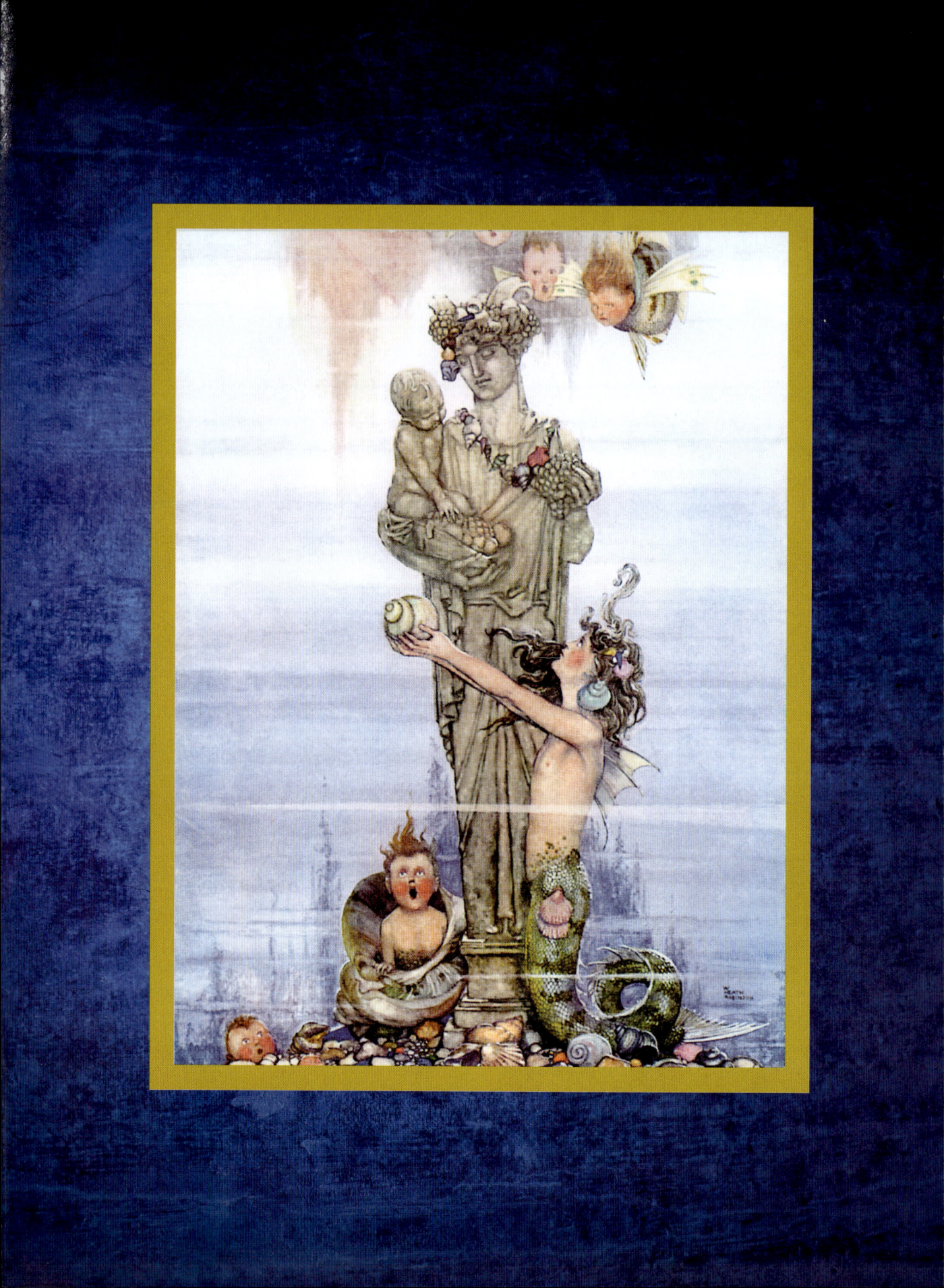

The Little Mermaid

Far out in the wide sea—where the water is blue as the loveliest cornflower, and clear as the purest crystal, where it is so deep that very, very many church-towers must be heaped one upon another in order to reach from the lowest depth to the surface above—dwell the Mer-people.

Now you must not imagine that there is nothing but sand below the water: no, indeed, far from it! Trees and plants of wondrous beauty grow there, whose stems and leaves are so light, that they are waved to and fro by the slightest motion of the water, almost as if they were living beings. Fishes, great and small, glide in and out among the branches, just as birds fly about among our trees.

Where the water is deepest stands the palace of the Mer-King. The walls of this palace are of coral, and the high, pointed windows are of amber; the roof, however, is composed of mussel-shells, which, as the billows pass over them, are continually opening and shutting. This looks exceedingly pretty, especially as each of these mussel-shells contains a number of bright, glittering pearls, one only of which would be the most costly ornament in the diadem of a King in the upper world.

The Mer-King, who lived in this palace, had been for many years a widower; his old mother managed the household affairs for him. She was, on the whole, a sensible sort of a lady, although extremely proud of her high birth and station, on which account she wore twelve oysters on her tail, whilst the other inhabitants of the sea, even those of distinction, were allowed only six. In every other respect she merited unlimited praise, especially for the affection she showed to the six little Princesses, her grand-daughters. These were all very beautiful children; the youngest was, however, the most lovely; her skin was as soft and delicate as a rose-leaf, her eyes were of as deep a blue as the sea, but like all other mermaids, she had no feet, her body ended in a tail like that of a fish.

The whole day long the children used to play in the spacious apartments of the palace, where beautiful flowers grew out of the walls on all sides around them. When the great amber windows were opened, fishes would swim into these apartments as swallows fly into our rooms; but the fishes were bolder than the swallows, they swam straight up to the little Princesses, ate from their hands, and allowed themselves to be caressed.

In front of the palace there was a large garden, full of fiery red and dark blue trees, whose fruit glittered like gold, and whose flowers resembled a bright, burning sun. The sand that formed the soil of the garden was of a bright blue color, something like flames of sulfur; and a strangely beautiful blue was spread over the whole, so that one might have fancied oneself raised very high in the air, with the sky at once above and below, certainly not at the bottom of the sea. When the waters were quite still, the sun might be seen looking like a purple flower, out of whose cup streamed forth the light of the world.

Each of the little Princesses had her own plot in the garden, where she might plant and sow at her pleasure. One chose hers to be made in the shape of a whale, another preferred the figure of a mermaid, but the youngest had hers quite round like the sun, and planted in it only those flowers that were red, as the sun seemed to her. She was certainly a singular child, very quiet and thoughtful. Whilst her sisters were adorning themselves with all sorts of gay things that came out of a ship which had been wrecked, she asked for nothing but a beautiful white marble statue of a boy, which had been found in it. She put the statue in her garden, and planted a red weeping willow by its side. The tree grew up quickly, and let its long boughs fall upon the bright blue ground, where ever-moving shadows played in violet hues, as if boughs and root were embracing.

Nothing pleased the little Princess more than to hear about the world of human beings living above the sea. She made her old grandmother tell her everything she knew about ships, towns, men, and land animals, and was particularly pleased when she heard that the flowers of the upper world had a pleasant fragrance (for the flowers of the sea are scentless), and that the woods were green, and the fishes fluttering among the branches of various gay colors, and that they could sing with a loud clear voice. The old lady meant birds, but she called them fishes, because her grandchildren, having never seen a bird, would not otherwise have understood her.

"When you have attained your fifteenth year," added she, "you will be permitted to rise to the surface of the sea; you will then sit by moonlight in the clefts of the rocks, see the ships sail by, and learn to distinguish towns and men."

The next year the eldest of the sisters reached this happy age, but the others—alas! the second sister was a year younger than the eldest, the third a year younger than the second, and so on; the youngest had still five whole years to wait till that joyful time should come when she also might rise to the surface of the water and see what was going on in the upper world; however, the eldest promised to tell the others of everything she might see, when the first day of her being of age arrived; for the grandmother gave them but little information, and there was so much that they wished to hear.

But none of all the sisters longed so ardently for the day when she should be released from childish restraint as the youngest, she who had longest to wait, and was so quiet and thoughtful. Many a night she stood by the open window, looking up through the clear blue water, whilst the fishes were leaping and playing around her. She could see the sun and the moon; their light was pale, but they appeared larger than they do to those who live in the upper world. If a shadow passed over them, she knew it must be either a whale or a ship sailing by full of human beings, who indeed little thought that, far beneath them, a little mermaid was passionately stretching forth her white hands towards their ship's keel.

The day had now arrived when the eldest Princess had attained her fifteenth year, and was therefore allowed to rise up to the surface of the sea.

When she returned she had a thousand things to relate. Her chief pleasure had been to sit upon a sandbank in the moonlight, looking at the large town which lay on the coast, where lights were beaming like stars, and where music was playing; she had heard the distant noise of men and carriages, she had seen the high church-towers, had listened to the ringing of the bells; and just because she could not go there she longed the more after all these things.

How attentively did her youngest sister listen to her words! And when she next stood at night-time by her open window, gazing upward through the blue waters, she thought so intensely of the great noisy city that she fancied she could hear the church-bells ringing.

Next year the second sister received permission to swim wherever she pleased. She rose to the surface of the sea, just when the sun was setting; and this sight so delighted her, that she declared it to be more beautiful than anything else she had seen above the waters.

"The whole sky seemed tinged with gold," said she, "and it is impossible for me to describe to you the beauty of the clouds. Now red, now violet, they glided over me; but still more swiftly flew over the water a flock of white swans, just where the sun was descending; I looked after them, but the sun disappeared, and the bright rosy light on the surface of the sea and on the edges of the clouds was gradually extinguished."

It was now time for the third sister to visit the upper world. She was the boldest of the six, and ventured up a river. On its shores she saw green hills covered with woods and vineyards, from among which arose houses and castles; she heard the birds singing, and the sun shone with so much power, that she was continually obliged to plunge below, in order to cool her burning face. In a little bay she met with a number of children, who were bathing and jumping about; she would have joined in their gambols, but the children fled back to land in great terror, and a little black animal barked at her in such a manner, that she herself was frightened at last, and swam back to the sea. She could not, however, forget the green woods, the verdant hills, and the pretty children, who, although they had no fins, were swimming about in the river so fearlessly.

The fourth sister was not so bold, she remained in the open sea, and said on her return home she thought nothing could be more beautiful. She had seen ships sailing by, so far off that they looked like sea-gulls, she had watched the merry dolphins gamboling in the water, and the enormous whales, sending up into the air a thousand sparkling fountains.

The year after, the fifth sister attained her fifteenth year. Her birthday happened at a different season to that of her sisters; it was winter, the sea was of a green color, and immense icebergs were floating on its surface. These, she said, looked like

The Little Mermaid

pearls; they were, however, much larger than the church-towers in the land of human beings. She sat down upon one of these pearls, and let the wind play with her long hair, but then all the ships hoisted their sails in terror, and escaped as quickly as possible. In the evening the sky was covered with sails; and whilst the great mountains of ice alternately sank and rose again, and beamed with a reddish glow, flashes of lightning burst forth from the clouds, and the thunder rolled on, peal after peal. The sails of all the ships were instantly furled, and horror and affright reigned on board, but the Princess sat still on the iceberg, looking unconcernedly at the blue zig-zag of the flashes.

The first time that either of these sisters rose out of the sea, she was quite enchanted at the sight of so many new and beautiful objects, but the novelty was soon over, and it was not long ere their own home appeared more attractive than the upper world, for there only did they find everything agreeable.

Many an evening would the five sisters rise hand in hand from the depths of the ocean. Their voices were far sweeter than any human voice, and when a storm was coming on, they would swim in front of the ships, and sing,—oh! how sweetly did they sing! describing the happiness of those who lived at the bottom of the sea, and entreating the sailors not to be afraid, but to come down to them.

The mariners, however, did not understand their words; they fancied the song was only the whistling of the wind, and thus they lost the hidden glories of the sea; for if their ships were wrecked, all on board were drowned, and none but dead men ever entered the Mer-King's palace.

Whilst the sisters were swimming at evening-time, the youngest would remain motionless and alone, in her father's palace, looking up after them. She would have wept, but mermaids cannot weep, and therefore, when they are troubled, suffer infinitely more than human beings do.

"Oh, if I were but fifteen!" sighed she, "I know that I should love the upper world and its inhabitants so much."

At last the time she had so longed for arrived.

"Well, now it is your turn," said the grandmother; "come here, that I may adorn you like your sisters." And she wound around her hair a wreath of white lilies, whose every petal was the half of a pearl, and then commanded eight large oysters to fasten themselves to the Princess's tail, in token of her high rank.

"But that is so very uncomfortable!" said the little Princess.

"One must not mind slight inconveniences when one wishes to look well," said the old lady.

How willingly would the Princess have given up all this splendor, and exchanged her heavy crown for the red flowers of her garden, which were so much more becoming to her. But she dared not do so. "Farewell," said she; and she rose from the sea, light as a flake of foam.

When, for the first time in her life, she appeared on the surface of the water, the sun had just sunk below the horizon, the clouds were beaming with bright golden and rosy hues, the evening star was shining in the pale western sky, the air was mild and refreshing, and the sea as smooth as a looking-glass. A large ship with three masts lay on the still waters; one sail only was unfurled, but not a breath was stirring, and the sailors were quietly seated on the cordage and ladders of the vessel. Music and song resounded from the deck, and after it grew dark hundreds of lamps all on a sudden burst forth into light, whilst innumerable flags were fluttering overhead. The little mermaid swam close up to the captain's cabin, and every now and then when the ship was raised by the motion of the water, she could look through the clear window panes. She saw within many richly dressed men; the handsomest among them was a young Prince with large black eyes. He could not certainly be more than sixteen years old, and it was in honor of his birthday that a grand festival was being celebrated. The crew were dancing on the deck, and when the young Prince appeared among them, a hundred rockets were sent up into the air, turning night into day, and so terrifying the little mermaid, that for some minutes she plunged beneath the water. However, she soon raised her little head again, and then it seemed as if all the stars were falling down upon her. Such a fiery shower she had never even seen before, never had she heard that men possessed such wonderful powers. Large suns revolved around her, bright fishes swam in the air, and everything was reflected perfectly on the clear surface of the sea. It was so light in the ship, that everything could be seen distinctly. Oh, how happy the young Prince was! He shook hands with the sailors, laughed and jested with them, whilst sweet notes of music mingled with the silence of night.

The Little Mermaid

It was now late, but the little mermaid could not tear herself away from the ship and the handsome young Prince. She remained looking through the cabin window, rocked to and fro by the waves. There was a foaming and fermentation in the depths beneath, and the ship began to move on faster; the sails were spread, the waves rose high, thick clouds gathered over the sky, and the noise of distant thunder was heard. The sailors perceived that a storm was coming on, so they again furled the sails. The great vessel was tossed about on the tempestuous ocean like a light boat, and the waves rose to an immense height, towering over the ship, which alternately sank beneath and rose above them. To the little mermaid this seemed most delightful, but the ship's crew thought very differently. The vessel cracked, the stout masts bent under the violence of the billows, the waters rushed in. For a minute the ship tottered to and fro, then the main-mast broke, as if it had been a reed; the ship turned over, and was filled with water. The little mermaid now perceived that the crew was in danger, for she herself was forced to beware of the beams and splinters torn from the vessel, and floating about on the waves. But at the same time it became pitch dark so that she could not distinguish anything; presently, however, a dreadful flash of lightning disclosed to her the whole of the wreck. Her eyes sought the young Prince—the same instant the ship sank to the bottom. At first she was delighted, thinking that the Prince must now come to her abode; but she soon remembered that man cannot live in water, and that therefore if the Prince ever entered her palace, it would be as a corpse.

"Die! no, he must not die!" She swam through the fragments with which the water was strewn regardless of the danger she was incurring, and at last found the Prince all but exhausted, and with great difficulty keeping his head above water. He had already closed his eyes, and must inevitably have been drowned, had not the little mermaid come to his rescue. She seized hold of him and kept him above water, suffering the current to bear them on together.

Towards morning the storm was hushed; no trace, however, remained of the ship. The sun rose like fire out of the sea; his beams seemed to restore color to the Prince's cheeks, but his eyes were still closed. The mermaid kissed his high forehead and stroked his wet hair away from his face. He looked like the marble statue in her garden; she kissed him again and wished most fervently that he might recover.

She now saw the dry land with its mountains glittering with snow. A green wood extended along the coast, and at the entrance of the wood stood a chapel or convent, she could not be sure which. Citron and lemon trees grew in the garden adjoining it, an avenue of tall palm trees led up to the door. The sea here formed a little bay, in which the water was quite smooth but very deep, and under the cliffs there were dry, firm sands. Hither swam the little mermaid with the seemingly dead Prince; she laid him upon the warm sand, and took care to place his head high, and to turn his face to the sun.

The bells began to ring in the large white building which stood before her, and a number of young girls came out to walk in the garden. The mermaid went away from the shore, hid herself behind some stones, covered her head with foam, so that her little face could not be seen, and watched the Prince with unremitting attention.

It was not long before one of the young girls approached. She seemed quite frightened at finding the Prince in this state, apparently dead; soon, however, she recovered herself, and ran back to call her sisters. The little mermaid saw that the Prince revived, and that all around smiled kindly and joyfully upon him—for her, however, he looked not, he knew not that it was she who had saved him, and when the Prince was taken into the house she felt so sad, that she immediately plunged beneath the water, and returned to her father's palace.

If she had been before quiet and thoughtful, she now grew still more so. Her sisters asked her what she had seen in the upper world, but she made no answer.

Many an evening she rose to the place where she had left the Prince. She saw the snow on the mountains melt, the fruits in the garden ripen and gathered, but the Prince she never saw, so she always returned sorrowfully to her subterranean abode. Her only pleasure was to sit in her little garden gazing on the beautiful statue so like the Prince. She cared no longer for her flowers; they grew up in wild luxuriance, covered the steps, and entwined their long stems and tendrils among the boughs of the trees, so that her whole garden became a bower.

At last, being unable to conceal her sorrow any longer, she revealed the secret to one of her sisters, who told it to the other Princesses, and they to some of their friends. Among them was a young mermaid who recollected the Prince, having been an eye-witness herself to the festivities in the ship; she knew also in what country the Prince lived, and the name of its King.

"Come, little sister!" said the Princesses, and embracing her, they rose together arm in arm, out of the water, just in front of the Prince's palace.

This palace was built of bright yellow stones, a flight of white marble steps led from it down to the sea. A gilded cupola crowned the building, and white marble figures, which might almost have been taken for real men and women, were placed among the pillars surrounding it. Through the clear glass of the high windows one might look into magnificent apartments hung with silken curtains, the walls adorned with magnificent paintings. It was a real treat to the little royal mermaids to behold so splendid an abode; they gazed through the windows of one of the largest rooms, and in the center saw a fountain playing, whose waters sprang up so high as to reach the glittering cupola above, through which the sunbeams fell dancing on the water, and brightening the pretty plants which grew around it.

The little mermaid now knew where her beloved Prince dwelt, and henceforth she went there almost every evening. She often approached nearer the land than her sisters had ventured, and even swam up the narrow channel that flowed under the marble balcony. Here on a bright moonlight night, she would watch the young Prince, who believed himself alone.

Sometimes she saw him sailing on the water in a gaily painted boat with many colored flags waving above. She would then hide among the green reeds which grew on the banks, listening to his voice, and if any one in the boat noticed the rustling of her long silver veil, which was caught now and then by the light breeze, they only fancied it was a swan flapping his wings.

Many a night when the fishermen were casting their nets by the beacon's light, she heard them talking of the Prince, and relating the noble actions he had performed. She was then so happy, thinking how she had saved his life when struggling with the waves, and remembering how his head had rested on her bosom, and how she had kissed him when he knew nothing of it, and could never even dream of such a thing.

Human beings became more and more dear to her every day; she wished that she were one of them. Their world seemed to her much larger than that of the mer-people;

they could fly over the ocean in their ships, as well as climb to the summits of those high mountains that rose above the clouds; and their wooded domains extended much farther than a mermaid's eye could penetrate.

There were many things that she wished to hear explained, but her sisters could not give her any satisfactory answer; she was again obliged to have recourse to the old Queen-Mother, who knew a great deal about the upper world, which she used to call "the country above the sea."

"Do men when they are not drowned live for ever?" she asked one day. "Do they not die as we do, who live at the bottom of the sea?"

"Yes," was the grandmother's reply, "they must die like us, and their life is much shorter than ours. We live to the age of three hundred years, but when we die, we become foam on the sea, and are not allowed even to share a grave among those that are dear to us. We have no immortal souls, we can never live again, and are like the grass which, when once cut down, is withered for ever. Human beings, on the contrary, have souls that continue to live when their bodies become dust, and as we rise out of the water to admire the abode of man, they ascend to glorious unknown dwellings in the skies which we are not permitted to see."

"Why have not *we* immortal souls?" asked the little mermaid. "I would willingly give up my three hundred years to be a human being for only one day, thus to become entitled to that heavenly world above."

"You must not think of that," answered her grandmother, "it is much better as it is; we live longer and are far happier than human beings."

"So I must die, and be dashed like foam over the sea, never to rise again and hear the gentle murmur of the ocean, never again see the beautiful flowers and the bright sun! Tell me, dear grandmother, are there no means by which I may obtain an immortal soul?"

"No!" replied the old lady. "It is true that if thou couldst so win the affections of a human being as to become dearer to him than either father or mother; if he loved thee with all his heart, and promised whilst the priest joined his hands with thine to be always faithful to thee; then his soul would flow into thine, and thou wouldst then become partaker of human bliss. But that can never be! for what in our eyes is the most beautiful part

The Little Mermaid

of our body, the tail, the inhabitants of the earth think hideous, they cannot bear it. To appear handsome to them, the body must have two clumsy props which they call legs."

The little mermaid sighed and looked mournfully at the scaly part of her form, otherwise so fair and delicate.

"We are happy," added the old lady, "we shall jump and swim about merrily for three hundred years; that is a long time, and afterwards we shall repose peacefully in death. This evening we have a court ball."

The ball which the Queen-Mother spoke of was far more splendid than any that earth has ever seen. The walls of the saloon were of crystal, very thick, but yet very clear; hundreds of large mussel-shells were planted in rows along them; these shells were some of rose-color, some green as grass, but all sending forth a bright light, which not only illuminated the whole apartment, but also shone through the glassy walls so as to light up the waters around for a great space, and making the scales of the numberless fishes, great and small, crimson and purple, silver and gold-colored, appear more brilliant than ever.

Through the center of the saloon flowed a bright, clear stream, on the surface of which danced mermen and mermaids to the melody of their own sweet voices, voices far sweeter than those of the dwellers upon earth. The little Princess sang more harmoniously than any other, and they clapped their hands and applauded her. She was pleased at this, for she knew well that there was neither on earth or in the sea a more beautiful voice than hers. But her thoughts soon returned to the world above her: she could not forget the handsome Prince; she could not control her sorrow at not having an immortal soul. She stole away from her father's palace, and whilst all was joy within, she sat alone lost in thought in her little neglected garden. On a sudden she heard the tones of horns resounding over the water far away in the distance, and she said to herself, "Now he is going out to hunt, he whom I love more than my father and my mother, with whom my thoughts are constantly occupied, and to whom I would so willingly trust the happiness of my life! All! all, will I risk to win him—and an immortal soul! Whilst my sisters are still dancing in the palace, I will go to the enchantress whom I have hitherto feared so much, but who is, nevertheless, the only person who can advise and help me."

So the little mermaid left the garden, and went to the foaming whirlpool beyond which dwelt the enchantress. She had never been this way before—neither flowers nor sea-grass bloomed along her path; she had to traverse an extent of bare grey sand till she reached the whirlpool, whose waters were eddying and whizzing like mill-wheels, tearing everything they could seize along with them into the abyss below. She was obliged to make her way through this horrible place, in order to arrive at the territory of the enchantress. Then she had to pass through a boiling, slimy bog, which the enchantress called her turf-moor: her house stood in a wood beyond this, and a strange abode it was. All the trees and bushes around were polypi, looking like hundred-headed serpents shooting up out of the ground; their branches were long slimy arms with fingers of worms, every member, from the root to the uttermost tip, ceaselessly moving and extending on all sides. Whatever they seized they fastened upon so that it could not loosen itself from their grasp. The little mermaid stood still for a minute looking at this horrible wood; her heart beat with fear, and she would certainly have returned without attaining her object, had she not remembered the Prince—and immortality. The thought gave her new courage, she bound up her long waving hair, that the polypi might not catch hold of it, crossed her delicate arms over her bosom, and, swifter than a fish can glide through the water, she passed these unseemly trees, who stretched their eager arms after her in vain. She could not, however, help seeing that every polypus had something in his grasp, held as firmly by a thousand little arms as if enclosed by iron bands. The whitened skeletons of a number of human beings who had been drowned in the sea, and had sunk into the abyss, grinned horribly from the arms of these polypi; helms, chests, skeletons of land animals were also held in their embrace; among other things might be seen even a little mermaid whom they had seized and strangled! What a fearful sight for the unfortunate Princess!

But she got safely through this wood of horrors, and then arrived at a slimy place, where immense, fat snails were crawling about, and in the midst of this place stood a house built of the bones of unfortunate people who had been shipwrecked. Here sat the witch caressing a toad in the same manner as some persons would a pet bird. The ugly fat snails she called her chickens, and she permitted them to crawl about her.

The Little Mermaid

"I know well what you would ask of me," said she to the little Princess. "Your wish is foolish enough, yet it shall be fulfilled, though its accomplishment is sure to bring misfortune on you, my fairest Princess. You wish to get rid of your tail, and to have instead two stilts like those of human beings, in order that a young Prince may fall in love with you, and that you may obtain an immortal soul. Is it not so?" Whilst the witch spoke these words, she laughed so violently that her pet toad and snails fell from her lap. "You come just at the right time," continued she; "had you come after sunset, it would not have been in my power to have helped you before another year. I will prepare for you a drink with which you must swim to land, you must sit down upon the shore and swallow it, and then your tail will fall and shrink up to the things which men call legs. This transformation will, however, be very painful; you will feel as though a sharp knife passed through your body. All who look on you after you have been thus changed will say that you are the loveliest child of earth they have ever seen; you will retain your peculiar undulating movements, and no dancer will move so lightly, but every step you take will cause you pain all but unbearable; it will seem to you as though you were walking on the sharp edges of swords, and your blood will flow. Can you endure all this suffering? If so, I will grant your request."

"Yes, I will," answered the Princess, with a faltering voice; for she remembered her dear Prince, and the immortal soul which her suffering might win.

"Only consider," said the witch, "that you can never again become a mermaid, when once you have received a human form. You may never return to your sisters, and your father's palace; and unless you shall win the Prince's love to such a degree that he shall leave father and mother for you, that you shall be mixed up with all his thoughts and wishes, and unless the priest join your hands, so that you become man and wife, you will never obtain the immortality you seek. The morrow of the day on which he is united to another will see your death; your heart will break with sorrow, and you will be changed to foam on the sea."

"Still I will venture!" said the little mermaid, pale and trembling as a dying person.

"Besides all this, I must be paid, and it is no slight thing that I require for my trouble. Thou hast the sweetest voice of all the dwellers in the sea, and thou thinkest by its means to charm the Prince; this voice, however, I demand as my recompense. The best thing thou possessest I require in exchange for my magic drink; for I shall be obliged to sacrifice my own blood, in order to give it the sharpness of a two-edged sword."

"But if you take my voice from me," said the Princess, "what have I left with which to charm the Prince?"

"Thy graceful form," replied the witch, "thy modest gait, and speaking eyes. With such as these, it will be easy to infatuate a vain human heart. Well now! hast thou lost courage? Put out thy little tongue, that I may cut it off, and take it for myself, in return for my magic drink."

"Be it so!" said the Princess, and the witch took up her caldron, in order to mix her potion. "Cleanliness is a good thing," remarked she, as she began to rub the caldron with a handful of toads and snails. She then scratched her bosom, and let the black blood trickle down into the caldron, every moment throwing in new ingredients, the smoke from the mixture assuming such horrible forms, as were enough to fill beholders with terror, and a moaning and groaning proceeding from it, which might be compared to the weeping of crocodiles. The magic drink at length became clear and transparent as pure water; it was ready.

"Here it is!" said the witch to the Princess, cutting out her tongue at the same moment. The poor little mermaid was now dumb: she could neither sing nor speak.

"If the polypi should attempt to seize you, as you pass through my little grove," said the witch, "you have only to sprinkle some of this magic drink over them, and their arms will burst into a thousand pieces." But the Princess had no need of this counsel, for the polypi drew hastily back, as soon as they perceived the bright phial, that glittered in her hand like a star; thus she passed safely through the formidable wood over the moor, and across the foaming mill-stream.

She now looked once again at her father's palace; the lamps in the saloon were extinguished, and all the family were asleep. She would not go in, for she could not speak if she did; she was about to leave her home for ever; her heart was ready to break with sorrow at the thought; she stole into the garden, plucked a flower from the bed of each of her sisters as a remembrance, kissed her hand again and again, and then rose through the dark blue waters to the world above.

The Little Mermaid

The sun had not yet risen when she arrived at the Prince's dwelling, and ascended those well-known marble steps. The moon still shone in the sky when the little mermaid drank off the wonderful liquid contained in her phial. She felt it run through her like a sharp knife, and she fell down in a swoon. When the sun rose, she awoke; and felt a burning pain in all her limbs, but—she saw standing close to her the object of her love, the handsome young Prince, whose coal-black eyes were fixed inquiringly upon her. Full of shame she cast down her own, and perceived, instead of the long fish-like tail she had hitherto borne, two slender legs; but she was quite naked, and tried in vain to cover herself with her long thick hair. The Prince asked who she was, and how she had got there; and she, in reply, smiled and gazed upon him with her bright blue eyes, for alas! she could not speak. He then led her by the hand into the palace. She found that the witch had told her true—she felt as though she were walking on the edges of sharp swords, but she bore the pain willingly; on she passed, light as a zephyr, and all who saw her wondered at her light, undulating movements.

When she entered the palace, rich clothes of muslin and silk were brought to her; she was lovelier than all who dwelt there, but she could neither speak nor sing. Some female slaves, gaily dressed in silk and gold brocade, sang before the Prince and his royal parents; and one of them distinguished herself by her clear sweet voice, which the Prince applauded by clapping his hands. This made the little mermaid very sad, for she knew that she used to sing far better than the young slave. "Alas!" thought she, "if he did but know that, for his sake, I have given away my voice for ever."

The slaves began to dance; our lovely little mermaiden then arose, stretched out her delicate white arms, and hovered gracefully about the room. Every motion displayed more and more the perfect symmetry and elegance of her figure; and the expression which beamed in her speaking eyes touched the hearts of the spectators far more than the song of the slaves.

All present were enchanted, but especially the young Prince, who called her his dear little foundling. And she danced again and again, although every step cost her excessive pain. The Prince then said she should always be with him; and accordingly a sleeping-place was prepared for her on velvet cushions in the anteroom of his own apartment.

The Prince caused a suit of male apparel to be made for her, in order that she might accompany him in his rides; so together they traversed the fragrant woods, where green boughs brushed against their shoulders, and the birds sang merrily among the fresh leaves. With him she climbed up steep mountains, and although her tender feet bled, so as to be remarked by the attendants, she only smiled, and followed her dear Prince to the heights, whence they could see the clouds chasing each other beneath them, like a flock of birds migrating to other countries.

During the night she would, when all in the palace were at rest, walk down the marble steps, in order to cool her feet in the deep waters; she would then think of those beloved ones who dwelt in the lower world.

One night, as she was thus bathing her feet, her sisters swam together to the spot, arm in arm and singing, but alas! so mournfully! She beckoned to them, and they immediately recognized her, and told her how great was the mourning in her father's house for her loss. From this time the sisters visited her every night; and once they brought with them the old grandmother, who had not seen the upper world for a great many years; they likewise brought their father, the Mer-King, with his crown on his head; but these two old people did not venture near enough to land to be able to speak to her.

The little mermaiden became dearer and dearer to the Prince every day; but he only looked upon her as a sweet, gentle child, and the thought of making her his wife never entered his head. And yet his wife she must be, ere she could receive an immortal soul; his wife she must be, or she would change into foam, and be driven restlessly over the billows of the sea!

"Dost thou not love me above all others?" her eyes seemed to ask, as he pressed her fondly in his arms, and kissed her lovely brow.

"Yes," the Prince would say, "thou art dearer to me than any other, for no one is as good as thou art! Thou lovest me so much; and thou art so like a young maiden whom I have seen but once, and may never see again. I was on board a ship, which was wrecked by a sudden tempest; the waves threw me on the shore, near a holy temple, where a number of young girls are occupied constantly with religious services. The youngest of them found me on the shore, and saved my life. I saw her only once, but her image is vividly impressed upon my memory, and her alone can I love. But she belongs to the holy temple; and thou who resemblest her so much hast been given to me for consolation; never will we be parted!"

"Alas! he does not know that it was I who saved his life," thought the little mermaiden, sighing deeply; "I bore him over the wild waves, into the wooded bay, where the holy temple stood; I sat behind the rocks, waiting till some one should come. I saw the pretty maiden approach, whom he loves more than me,"—and again she heaved a deep sigh, for she could not weep. "He said that the young girl belongs to the holy temple; she never comes out into the world, so they cannot meet each other again,—and I am always with him, see him daily; I will love him, and devote my whole life to him."

"So the Prince is going to be married to the beautiful daughter of the neighboring King," said the courtiers, "that is why he is having that splendid ship fitted out. It is announced that he wishes to travel, but in reality he goes to see the Princess; a numerous retinue will accompany him." The little mermaiden smiled at these and similar conjectures, for she knew the Prince's intentions better than any one else.

"I must go," he said to her, "I must see the beautiful Princess; my parents require me to do so; but they will not compel me to marry her, and bring her home as my bride. And it is quite impossible for me to love her, for she cannot be so like the beautiful girl in the temple as thou art; and if I were obliged to choose, I should prefer thee, my little silent foundling, with the speaking eyes." And he kissed her rosy lips, played with her locks, and folded her in his arms, whereupon arose in her heart a sweet vision of human happiness, and immortal bliss.

"Thou art not afraid of the sea, art thou, my sweet silent child?" asked he tenderly, as they stood together in the splendid ship, which was to take them to the country of the neighboring King. And then he told her of the storms that sometimes agitate the waters; of the strange fishes that inhabit the deep, and of the wonderful things seen by divers. But she smiled at his words, for she knew better than any child of earth what went on in the depths of the ocean.

At night-time, when the moon shone brightly, and when all on board were fast asleep, she sat in the ship's gallery, looking down into the sea. It seemed to her, as she gazed through the foamy track made by the ship's keel, that she saw her father's palace, and her grandmother's silver crown. She then saw her sisters rise out of the water, looking sorrowful and stretching out their hands towards her. She nodded to them, smiled, and would have explained that everything was going on quite according to her wishes; but just then the cabin boy approached, upon which the sisters plunged beneath the water so suddenly that the boy thought what he had seen on the waves was nothing but foam.

The next morning the ship entered the harbor of the King's splendid capital. Bells were rung, trumpets sounded, and soldiers marched in procession through the city, with waving banners, and glittering bayonets. Every day witnessed some new entertainments, balls and parties followed each other; the Princess, however, was not yet in the town; she had been sent to a distant convent for education, and had there been taught the practice of all royal virtues. At last she arrived at the palace.

The little mermaid had been anxious to see this unparalleled Princess; and she was now obliged to confess that she had never before seen so beautiful a creature.

The skin of the Princess was so white and delicate that the veins might be seen through it, and her dark eyes sparkled beneath a pair of finely formed eye-brows.

"It is herself!" exclaimed the Prince, when they met, "it is she who saved my life, when I lay like a corpse on the sea shore!" and he pressed his blushing bride to his beating heart.

"Oh, I am all too happy!" said he to his dumb foundling. "What I never dared to hope for has come to pass. Thou must rejoice in my happiness, for thou lovest me more than all others who surround me."—And the little mermaid kissed his hand in silent sorrow; it seemed to her as if her heart was breaking already, although the morrow of his marriage-day, which must inevitably see her death, had not yet dawned.

Again rung the church-bells, whilst heralds rode through the streets of the capital, to announce the approaching bridal. Odorous flames burned in silver candlesticks on all the altars; the priests swung their golden censers; and bride and bridegroom joined hands, whilst the holy words that united them were spoken. The little mermaid, clad in silk and cloth of gold, stood behind the Princess, and held the train of the bridal dress; but her ear heard nothing of the solemn music; her eye saw not the holy ceremony; she remembered her approaching end, she remembered that she had lost both this world and the next.

That very same evening bride and bridegroom went on board the ship; cannons were fired, flags waved with the breeze, and in the center of the deck stood a magnificent pavilion of purple and cloth of gold, fitted up with the richest and softest couches. Here the princely pair were to spend the night. A favorable wind swelled the sails, and the ship glided lightly over the blue waters.

As soon as it was dark, colored lamps were hung out and dancing began on the deck. The little mermaid was thus involuntarily reminded of what she had seen the first time she rose to the upper world. The spectacle that now presented itself was equally splendid—and she was obliged to join in the dance, hovering lightly as a bird over the ship boards. All applauded her, for never had she danced with more enchanting grace. Her little feet suffered extremely, but she no longer felt the pain; the anguish her heart suffered was much greater. It was the last evening she might see him, for whose sake she had forsaken her home and all her family, had given away her beautiful voice, and suffered daily the most violent pain—all without his having the least suspicion of it. It was the last evening that she might breathe the same atmosphere in which he, the beloved one, lived; the last evening when she might behold the deep blue sea, and the starry heavens—an eternal night, in which she might neither think nor dream, awaited her. And all was joy in the ship; and she, her heart filled with thoughts of death and annihilation, smiled and danced with the others, till past midnight. Then the Prince kissed his lovely bride, and arm in arm they entered the magnificent tent prepared for their repose.

All was now still; the steersman alone stood at the ship's helm. The little mermaid leaned her white arms on the gallery, and looked towards the east, watching for the dawn; she well knew that the first sunbeam would witness her dissolution. She saw her sisters rise out of the sea; deadly pale were their features; and their long hair no more fluttered over their shoulders, it had all been cut off.

"We have given it to the witch," said they, "to induce her to help thee, so that thou mayest not die. She has given to us a penknife: here it is! Before the sun rises, thou must plunge it into the Prince's heart; and when his warm blood trickles down upon thy feet they will again be changed to a fish-like tail; thou wilt once more become a mermaid, and wilt live thy full three hundred years, ere thou changest to foam on the sea. But hasten! either he or thou must die before sunrise. Our aged mother mourns for thee so much her grey hair has fallen off through sorrow, as ours fell before the scissors of the witch. Kill the Prince, and come down to us! Hasten! hasten! dost thou not see the red streaks on the eastern sky, announcing the near approach of the sun? A few minutes more and he rises, and then all will be over with thee." At these words they sighed deeply and vanished.

The little mermaid drew aside the purple curtains of the pavilion, where lay the bride and bridegroom; bending over them, she kissed the Prince's forehead, and then glancing at the sky, she saw that the dawning light became every moment brighter. The Prince's lips unconsciously murmured the name of his bride—he was dreaming of her, and her only, whilst the fatal penknife trembled in the hand of the unhappy mermaid. All at once, she threw far out into the sea that instrument of death; the waves rose like bright blazing flames around, and the water where it fell seemed tinged with blood. With eyes fast becoming dim and fixed, she looked once more at her beloved Prince; then plunged from the ship into the sea, and felt her body slowly but surely dissolving into foam.

The sun rose from his watery bed; his beams fell so softly and warmly upon her, that our little mermaid was scarcely sensible of dying. She still saw the glorious sun; and over her head hovered a thousand beautiful, transparent forms; she could still distinguish the white sails of the ship, and the bright red clouds in the sky; the voices of those airy creatures above her had a melody so sweet and soothing, that a human ear would be as little able to catch the sound as her eye was capable of distinguishing their forms; they hovered around her without wings, borne by their own lightness through the air. The little mermaid at last saw that she had a body as transparent as theirs; and felt herself raised gradually from the foam of the sea to higher regions.

"Where are they taking me?" asked she, and her words sounded just like the voices of those heavenly beings.

"Speak you to the daughters of air?" was the answer. "The mermaid has no immortal soul, and can only acquire that heavenly gift by winning the love of one of the sons of men; her immortality depends upon union with man. Neither do the daughters of air possess immortal souls, but they can acquire them by their own good deeds. We fly to hot countries, where the children of earth are sinking under sultry pestilential breezes—our fresh cooling breath revives them. We diffuse ourselves through the atmosphere; we perfume it with the delicious fragrance of flowers; and thus spread delight and health over the earth. By doing good in this manner for three hundred years, we win immortality, and receive a share of the eternal bliss of human beings. And thou, poor little mermaid! who, following the impulse of thine own heart, hast done and suffered so much, thou art now raised to the airy world of spirits, that by performing deeds of kindness for three hundred years, thou mayest acquire an immortal soul."

The little mermaid stretched out her transparent arms to the sun; and, for the first time in her life, tears moistened her eyes.

And now again all were awake and rejoicing in the ship; she saw the Prince, with his pretty bride; they had missed her; they looked sorrowfully down on the foamy waters, as if they knew she had plunged into the sea; unseen she kissed the bridegroom's forehead, smiled upon him, and then, with the rest of the children of air, soared high above the rosy cloud which was sailing so peacefully over the ship.

"After three hundred years we shall fly in the Kingdom of Heaven!"

"We may arrive there even sooner," whispered one of her sisters. "We fly invisibly through the dwellings of men, where there are children; and whenever we find a good child, who gives pleasure to his parents and deserves their love, the good God shortens our time of probation. No child is aware that we are flitting about his room, and that whenever joy draws from us a smile, a year is struck out of our three hundred. But when we see a rude naughty child, we weep bitter tears of sorrow, and every tear we shed adds a day to our time of probation."

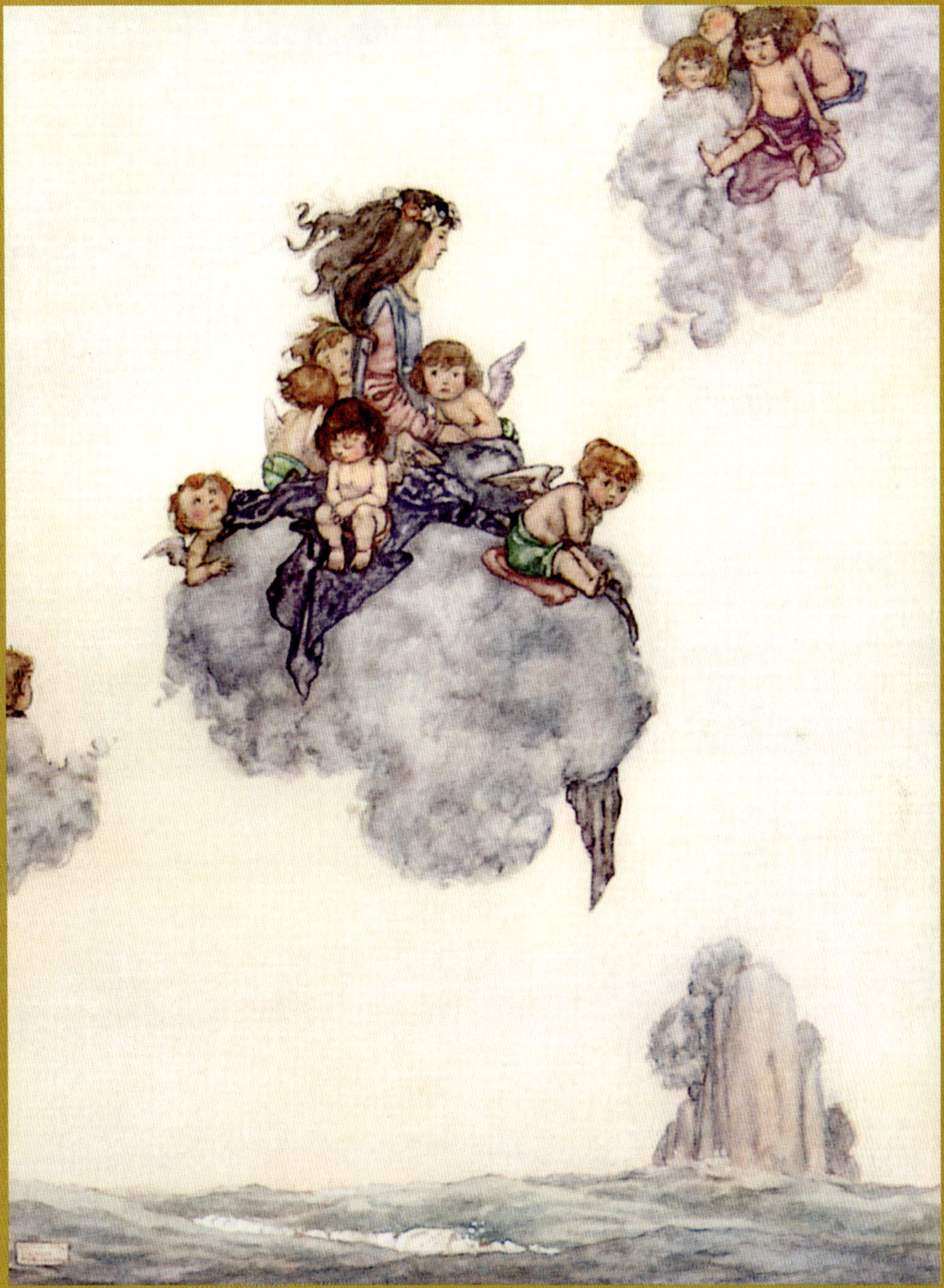

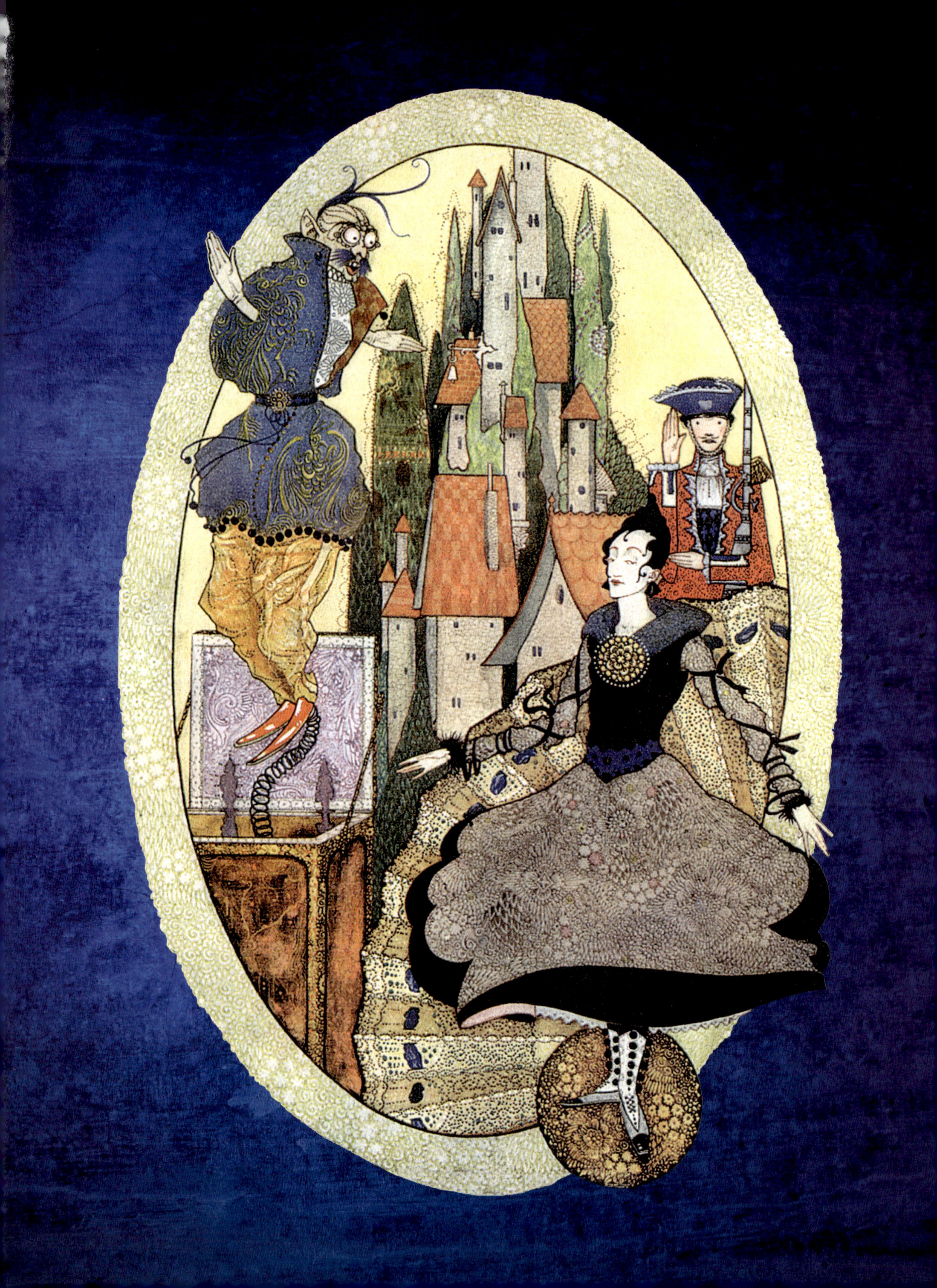

The Steadfast Tin Soldier

There were once five and twenty tin soldiers; they were all brothers, for they had all been born of one old tin spoon. They shouldered their muskets, and looked straight before them: their uniform was red and blue, and very splendid. The first thing they had heard in the world, when the lid was taken off their box, had been the words "Tin soldiers!" These words were uttered by a little boy, clapping his hands: the soldiers had been given to him, for it was his birthday; and now he put them upon the table. Each soldier was exactly like the rest; but one of them had been cast last of all, and there had not been enough tin to finish him; but he stood as firmly upon his one leg as the others on their two; and it was just this Soldier who became remarkable.

On the table on which they had been placed stood many other playthings, but the toy that attracted most attention was a neat castle of cardboard. Through the little windows one could see straight into the hall. Before the castle some little trees were placed round a little looking-glass, which was to represent a clear lake. Waxen swans swam on this lake, and were mirrored in it. This was all very pretty; but the prettiest of all was a little lady, who stood at the open door of the castle: she was also cut out in paper, but she had a dress of the clearest gauze, and a little narrow blue ribbon over her shoulders, that looked like a scarf; and in the middle of this ribbon was a shining tinsel rose as big as her whole face. The little lady stretched out both her arms, for she was a dancer; and then she lifted one leg so high that the Tin Soldier could not see it at all, and thought that, like himself, she had but one leg.

"That would be the wife for me," thought he; "but she is very grand. She lives in a castle, and I have only a box, and there are five-and-twenty of us in that. It is no place for her. But I must try to make acquaintance with her."

And then he lay down at full length behind a snuff-box which was on the table; there he could easily watch the little dainty lady, who continued to stand on one leg without losing her balance.

When the evening came, all the other tin soldiers were put into their box, and the people in the house went to bed. Now the toys began to play at "visiting," and at "war," and "giving balls." The tin soldiers rattled in their box, for they wanted to join, but could not lift the lid. The nutcracker threw somersaults, and the pencil amused itself on the table: there was so much noise that the canary woke up, and began to speak too, and even in verse. The only two who did not stir from their places were the Tin Soldier and the dancing lady: she stood straight up on the point of one of her toes, and stretched out both her arms; and he was just as enduring on his one leg; and he never turned his eyes away from her.

Now the clock struck twelve—and, bounce!—the lid flew off the snuff-box; but there was not snuff in it, but a little black Goblin: you see it was a trick.

"Tin Soldier!" said the Goblin, "don't stare at things that don't concern you."

But the Tin Soldier pretended not to hear him.

"Just you wait till to-morrow!" said the Goblin

But when the morning came, and the children got up, the Tin Soldier was placed in the window; and whether it was the Goblin or the draught that did it, all at once the window flew open, and the Soldier fell head over heels out of the third story. That was a terrible passage! He put his leg straight up, and stuck with his helmet downward and his bayonet between the paving-stones.

The servant-maid and the little boy came down directly to look for him, but though they almost trod upon him they could not see him. If the Soldier had cried out, "Here

The Steadfast Tin Soldier

I am!" they would have found him; but he did not think it fitting to call out loudly, because he was in uniform.

Now it began to rain; the drops soon fell thicker, and at last it came down in a complete stream. When the rain was past, two street boys came by.

"Just look!" said one of them, "there lies a tin soldier. He must come out and ride in the boat."

And they made a boat out of a newspaper, and put the Tin Soldier in the middle of it; and so he sailed down the gutter, and the two boys ran beside him and clapped their hands. Goodness preserve us! how the waves rose in that gutter, and how fast the stream ran! But then it had been a heavy rain. The paper boat rocked up and down, and sometimes turned round so rapidly that the Tin Soldier trembled; but he remained firm, and never changed countenance, and looked straight before him, and shouldered his musket.

All at once the boat went into a long drain, and it became as dark as if he had been in his box.

"Where am I going now?" he thought. "Yes, yes, that's the Goblin's fault. Ah! if the little lady only sat here with me in the boat, it might be twice as dark for what I should care."

Suddenly there came a great Water Rat, which lived under the drain.

"Have you a passport?" said the Rat. "Give me your passport."

But the Tin Soldier kept silence, and held his musket tighter than ever.

The boat went on, but the Rat came after it. Hu! how he gnashed his teeth, and called out to the bits of straw and wood:

"Hold him! hol him! he hasn't paid toll—he hasn't shown his passport!"

But the stream became stronger and stronger. The Tin Soldier could see the bright daylight where the arch ended; but he heard a roaring noise, which might well frighten a bolder man. Only think—just where the tunnel ended, the drain ran into a great canal; and for him that would have been as dangerous as for us to be carried down a great waterfall.

Now he was already so near it that he could not stop. The boat was carried out, the poor Tin Soldier stiffening himself as much as he could, and no one could say that he moved an eyelid. The boat whirled round three or four times, and was full of water to the very edge—it must sink. The Tin Soldier stood up to his neck in water, and the boat sank deeper and deeper, and the paper was loosened more and more; and now the water closed over the Soldier's head. Then he thought of the pretty little dancer, and how he should never see her again; and it sounded in the Soldier's ears:

> "Farewell, farewell, thou warrior brave,
> For this day thou must die!"

And now the paper parted, and the Tin Soldier fell out; but at that moment he was snapped up by a great fish.

Oh, how dark it was in that fish's body! It was darker yet than in the drain tunnel; and then it was very narrow too. But the Tin Soldier remained unmoved, and lay at full length shouldering his musket.

The fish swam to and fro; he made the most wonderful movements, and then became quite still. At last something flashed through him like lightning. The daylight shone quite clear, and a voice said aloud, "The Tin Soldier!" The fish had been caught, carried to market, bought, and taken into the kitchen, where the cook cut him open with a large knife. She seized the Soldier round the body with both her hands, and carried him into the room, where all were anxious to see the remarkable man who had traveled about in the inside of a fish; but the Tin Soldier was not at all proud. They placed him on the table, and there—no! What curious things may happen in the world! The Tin Soldier was in the very room in which he had been before! He saw the same children, and the same toys stood on the table; and there was the pretty castle with the graceful little dancer. She was still balancing herself on one leg, and held the other extended in the air. She was hardy too. That moved the Tin Soldier: he was very nearly weeping tin tears, but that would not have been proper. He looked at her, but they said nothing to each other.

Then one of the little boys took the Tin Soldier and flung him into the stove. He gave no reason for doing this. It must have been the fault of the Goblin in the snuff-box.

The Tin Soldier stood there quite illuminated, and felt a heat that was terrible; but whether this heat proceeded from the real fire or from love he did not know. The colors had quite gone off from him; but whether that had happened on the journey, or had been caused by grief, no one could say. He looked at the little lady, she looked at him, and he felt that he was melting; but he still stood firm, shouldering his musket. Then suddenly the door flew open, and the draught of air caught the dancer, and she flew like a sylph just into the stove to the Tin Soldier, and flashed up in a flame, and she was gone. Then the Tin Soldier melted down into a lump, and when the servant-maid took the ashes out next day, she found him in the shape of a little tin heart. But of the dancer nothing remained but the tinsel rose, and that was burned as black as a coal.

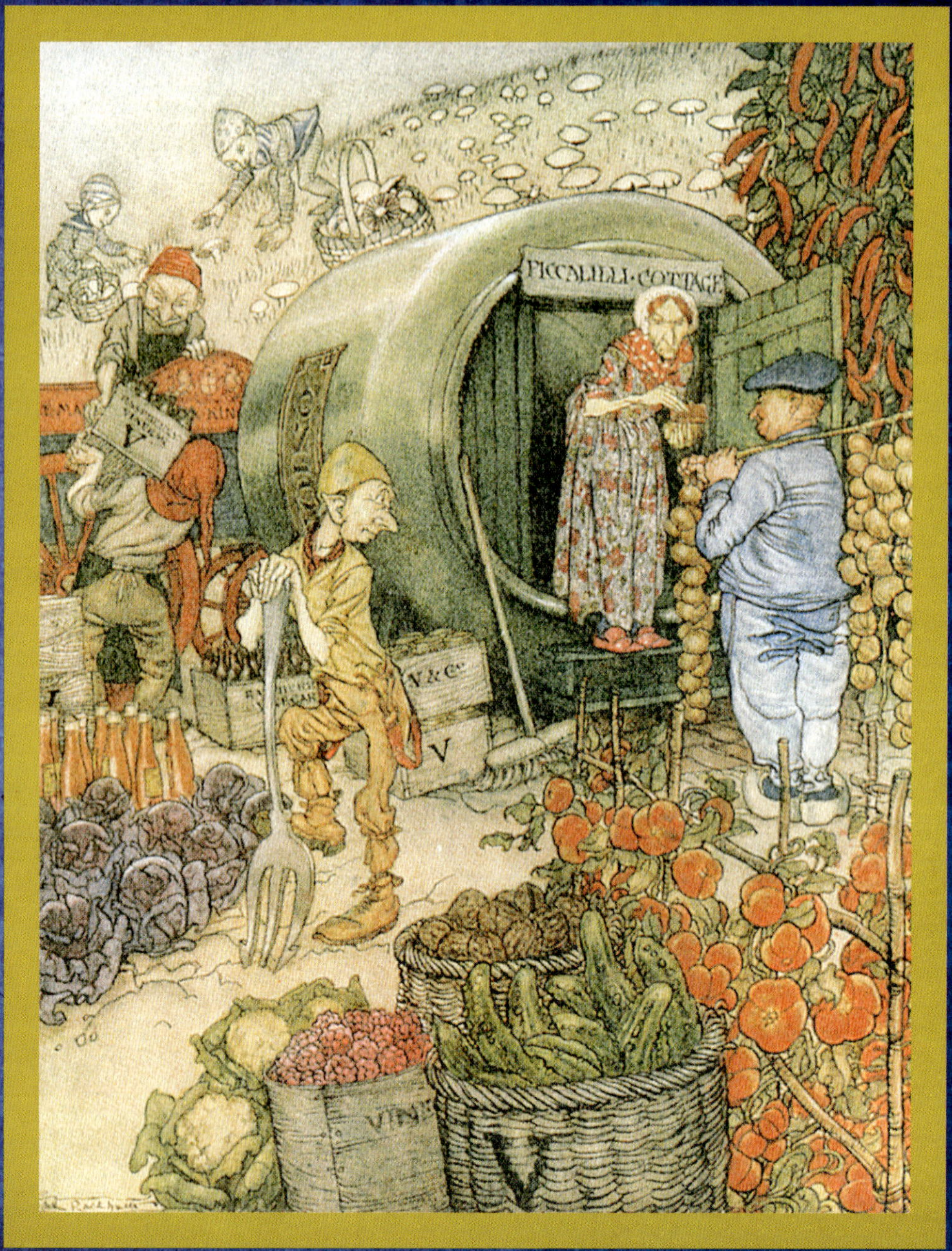
PICCALILLI·COTTAGE

Mr. and Mrs. Vinegar

Mr. and Mrs. Vinegar, a worthy couple, lived in a glass pickle-jar. The house, though small, was snug, and so light that each speck of dust on the furniture showed like a mole-hill; so while Mr. Vinegar tilled his garden with a pickle-fork and grew vegetables for pickling, Mrs. Vinegar, who was a sharp, bustling, tidy woman, swept, brushed, and dusted, brushed and dusted and swept to keep the house clean as a new pin. Now one day she lost her temper with a cobweb and swept so hard after it that bang! bang! the broom-handle went right through the glass, and crash! crash! clitter! clatter! there was the pickle-jar house about her ears all in splinters and bits.

She picked her way over these as best she might, and rushed into the garden.

"Oh, Vinegar, Vinegar!" she cried. "We are clean ruined and done for! Quit these vegetables! they won't be wanted! What is the use of pickles if you haven't a pickle-jar to put them in, and—I've broken ours—into little bits!" And with that she fell to crying bitterly.

But Mr. Vinegar was of different mettle; though a small man, he was a cheerful one, always looking at the best side of things, so he said, "Accidents will happen, lovey! But there are as good pickle-bottles in the shop as ever came out of it. All we need is money to buy another. So let us go out into the world and seek our fortunes."

"But what about the furniture?" sobbed Mrs. Vinegar.

"I will take the door of the house with me, lovey," quoth Mr. Vinegar stoutly. "Then no one will be able to open it, will they?"

Mrs. Vinegar did not quite see how this fact would mend matters, but, being a good wife, she held her peace. So off they trudged into the world to seek fortune, Mr. Vinegar bearing the door on his back like a snail carries its house.

Well, they walked all day long, but not a brass farthing did they make, and when night fell, they found themselves in a dark, thick forest. Now Mrs. Vinegar, for all she was a smart, strong woman, was tired to death, and filled with fear of wild beasts, so she began once more to cry bitterly; but Mr. Vinegar was cheerful as ever.

"Don't alarm yourself, lovey," he said. "I will climb into a tree, fix the door firmly in a fork, and you can sleep there as safe and comfortable as in your own bed."

So he climbed the tree, fixed the door, and Mrs. Vinegar lay down on it, and being dead tired was soon fast asleep. But her weight tilted the door sideways, so, after a time, Mr. Vinegar, being afraid she might slip off, sat down on the other side to balance her and keep watch.

Now in the very middle of the night, just as he was beginning to nod, what should happen but that a band of robbers should meet beneath that very tree in order to divide their spoils. Mr. Vinegar could hear every word said quite distinctly, and began to tremble like an aspen as he listened to the terrible deeds the thieves had done to gain their ends.

"Don't shake so!" murmured Mrs. Vinegar, half asleep. "You'll have me off the bed."

"I'm not shaking, lovey," whispered back Mr. Vinegar in a quaking voice. "It is only the wind in the trees."

But for all his cheerfulness he was not really very brave inside, so he went on trembling and shaking and shaking and trembling, till, just as the robbers were beginning to parcel out the money, he actually shook the door right out of the tree-fork, and down it came—with Mrs. Vinegar still asleep upon it—right on top of the robbers' heads!

As you may imagine, they thought the sky had fallen, and made off as fast as their legs would carry them, leaving their booty behind them. But Mr. Vinegar, who had saved himself from the fall by clinging to a branch, was far too frightened to go down in the dark to see what had happened. So up in the tree he sat like a big bird until dawn came.

Then Mrs. Vinegar woke, rubbed her eyes, yawned, and said, "Where am I?"

"On the ground, lovey," answered Mr. Vinegar, scrambling down.

And when they lifted up the door, what do you think they found?

One robber squashed flat as a pancake and forty golden guineas all scattered about!

My goodness! How Mr. and Mrs. Vinegar jumped for joy!

"Now, Vinegar!" said his wife when they had gathered up all the gold pieces, "I will tell you what we must do. You must go to the next market-town and buy a cow; for, see you, money makes the mare to go, truly; but it also goes itself. Now a cow won't run away, but will give us milk and butter, which we can sell. So we shall live in comfort for the rest of our days."

"What a head you have, lovey," said Mr. Vinegar admiringly, and started off on his errand.

"Mind you make a good bargain," bawled his wife after him.

"I always do," bawled back Mr. Vinegar. "I made a good bargain when I married such a clever wife, and I made a better one when I shook her down from the tree. I am the happiest man alive!"

So he trudged on, laughing and jingling the forty gold pieces in his pocket.

Now the first thing he saw in the market was an old red cow.

"I am in luck to-day," he thought, "that is the very beast for me. I shall be the happiest of men if I get that cow." So he went up to the owner, jingling the gold in his pocket.

"What will you take for your cow?" he asked.

And the owner of the cow, seeing he was a simpleton, said, "What you've got in your pocket."

"Done!" said Mr. Vinegar, handed over the forty guineas and led off the cow, marching her up and down the market, much against her will, to show off his bargain.

Now, as he drove it about, proud as Punch, he noticed a man who was playing the bagpipes. He was followed about by a crowd of children who danced to the music, and a perfect shower of pennies fell into his cap every time he held it out.

"Ho, ho!" thought Mr. Vinegar. "That is an easier way of earning a livelihood than by driving about a beast of a cow! Then the feeding, and the milking, and the churning! Ah, I should be the happiest man alive if I had those bagpipes!"

So he went up to the musician and said, "What will you take for your bagpipes?"

"Well," replied the musician, seeing he was a simpleton, "it is a beautiful instrument and I make so much money by it, that I cannot take anything less than that red cow."

"Done!" cried Mr. Vinegar in a hurry, lest the man should repent of his offer.

So the musician walked off with the red cow, and Mr. Vinegar tried to play the bagpipes. But, alas, and alack! Though he blew till he almost burst, not a sound could he make at first, and when he did at last, it was such a terrific squeal and screech that all the children ran away frightened, and the people stopped their ears.

But he went on and on, trying to play a tune, and never earning anything, save hootings and peltings, until his fingers were almost frozen with the cold, when of course the noise he made on the bagpipes was worse than ever.

Then he noticed a man who had on a pair of warm gloves, and he said to himself, "Music is impossible when one's fingers are frozen. I believe I should be the happiest man alive if I had those gloves."

So he went up to the owner and said, "You seem, sir, to have a very good pair of gloves." And the man replied, "Truly, sir, my hands are as warm as toast this bitter November day."

That quite decided Mr. Vinegar, and he asked at once what the owner would take for them; and the owner, seeing he was a simpleton, said, "As your hands seem frozen, sir, I will, as a favor, let you have them for your bagpipes."

"Done!" cried Mr. Vinegar, delighted, and made the exchange.

Then he set off to find his wife, quite pleased with himself. "Warm hands, warm heart!" he thought. "I'm the happiest man alive!"

But as he trudged he grew very, very tired, and at last began to limp. Then he saw a man coming along the road with a stout stick.

"I should be the happiest man alive if I had that stick," he thought. "What is the use of warm hands if your feet ache!" So he said to the man with the stick, "What will you take for your stick?" and the man, seeing he was a simpleton, replied:

Mr. and Mrs. Vinegar

"Well, I don't want to part with my stick, but as you are so pressing I'll oblige you, as a friend, for those warm gloves you are wearing."

"Done for you!" cried Mr. Vinegar delightedly; and trudged off with the stick, chuckling to himself over his good bargain.

But as he went along a magpie fluttered out of the hedge and sat on a branch in front of him, and chuckled and laughed as magpies do. "What are you laughing at?" asked Mr. Vinegar.

"At you, forsooth!" chuckled the magpie, fluttering just a little further. "At you, Mr. Vinegar, you foolish man—you simpleton—you blockhead! You bought a cow for forty guineas when she wasn't worth ten, you exchanged her for bagpipes you couldn't play—you changed the bagpipes for a pair of gloves, and the pair of gloves for a miserable stick. Ho, ho! Ha, ha! So you've nothing to show for your forty guineas save a stick you might have cut in any hedge. Ah, you fool! you simpleton! you blockhead!"

And the magpie chuckled, and chuckled, and chuckled in such guffaws, fluttering from branch to branch as Mr. Vinegar trudged along, that at last he flew into a violent rage and flung his stick at the bird. And the stick stuck in a tree out of his reach; so he had to go back to his wife without anything at all.

But he was glad the stick had stuck in a tree, for Mrs. Vinegar's hands were quite hard enough.

When it was all over Mr. Vinegar said cheerfully, "You are too violent, lovey. You broke the pickle-jar, and now you've nearly broken every bone in my body. I think we had better turn over a new leaf and begin afresh. I shall take service as a gardener, and you can go as a housemaid until we have enough money to buy a new pickle-jar. There are as good ones in the shop as ever came out of it."

And that is the story of Mr. and Mrs. Vinegar.

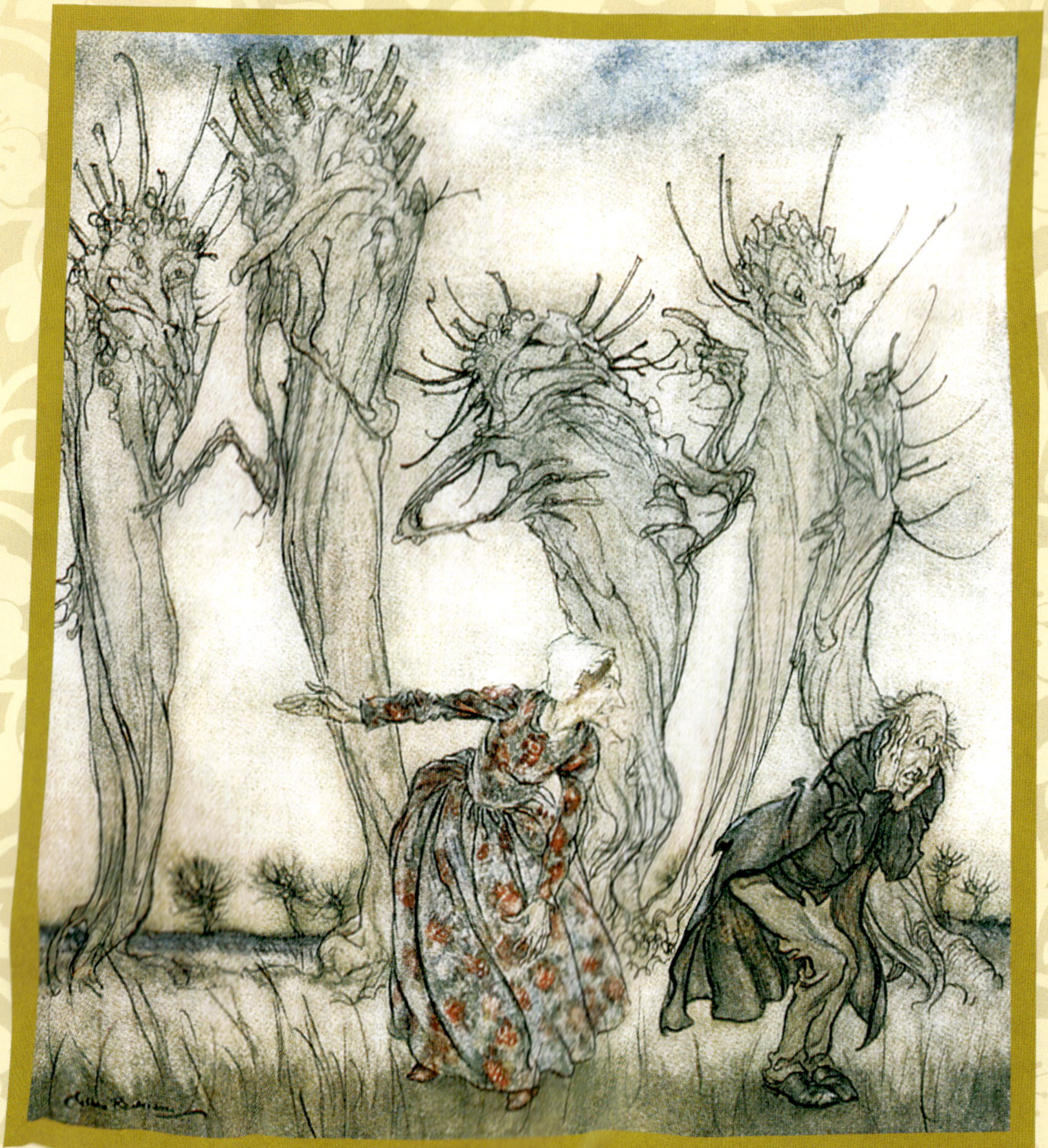

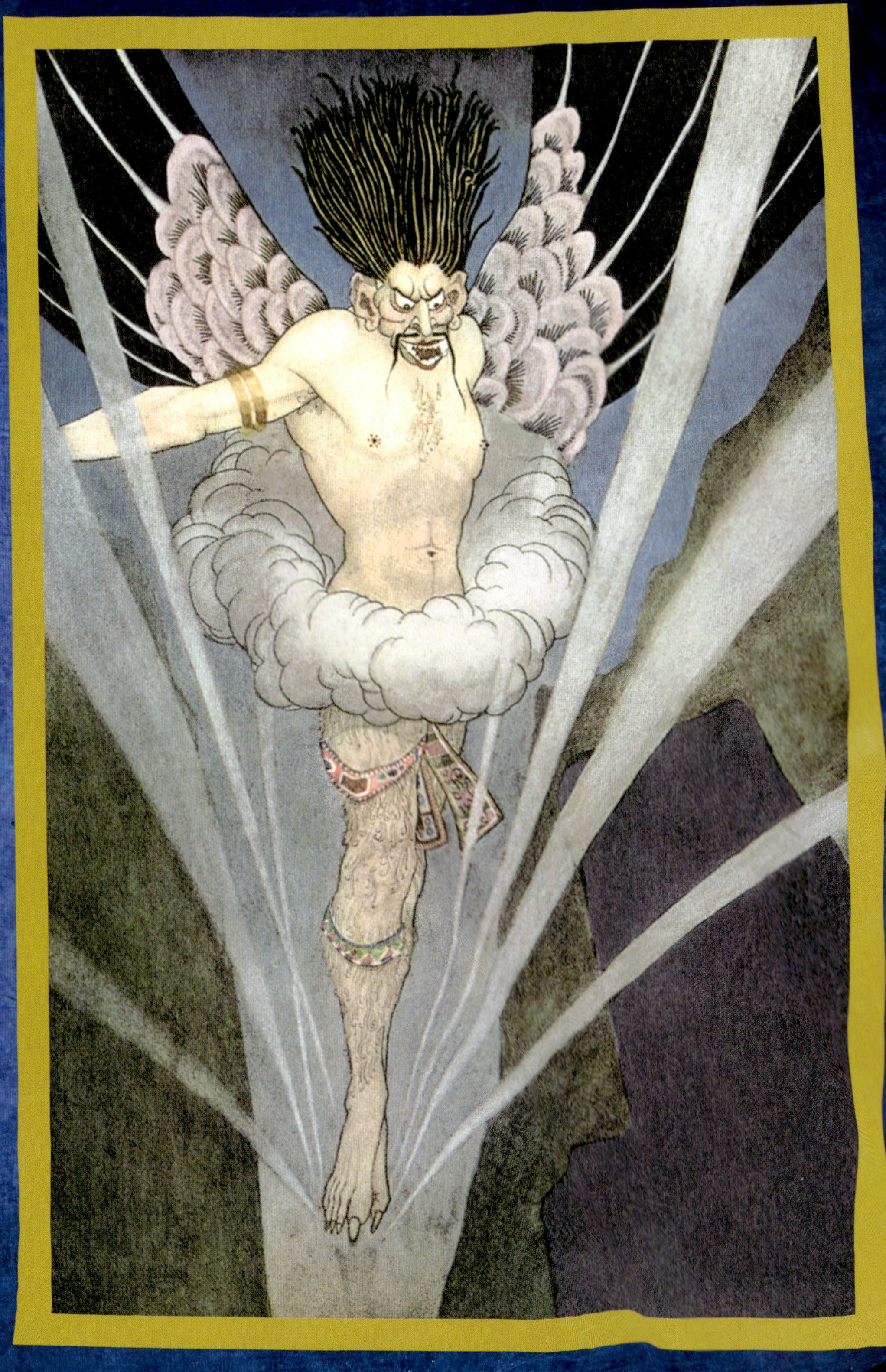

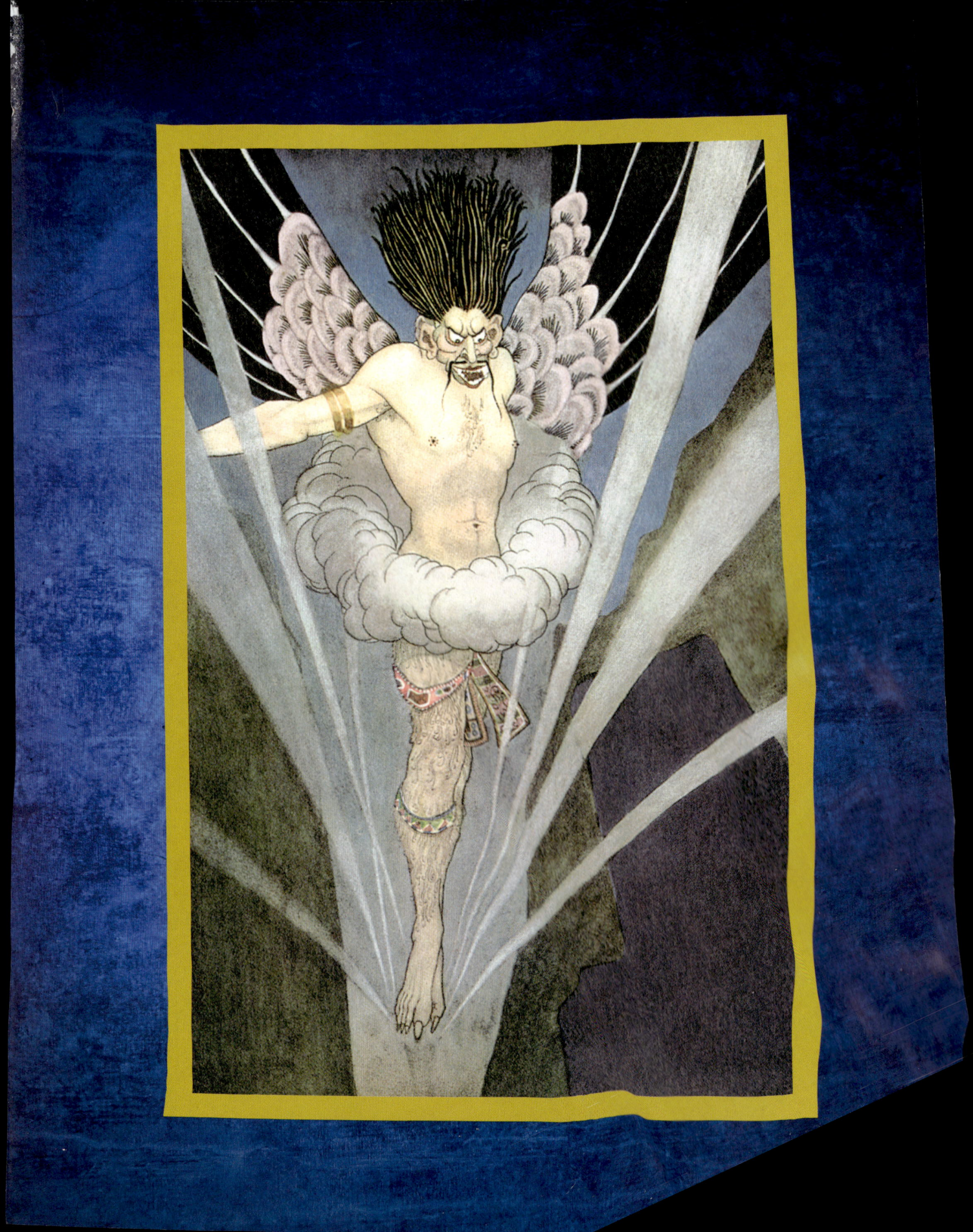

Aladdin and the Magic Lamp

Once there lived a tailor, by name Mustapha, in one of the wealthy cities of China, who was so poor that he could hardly maintain himself and his family, which consisted only of a wife and son.

His son, who was called Aladdin, was a good-for-nothing, and caused his father much trouble, for he used to go out early in the morning, and stay out all day, playing in the streets with idle children of his own age.

When he was old enough to learn a trade, his father took him into his own shop, and taught him how to use his needle, but to no purpose; for as soon as his back turned, Aladdin was gone for that day. Mustapha chastised him, but Aladdin was incorrigible, and his father was so much troubled about him that he became ill, and died in a few months.

Aladdin, no longer restrained by the fear of his father, gave himself entirely over to his idle habits, and was never out of the streets. This course he followed till he was fifteen years old, without giving his mind to any useful pursuit. As he was one day playing in the street, with his vagabond associates, a stranger passing by stood and watched him closely. The stranger was a sorcerer, known as the African magician, and had been but two days in the city.

The African magician, perceiving that Aladdin was a boy well-suited for his purpose, made inquiries about him; and, after he had learned his history, called him aside, and said: Child, was not your father called Mustapha the tailor? Yes, sir, answered the boy, but he has been dead a long time.

At these words, the African magician threw his arms about Aladdin's neck, and kissing him with tears in his eyes, said, I am your uncle; your worthy father was my own brother. You are so like him that I knew you at first sight. Then he gave Aladdin a handful of small coins, saying, Go, my son, to your mother, give my love to her, and tell her that I will visit her to-morrow, that I may see where my good brother lived so long, and ended his days.

Aladdin ran to his mother, overjoyed at his uncle's gift. Mother, said he, have I an uncle? No, child, replied his mother, you have no uncle by your father's side, or mine. I am just now come, said Aladdin, from a man who says he is my uncle, my father's brother. He cried and kissed me when I told him my father was dead, and gave me money; also bade me give you his love and say that he will come to see you, that he may be shown the house wherein my father lived and died. Indeed, child, replied the mother, your father had a brother, but he has been dead a long time, and I never heard of another.

The next day Aladdin's uncle found him playing in another part of the town, and embracing him as before, put two pieces of gold into his hand, and said to him, Carry this, child, to your mother, tell her that I will come and see her to-night, and bid her get us something for supper; but first show me the house where you live.

Aladdin showed the magician the house, and carried the two pieces of gold to his mother, and when he had told her of his uncle's intention, she went out and bought provisions, and borrowed various utensils of her neighbors. She spent the whole day in preparing the supper; and at night, when it was ready, said to her son, Perhaps your uncle will not find the way to our house; go and bring him with you if you meet him.

Aladdin was ready to start, when the magician came in loaded with wine, and all sorts of fruits, for dessert. After the African magician had given what he brought into Aladdin's hands, he saluted his mother, and desired her to show him the place where his brother Mustapha used to sit on the sofa; and when she had so done, he bowed his head down, and kissed it, crying out repeatedly with tears in his eyes, My poor brother! How unhappy am I not to have come soon enough to give you one last embrace. Aladdin's mother desired

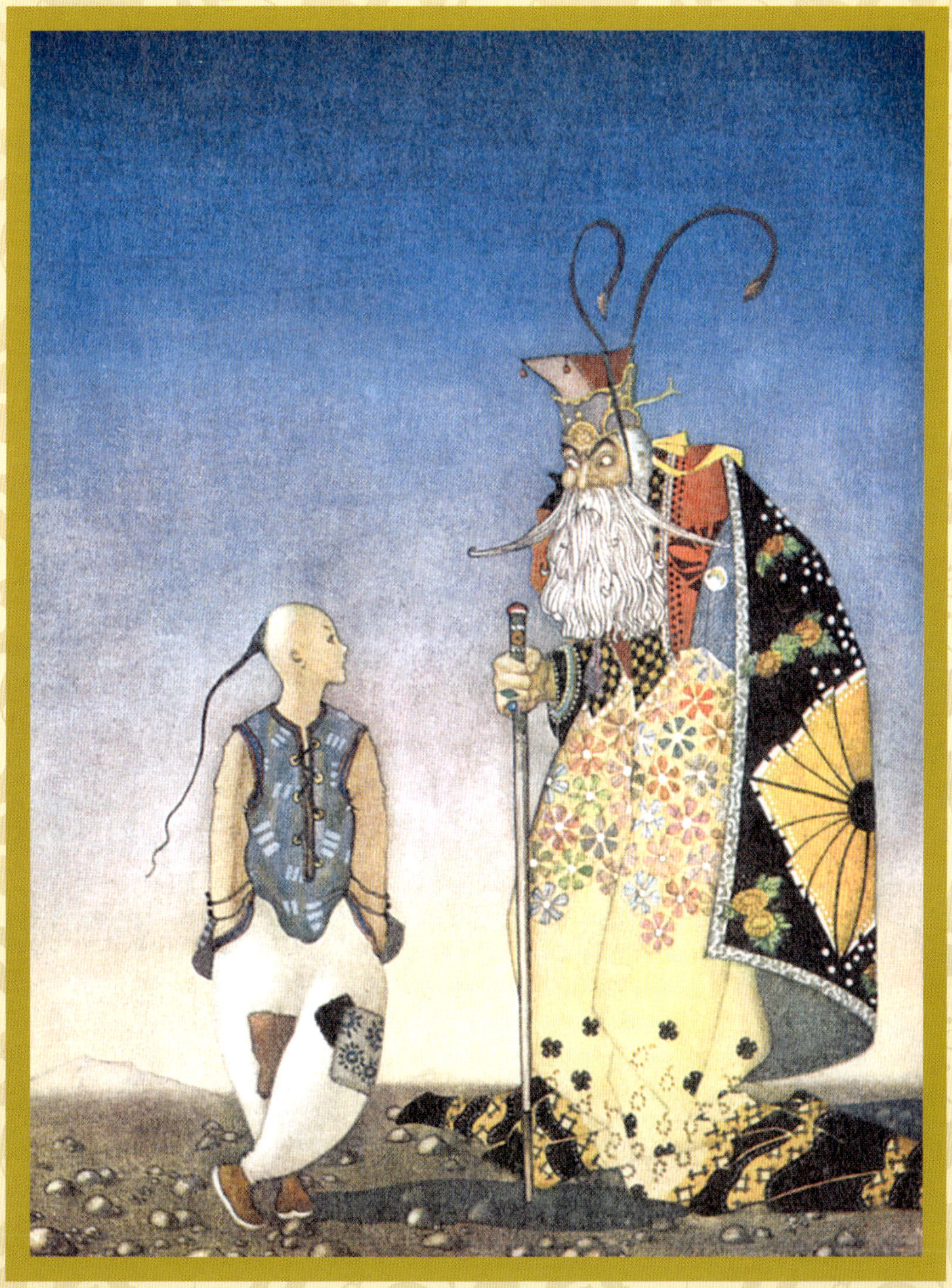

him to sit down in the same place, but he declined. No, said he, I shall not do that; but let me sit opposite to it, that although I may not see the master of a family so dear to me, I may at least have the pleasure of beholding the place where he used to sit.

When the magician had sat down, he began to enter into discourse with Aladdin's mother: My good sister, said he, do not be surprised at your never having seen me all the time you have been married to my brother Mustapha, of happy memory. I have been forty years absent from this country; and during that time have traveled into the Indies, Persia, Arabia, Syria, and Egypt, and afterwards crossed over into Africa, where I settled. Being desirous to see my native land once more, and to embrace my brother, I made the necessary preparations, and set out. It was a long and painful journey, but my greatest grief was the news of my brother's death. But it is a comfort for me to find, as it were, my brother in a son, who has his most remarkable features.

The African magician perceiving that the widow began to weep at the remembrance of her husband, changed the conversation, and turning towards her son, asked him his name, and what business he followed.

At this question the youth hung down his head, and was not a little abashed when his mother answered, Aladdin is an idle fellow. His father when alive, strove to teach him his trade, but could not succeed. Since his death he does nothing but idles away his time in the streets, as you saw him, without considering he is no longer a child; and if you do not make him ashamed of it, I despair of his ever coming to any good. For my part, I am resolved one of these days to turn him out of doors, and let him provide for himself.

After these words, Aladdin's mother burst into tears; and the magician said, This is not well, nephew; you must think of helping yourself, and getting your livelihood. There are many sorts of trades: if you have any choice, I will endeavor to help you. Or if you have no mind to learn any handicraft, I will take a shop for you, furnish it with all sorts of fine stuffs and linens; and with the money you make of them lay in fresh goods, and then you will live in an honorable way. Tell me freely what you think of my proposal; you shall always find me ready to keep my word.

This plan greatly pleased Aladdin, who hated work. He told the magician he had a greater inclination to that business than to any other, and that he should be much obliged to him for his kindness. Very well, said the African magician, I will carry you with me to-morrow, clothe you as handsomely as the best merchants in the city, and afterwards we will open a shop.

The widow, who never till then could believe that the magician was her husband's brother, no longer doubted after his promises of kindness to her son. She thanked him for his good intentions; and after having exhorted Aladdin to render himself worthy of his uncle's favor by good behavior, served up supper, and afterwards the magician took his leave, and retired.

He came again the next day, as he had promised, and took Aladdin with him to a merchant, who sold all sorts of clothes, and a variety of fine stuffs. He bade Aladdin choose those he preferred, and paid for them immediately.

Aladdin was much delighted by his new dress, and thanked his uncle warmly. Then the magician replied: As you are soon to be a merchant, it is proper you should frequent these shops, and be acquainted with them. He then showed him the largest and finest mosques, carried him to the khans, and afterwards to the sultan's palace, where he had free access; and at last brought him to his own khan, where meeting with some merchants he had become acquainted with since his arrival, he introduced his pretended nephew to them.

This entertainment lasted till night, when Aladdin would have taken leave of his uncle to go home; the magician would not let him go by himself, but conducted him to his mother, who, as soon as she saw him so well dressed, was transported with joy, and bestowed a thousand blessings upon the magician.

Early the next morning the magician took Aladdin out, saying that he would show him the country road, and that on the following day he would purchase the shop. He then led him out at one of the gates of the city, to some magnificent palaces, to each of which belonged beautiful gardens, into which anybody might enter. At every building he came to, he asked Aladdin if he did not think it fine; and the youth was ready to answer when any one presented itself, crying out, Here is a finer house, uncle, than any we have seen yet. By this artifice, the cunning magician led Aladdin some way into the country; and as he meant to carry him farther, to execute his design, he took an opportunity to sit down in one of the gardens on the brink of a fountain of clear water, which discharged itself by a lion's mouth of bronze into a basin, pretending to be tired: Come, nephew, said he, you must be weary as well as I; let us rest ourselves, and we shall be better able to pursue our walk.

The magician then pulled from his girdle a handkerchief with cakes and fruit, which he had provided, and laid them on the edge of the basin. While they were partaking of this short repast the magician spoke gravely to his nephew, urging him to give up his evil companions and to seek the company of wise men from whose society he would benefit. When he had finished his advice they resumed their walk through the gardens. The African magician drew Aladdin beyond the gardens, and crossed the country, till they reached the mountains.

At last they arrived between two mountains of moderate height, and equal size, divided by a narrow valley, which was the place where the magician intended to execute the design that had brought him from Africa to China. We will go no farther now, said he. I will show you here some extraordinary things, which you will thank me to have seen: but while I strike a light, gather up all the loose dry sticks you can see, to kindle a fire.

Aladdin collected a great heap; the magician set them on fire; and when they were in a blaze, threw in some incense, and pronounced several magical words which Aladdin did not understand.

At the same time the earth trembling, opened just before the magician, and uncovered a stone, with a brass ring fixed in the middle. Aladdin was so frightened, that he would have run away, but the magician caught hold of him, abused him, and gave him such a box on the ear, that he knocked him down. Aladdin got up trembling, and with tears in his eyes, said, What have I done, uncle, to be treated in this severe manner? I supply the place of your father, replied the magician, and you ought to make no reply. But, child, added he, softening, do not be afraid; for I shall not ask anything of you, but that you obey me punctually, if you would reap the advantages which I intend you. Know then, that under this stone there is hidden a treasure, destined to be yours, and which will make you richer than the greatest monarch in the world. No person but yourself is permitted to lift this stone, or enter the cave; so you must punctually execute what I may command, for it is a matter of great consequence both to you and me.

Aladdin and the Magic Lamp

Aladdin, amazed at all he saw and heard, forgot what was past, and rising, said, Well, uncle, what is to be done? Command me, I am ready to obey. I am overjoyed, child, said the magician, embracing him. Take hold of the ring, and lift up that stone. Indeed, uncle, replied Aladdin, I am not strong enough; you must help me. Then we shall be able to do nothing, replied the magician. Take hold of the ring, pronounce the names of your father and grandfather, then lift it up, and you will find it will come easily. Aladdin did as the magician bade him, raised the stone with ease, and laid it on one side.

When the stone was pulled up, there appeared a little door, and steps to go down lower. Descend into the cave, said the magician, and you will find three great halls, in each of which you will see four large brass cisterns placed on each side, full of gold and silver; but take care you do not meddle with them. Before you enter the first hall, be sure to tuck up your robe, wrap it about you, and then pass through the second into the third without stopping. Above all things, have a care that you do not touch the walls, so much as with your clothes; for if you do, you will die instantly. At the end of the third hall, you will find a door which opens into a garden planted with fine trees loaded with fruit; walk across the garden to five steps that will bring you upon a terrace, where you will see a lighted lamp in a niche before you. Take the lamp down, and extinguish it. When you have thrown away the wick, and poured out the liquor, put it in your girdle and bring it to me. Do not be afraid that the liquor will spoil your clothes, for it is not oil; and the lamp will be dry as soon as it is thrown out.

After these words, the magician drew a ring off his finger, and put it on one of Aladdin's, telling him that it was a talisman. Then he added, Go down boldly, and we shall both be rich all our lives.

Aladdin descended, and found the three halls just as the African magician had described. He went through them with all the precaution the fear of death could inspire, crossed the garden without stopping, took down the lamp from the niche, emptied it, and put it in his girdle. As he came down from the terrace, he stopped in the garden to observe the trees, which were loaded with extraordinary fruit, of different colors on each tree. Some bore fruit entirely white, and some clear and transparent as crystal; some pale red, and others deeper; some green, blue, and purple, and others yellow: in

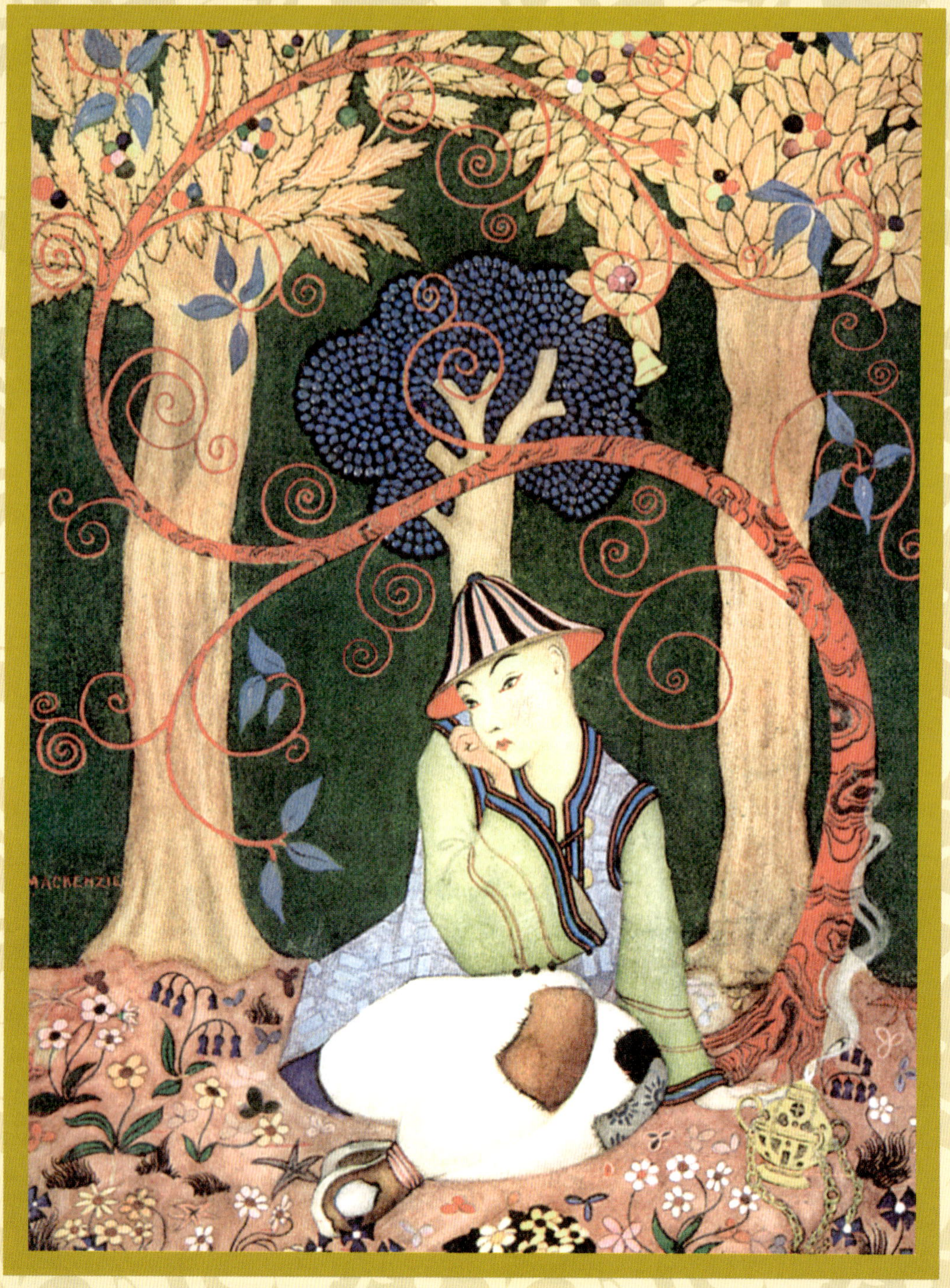
MACKENZIE

short, there was fruit of all colors. The white were pearls; the clear and transparent, diamonds; the deep red, rubies; the paler, ballas rubies; the green, emeralds; the blue, turquoises; the purple, amethysts; and the yellow, sapphires. Aladdin was ignorant of their worth, and would have preferred figs and grapes, or any other fruits. But thinking them pretty, he collected as many of each sort as he could carry, and filled his purses and the flaps of his robe.

Aladdin having thus loaded himself with riches he knew not the value of, returned through the three halls with the same precaution, and soon arrived at the mouth of the cave, where the magician expected him with the utmost impatience. As soon as Aladdin saw him, he cried out, Pray, uncle, lend me your hand, to help me out. Give me the lamp first, replied the magician; it will be troublesome to you. Indeed, uncle, answered Aladdin, I cannot now; but I will as soon as I am up. The African magician was resolved to have the lamp before he would help him up; and Aladdin, who had encumbered himself so much with his fruit that he could not well get at it, refused to give it to him till he was out of the cave. The magician, provoked at this obstinate refusal, flew into a passion, threw a little of his incense into the fire, and pronounced two magical words. Immediately the stone moved into its place, with the earth over it in the same manner as it lay at the arrival of the magician and Aladdin.

This action plainly showed that the magician was not his uncle, but some adventurer who sought to possess the lamp, of which he had read in the magic books. And, moreover, it was but recently that he had learned where the wonderful lamp was concealed. He had also discovered that he must receive the lamp from another's hand, so he chanced to select Aladdin, whose life he reckoned as nought.

When the magician saw that all his hopes were frustrated, he returned the same day to Africa; but kept away from the town, lest Aladdin's absence should be noticed and questions asked. When Aladdin found himself shut in, he cried, and called out to his uncle, to tell him he was ready to give him the lamp; but in vain, since his cries could not be heard. He descended to the bottom of the steps, with a design to get into the garden, but the door, which was opened before by enchantment, was now shut by the same means. He then redoubled his cries and tears, sat down on the steps, without any hopes of ever seeing light again, and in a melancholy certainty of passing from the present darkness into that of a speedy death. Clasping his hands with an entire resignation to the will of God, he said, There is no strength or power but in the great and high God, and in joining his hands he rubbed the ring which the magician had put on his finger. Immediately a genie of frightful aspect rose out of the earth, his head reaching the roof of the vault, and said to him, What wouldst thou have? I am ready to obey thee as thy slave, and the slave of all who may possess the ring on thy finger; I, and the other slaves of that ring.

At another time, Aladdin would have been so frightened at the sight of so extraordinary a figure that he would not have been able to speak; but the danger he was in made him answer without hesitation, Deliver me from this place. He had no sooner spoken these words, than he found himself on the very spot where the magician had caused the earth to open. Aladdin was greatly astonished; and, returning good thanks to find himself once more in the world, he made the best of his way home. When he got within his mother's door, the joy to see her and his weakness for want of sustenance for three days made him faint, and he remained for a long time as dead. As soon as he recovered, he related to his mother all that had happened, and she was very bitter in her execrations of the magician. Aladdin then retired to rest, and slept till late the next morning; when the first thing he said to his mother was, that he wanted something to eat. Alas! child, said she, I have not a bit of bread to give you; but I have a little cotton, which I have spun, I will go and sell it, buy bread, and something for our dinner. Mother, replied Aladdin, keep your cotton for another time, and give me the lamp I brought home with me yesterday; I will go and sell it, and the money I shall get for it will serve both for breakfast and dinner, and perhaps supper too.

Aladdin's mother took the lamp, and said to her son, Here it is, but it is very dirty; if it was a little cleaner I believe it would bring something more. She took some fine sand and water to clean it; but had no sooner begun to rub it, than in an instant a hideous genie of gigantic size appeared before her, and said in a voice like thunder, What wouldst thou have? I am ready to obey thee as thy slave, and the slave of all those who have that lamp in their hands; I, and the other slaves of the lamp.

Aladdin's mother, terrified at the sight of the genie, fainted; when Aladdin, who had seen such a phantom in the cavern, snatched the lamp out of his mother's hand,

and said to the genie boldly, I am hungry, bring me something to eat. The genie disappeared immediately, and in an instant returned with a large silver tray, holding twelve covered dishes of the same metal, which contained the most delicious viands; six large white bread cakes on two plates, two flagons of wine, and two silver cups. All these he placed upon a carpet, and disappeared: this was done before Aladdin's mother recovered from her swoon.

Aladdin fetched some water, and sprinkled it in her face, to restore her; and it was not long before she came to herself. Mother, said Aladdin, do not be alarmed: here is what will put you in heart, and at the same time satisfy my extreme hunger.

His mother was much surprised to see the repast spread. Child, said she, to whom are we obliged for this great plenty and liberality? Has the sultan been made acquainted with our poverty, and had compassion on us? It is no matter, mother, said Aladdin, let us sit down and eat; for you have as much need of a good breakfast as myself; when we have done, I will tell you. Accordingly both mother and son sat down, and ate with the better relish as the table was so well furnished. But all the time Aladdin's mother could not forbear looking at and admiring the tray and dishes, though she could not judge whether they were silver or any other metal, and the novelty more than the value attracted her attention.

When Aladdin's mother had taken away and set by what was left, she went and sat down by her son on the sofa, saying: I expect now that you should satisfy my impatience, and tell me exactly what passed between the genie and you while I was in a swoon; which he readily complied with.

She was in as great amazement at what her son told her, as at the appearance of the genie; and said to him: But, son, what have we to do with genii? How came that vile genie to address himself to me, and not to you, to whom he had appeared before in the cave? Mother, answered Aladdin, the genie you saw is not the one who appeared to me, though he resembles him in size; no, they had quite different persons and habits: they belong to different masters. If you remember, he that I first saw called himself the slave of the ring on my finger; and this you saw, called himself the slave of the lamp you had in your hand: but I believe you did not hear him, for I think you fainted as soon as he began to speak.

What! cried the mother, was your lamp then the occasion of the genie's addressing himself rather to me than to you? Ah! my son, take it out of my sight, and put it where you please. I had rather you would sell it, than run the hazard of being frightened to death again by touching it: and if you would take my advice, you would part also with the ring, and not have anything to do with genii, who, as our prophet has told us, are only devils.

With your leave, mother, replied Aladdin, I shall now take care how I sell a lamp, which may be so serviceable both to you and me. That false and wicked magician would not have undertaken so tedious a journey, if he had not known the value of this wonderful lamp. And since chance hath given it to us, let us make a profitable use of it, without making any great show, and exciting the envy and jealousy of our neighbors. However, since the genii frighten you so much, I will take it out of your sight, and put it where I may find it when I want it. The ring I cannot resolve to part with; for without that you had never seen me again; and though I am alive now, perhaps, if it was gone, I might not be so some moments hence; therefore I hope you will give me leave to keep it, and to wear it always on my finger. She replied, that he might do what he pleased: for her part, she would have nothing to do with genii, and never say anything more about them.

By the next night they had eaten all the provisions the genie had brought: and the next day Aladdin, who could not bear the thoughts of hunger, putting one of the silver dishes under his vest, went out early to sell it, and addressing himself to a merchant whom he met in the streets, took him aside, and pulling out the plate, asked I him if he would buy it. The cunning merchant took the dish, examined it, and as soon as he found that it was good silver, asked Aladdin at how much he valued it. Aladdin, who knew not its value, and never had been used to such traffic, told him he would trust to his judgment and honor. The merchant was somewhat confounded at this plain dealing; and doubting whether Aladdin understood the material or the full value of what he offered to sell, took a piece of gold out of his purse and gave it him, though it was but the sixtieth part of the worth of the plate. Aladdin, taking the money very eagerly, retired with so much haste, that the merchant, not content with the exorbitancy of his profit, was vexed he had not penetrated into his ignorance,

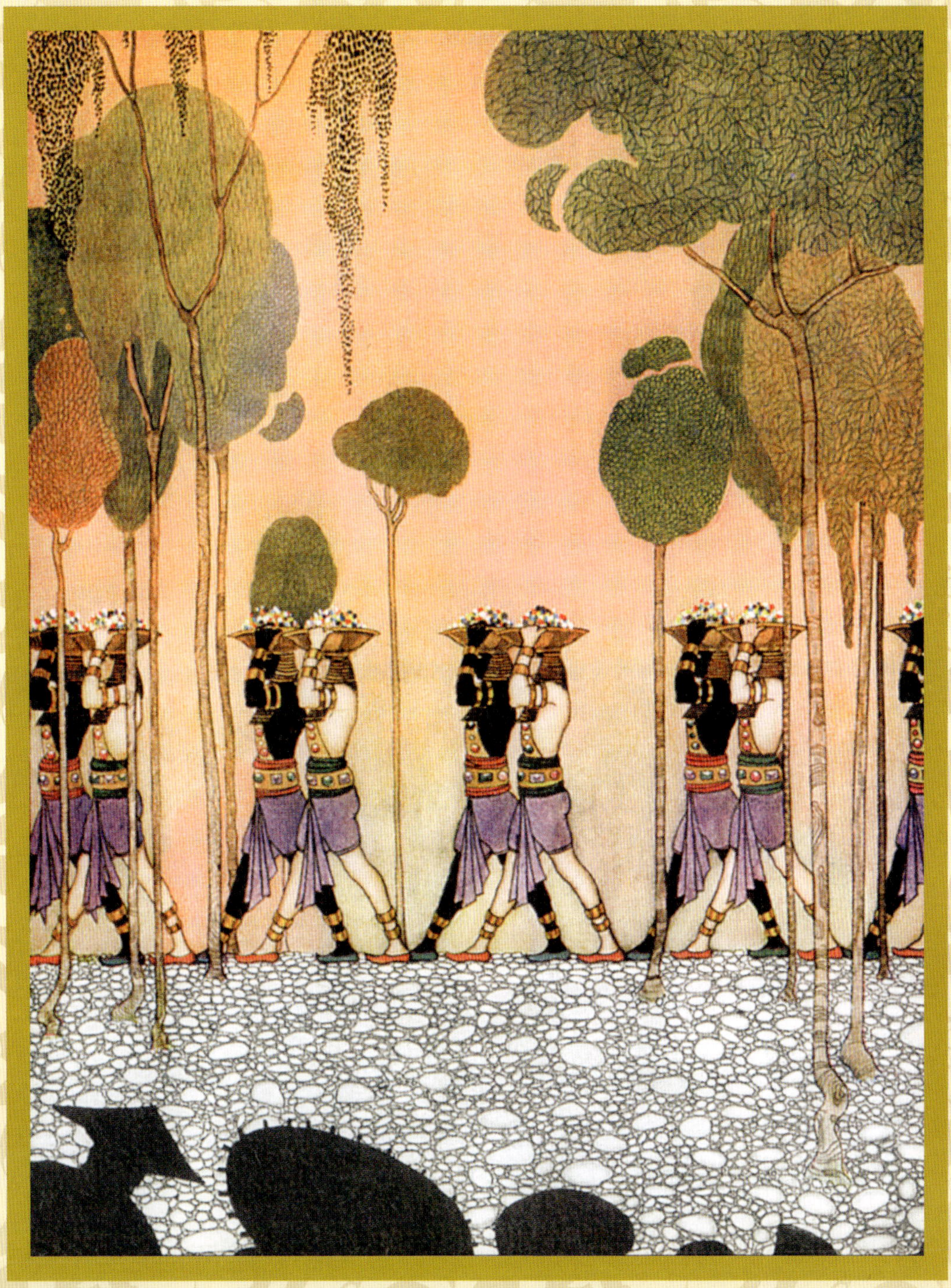

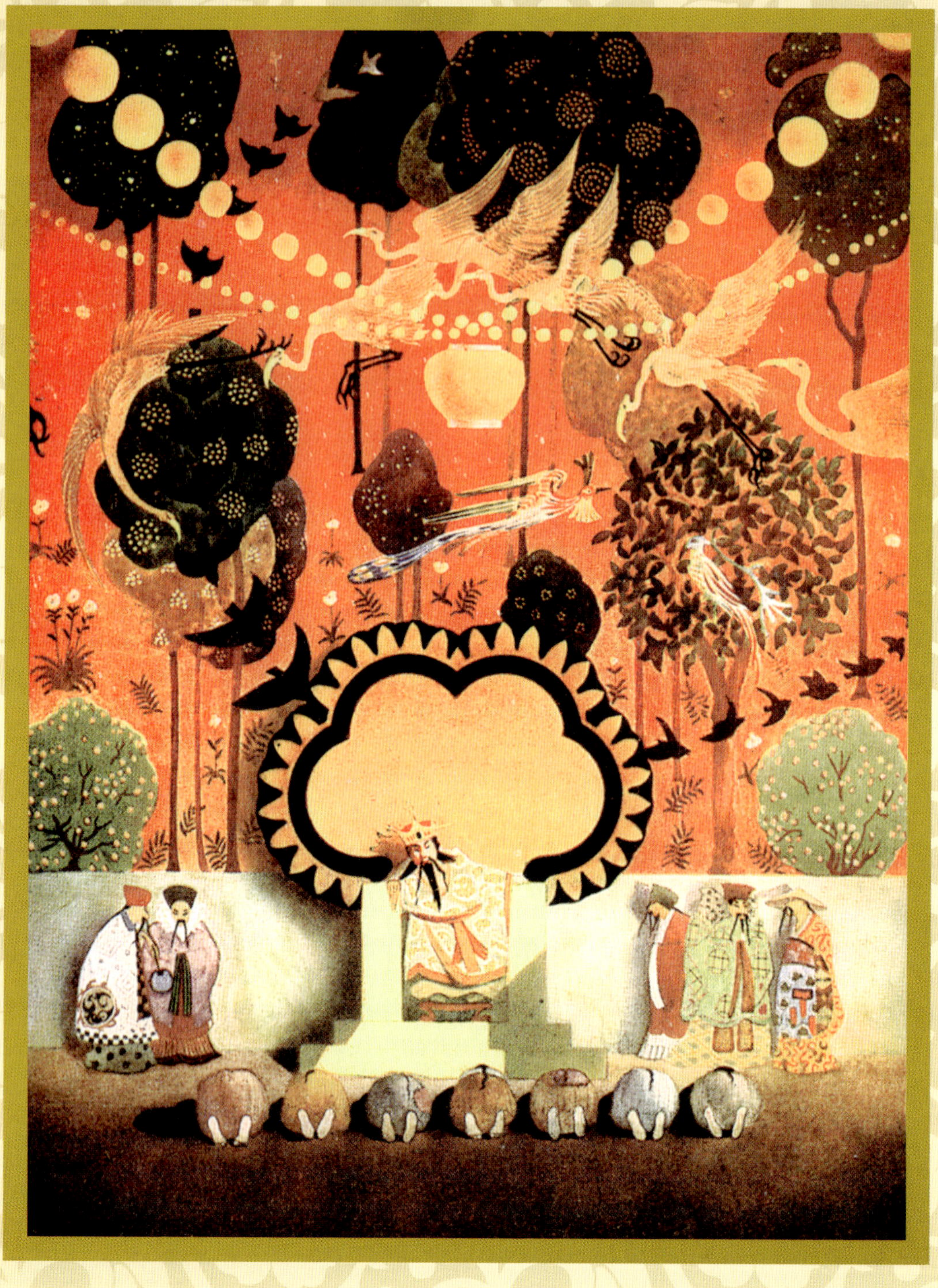

and was going to run after him, to endeavor to get some change out of the piece of gold; but he ran so fast, and had got so far, that it would have been impossible for him to overtake him.

Before Aladdin went home, he called at a baker's, bought some cakes of bread, changed his money, and on his return gave the rest to his mother, who went and purchased provisions enough to last them some time. After this manner they lived, till Aladdin had sold the twelve dishes singly, as necessity pressed, to the merchant, for the same money; who, after the first time, durst not offer him less, for fear of losing so good a bargain. When he had sold the last dish, he had recourse to the tray, which weighed ten times as much as the dishes, and would have carried it to his old purchaser, but that it was too large and cumbersome; therefore he was obliged to bring him home with him to his mother's, where, after the merchant had examined the weight of the tray, he laid down ten pieces of gold, with which Aladdin was very well satisfied.

When all the money was spent, Aladdin had recourse again to the lamp. He took it in his hand and rubbed it, when the genie immediately appeared, and repeated the same words that he had used before. I am hungry, said Aladdin, bring me something to eat. The genie disappeared, and presently returned with a tray, the same number of covered dishes as before, set them down, and vanished.

As soon as Aladdin found that their provisions were expended, he took one of the dishes, and went to look for his merchant chapman; but passing by a goldsmith's shop, the goldsmith perceiving him, called to him, and said, My lad, I imagine that you carry something which you sell to that merchant with whom I see you speak; but perhaps you do not know that he is the greatest rogue among the merchants. I will give you the full worth of it; or I will direct you to other merchants who will not cheat you.

The hopes of getting more money for his plate induced Aladdin to pull it from under his vest and show it to the goldsmith, who at first sight seeing that it was made of the finest silver, asked him if he had sold such as that to the merchant, when Aladdin told him that he had sold him twelve such, for a piece of gold each. What a villain! cried the goldsmith; but, added he, my son, what is past cannot be recalled. By showing you the value of this plate, which is of the finest silver we use in our shops, I will let you see how much the merchant has cheated you.

The goldsmith took a pair of scales, weighed the dish, and after he had mentioned how much an ounce of fine silver cost, assured him that his plate would fetch by weight sixty pieces of gold, which he offered to pay down immediately.

Aladdin thanked him for his fair dealing, and sold him all his dishes and the tray, and had as much for them as the weight came to.

Though Aladdin and his mother had an inexhaustible treasure in their lamp, and might have had whatever they wished for, yet they lived with the same frugality as before, and it may easily be supposed that the money for which Aladdin had sold the dishes and tray was sufficient to maintain them for some time.

During this interval, Aladdin frequented the shops of the principal merchants, where they sold cloth of gold and silver, linens, silk stuffs, and jewelry, and oftentimes joining in their conversation, acquired a knowledge of the world. By his acquaintance among the jewelers, he came to know that the fruits which he had gathered when he took the lamp were, instead of colored glass, stones of inestimable value; but he had the prudence not to mention this to any one, not even to his mother.

One day as Aladdin was walking about the town, he heard an order proclaimed, commanding the people to shut up their shops and houses, and keep within doors, while the Princess Buddir al Buddoor, the sultan's daughter, went to the baths and returned.

This proclamation inspired Aladdin with curiosity to see the Princess's face. To achieve this he placed himself behind the door of the bath, which was so situated that he could not fail of seeing her face. Aladdin had not waited long before the Princess came. She was attended by a great crowd of ladies and slaves, who walked on each side, and behind her. When she came within three or four paces of the door of the baths, she took off her veil, and gave Aladdin an opportunity of a full view.

The Princess was the most beautiful brunette in the world: her eyes were large and sparkling; her looks sweet and modest; her nose faultless; her mouth small; her lips vermilion; and her figure perfect. It is not, therefore, surprising that Aladdin was dazzled and enchanted.

After the Princess had passed by, and entered the baths, Aladdin left his hiding place and went home. His mother perceived that he was much more thoughtful and

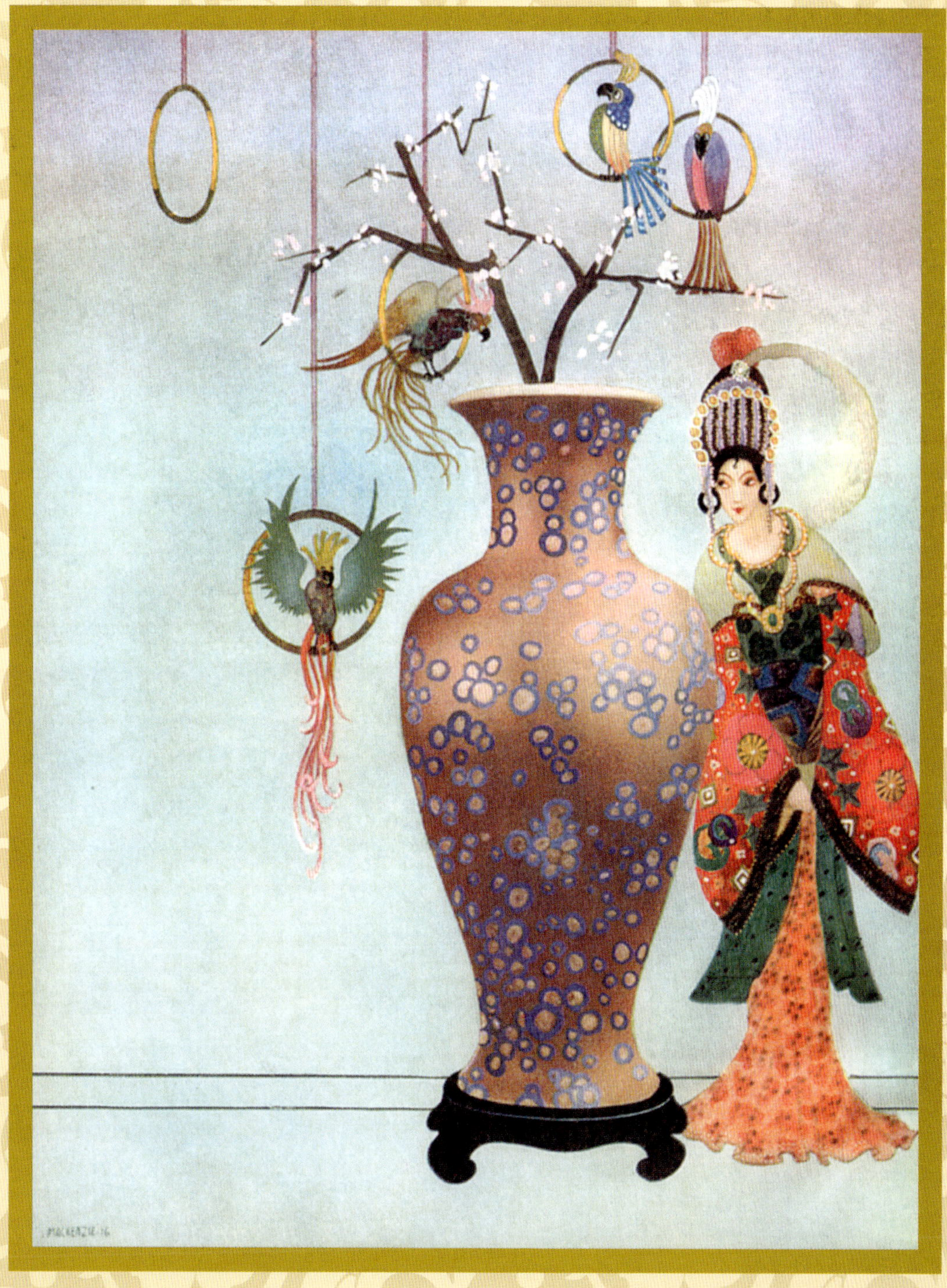

melancholy than usual; and asked what had happened to make him so, or if he was ill. For some time he remained silent, but at length he told her all, saying in conclusion, I love the Princess, and am resolved to ask her in marriage of the sultan.

Aladdin's mother listened with surprise to what her son told her; but when he talked of asking the Princess in marriage, she said: Child, what are you thinking of? You must be mad to talk thus. I assure you, mother, replied Aladdin, that I am in my right senses. I foresaw that you would reproach me with folly and extravagance, but I must tell you once more, that I am resolved to demand the Princess of the sultan in marriage, and your remonstrances shall not prevent me. As for a present worthy of the sultan's acceptance, those pieces of glass which I brought with me from the subterranean storehouse are in reality jewels of inestimable value, and fit for the greatest monarchs. I know the worth of them by frequenting the shops; and you may take my word that none of the jewelers have stones to be compared to those we have, either for size or beauty, and yet they value theirs at an excessive price. So I am persuaded that they will be received very favorably by the sultan. You have a large porcelain dish fit to hold them; fetch it, and let us see how they will look, when we have arranged them according to their different colors.

Aladdin's mother brought the china dish, when he took the jewels out of the two purses in which he had kept them, and placed them in order according to his fancy. But the brightness and luster they emitted in the day-time, and the variety of the colors, so dazzled their eyes that they were astonished beyond measure. The sight of all these precious stones, of which she knew not the value, only partially removed her anxiety; but, fearing that Aladdin might do something rash, she promised to go to the palace the next morning. Aladdin rose before daybreak, awakened his mother, pressing her to get herself dressed to go to the sultan's palace, and to get admittance, if possible, before the grand vizier and the great officers of state went in to take their seats in the divan, where the sultan held his court.

Aladdin's mother took the china dish, in which they had put the jewels the day before, wrapped in two napkins, and set forwards for the sultan's palace. When she came to the gates, the grand vizier, and the most distinguished lords of the court, were just gone in; but, notwithstanding the crowd of people, she got into the divan, a spacious hall, the entrance into which was very magnificent. She placed herself just before the sultan, grand vizier, and the great lords, who sat in council on his right and left hand. Several causes were called, according to their order, pleaded and adjudged, until the time the divan generally broke up, when the sultan rising, returned to his apartment, attended by the grand vizier.

Aladdin's mother, seeing the sultan retire, and all the people depart, judged rightly that he would not sit again that day, and resolved to go home. Aladdin was greatly disappointed when he heard of her failure, but she soothed him by saying, I will go again to-morrow; perhaps the sultan may not be so busy.

The next morning she repaired to the sultan's palace with the present, as early as the day before, but when she came there, she found the gates of the divan shut, and understood that the council sat but every other day, therefore she must come again the next. She went six times afterwards on the days appointed, placed herself always directly before the sultan, but with as little success as the first morning.

On the sixth day, however, after the divan was broken up, when the sultan returned to his own apartment, he said to his grand vizier, I have for some time observed a certain woman, who attends constantly every day that I give audience, with something wrapped up in a napkin; she always stands up from the beginning to the breaking up of the audience, and affects to place herself just before me. If she comes to our next audience, do not fail to call her, that I may hear what she has to say. The grand vizier made answer by lowering his hand, and then lifting it up above his head, signifying his willingness to lose it if he failed.

The next audience-day Aladdin's mother went to the divan, and placed herself in front of the sultan as usual. The grand vizier immediately called the chief of the mace-bearers, and pointing to her, bade him tell her to come before the sultan. The widow promptly followed him; and when she reached the throne she bowed her head to the ground, and waited for the sultan's command to rise. The sultan immediately said to her, Good woman, I have observed you to stand a long time, from the beginning to the rising of the divan; what business brings you here?

After these words, Aladdin's mother prostrated herself a second time, and said, Monarch of monarchs, I beg of you to pardon the boldness of my request, and to assure me first of your pardon and forgiveness. Well, replied the sultan, I will forgive you, be it what it may, and no hurt shall come to you: speak boldly.

When Aladdin's mother had taken all these precautions, she told him faithfully the errand on which she had come, and made many apologies and explanations in extenuation of her son's love for the Princess.

The sultan hearkened to this discourse without showing the least anger; but before he gave her any answer, asked her what she had brought tied up in the napkin. She took the china dish, which she had set down at the foot of the throne, untied it, and presented it to the sultan.

The sultan's amazement and surprise were inexpressible, when he saw so many large, beautiful, and valuable jewels collected in the dish. He remained for some time motionless with admiration. Then he received the present from Aladdin's mother's hand, crying out in a transport of joy, How rich, how beautiful! After he had admired and handled all the jewels, one after another, he turned to his grand vizier, and showing him the dish, said, Behold, admire, wonder, and confess that your eyes never beheld jewels so rich and beautiful before! The vizier was charmed. Well, continued the sultan, what sayest thou to such a present? Is it not worthy of the Princess my daughter? And ought I not to bestow her on one who values her at so great price? I cannot but own, replied the grand vizier, that the present is worthy of the Princess; but I beg of your majesty to grant me three months before you come to a final resolution. I hope, before that time, my son, whom you have regarded favorably, will be able to make a nobler present than Aladdin, who is an entire stranger to your majesty.

The sultan readily granted this request, and said to the widow: Good woman, go home, and tell your son that I agree to the proposal you have made me; but I cannot marry the Princess my daughter for the next three months; but at the expiration of that time come again.

Aladdin's mother returned home much more gratified than she had expected, since she had met with a favorable answer, and told her son that she was to attend at the court in three months to hear the sultan's decision.

Aladdin thought himself the most happy of men at hearing this news, and thanked his mother for the pains she had taken in the affair, the good success of which was of so

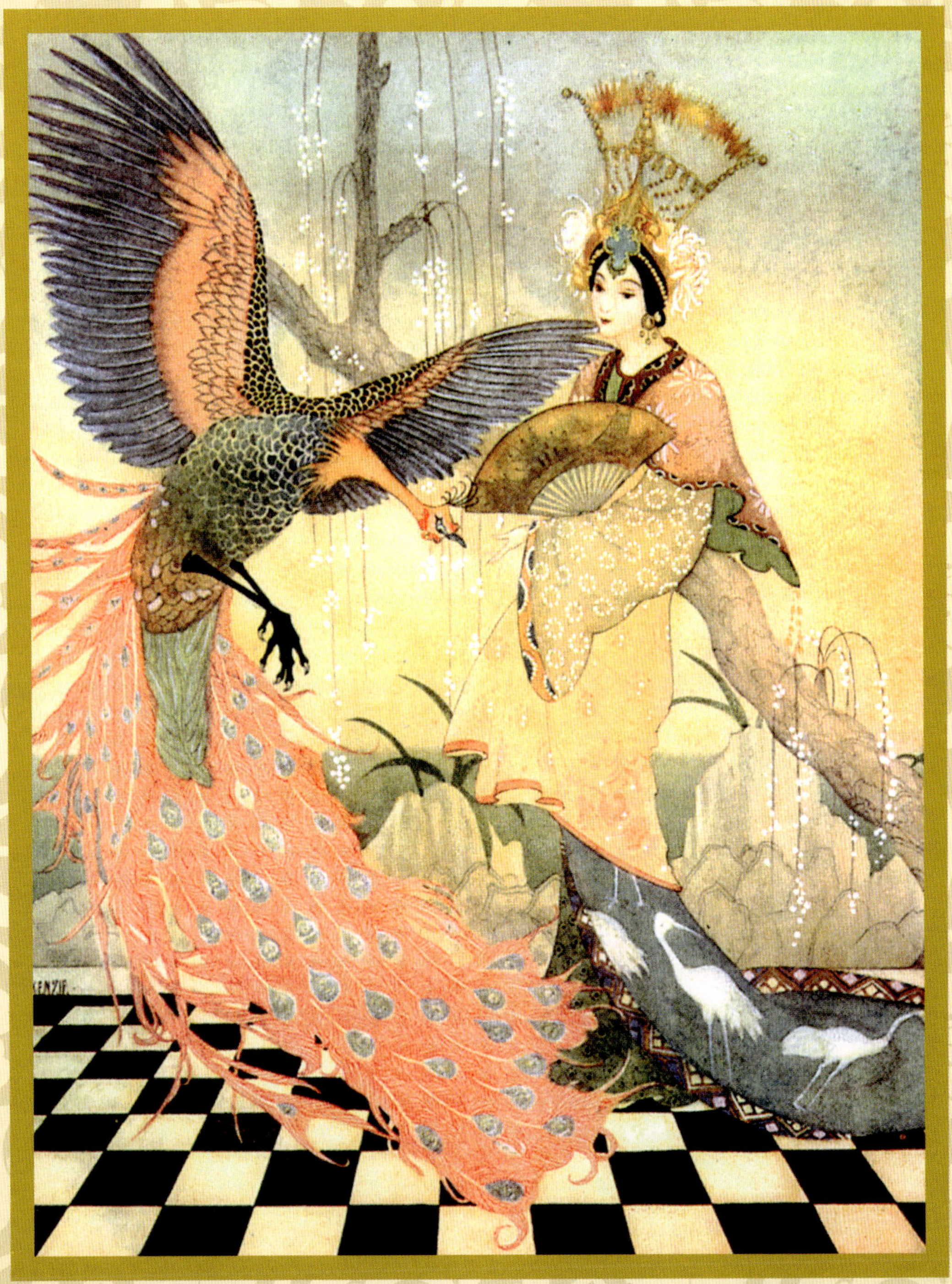

great importance to his peace. When two of the three months were passed, his mother one evening went into the town, and found the shops dressed with foliage, silks, and carpeting, and everyone rejoicing. The streets were crowded with officers in habits of ceremony, mounted on horses richly caparisoned, each attended by a great many footmen. Aladdin's mother asked what was the meaning of all this preparation of public festivity. Whence came you, good woman, said one, that you don't know that the grand vizier's son is to marry the Princess Buddir al Buddoor, the sultan's daughter, to-night? She will presently return from the baths; and these officers whom you see are to assist at the cavalcade to the palace, where the ceremony is to be solemnized.

The widow hastened home to inform Aladdin: Child, cried she, you are undone! the sultan's fine promises will come to nothing. This night the grand vizier's son is to marry the Princess.

At this account Aladdin was thunderstruck, but with a sudden hope he bethought himself of the lamp, vowing to stop the marriage. He therefore went to his chamber, took the lamp, and rubbed it, when immediately the genie appeared, and said to him, What wouldst thou have? Hear me, said Aladdin; thou hast hitherto served me well; but now I entrust to thee a matter of great importance. The sultan's daughter, who was to have been mine, is to-night to wed the son of the grand vizier. It shall not be. Bring them both to me ere the marriage takes place. Master, replied the genie, I will obey you.

Aladdin supped with his mother as usual; he then retired to his own chamber again, and waited for the genie to execute his orders.

At the sultan's palace the greatest rejoicings prevailed at the wedding festivities, which were kept up until midnight. The bride and bridegroom retired to their apartments. They had scarcely entered the room when the genie seized them, and bore them straight to Aladdin's chamber, much to the terror of both, as they could not see by what means they were transported. Remove the bridegroom, said Aladdin, and keep him in close custody until dawn to-morrow, when you shall return with him. Aladdin then tried to soothe the Princess's fears by explaining how ill he had been treated; but he did not succeed over well, as the Princess knew nothing of the matter.

At dawn the genie appeared with the vizier's son, who had been kept in a house all night, near at hand, merely by being breathed upon by the genie. He was left motionless and entranced at the chamber door. At a word from Aladdin the slave of the lamp took the couple and bore them back to the palace.

The genie had only just deposited them in safety when the sultan tapped at the door to wish them good morning. The grand vizier's son, who was almost perished with cold, by standing in his thin undergarment all night, no sooner heard the knocking at the door than he ran into the robing-chamber, where he had undressed himself the night before.

The sultan, having opened the door, went to the bedside, kissed the Princess on the forehead, but was extremely surprised to see her so melancholy. She only cast at him a sorrowful look, expressive of great affliction. He suspected that there was something extraordinary in this silence, and thereupon went immediately to the sultana's apartment, told her in what a state he had found the Princess, and how she had received him. Sir, said the sultana, I will go and see her; she will not receive me in the same manner.

The Princess was quite as reserved when her mother came; but when the sultana pressed her to speak she said, with a deep sigh and many tears, I am very unhappy. She then narrated all that had taken place. Daughter, replied the sultana, you must keep all this to yourself, for no one would believe that you were sane if you told this strange tale. The sultana then questioned the vizier's son; but he, being proud of the alliance he had made, denied everything, and so the celebrations of the marriage went forward that day with equal splendor.

That night Aladdin again summoned the genie, and had the Princess and the vizier's son brought to him as before. And on the following morning they were conveyed back to the palace, just in time to receive the visit of the sultan. The Princess answered his inquiries with tears, and at last told him everything that had happened. The sultan consulted with the grand vizier; and, learning that his son had suffered even worse than the Princess, he ordered the marriage to be cancelled, and all the festivities—which should have lasted for several days more—were stopped throughout the kingdom.

This sudden stopping of the wedding celebrations gave rise to much gossip, but nothing could be discovered: and this sudden and unexpected change gave rise both in the city and kingdom to various speculations and inquiries; but no other account could be given of it, except that both the vizier and his son went out of the palace very much dejected. Nobody but Aladdin alone knew the secret, and he kept it most cunningly to himself, so that neither the sultan nor the grand vizier, who had forgotten Aladdin and his request, had the slightest suspicion that he was the cause of all the trouble.

Three months had now elapsed since the sultan had made his promise to Aladdin's mother, and so she again repaired to the palace to hear his decision. The sultan at once recognized her, and bade the grand vizier bring her to him.

Sir, said the widow, bowing to the ground before him, I have come, as you directed, at the end of the three months, to plead for my son. The sultan, when he had fixed a time to answer the request of this good woman, little thought of hearing any more of a marriage; but he was loath to break his word. Therefore he consulted his vizier, who advised that such conditions should be imposed that no one in Aladdin's position could fulfill them. This suggestion seemed wise, so the sultan said: Good woman, it is true sultans ought to abide by their word, and I am ready to keep mine, by making your son happy in marriage with my daughter. But as I cannot marry her without some further valuable consideration from your son, you may tell him, I will fulfill my promise as soon as he shall send me forty trays of massive gold, full of the same sort of jewels you have already made me a present of, and carried by the like number of black slaves, who shall be led by as many young and handsome white slaves, all dressed magnificently. On these conditions I am ready to bestow the Princess upon him; go, and tell him so, and I will wait till you bring me his answer.

Aladdin's mother prostrated herself a second time before the throne, and retired. On her way home, she laughed within herself at her son's foolish imagination. Where, said she, can he get all that the sultan demands? When she came home, she told her son the message she had been commanded to deliver, adding, The sultan expects your answer immediately; but, continued she, laughing, I believe he may wait long enough.

Not so long, mother, as you imagine, replied Aladdin. I am very well pleased; his demand is but a trifle to what I could have done for her. I will at once provide these things.

Aladdin promptly withdrew and summoned the genie, to whom he made known his wants. The genie told him his command should be immediately obeyed, and disappeared. In a very short time the genie returned with forty black slaves, each bearing on his head a heavy tray of pure gold, full of pearls, diamonds, rubies, emeralds, and every sort of precious stones, all larger and more beautiful than those presented to the sultan. Mother, said Aladdin, let us lose no time; before the sultan and the divan rise, I would have you return to the palace with this present as the dowry demanded for the Princess, that he may judge by my diligence and exactness of the ardent and sincere desire I have to procure myself the honor of this alliance.

So magnificent was this procession that as it passed through the streets crowds of people came out to look in wonder. The splendor of the dress of the slaves, which glistened with precious stones, made the people think that they were so many kings or Princes. They walked sedately, Aladdin's mother at their head, towards the palace, and were all so much alike that the spectators marveled.

As the sultan, who had been informed of their approach, had given orders for them to be admitted, they met with no obstacle, but went into the divan in regular order, one part filing to the right, and the other to the left. After they were all entered, and had formed a semicircle before the sultan's throne, the black slaves laid the golden trays on the carpet, prostrated themselves, touching the carpet with their foreheads, and at the same time the white slaves did the same. When they rose, the black slaves uncovered the trays, and then all stood with their arms crossed over their breasts.

In the meantime Aladdin's mother advanced to the foot of the throne, and having paid her respects, said to the sultan, Sir, my son feels that this present is much below the Princess Buddir al Buddoor's worth; but hopes, nevertheless, that your majesty will accept of it, and make it agreeable to the Princess, and with the greater confidence since he has endeavored to conform to the conditions you were pleased to impose.

The sultan made no longer hesitation: he was overjoyed at the sight of Aladdin's rich present. Go, said he, and tell your son that I wait with open arms to embrace him, and the more haste he makes to come and receive the Princess my daughter from my hands, the greater pleasure he will do me. As soon as the tailor's widow had retired, the sultan put an end to the audience; and rising from his throne, ordered that the Princess's servants should come and carry the trays into their mistress's apartment, whither he went himself to examine them with her at his leisure. The fourscore slaves were conducted into the palace; and the sultan, telling the Princess of their magnificent appearance, ordered them to be brought before her apartment, that she might see through the lattices he had not exaggerated in his account of them.

In the meantime Aladdin's mother got home, and showed in her air and countenance the good news she brought her son. My son, said she to him, rejoice, for you have arrived at the height of your desires. The sultan has declared that you are worthy to possess the Princess Buddir al Buddoor, and waits with impatience to embrace you, and conclude your marriage.

Aladdin, enraptured with this news, retired to his chamber, and summoned the slave of the lamp as usual. Genie, said he, I want to bathe immediately, and you must afterwards provide me the richest and most magnificent habit ever worn by a monarch. No sooner were the words out of his mouth than the genie rendered him, as well as himself, invisible, and transported him into a saloon of the finest marble of all sorts of colors; where he bathed in scented water. And when he returned into the hall he found, instead of his own, a suit the magnificence of which astonished him. The genie helped him to dress, and, when he had done, transported him back to his own chamber, where he asked him if he had any other commands. Yes, answered Aladdin, bring me a charger that surpasses in beauty and goodness the best in the sultan's stables, with a saddle, bridle, and other caparisons worth a million of money. I want also twenty slaves, as richly clothed as those who carried the present to the sultan, to walk by my side and follow me, and twenty more to go before me in two ranks. Besides these, bring my mother six women slaves to attend her, as richly dressed at least as any of the Princess Buddir al Buddoor's, each carrying a complete dress fit for any sultana. I want also ten thousand pieces of gold in ten purses; go, and make haste.

As soon as Aladdin had given these orders, the genie disappeared, but presently returned with the horse, the forty slaves, ten of whom carried each a purse containing ten thousand pieces of gold, and six women slaves, each carrying on her head a different dress for Aladdin's mother, wrapped up in a piece of silver tissue, and presented them all to Aladdin.

Aladdin took four of the purses, which he presented to his mother, together with the six women slaves who carried the dresses, telling her to spend the money as she wished; the other six he left with the slaves, and bade them cast handfuls among the people as they walked. And after this, when all was ready, he set out for the palace, mounted upon the charger, three of the purse-bearers walking on his right hand, and three on his left. Although Aladdin never was on horseback before, he appeared with such extraordinary grace, that the most experienced horseman would not have taken him for a novice. The streets through which he was to pass were filled with an innumerable concourse of people, who made the air echo with their acclamations, especially every time the six slaves who carried the purses threw handfuls of gold among the populace. The sultan, much surprised by the magnificence of Aladdin's dress and the splendor of his cortege, received him with joy, and did everything in his power to honor him. After they had feasted, the marriage contract was drawn up and duly signed, and the sultan was anxious that the nuptials should be completed at once. But Aladdin said, Sir, I beg of you to grant me sufficient land near your palace on which I may build a home worthy of the Princess, before our wedding takes place. You may judge of my eagerness to claim the Princess by the expedition with which the castle shall be erected.

The sultan readily granted this request; and, having embraced Aladdin, he allowed him to return home.

Aladdin withdrew with a most courtly bow, and hastened home, amid the cheers of the people, to consult the genie. And as soon as he reached his house he went to his chamber, and took the lamp and rubbed it. Immediately the genie appeared, professed his allegiance, and Aladdin said to him: Genie, build me a palace fit to receive my spouse the Princess Buddir al Buddoor. Let it be built of porphyry, jasper, agate, lapis lazuli, and the finest marble of various colors. On the roof of the palace build a large, dome-crowned hall, having four equal fronts; and instead of bricks, let the walls be formed of layers of massive gold and silver, laid alternately; let each front contain six windows. The lattices of these, except one, which must be left unfinished, must be so enriched with diamonds, rubies, and emeralds, that they shall exceed everything of the kind ever seen in the world. There must also be an inner and outer court in front of the palace, and a spacious garden; but, above all things, provide and fill an ample treasure-house well supplied with gold and silver. Let nothing be lacking in the kitchens and storehouses; and let the stables be filled with the best horses. Finally, see that there is a royal staff of servants. Go, execute my orders.

It was about the hour of sunset when Aladdin gave these orders, and the next morning, before break of day, the genie presented himself, and said, Sir, your palace is finished. At a word from Aladdin the genie carried him to the palace, and led him through all the apartments, all of which, as well as the servants, delighted him. The genie then showed him the treasury, which was opened by a treasurer, where Aladdin saw heaps of purses, of different sizes, piled up to the top of the ceiling, and disposed in most excellent order. The genie thence led him to the stables, where he showed him some of the finest horses in the world, and the grooms busy in dressing them; from thence they went to the storehouses, which were filled with all things necessary, both for food and ornament.

When Aladdin had thoroughly examined the palace, he said, Genie, no one can be better satisfied than I am. There is only one thing wanting: that is, a carpet of fine velvet for the Princess to walk upon from the sultan's palace here. The genie immediately disappeared, and Aladdin saw what he desired executed in an instant. The genie then returned, and carried him home before the gates of the sultan's palace were opened.

When the sultan's porters came to open the gates, they were amazed to find a magnificent palace erected, and to see a carpet of velvet spread from the grand entrance. They immediately informed the grand vizier, who hastened to tell the sultan. It must be Aladdin's palace, exclaimed the sultan, which I gave him leave to build. He has done this as a surprise for me, to show what can be done in one night.

When Aladdin had been conveyed home, he requested his mother to go to the Princess Buddir al Buddoor to inform her that the palace would be ready for her reception that evening. She at once set out, attended by her women slaves. The widow was sitting with the Princess when the sultan came in. He was much surprised to see the change that had taken place in her, and was greatly pleased. Aladdin had, meanwhile, set out to his new home, being careful to take the lamp and the ring, both of which had served him in such good stead. Great were the rejoicings, and loud the sounds of music, when Princess Buddir al Buddoor set out from the sultan's palace in the evening. A wonderful procession attended her to the door of Aladdin's palace,

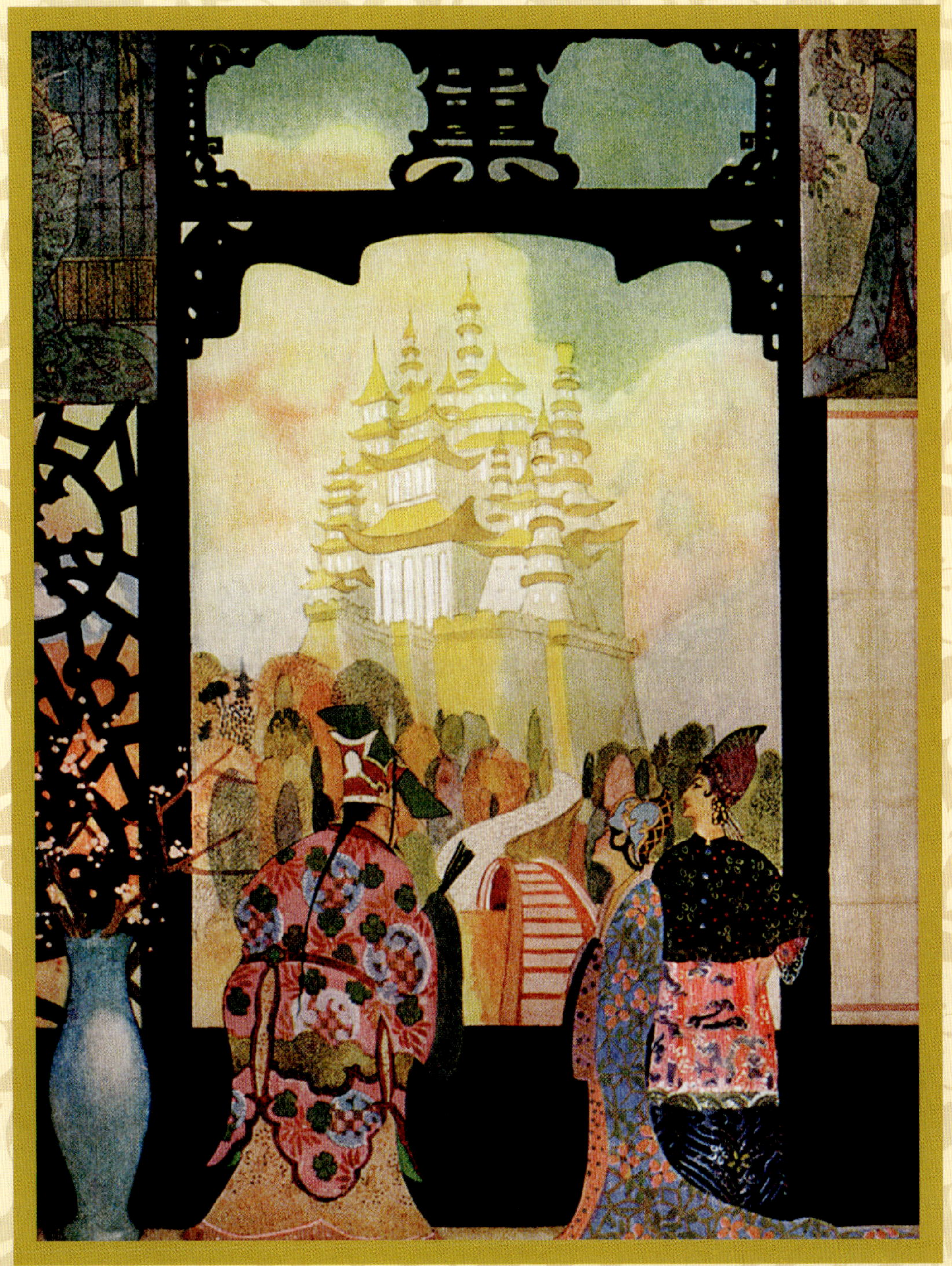

where he stood ready to receive her with all honor. He conducted her into a large hall, the wealth of which astonished her beyond measure, and then the festivities were kept up until a late hour.

The next morning, as soon as he was dressed, Aladdin set out to invite the sultan and his court to come to his palace. The sultan willingly consented, and, attended by his grand vizier and all the great lords of his court, he accompanied Aladdin. The nearer the sultan approached Aladdin's palace, the more he was struck with its beauty. But when he came into the hall, and saw the windows, enriched with diamonds, rubies, emeralds—all large, perfect stones—he was so much surprised that he remained some time motionless. Son, said the sultan, this hall is the most worthy of admiration of any in the world; there is only one thing that surprises me, which is to find one of the windows unfinished. Sir, Aladdin, the omission was by design, since I wished that your majesty should have the glory of finishing this hall. I take it kindly, the sultan, and will give orders about it immediately.

When the sultan arose from the repast that had been prepared, he was informed that the jewelers and goldsmiths attended; upon which he returned to the hall, and showed them the window which was unfinished. I sent for you, said he, to fit up this window in as great perfection as the rest; and make all the dispatch you can.

The jewelers and goldsmiths examined the three-and-twenty windows with great attention, and after they had consulted together, to know what each could furnish, they returned, and presented themselves before the sultan, whose principal jeweler, undertaking to speak for the rest, said, Sir, we are all willing to exert our utmost care to obey your majesty; but among us all we cannot furnish jewels for so great a work. I have more than are necessary, said the sultan; come to my palace, and you shall choose what may answer your purpose.

When the sultan returned to his palace, he ordered his jewels to be brought out, and the jewelers took a great quantity, particularly those Aladdin had made him a present of, which they soon used, without making any great advance in their work. They came again several times for more, and in a month's time had not finished half their work. In short, they used all the jewels the sultan had, and borrowed of the vizier, but yet the work was not half done.

Aladdin, who knew that all the sultan's endeavors to make this window like the rest were in vain, sent for the jewelers and goldsmiths, and not only commanded them to desist from their work, but ordered them to undo what they had begun, and to carry all their jewels back to the sultan and to the vizier. They undid in a few hours what they had been six weeks about, and retired, leaving Aladdin alone in the hall. He took the lamp, which he carried about him, rubbed it, and presently the genie appeared. Genie, said Aladdin, I ordered thee to leave one of the four and twenty windows of this hall imperfect, and thou hast executed my commands punctually; now I would have thee make it like the rest. The genie immediately disappeared. Aladdin went out of the hall, and returning soon after, found the window, as he wished it to be, like the others.

In the meantime the jewelers and goldsmiths repaired to the palace, and were introduced into the sultan's presence; where the chief jeweler presented the precious stones which he had brought back. The sultan asked them if Aladdin had given them any reason for so doing, and they answering that he had given them none, he ordered a horse to be brought, which he mounted, and rode to his son-in-law's palace, with some few attendants on foot. Aladdin met him at the gate, and, instead of answering his question, led him to the great hall, when the sultan was much surprised to find the window finished just like the others. He fancied at first that he had mistaken the window, but, having examined all the others, he found that it had been completed in a few minutes, whereas the jewelers had spent weeks upon it without finishing the work. My son, said he, what a man you are to do such surprising things always in the twinkling of an eye: there is not your fellow in the world; the more I know, the more I admire you.

Aladdin did not confine himself in his palace, but took care to show himself once or twice a week in the town, by going sometimes to one mosque, and sometimes to another, to prayers, or to visit the grand vizier, or the principal lords of the court. Every time he went out, he caused two slaves, who walked by the side of his horse, to throw handfuls of money among the people as he passed through the streets and squares. This generosity gained him the love and blessings of the people: and it was common for them to swear by his head. Thus he won the affections of the people, and was more beloved than the sultan himself.

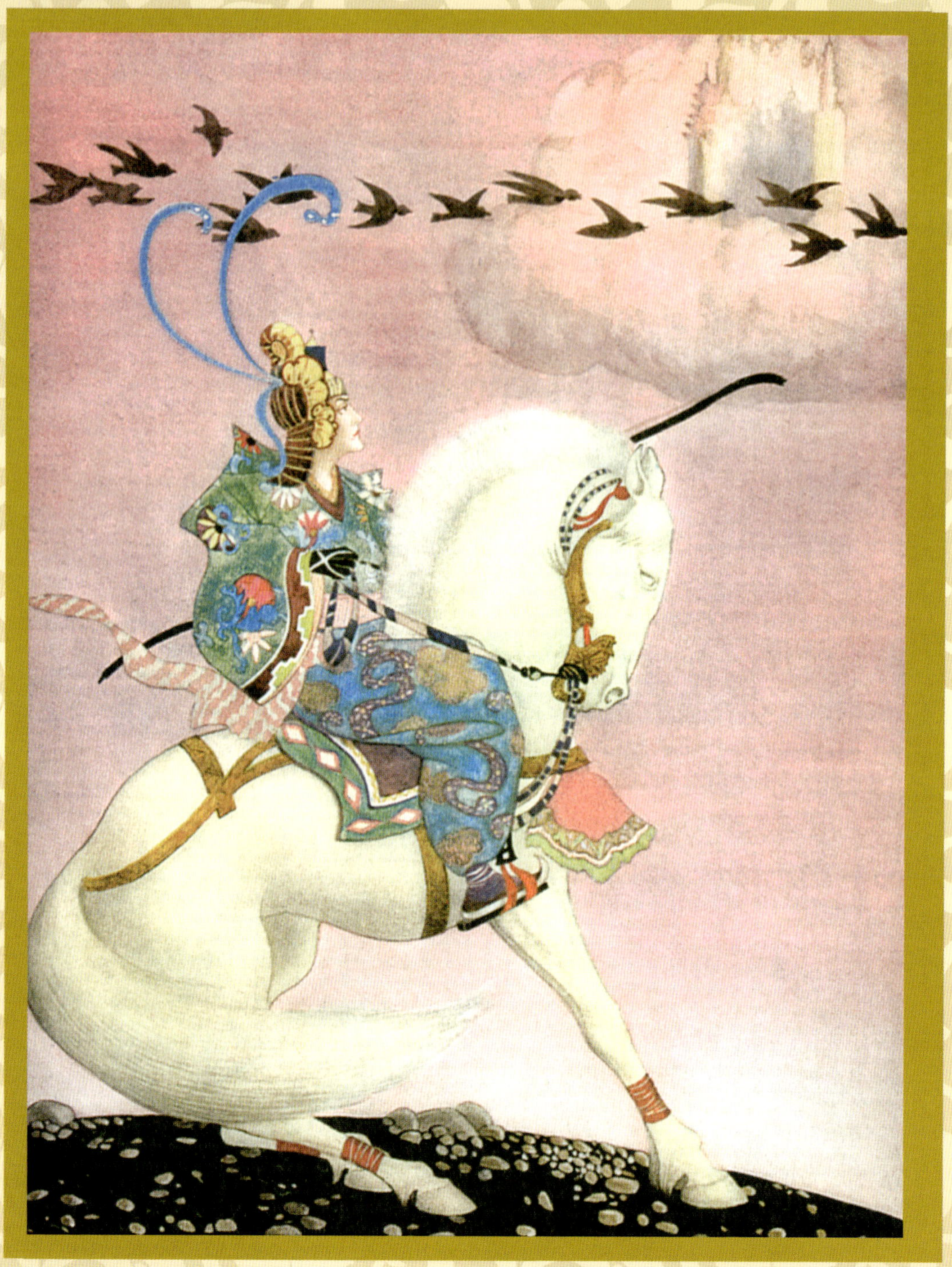

Aladdin and the Magic Lamp

Aladdin had conducted himself in this manner several years, when the African magician recalled him to his recollection in Africa, and, though he thought him dead in the cave where he had left him, he resolved to find out for certain. After a long and careful course of magical inquiries, he discovered that Aladdin had escaped, and lived in great splendor, all of which he owed to the wonderful lamp.

Directly the magician found out this, he set out in hot haste for the capital of China; and when he arrived, he went to a khan, where he rested after his long journey.

He made inquiries, which revealed to him Aladdin's enormous wealth, and heard of all his charities and of the magnificent palace he had built. The magician, when he saw the palace, knew that none but genies could have erected it, and he was exceeding annoyed to think how he had been worsted. He returned to the khan, determined to find out where the lamp was kept; and by the magic knowledge he possessed he was enabled to discover what he wanted to know. When, to his great delight, he learned that the lamp was in the palace—not, as he feared, about Aladdin's person—Now, said he, I shall have the lamp, and will be revenged upon this fellow, who shall be degraded to his original mean station in life.

The magician also learned that Aladdin had set out on a hunting expedition, three days before, which was to last for eight days. This knowledge was sufficient to enable the magician to carry out his plans, which he straightway did.

First he went to a coppersmith, from whom he purchased a dozen lamps, which he put into a basket, and then he set out to Aladdin's palace again. As he drew near he called out: Who will change old lamps for new? The Princess happened to hear the cries, though she heard not his words. Curious to learn why the people collected around him, she sent one of her women to inquire what he sold.

The slave soon returned, laughing so heartily that the Princess was angry. Madam, said the slave, laughing still, this fellow has a basket on his arm, full of fine new lamps, asking to change them for old ones; the children and mob, crowding about him so that he can hardly stir, make all the noise they can in derision of him.

Another female slave, hearing this, said, Now you speak of lamps, I know not whether the Princess may have observed it, but there is an old one upon a shelf of the Prince's robing room, and whoever owns it will not be sorry to find a new one in its stead.

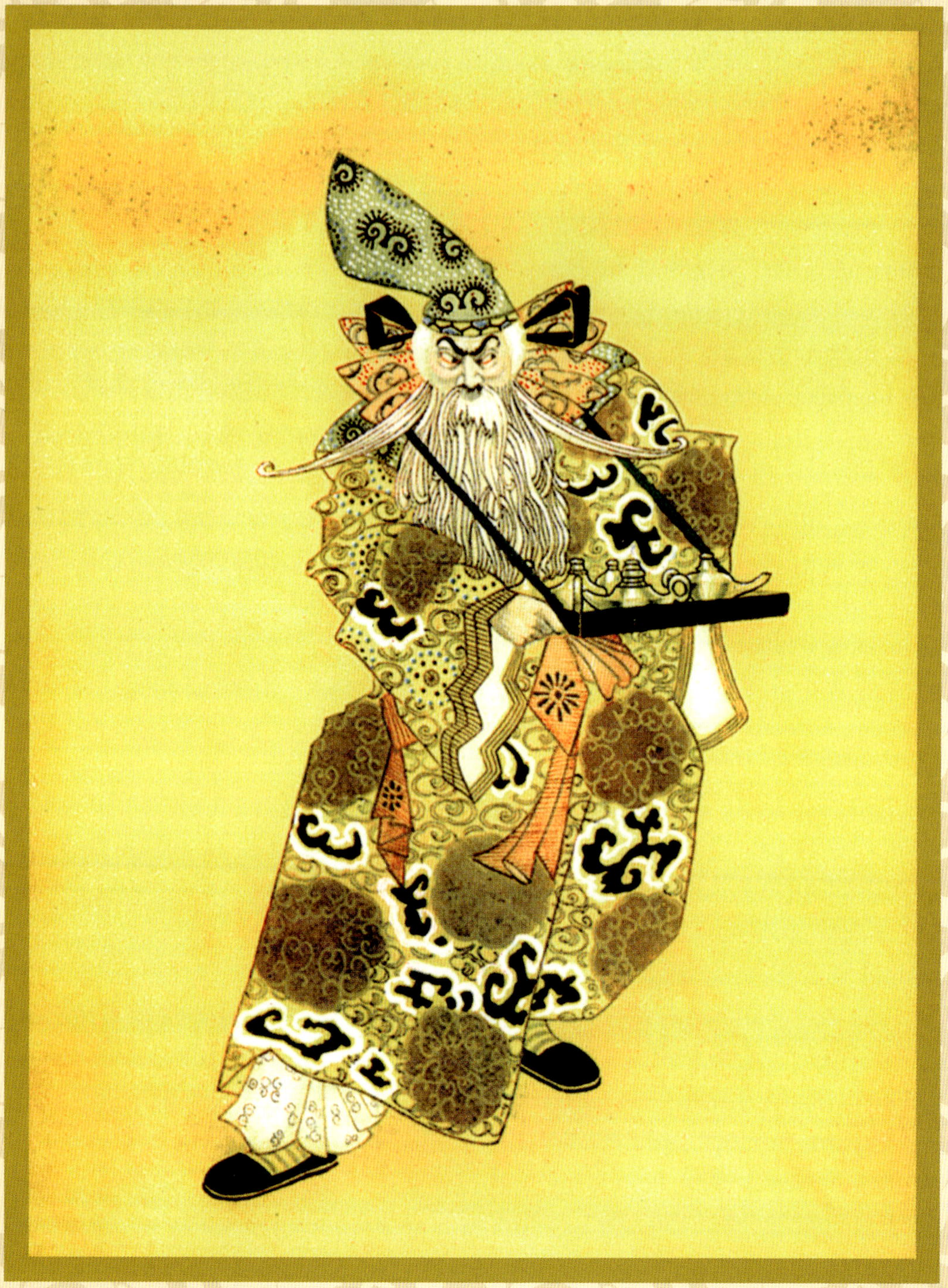

Aladdin and the Magic Lamp

The Princess, who knew not the value of this lamp, commanded a slave to take it, and make the exchange. The slave obeyed, went out of the hall, and no sooner got to the palace gates than he saw the African magician, called to him, and showing him the old lamp, said, Give me a new lamp for this.

The magician never doubted but this was the lamp he wanted. There could be no other such in this palace, where every utensil was gold or silver. He snatched it eagerly out of the slave's hand, and thrusting it as far as he could into his breast, offered him his basket, and bade him choose which he liked best. The slave picked out one, and carried it to the Princess; but the exchange was no sooner made than the place rang with the shouts of the children, deriding the magician's folly.

The African magician gave everybody leave to laugh as much as they pleased; and as soon as he was out of the square between the two palaces, he hastened down the streets which were the least frequented; and having no more occasion for his lamps or basket, set all down in an alley where nobody saw him: then going down another street or two, he walked till he came to one of the city gates, and pursuing his way through the suburbs, at length reached a lonely spot, where he passed the remainder of the day. When night came he pulled the lamp out of his breast and rubbed it. At that summons the genie appeared, and said, What wouldst thou have? I am ready to obey thee as thy slave, and the slave of all those who have that lamp in their hands, both I and the other slaves of the lamp. I command thee, replied the magician, to transport me immediately and the palace which thou and the other slaves of the lamp have built in this city, with all the people in it, to Africa. The genie made no reply, but immediately transported him and the palace entire, to the spot whither he was desired to convey it.

The sultan was so surprised at not finding the palace upon which he was used to gaze, that he called the grand vizier to him in order that he might give his opinion. The grand vizier, who feared and disliked Aladdin, was not slow to advise the sultan to have him arrested. He would have had him put to death but that the people threatened to rebel if this were done.

The sultan in his wrath sent for Aladdin, and said to him: Where is your palace? Indeed, answered Aladdin, I cannot tell you; but pray, sir, give me forty days, and if at the end of that time I do not restore it to its place, I offer my head as a forfeit. Go then, said the sultan, but forget not to return in forty days.

Aladdin went out of the sultan's presence in great humiliation, so that he durst not lift up his eyes. The principal officers of the court, who had all professed themselves his friends, turned their backs to avoid seeing him. He was quite distraught, and wandered about the city vainly asking if any one had seen his palace.

Having spent three days in this way, he at length went into the country, determined to end his life. As he approached the river in which he intended to drown himself, he slipped and fell, and in falling rubbed the magic ring, which he still wore, but of which he had forgotten the power. Immediately the genie whom he had seen in the cave appeared, and said: What wouldst thou? I am thy slave; the slave of the ring. Genie, said Aladdin, agreeably surprised at this unexpected help, transport me immediately to the spot whither my palace has been removed. No sooner were these words spoken than Aladdin found himself in Africa, beside his own palace, under the Princess's window.

It so happened that shortly after the Princess Buddir al Buddoor came to the window, and seeing Aladdin was overcome with joy. Come, she cried, to the private door, and hasten to me. Aladdin's joy was no less than that of the Princess; he tenderly embraced her, and then asked: Tell me what has become of the lamp that stood on the shelf in my room. Alas, replied the Princess, I foolishly changed it for a new one, not knowing its power, and the next morning found myself in this place, which I am told is Africa. Then, since we are in Africa, said Aladdin, I know that this must be the doing of the African magician. Can you tell me where he keeps the lamp?

The Princess told him that the magician always carried the lamp in the bosom of his dress, for that he had shown it to her. Then, said Aladdin, we may yet punish this wicked magician. Let the private door be opened to me directly I return: for the first thing is to secure the lamp.

Aladdin set out and soon descried a wayfarer who was overjoyed to change clothes with him, and went to a druggist's and asked for a certain powder, which was very costly. The druggist looked askance, but Aladdin showed him a purse full of gold and demanded half a dram, with which he returned quickly to the palace. He entered by the private door; and hastening to the Princess's apartment he said to her: When the magician comes to visit you, you must be most gracious to him. Entertain him as becomes you, and ere he leaves request him to drink to you. Then give him this cup, in which there is a powder that will send him to sleep. While he sleeps we can secure the lamp, whose slaves will do our bidding, and we shall be restored to China once more.

The Princess most carefully performed all that Aladdin had directed, and when the magician came as usual to pay her a visit, he was agreeably surprised to find her waiting to receive him with a smile. He spent some time with her; and then, at her request, drank the cup of wine before leaving. Immediately he had swallowed it he fell back on the sofa dead, and the Princess gave the signal which she had arranged with Aladdin.

As soon as Aladdin entered the hall, the Princess rose from her seat, and ran overjoyed to embrace him; but he stopped her, and said, Princess, it is not yet time; oblige me by retiring to your apartment; and let me be left alone a moment, while I endeavor to transport you back to China as speedily as you were brought from thence.

When the Princess and her women were gone out of the hall, Aladdin shut the door, and going directly to the dead body of the magician, opened his vest, took out the lamp—which was carefully wrapped up, as the Princess had told him—and unfolding and rubbing it, the genie immediately appeared. Genie, said Aladdin, I command thee to transport this palace instantly into China, to the place from whence it was brought hither. Immediately the palace was transported into China, and its removal was only felt by two little shocks—the one when it was lifted up, the other when it was set down, and both in a very short interval of time.

The sultan, who rose early, looked, as was his wont, to sorrow over the empty space; but perceiving that the palace had been replaced, he was overjoyed. He at once called for his horse and rode over to the palace, to welcome the return of his daughter and Aladdin. Aladdin, who had foreseen this visit, had risen early, and was ready to receive the sultan in the hall, clothed in a most magnificent garment. He led the sultan straight to the Princess's apartment, where the happy father fondly embraced his child. Son, said he, turning to Aladdin, forgive the harshness of my conduct towards you, which was inspired by paternal affection. Sir, replied Aladdin, you are not to blame; that base magician was alone the cause of all my troubles.

Although the African magician was dead, he had a younger brother, who was equally skillful as a necromancer, and even surpassed him in villainy and pernicious designs. These two brothers did not live together, but each year they communicated by means of their magic arts. Not having received any tidings of his elder brother, the younger one made an astrological inquiry, by which he discovered that he had been poisoned; and, by a further investigation, he discovered that he was buried in the capital of China, near the dwelling of the man who had murdered him: who, he learned, was married to the sultan's daughter.

He at once set out to the capital of China to avenge his brother's death, and after a long and fatiguing journey reached the city, where he soon discovered that Aladdin was the poisoner whom he sought. He took a lodging in a khan, where he heard of the virtue and piety of a woman called Fatima, who was retired from the world, and of the miracles she wrought. As he fancied that this woman might be serviceable to him in the project he had conceived, he requested to be informed more particularly who that holy woman was, and what sort of miracles she performed.

What! said the person whom he addressed, have you never seen or heard of her? She is the admiration of the whole town, for her fasting, her austerities, and her exemplary life. Except Mondays and Fridays, she never stirs out of her little cell; and on those days on which she comes into the town she does an infinite deal of good; for there is not a person but is cured by her laying her hand upon them.

That very night the magician went to Fatima's cell; and, having murdered her, he put on her clothes and went to the palace of Aladdin, bent upon revenge.

As soon as the people saw the holy woman, as they imagined him to be, they presently gathered about him in a great crowd. Some begged his blessing, others kissed his hand, and others, more reserved, only the hem of his garment; while others stooped for him to lay his hands upon them; which he did, muttering some words in form of prayer, and, in short, counterfeited so well, that everybody took him for the holy woman.

Though the progress was slow the magician at length reached the square in front of the palace. The Princess happening to hear that the holy woman was there, and being desirous of seeing her, sent some of her slaves to bid her enter. The people, seeing the slave approach, fell back to allow him to approach Fatima. Holy woman, said he, the

Princess wishes to see you. The Princess does me too great an honor, replied the false Fatima. I am ready to obey her command: and at the same time followed the slave to the palace, greatly delighted at the success of his plot.

When they had conversed, the Princess said: My good mother, I have one thing to request, which you must not refuse me; it is, to stay with me, that you may edify me with your way of living; and that I may learn from your good example. Princess, said the counterfeit Fatima, I beg of you not to ask what I cannot consent to, without neglecting my prayers and devotion. That shall be no hindrance to you, answered the Princess; I have a great many apartments unoccupied; you shall choose which you like best, and have as much liberty to perform your devotions as if you were in your own cell.

The magician, who desired nothing more than to introduce himself into the palace, where it would be a much easier matter for him to execute his designs, said, after a pause: Princess, whatever resolution a poor wretched woman as I am may have made to renounce the pomp and grandeur of this world, I dare not presume to oppose the will and commands of so pious and charitable a Princess. He accordingly followed her with tottering gait.

Afterwards the Princess requested him to dine with her; but he, considering that he should then be obliged to show his face, which he had always taken care to conceal; and fearing that the Princess should find out that he was not Fatima, begged of her earnestly to excuse him, telling her that he never ate anything but bread and dried fruits, and desiring to eat that slight repast in his own apartment. The Princess granted his request, saying, You may be as free here, good mother, as if you were in your own cell: I will order you a dinner, but remember I expect you as soon as you have finished your repast.

After the Princess had dined, and the false Fatima had been informed by one of the slaves that she was risen from table, he failed not to wait upon her. My good mother, said the Princess, I am overjoyed to have the company of so holy a woman as yourself, who will confer a blessing upon this palace. But now I am speaking of the palace, Pray how do you like it? And before I show it all to you, tell me first what you think of this hall.

Upon this question, the counterfeit Fatima surveyed the hall from one end to the other, and said, As far as such a solitary being as I am, who am unacquainted with what the world calls beautiful, can judge, this hall is truly admirable and most beautiful; there wants but one thing. What is that, good mother? demanded the Princess; tell me, I conjure you. For my part, I always believed, and have heard say, it wanted nothing; but if it does, it shall be supplied.

Princess, said the false Fatima, with great dissimulation, forgive me the liberty I have taken; but my opinion is, if it can be of any importance, that if a roc's egg were hung up in the middle of the dome, this hall would have no parallel in the four quarters of the world, and your palace would be the wonder of the universe.

My good mother, said the Princess, what bird is a roc, and where may one get an egg? Princess, replied the pretended Fatima, it is a bird of prodigious size, which inhabits the summit of Mount Caucasus; the architect who built your palace can get you one.

The Princess often thought of the roc's egg, and it annoyed her to think that any thing was lacking from her palace; so when Aladdin returned she received him coldly, and said: I always believed that our palace was the most superb, magnificent, and complete in the world-; but I will tell you now what I find fault with upon examining the hall of four-and-twenty windows. Do not you think with me that it would be complete if a roc's egg were hung up in the midst of the dome? Princess, replied Aladdin, it is enough that you think there wants such an ornament; you shall see by the diligence used to supply that deficiency that there is nothing which I would not do for your sake.

Aladdin left the Princess Buddir al Buddoor that moment, and went up into the hall of four-and-twenty windows, where, pulling out of his bosom the lamp which, after the danger he had been exposed to, he always carried about him, he rubbed it, upon which the genie immediately appeared. Genie, said Aladdin, there wants a roc's egg to be hung up in the midst of the dome; I command thee, in the name of this lamp, to repair the deficiency. Aladdin had no sooner pronounced these words, than the genie gave so loud and terrible a cry that the hall shook, and Aladdin could scarcely stand upright. What! wretch, said the genie, in a voice that would have made the most undaunted man tremble, is it not enough that I and my companions have done everything for you, but you, by an unheard-of ingratitude, must command me to bring my master and hang him up in the midst of this dome? This attempt deserves that you,

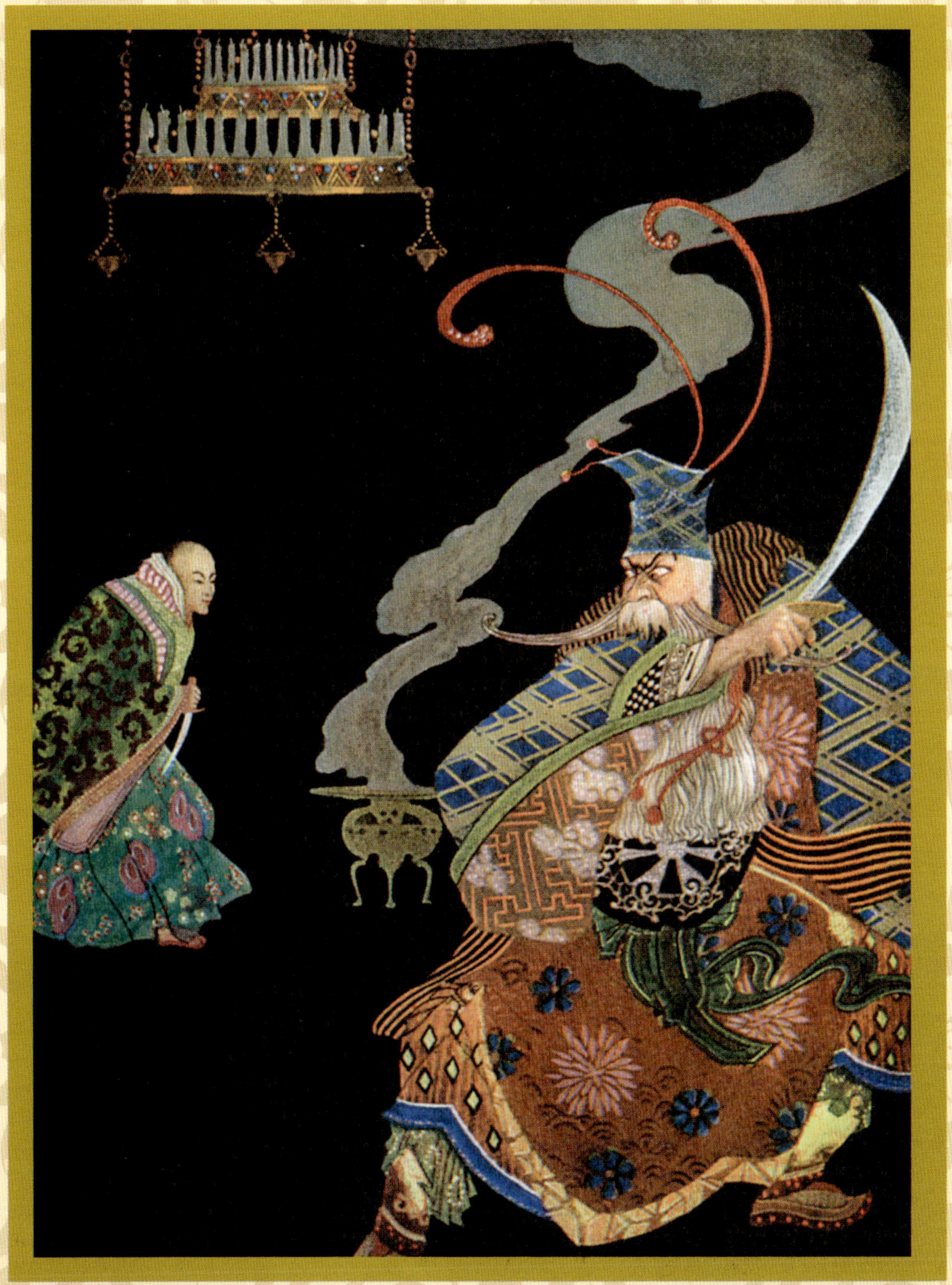

your wife, and your palace, should be immediately reduced to ashes: but you are happy that this request does not come from yourself. Know then, that the true author is the brother of the African magician, your enemy, whom you have destroyed as he deserved. He is now in your palace, disguised in the habit of the holy woman Fatima, whom he has murdered; and it is he who has suggested to your wife to make this pernicious demand. His design is to kill you, therefore take care of yourself. After these words the genie disappeared.

Aladdin quickly resolved what to do. He returned to the Princess and pretended to be suddenly taken ill. The Princess, remembering Fatima's power, at once sent for her, and she came with all speed. In the meantime the Princess explained how the holy woman came into the palace, and when she appeared Aladdin smiled and bade her welcome at so opportune a moment. Surely, good woman, said he, you can cure me as you have others.

The counterfeit Fatima advanced towards him, with his hand all the time on a dagger concealed in his girdle under his gown. Aladdin perceived this, and snatched the weapon from his hand, and slew him on the spot.

My dear husband, what have you done? cried the Princess in surprise. You have killed the holy woman. No, my Princess, answered Aladdin with emotion, I have not killed Fatima, but a villain, who would have assassinated me if I had not prevented him. This wicked wretch, added he, uncovering his face, is brother to the African magician.

Thus was Aladdin delivered from the persecution of two brothers, who were magicians. Within a few years afterwards the sultan died in a good old age, and as he left no male children the Princess Buddir al Buddoor succeeded him, and she and Aladdin reigned together many years, and left a numerous and illustrious posterity.

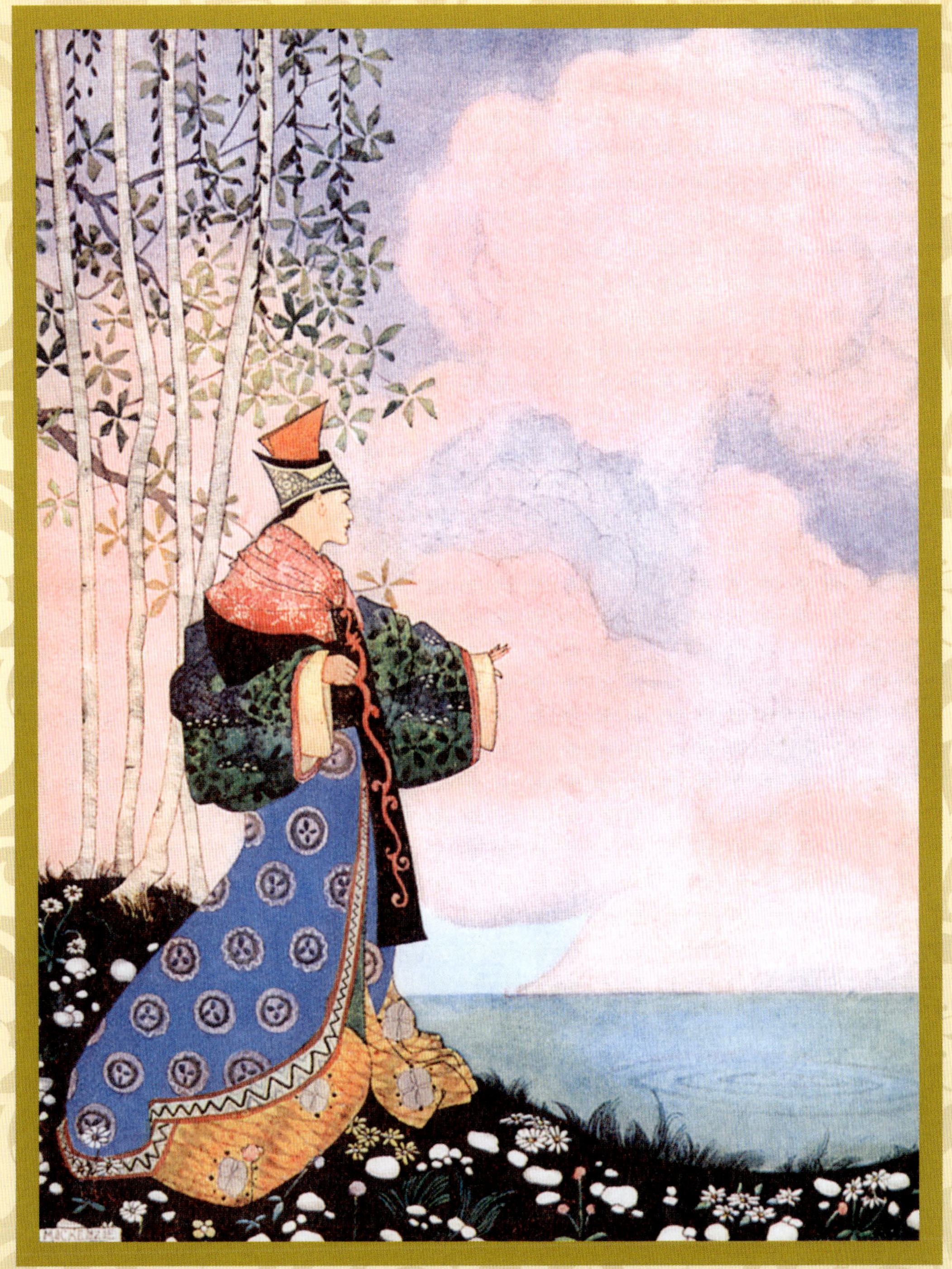

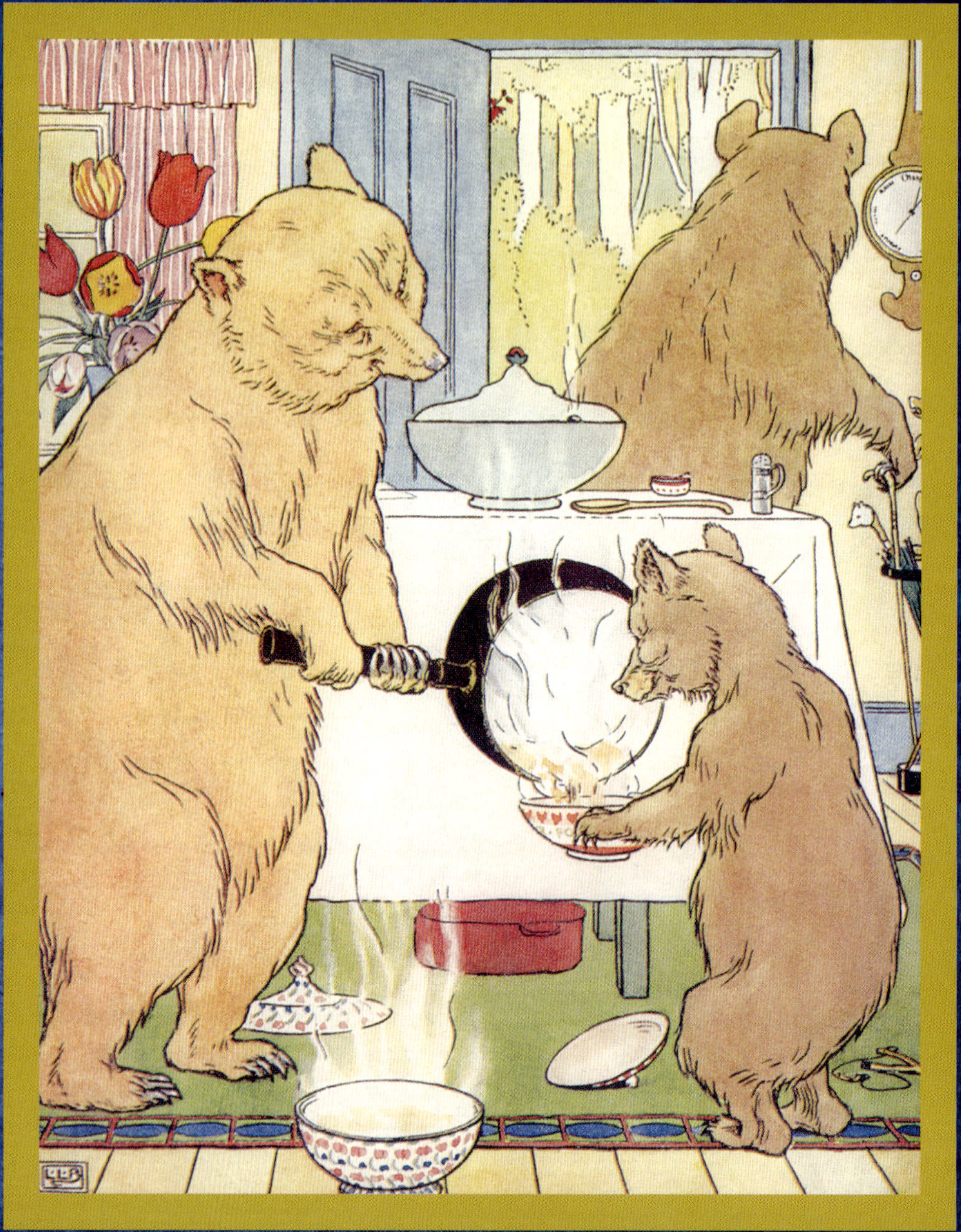

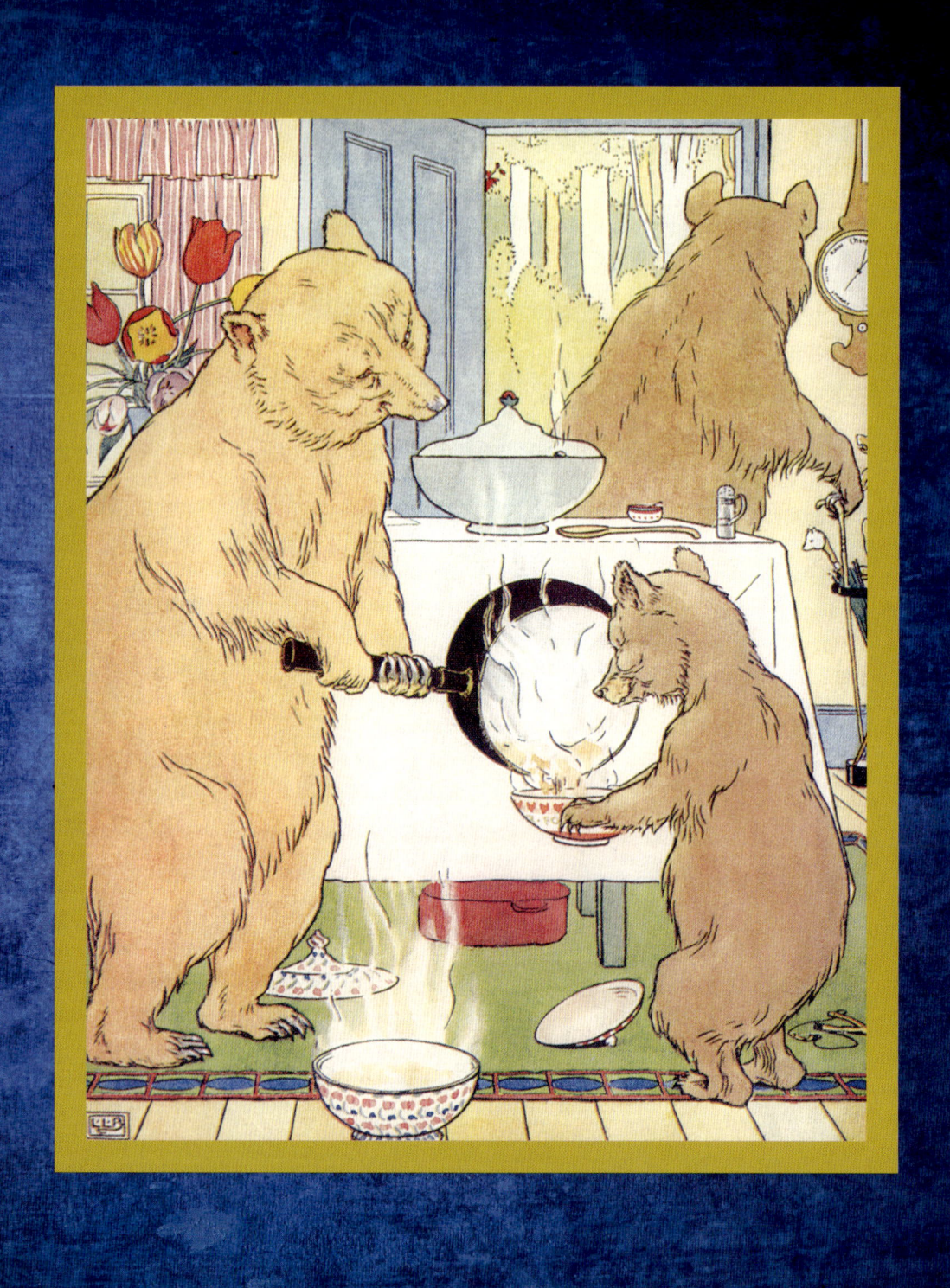

Goldilocks and the Three Bears

ONCE UPON A TIME THERE WERE THREE BEARS, WHO LIVED TOGETHER in a house of their own, in a wood. One of them was a Little, Small, Wee Bear; and one was a Middle-sized Bear, and the other was a Great, Huge Bear. They had each a pot for their porridge; a little pot for the Little, Small, Wee Bear; and a middle-sized pot for the Middle Bear, and a great pot for the Great, Huge Bear. And they had each a chair to sit in; a little chair for the Little, Small, Wee Bear; and a middle-sized chair for the Middle Bear, and a great chair for the Great, Huge Bear. And they had each a bed to sleep in; a little bed for the Little, Small, Wee Bear; and a middle-sized bed for the Middle Bear, and a great bed for the Great, Huge Bear.

One day, after they had made the porridge for their breakfast, and poured it into their porridge-pots, they walked out into the wood while the porridge was cooling, that they might not burn their mouths by beginning too soon to eat it. And while they were walking, a little girl called Goldilocks came to the house. First she looked in at the window, and then she peeped in at the keyhole; and seeing nobody in the house, she turned the handle of the door. The door was not fastened, because the Bears were good Bears, who did nobody any harm, and never suspected that anybody would harm them. So Goldilocks opened the door, and went in; and well pleased she was when she saw the porridge on the table. If she had been a thoughtful little girl, she would have waited till the Bears came home, and then, perhaps, they would have asked her to breakfast; for they were good Bears—a little rough or so, as the manner of Bears is, but for all that very good-natured and hospitable. But the porridge looked tempting, and she set about helping herself.

So first she tasted the porridge of the Great, Huge Bear, and that was too hot for her. And then she tasted the porridge of the Middle Bear, and that was too cold for her. And then she went to the porridge of the Little, Small, Wee Bear, and tasted that; and that was neither too hot nor too cold, but just right, and she liked it so well that she ate it all up.

Then Goldilocks sat down in the chair of the Great, Huge Bear, and that was too hard for her. And then she sat down in the chair of the Middle Bear, and that was too soft for her. And then she sat down in the chair of the Little, Small, Wee Bear, and that was neither too hard nor too soft, but just right. So she seated herself in it, and there she sat till the bottom of the chair came out, and down she came plump upon the ground.

Then Goldilocks went upstairs into the bedchamber in which the three Bears slept. And first she lay down upon the bed of the Great, Huge Bear, but that was too high at the head for her. And next she lay down upon the bed of the Middle Bear, and that was too high at the foot for her. And then she lay down upon the bed of the Little, Small, Wee Bear; and that was neither too high at the head nor at the foot, but just right. So she covered herself up comfortably, and lay there till she fell fast asleep.

THE FAMILY TREE
BEAR AND FORBEAR
MAJOR URSA D.S.O.
THE BEAR TRUTH

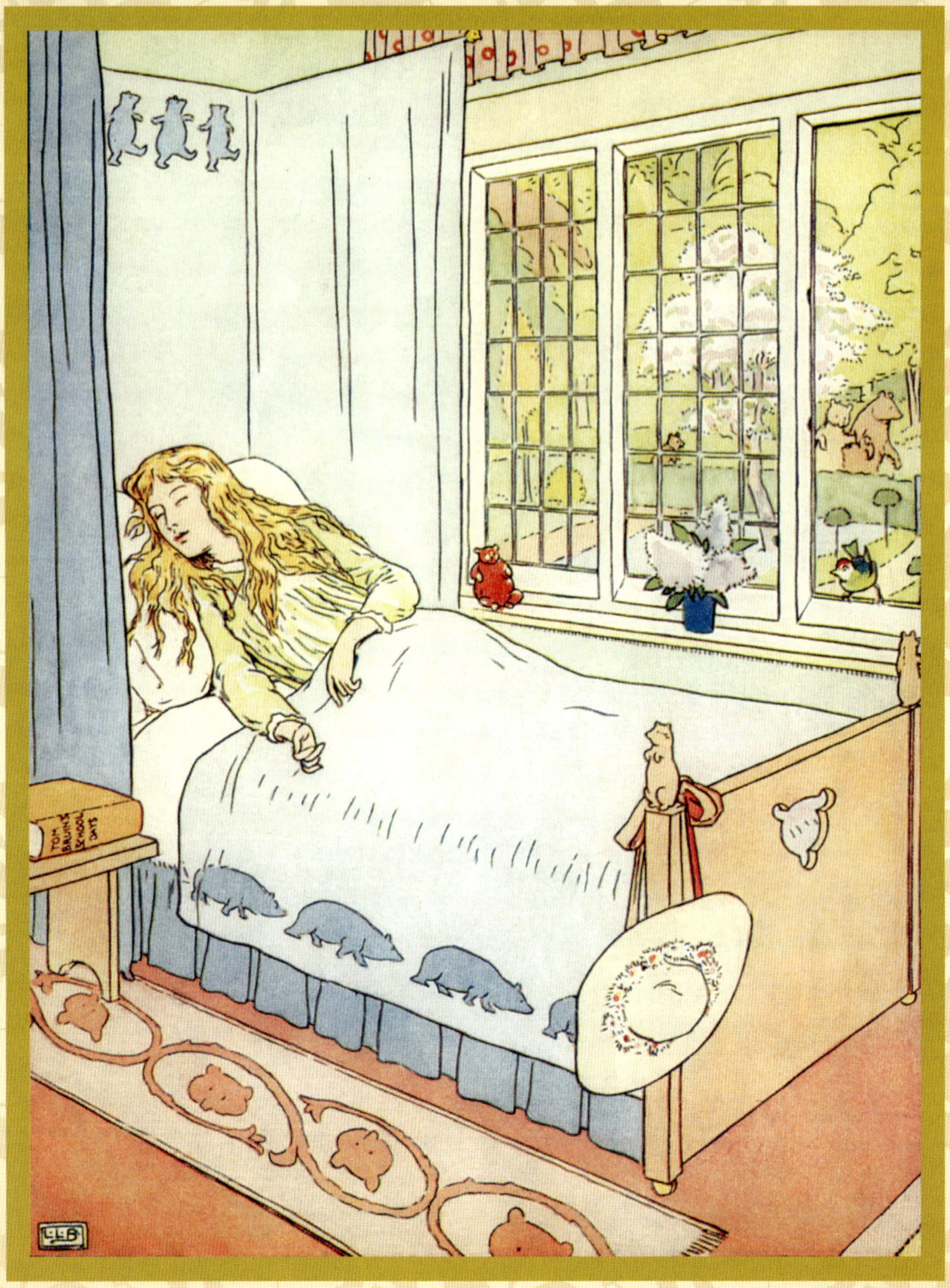
TOM BRUIN'S SCHOOL DAYS

By this time the Three Bears thought their porridge would be cool enough; so they came home to breakfast. Now Goldilocks had left the spoon of the Great, Huge Bear standing in his porridge.

"SOMEBODY HAS BEEN AT MY PORRIDGE!"

said the Great, Huge Bear, in his great, rough, gruff voice. And when the Middle Bear looked at hers, she saw that the spoon was standing in it too.

"Somebody has been at my porridge!"

said the Middle Bear, in her middle voice. Then the Little, Small, Wee Bear looked at his, and there was the spoon in the porridge-pot, but the porridge was all gone.

"Somebody has been at my porridge, and has eaten it all up!"

said the Little, Small, Wee Bear, in his little, small, wee voice.

Upon this the Three Bears, seeing that someone had entered their house, and eaten up the Little, Small, Wee Bear's breakfast, began to look about them. Now Goldilocks had not put the hard cushion straight when she rose from the chair of the Great, Huge Bear.

"SOMEBODY HAS BEEN SITTING IN MY CHAIR!"

said the Great, Huge Bear, in his great, rough, gruff voice.

And Goldilocks had squatted down the soft cushion of the Middle Bear.

"Somebody has been sitting in my chair!"

said the Middle Bear, in her middle voice.
And you know what Goldilocks had done to the third chair.

"Somebody has been sitting in my chair and has sat the bottom out of it!"

said the Little, Small, Wee Bear, in his little, small, wee voice.
Then the Three Bears thought it necessary that they should make further search; so they went upstairs into their bedchamber. Now Goldilocks had pulled the pillow of the Great, Huge Bear out of its place.

"SOMEBODY HAS BEEN LYING IN MY BED!"

said the Great, Huge Bear, in his great, rough, gruff voice.
And Goldilocks had pulled the bolster of the Middle Bear out of its place.

"Somebody has been lying in my bed!"

said the Middle Bear, in her middle voice. And when the Little, Small, Wee Bear came to look at his bed, there was the bolster in its place; and the pillow in its place upon the bolster; and upon the pillow was the head of Goldilocks—which was not in its place, for she had no business there.

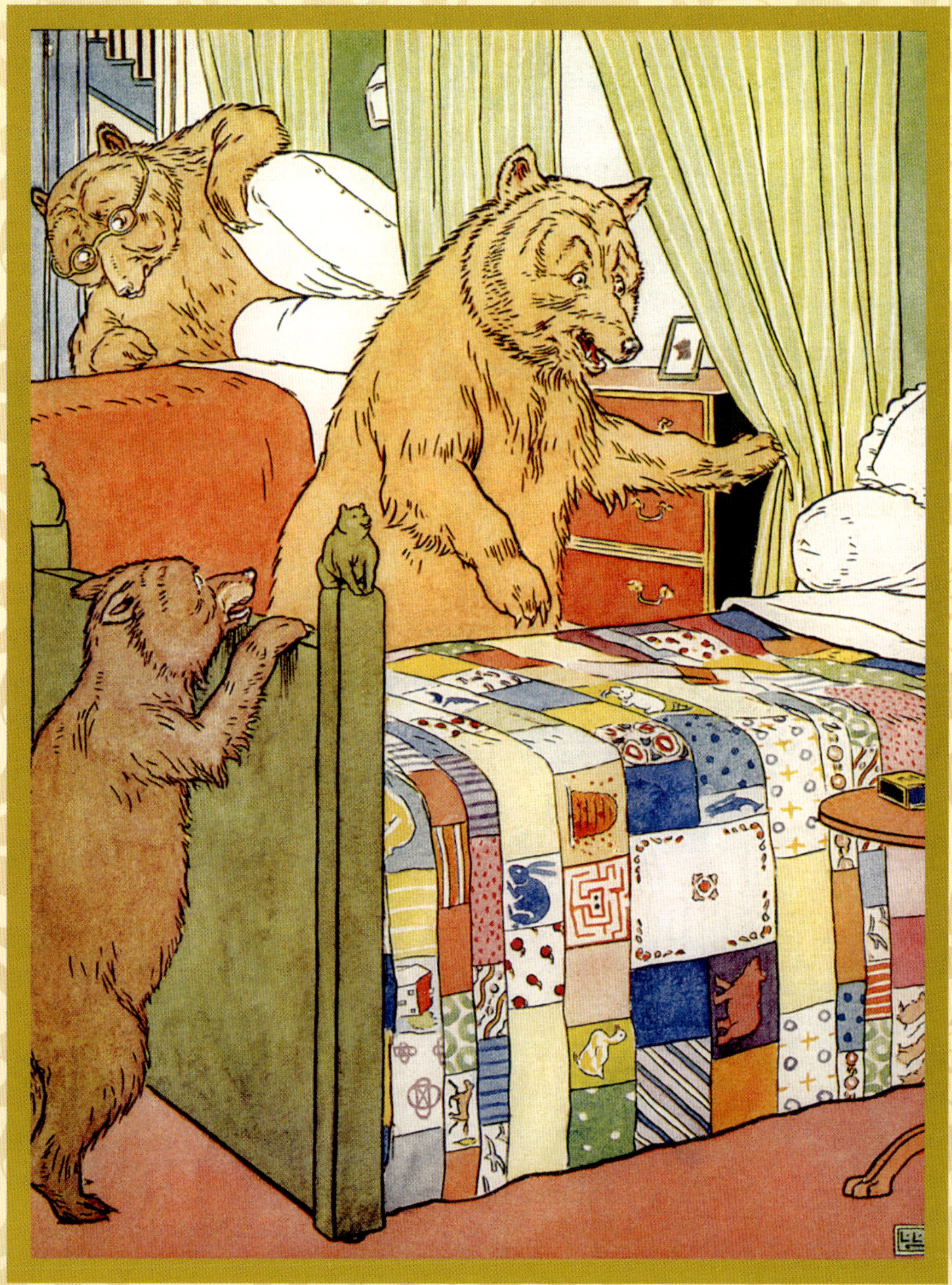

"Somebody has been lying in my bed—and here she is!"

said the Little, Small, Wee Bear, in his little, small, wee voice.

Goldilocks had heard in her sleep the great, rough, gruff voice of the Great, Huge Bear, and the middle voice of the Middle Bear, but it was only as if she had heard someone speaking in a dream. But when she heard the little, small, wee voice of the Little, Small, Wee Bear, it was so sharp, and so shrill, that it awakened her at once. Up she started; and when she saw the Three Bears on one side of the bed she tumbled herself out at the other, and ran to the window. Now the window was open, because the Bears, like good, tidy Bears, as they were, always opened their bedchamber window when they got up in the morning. Out Goldilocks jumped, and ran away as fast as she could run—never looking behind her; and what happened to her afterward I cannot tell. But the Three Bears never saw anything more of her.

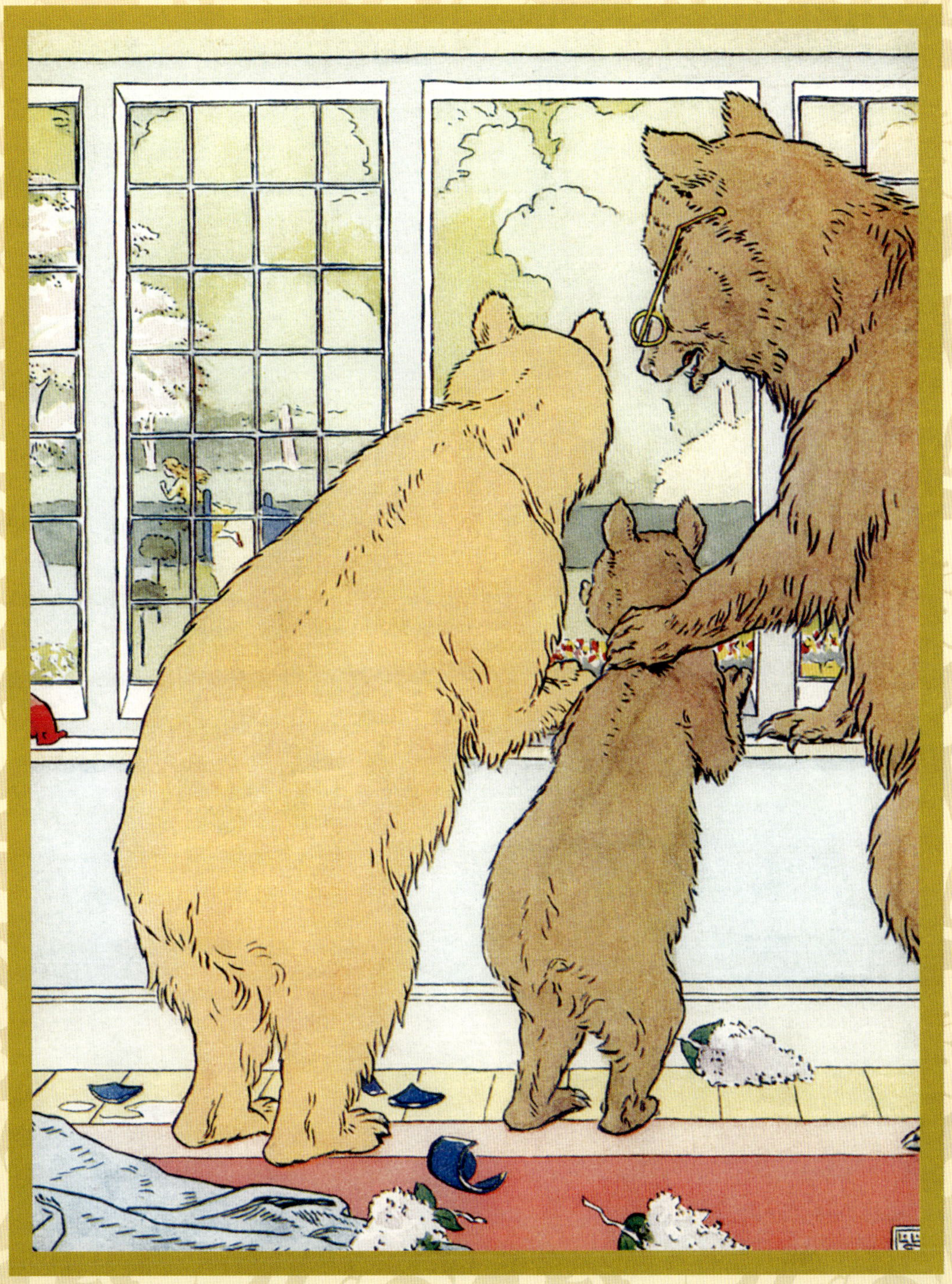

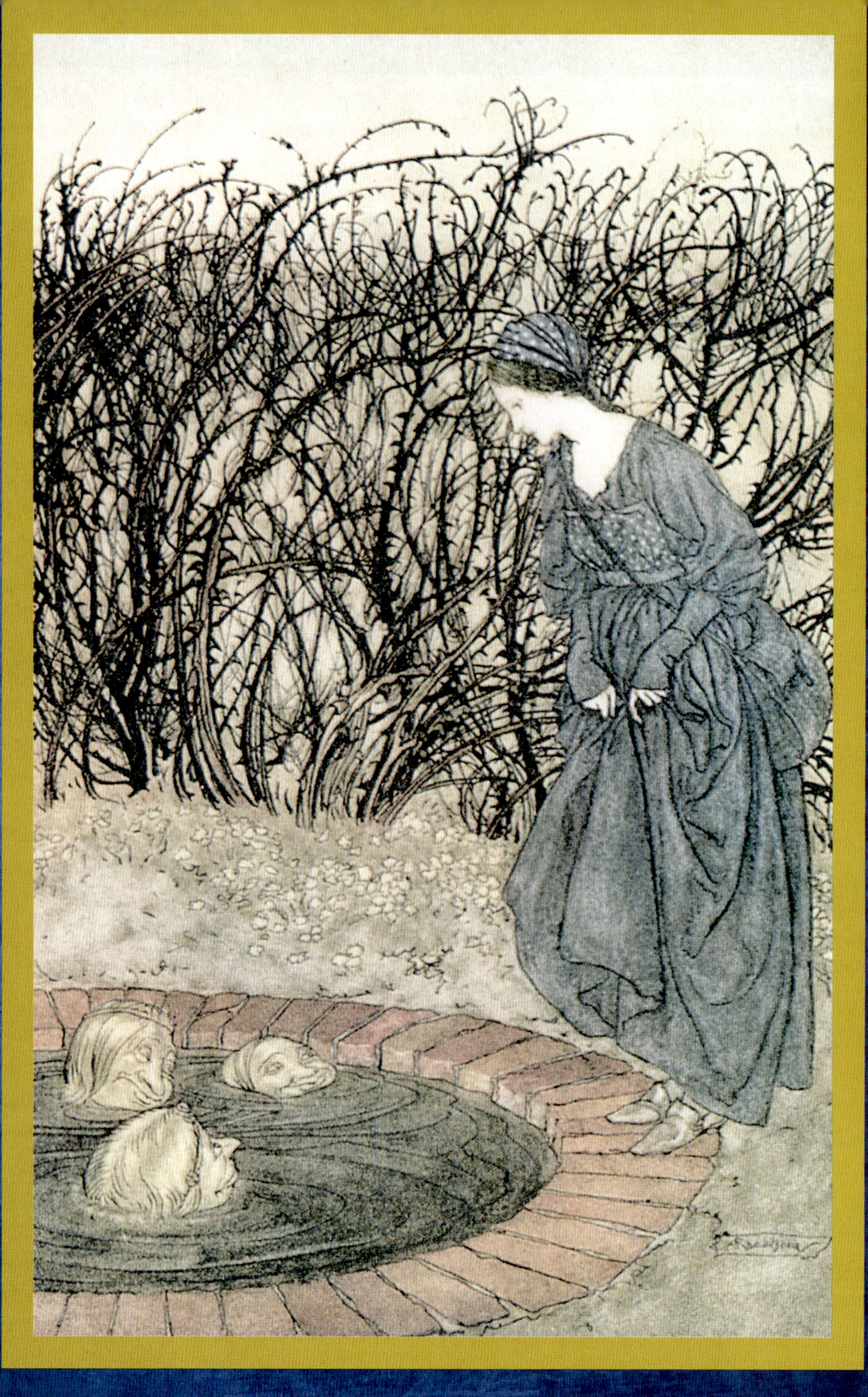

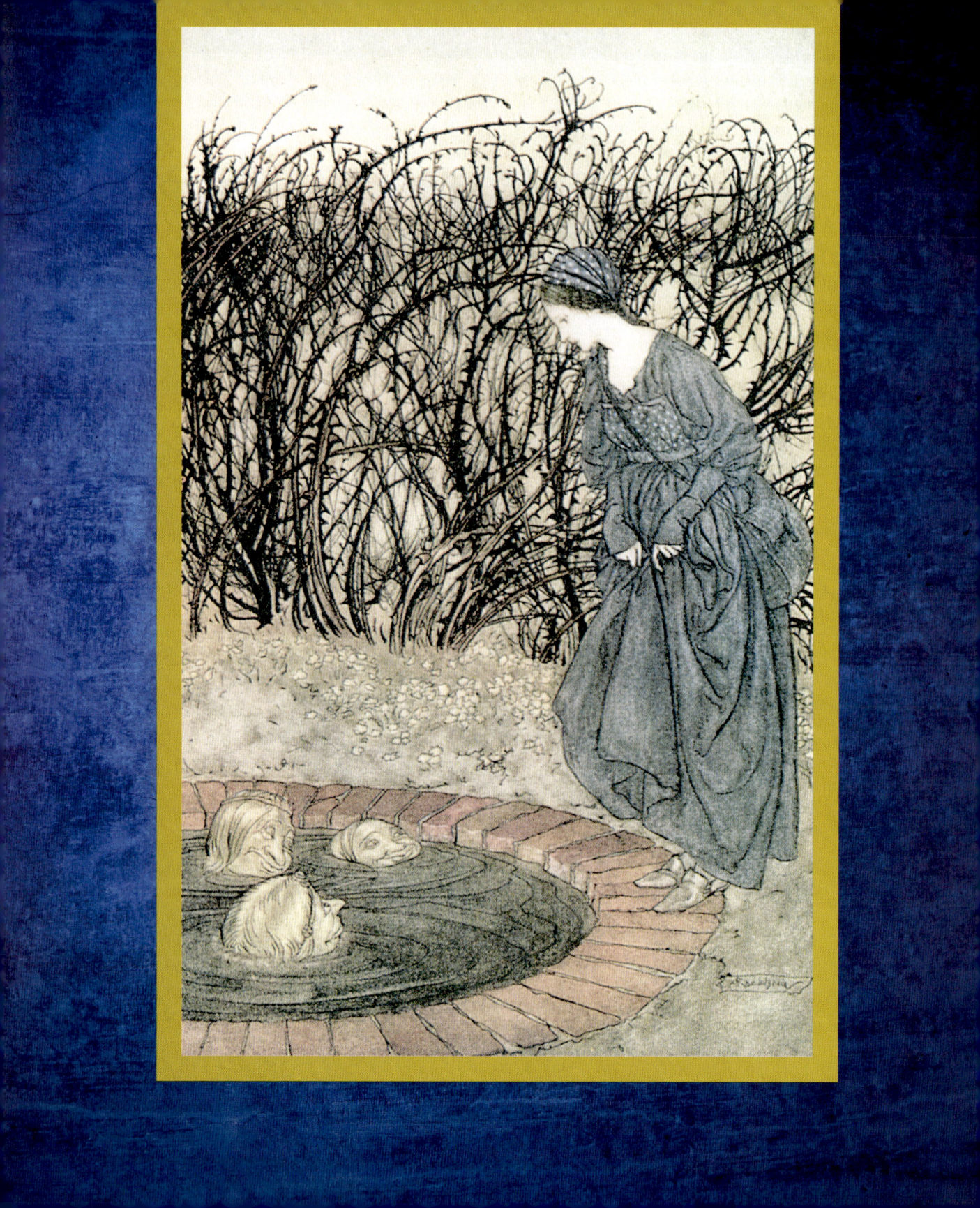

The Three Heads of the Well

Once upon a time there reigned a King in Colchester, valiant, strong, wise, famous as a good ruler.

But in the midst of his glory his dear Queen died, leaving him with a daughter just touching woman's estate; and this maiden was renowned, far and wide, for beauty, kindness, grace. Now strange things happen, and the King of Colchester, hearing of a lady who had immense riches, had a mind to marry her, though she was old, ugly, hook-nosed, and ill-tempered; and though she was, furthermore, possessed of a daughter as ugly as herself. None could give the reason why, but only a few weeks after the death of his dear Queen, the King brought this loathly bride to Court, and married her with great pomp and festivities. Now the very first thing she did was to poison the King's mind against his own beautiful, kind, gracious daughter, of whom, naturally, the ugly Queen and her ugly daughter were dreadfully jealous.

Now when the young Princess found that even her father had turned against her, she grew weary of Court life, and longed to get away from it; so, one day, happening to meet the King alone in the garden, she went down on her knees, and begged and prayed him to give her some help, and let her go out into the world to seek her fortune. To this the King agreed, and told his consort to fit the girl out for her enterprise in proper fashion. But the jealous woman only gave her a canvas bag of brown bread and hard cheese, with a bottle of small-beer.

Though this was but a pitiful dowry for a King's daughter, the Princess was too proud to complain; so she took it, returned her thanks, and set off on her journey through woods and forests, by rivers and lakes, over mountain and valley.

At last she came to a cave at the mouth of which, on a stone, sat an old, old man with a white beard.

"Good morrow, fair damsel," he said, "whither away so fast?"

"Reverend father," replies she, "I go to seek my fortune."

"And what hast thou for dowry, fair damsel?" said he, "in thy bag and bottle?"

"Bread and cheese and small-beer, father," says she, smiling. "Will it please you to partake of either?"

"With all my heart," says he, and when she pulled out her provisions he ate them nearly all. But once again she made no complaint, but bade him eat what he needed, and welcome.

Now, when he had finished he gave her many thanks, and said:

"For your beauty, and your kindness, and your grace, take this wand. There is a thick thorny hedge before you which seems impassable. But strike it thrice with this wand, saying each time, 'Please, hedge, let me through,' and it will open a pathway for you. Then, when you come to a well, sit down on the brink of it, do not be surprised at anything you may see, but, whatever you are asked to do, that do!"

So saying the old man went into the cave and she went on her way. After a while she came to a high, thick thorny hedge; but when she struck it three times with the wand, saying, "Please, hedge, let me through," it opened a wide pathway for her. So she came to the well, on the brink of which she sat down, and no sooner had she done so, than a golden head without any body came up through the water, singing as it came:

"Wash me, and comb me, lay me on a bank to dry
Softly and prettily to watch the passers-by."

"Certainly," she said, pulling out her silver comb. Then, placing the head on her lap, she began to comb the golden hair. When she had combed it, she lifted the golden head softly, and laid it on a primrose bank to dry. No sooner had she done this than another golden head appeared, singing as it came:

> "Wash me, and comb me, lay me on a bank to dry
> Softly and prettily to watch the passers-by."

"Certainly," says she, and after combing the golden hair, placed the golden head softly on the primrose bank, beside the first one.

Then came a third head out of the well, and it said the same thing:

> "Wash me, and comb me, lay me on a bank to dry
> Softly and prettily to watch the passers-by."

"With all my heart," says she, graciously, and after taking the head on her lap, and combing its golden hair with her silver comb, there were the three golden heads in a row on the primrose bank. And she sat down to rest herself and looked at them, they were so quaint and pretty; and as she rested she cheerfully ate and drank the meager portion of the brown bread, hard cheese, and small-beer which the old man had left to her; for, though she was a King's daughter, she was too proud to complain.

Then the first head spoke. "Brothers, what shall we weird for this damsel who has been so gracious unto us? I weird her to be so beautiful that she shall charm every one she meets."

"And I," said the second head, "weird her a voice that shall exceed the nightingale's in sweetness."

"And I," said the third head, "weird her to be so fortunate that she shall marry the greatest King that reigns."

"Thank you with all my heart," says she; "but don't you think I had better put you back in the well before I go on? Remember you are golden, and the passers-by might steal you."

To this they agreed; so she put them back. And when they had thanked her for her kind thought and said good-bye, she went on her journey.

Now she had not traveled far before she came to a forest where the King of the country was hunting with his nobles, and as the gay cavalcade passed down the glade she stood back to avoid them; but the King caught sight of her, and drew up his horse, fairly amazed at her beauty.

"Fair maid," he said, "who art thou, and whither goest thou through the forest thus alone?"

"I am the King of Colchester's daughter, and I go to seek my fortune," says she, and her voice was sweeter than the nightingale's.

Then the King jumped from his horse, being so struck by her that he felt it would be impossible to live without her, and falling on his knee begged and prayed her to marry him without delay.

And he begged and prayed so well that at last she consented. So, with all courtesy, he mounted her on his horse behind him, and commanding the hunt to follow, he returned to his palace, where the wedding festivities took place with all possible pomp and merriment. Then, ordering out the royal chariot, the happy pair started to pay the King of Colchester a bridal visit: and you may imagine the surprise and delight with which, after so short an absence, the people of Colchester saw their beloved, beautiful, kind, and gracious Princess return in a chariot all gemmed with gold, as the bride of the most powerful King in the world. The bells rang out, flags flew, drums beat, the people huzzaed, and all was gladness, save for the ugly Queen and her ugly daughter, who were ready to burst with envy and malice; for, see you, the despised maiden was now above them both, and went before them at every Court ceremonial.

So, after the visit was ended, and the young King and his bride had gone back to their own country, there to live happily ever after, the ugly ill-natured Princess said to her mother, the ugly Queen:

"I also will go into the world and seek my fortune. If that drab of a girl with her mincing ways got so much, what may I not get?"

So her mother agreed, and furnished her forth with silken dresses and furs, and gave her as provisions, sugar, almonds, and sweetmeats of every variety, besides a large flagon of Malaga sack. Altogether a right royal dowry.

The Three Heads of the Well

Armed with these she set forth, following the same road as her step-sister. Thus she soon came upon the old man with a white beard, who was seated on a stone by the mouth of a cave.

"Good morrow," says he. "Whither away so fast?"

"What's that to you, old man?" she replied rudely.

"And what hast thou for dowry in bag and bottle?" he asked quietly.

"Good things with which you shall not be troubled," she answered pertly.

"Wilt thou not spare an old man something?" he said.

Then she laughed. "Not a bite, not a sup, lest they should choke you: though that would be small matter to me," she replied with a toss of her head.

"Then ill luck go with thee," remarked the old man as he rose and went into the cave.

So she went on her way, and after a time came to the thick thorny hedge, and seeing what she thought was a gap in it, she tried to pass through; but no sooner had she got well into the middle of the hedge than the thorns closed in around her so that she was all scratched and torn before she went her way. Thus, streaming with blood, she went on to the well, and seeing water, sate on the brink intending to cleanse herself. But just as she dipped her hands, up came a golden head singing as it came:

> "Wash me, and comb me, lay me on the bank to dry
> Softly and prettily to watch the passers-by."

"A likely story," says she. "I'm going to wash myself." And with that she gave the head such a bang with her bottle that it bobbed below the water. But it came up again, and so did a second head, singing as it came:

> "Wash me, and comb me, lay me on the bank to dry
> Softly and prettily to watch the passers-by."

"Not I," scoffs she. "I'm going to wash my hands and face and have my dinner." So she fetches the second head a cruel bang with the bottle, and both heads ducked down in the water.

But when they came up again all draggled and dripping, the third head came also, singing as it came:

> "Wash me, and comb me, lay me on the bank to dry
> Softly and prettily to watch the passers-by."

By this time the ugly Princess had cleansed herself, and seated on the primrose bank had her mouth full of sugar and almonds.

"Not I," says she as well as she could. "I'm not a washerwoman nor a barber. So take that for your washing and combing."

And with that, having finished the Malaga sack, she flung the empty bottle at the three heads.

But this time they didn't duck. They looked at each other and said, "How shall we weird this rude girl for her bad manners?" Then the first head said:

The Three Heads of the Well

"I weird that to her ugliness shall be added blotches on her face."

And the second head said:

"I weird that she shall ever be hoarse as a crow and speak as if she had her mouth full."

Then the third head said:

"And I weird that she shall be glad to marry a cobbler."

Then the three heads sank into the well and were no more seen, and the ugly Princess went on her way. But lo and behold! when she came to a town, the children ran from her ugly blotched face screaming with fright, and when she tried to tell them she was the King of Colchester's daughter, her voice squeaked like a corn-crake's, was hoarse as a crow's, and folk could not understand a word she said, because she spoke as if her mouth was full!

Now in the town there happened to be a cobbler who not long before had mended the shoes of a poor old hermit, and the latter, having no money, had paid for the job by the gift of a wonderful ointment which would cure blotches on the face, and a bottle of medicine that would banish any hoarseness.

So, seeing the miserable, ugly Princess in great distress, he went up to her and gave her a few drops out of his bottle; and then understanding from her rich attire and clearer speech that she was indeed a King's daughter, he craftily said that if she would take him for a husband, he would undertake to cure her.

"Anything! Anything!" sobbed the miserable Princess.

So they were married, and the cobbler straightway set off with his bride to visit the King of Colchester. But the bells did not ring, the drums did not beat, and the people, instead of huzzaing, burst into loud guffaws at the cobbler in leather, and his wife in silks and satins.

As for the ugly Queen, she was so enraged and disappointed that she went mad, and hanged herself in wrath. Whereupon the King, really pleased at getting rid of her so soon, gave the cobbler a hundred pounds and bade him go about his business with his ugly bride.

Which he did quite contentedly, for a hundred pounds means much to a poor cobbler. So they went to a remote part of the Kingdom and lived unhappily for many years, he cobbling shoes, and she spinning the thread for him.

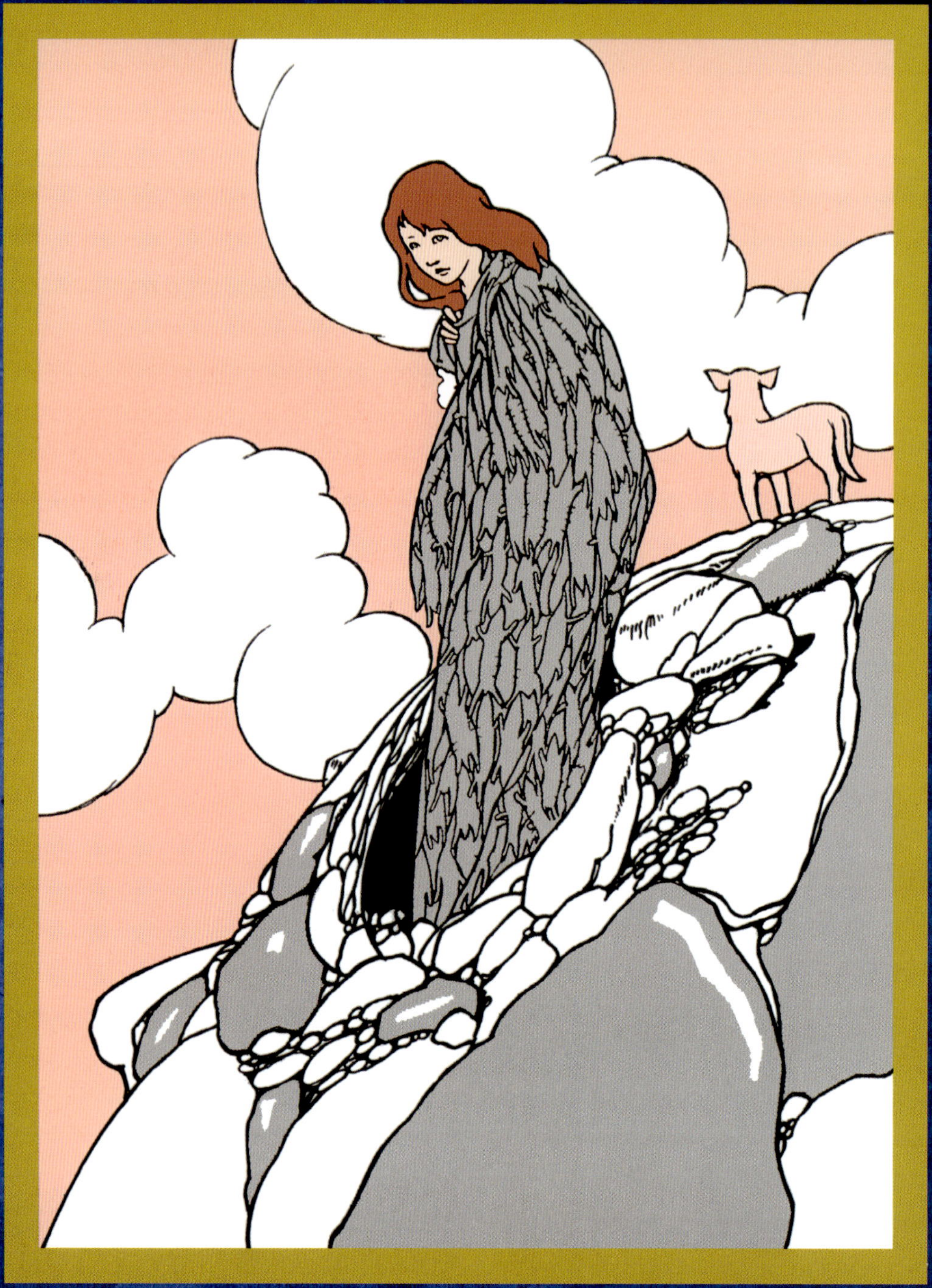

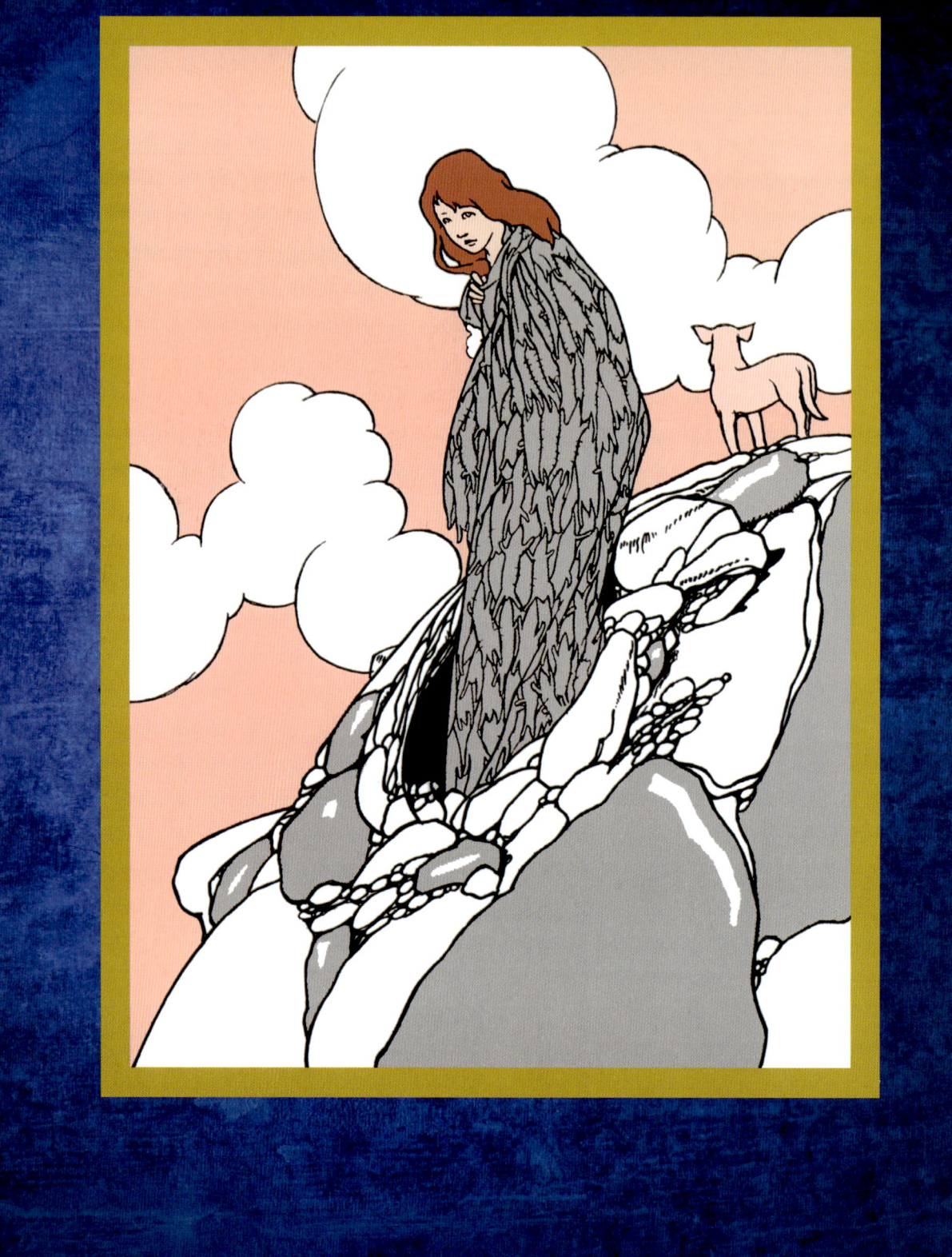

Mouseskin

Once a nobleman had an only daughter, whom he placed in a mount, there to remain as long as there was war in the country. The father had secretly caused a room to be built for her in the mount, and had laid in a stock of provisions, and wood enough to last for seven years; and she was not to come out until he fetched her; but if at the end of seven years he did not come for her, she might conclude that he was dead, and might then leave the mount. A little dog was her only companion.

The damsel occupied herself with spinning, weaving, and sewing; and thus one year passed after another. She made a number of fine clothes, some of which were embroidered with gold, and others with silver; but when she had no longer anything to spin or employ her, the time began to be tedious. Her stock of food was nearly exhausted, and she was fearful that her father would not return. As the time that she was to remain in the mount had nearly expired, and he had not come to fetch her, she concluded that he was dead. She now began to dig her way out, but this was very slow work, and no easy task for.

In the meantime all her provisions were consumed. But the mount was full of mice, and her little dog destroyed a great many every day; these she skinned, roasted, and ate the meat, and gave the bones to her little dog. She stitched all the skins together, and made herself a cloak or garment, which was so large that she could quite wrap herself up in it. Every day she labored at the aperture, and at length succeeded so far as to be able once more to see the light of day. She then closed up the opening, and left the hill with her little dog, and went through the wood, and there was much she found changed in the seven years she had lived underground. She had her silver and her gold dresses on, and over them she wore the mouseskin cloak, which quite covered her, so that she had more the appearance of a poor man's child than a young lady of rank. At the first house she came to she inquired who lived at the manor. She was told it was the young lord, who had inherited it after the death of the former proprietor.

"How then did he die?" asked she, hardly able to conceal her feelings.

She received for answer, that he was a brave soldier, and drove the enemy out of the country, but was killed in the last battle; that his only child was a daughter who had been carried off before that time, and no one had since ever heard anything of her.

The young maiden then asked, if they could tell her where she could be employed, as she wanted work.

"Our young master is soon to be married," said the people; "his bride, with her father and mother, are arrived at the mansion to make preparations for the wedding; if you only go up there, you will surely find something to do."

The young girl then went up to her father's abode, and her little dog was so happy; for it knew the place again; but its mistress wept with grief, as she humbly knocked at the door. When the people heard that she wished to be employed, they gladly engaged her, and set her to sweep the yard, and the steps, and do other menial work.

The day before the wedding the bride sent for her, and told her that she had a great favor to ask: "Thou art of the same height as I am," said she; "thou must to-morrow put on my bridal dress and veil, and drive to the church, and be wedded to the bridegroom, instead of me." The young girl could not imagine why the other objected to be wedded to the handsome young lord. The bride then told her, that there was another lover, to whom she had previously betrothed herself; but that her parents wanted to force her to marry this rich young lord; that she was afraid of disobeying them, but that she had agreed with her first beloved, that on the wedding day she would elope with him. This she could not do, if she were wedded at the altar to another; but if she sent some one in her place, everything might end well. The young maiden promised to do all that the bride requested of her.

The next day the bride was attired in the most costly dress, and all the people in the house came into her chamber to look at her; at length she said: "Now call that poor young girl that sweeps the yard, and let her also see me." The girl in the mousekin dress came up accordingly, and, when they were alone together, the bride locked the door, dressed her in the beautiful clothes, with the bridal veil over her head, and then wrapped herself in the young girl's large mouseskin cloak.

The late lord's daughter was then conducted to a chariot, in which was the bridegroom, and they drove to church together, accompanied by all the bridal guests. On the road they passed the mount, where she had lived so long concealed. She sighed beneath her veil, and said:

> "Yonder stands yet every pin,
> With every little mouse's skin,
> Where seven long years I pined in sadness
> In the dark mount, and knew no gladness."

"What sayest thou, dearest of my heart?" asked the bridegroom.

"Oh! I am only talking a little to myself," answered the bride.

When she entered the church, she saw the portraits of her parents suspended on each side of the altar; but it appeared to her as if they turned from her, as she wept beneath her veil while gazing on them; she then said:

"Turn, turn again, ye pictures dear; dear father and mother, turn again";

and then the pictures turned again.

"What sayest thou, my dear bride?" asked the bridegroom.

"Oh! I am only talking a little to myself," answered she.

They were then wedded in the church, the young lord put a ring upon her finger, and they drove home. As soon as the bride alighted from the carriage she hurried up into the lady's chamber, as they had agreed, where they changed dresses once more, but the wedding ring which she had on her finger she kept.

In the evening there was dancing, and the young lord danced with her who he thought was his bride; but when he took her hand, he said: "Where is the ring I put on your finger in the church?"

The bride was at first embarrassed, but said quickly: "I took it off and left it in my chamber, but now I will run and fetch it."

She then ran out of the room, called the real bride, and demanded the ring.

"No," answered the maiden, "the ring I will not part with, it belongs to the hand that was given away at the altar. But I will go with you to the door, then you can call him, and we will both stand in the passage; when he comes we will extinguish the light that is there, and I will stretch forth my hand in at the door, so that he can see the ring." Thus it was arranged.

The bridegroom was standing near the door, when the bride called him into the passage, and said: "See! here is the ring." At the same moment as the one damsel extinguished the light, the other stretched forth her hand with the ring.

But the bridegroom was not satisfied with merely seeing the ring, he seized the hand, and drew the young girl into the room, and then, to his astonishment, saw it was the damsel in the mouseskin dress. All the guests flocked round them, and were eager to know how it had all happened.

She then threw off her mouseskin dress, and stood clad in her beautiful gold embroidery, and was more lovely to look at than the other bride. Every one was impatient to hear her story; and she was obliged to relate to them, how long she had remained in the mount, and that her father had been their former lord. The little dog was fetched from her miserable room, and many of the neighbors knew it again.

Hereupon there was great joy and wonder. Everybody revered her father, who had fought so bravely for his country, and all were unanimous that the estate belonged to her. Her sorrow was now turned into joy, and as she wished every one to be as happy as herself, she bestowed land and money on the other bride, that she might marry the man of her choice, to whom she had secretly given her heart. The parents were contented with this arrangement, and now the marriage feast was gay, when the young lord danced with his true bride, to whom he had been wedded in the church, and to whom he had given the ring.

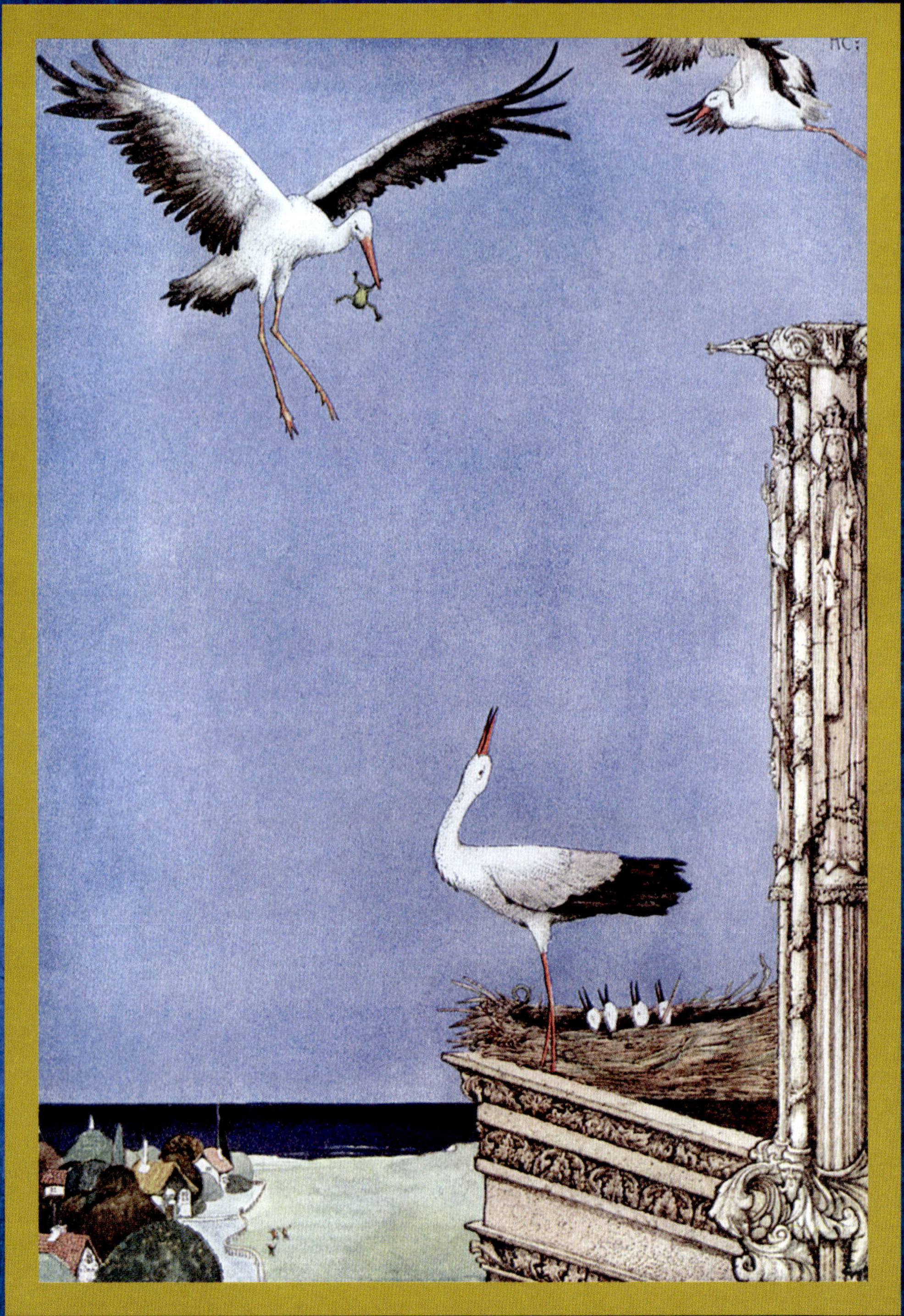

The Storks

On the last house in a little village stood a Stork's nest. The Mother-Stork sat in it with her four young ones, who stretched out their heads with the pointed black beaks, for their beaks had not yet turned red. A little way off stood the Father-Stork, all alone on the ridge of the roof, quite upright and stiff; he had drawn up one of his legs, so as not to be quite idle while he stood sentry. One would have thought he had been carved out of wood, so still did he stand. He thought, "It must look very grand, that my wife has a sentry standing by her nest. They can't tell that it is her husband. They certainly think I have been commanded to stand here. That looks so aristocratic!" And he went on standing on one leg.

Below in the street a whole crowd of children were playing; and when they caught sight of the Storks, one of the boldest of the boys, and afterward all of them, sang the old verse about the Storks. But they only sang it just as he could remember it:

> "Stork, stork, fly away;
> Stand not on one leg to-day.
> Thy dear wife is in the nest,
> Where she rocks her young to rest.
>
> "The first he will be hanged,
> The second will be hit,
> The third he will be shot,
> And the fourth put on the spit."

"Just hear what those boys are saying!" said the little Stork-children. "They say we're to be hanged and killed."

"You're not to care for that!" said the Mother-Stork. "Don't listen to it, and then it won't matter."

But the boys went on singing, and pointed at the Storks mockingly with their fingers; only one boy, whose name was Peter, declared that it was a sin to make a jest of animals, and he would not join in it at all.

The Mother-Stork comforted her children. "Don't you mind it at all," she said; "see how quiet your father stands, though it's only on one leg."

"We are very much afraid," said the young Storks: and they drew their heads far back into the nest.

Now to-day, when the children came out again to play, and saw the Storks, they sang their song:

> "The first he will be hanged,
> The second will be hit . . ."

"Shall we be hanged and beaten?" asked the young Storks.

"No, certainly not," replied the mother. "You shall learn to fly; I'll exercise you; then we shall fly out into the meadows and pay a visit to the frogs; they will bow before us in the water, and sing, 'Co-ax! co-ax!' and then we shall eat them up. That will be a real pleasure."

"And what then?" asked the young Storks.

"Then all the Storks will assemble, all that are here in the whole country, and the autumn exercises begin: then one must fly well, for that is highly important, for whoever cannot fly properly will be thrust dead by the general's beak; so take care and learn well when the exercising begins."

"But then we shall be killed, as the boys say—and only listen, now they're singing again."

"Listen to me, and not to them," said the Mother-Stork. "After the great review we shall fly away to the warm countries, far away from here, over mountains and forests.

We shall fly to Egypt, where there are three covered houses of stone, which curl in a point and tower above the clouds; they are called pyramids, and are older than a stork can imagine. There is a river in that country which runs out of its bed, and then all the land is turned to mud. One walks about in the mud, and eats frogs."

"Oh!" cried all the young ones.

"Yes, it is glorious there! One does nothing all day long but eat; and while we are so comfortable over there, here there is not a green leaf on the trees; here it is so cold that the clouds freeze to pieces, and fall down in little white rags!"

It was the snow that she meant, but she could not explain it in any other way.

"And do the naughty boys freeze to pieces?" asked the young Storks.

"No, they do not freeze to pieces; but they are not far from it, and must sit in the dark room and cower. You, on the other hand, can fly about in foreign lands, where there are flowers, and the sun shines warm."

Now some time had elapsed, and the nestlings had grown so large that they could stand upright in the nest and look far around; and the Father-Stork came every day with delicious frogs, little snakes, and all kinds of stork-dainties as he found them. Oh! it looked funny when he performed feats before them! He laid his head quite back upon his tail, and clapped with his beak as if he had been a little clapper; and then he told them stories, all about the marshes.

"Listen! now you must learn to fly," said the Mother-Stork one day; and all the four young ones had to go out on the ridge of the roof. Oh, how they tottered! how they balanced themselves with their wings, and yet they were nearly falling down.

"Only look at me," said the mother. "Thus you must hold your heads! Thus you must pitch your feet! One, two! one, two! That's what will help you on in the world."

Then she flew a little way, and the young ones made a little clumsy leap. Bump!— there they lay, for their bodies were too heavy. "I will not fly!" said one of the young Storks, and crept back into the nest; "I don't care about getting to the warm countries."

"Do you want to freeze to death here, when the winter comes? Are the boys to come and hang you, and singe you, and roast you? Now I'll call them."

"Oh no!" cried the young Stork, and hopped out on to the roof again like the rest.

On the third day they could actually fly a little, and then they thought they could also soar and hover in the air. They tried it, but—bump!—down they tumbled, and they had to shoot their wings again quickly enough. Now the boys came into the street again, and sang their song:

"Stork, stork, fly away!"

"Shall we fly down and pick their eyes out?" asked the young Storks.

"No," replied the mother, "let them alone. Only listen, to me, that's far more important. One, two, three!—now we fly round to the right. One, two, three!—now to the left round the chimney! See, that was very good! the last kick with the feet was so neat and correct that you shall have permission to-morrow to fly with me to the marsh! Several nice stork families go there with their young: show them that mine are the nicest, and that you can start proudly; that looks well, and will get you consideration."

"But are we not to take revenge on the rude boys?" asked the young Storks.

"Let them scream as much as they like. You will fly up to the clouds, and get to the land of the pyramids, when they will have to shiver, and not have a green leaf or a sweet apple."

"Yes, we will revenge ourselves!" they whispered to one another; and then the exercising went on.

Among all the boys down in the street, the one most bent upon singing the teasing song was he who had begun it, and he was quite a little boy. He could hardly be more than six years old. The young Storks certainly thought he was a hundred, for he was much bigger than their mother and father; and how should they know how old children and grown-up people can be? Their revenge was to come upon this boy, for it was he who had begun, and he always kept on. The young Storks were very angry; and as they grew bigger they were less inclined to bear it: at last their mother had to promise them that they should be revenged, but not till the last day of their stay.

"We must first see how you behave at the grand review. If you get through badly, so that the general stabs you through the chest with his beak, the boys will be right, at least in one way. Let us see."

The Storks

"Yes, you shall see!" cried the young Storks; and then they took all imaginable pains. They practiced every day, and flew so neatly and so lightly that it was a pleasure to see them.

Now the autumn came on; all the Storks began to assemble, to fly away to the warm countries while it is winter here. That was a review. They had to fly over forests and villages, to show how well they could soar, for it was a long journey they had before them. The young Storks did their part so well that they got as a mark, "Remarkably well, with frogs and snakes." That was the highest mark; and they might eat the frogs and snakes; and that is what they did.

"Now we will be revenged!" they said.

"Yes, certainly!" said the Mother-Stork. "What I have thought of will be the best. I know the pond in which all the little mortals lie till the stork comes and brings them to their parents. The pretty little babies lie there and dream so sweetly as they never dream afterward. All parents are glad to have such a child, and all children want to have a sister or a brother. Now we will fly to the pond, and bring one for each of the children who have not sung the naughty song and laughed at the Storks."

"But he who began to sing—that naughty, ugly boy!" screamed the young Storks; "what shall we do with him?"

"There is a little dead child in the pond, one that has dreamed itself to death; we will bring that for him. Then he will cry because we have brought him a little dead brother. But that good boy—you have not forgotten him, the one who said, 'It is wrong to laugh at animals!' for him we will bring a brother and a sister too. And as his name is Peter, all of you shall be called Peter too."

And it was done as she said; all the storks were named Peter, and so they are all called even now.

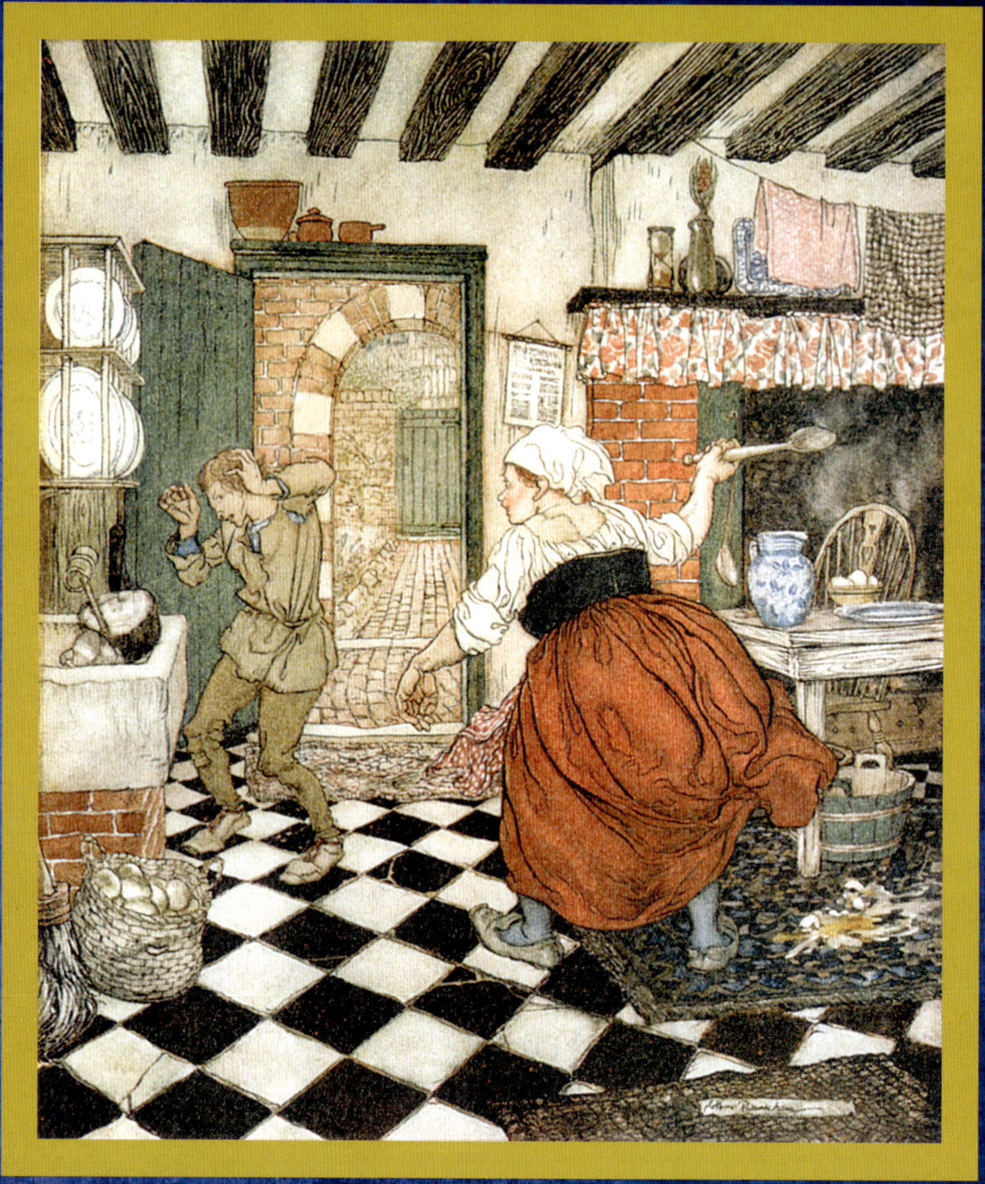

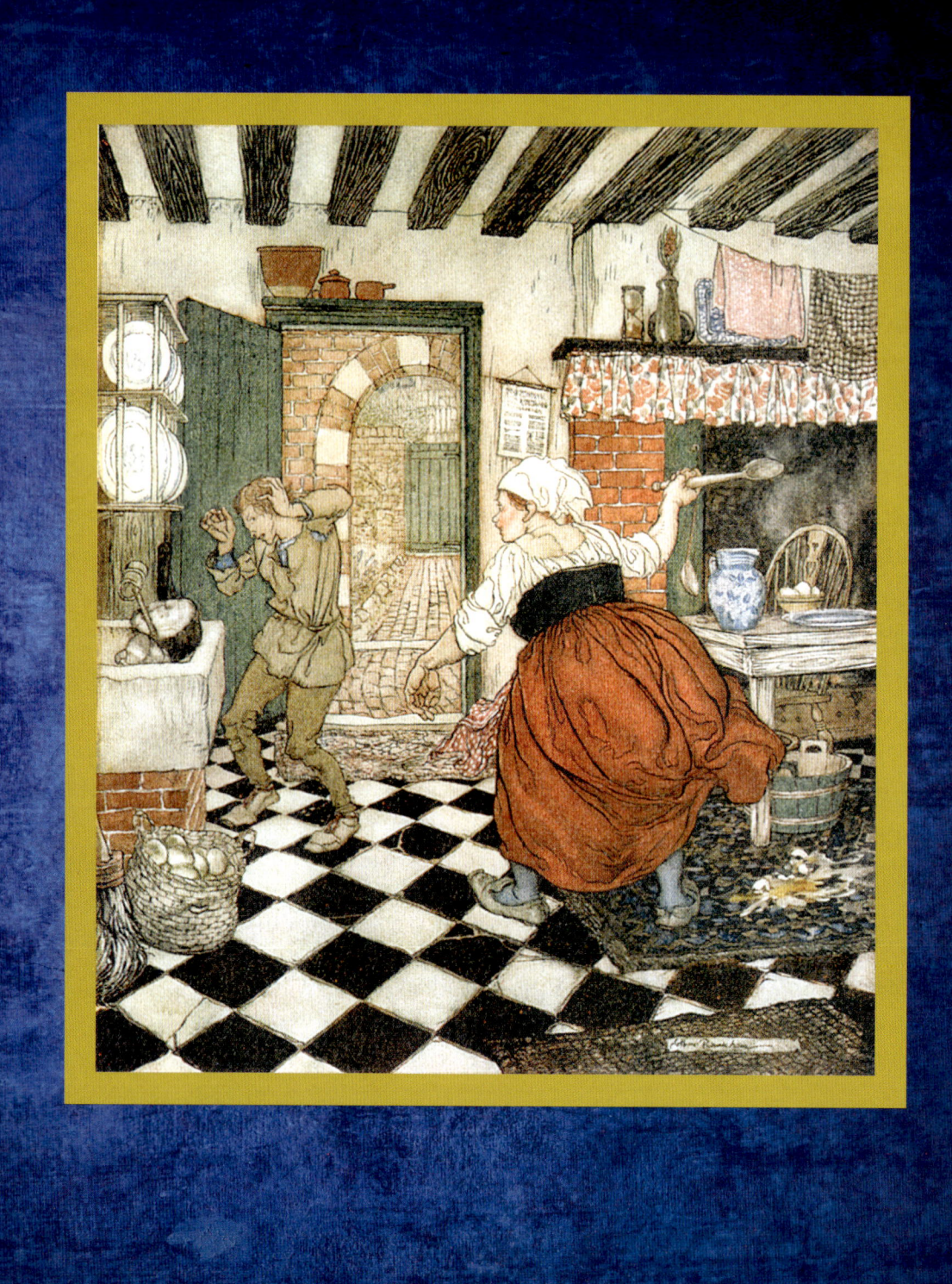

Dick Whittington and His Cat

MORE THAN FIVE HUNDRED YEARS AGO THERE WAS A LITTLE BOY NAMED Dick Whittington, and this is true. His father and mother died when he was too young to work, and so poor little Dick was very badly off. He was quite glad to get the parings of the potatoes to eat and a dry crust of bread now and then, and more than that he did not often get, for the village where he lived was a very poor one and the neighbors were not able to spare him much.

Now the country folk in those days thought that the people of London were all fine ladies and gentlemen, and that there was singing and dancing all the day long, and so rich were they there that even the streets, they said, were paved with gold. Dick used to sit by and listen while all these strange tales of the wealth of London were told, and it made him long to go and live there and have plenty to eat and fine clothes to wear instead of the rags and hard fare that fell to his lot in the country.

So one day when a great wagon with eight horses stopped on its way through the village, Dick made friends with the wagoner and begged to be taken with him to London. The man felt sorry for poor little Dick when he heard that he had no father or mother to take care of him, and saw how ragged and how badly in need of help he was. So he agreed to take him, and off they set.

How far it was and how many days they took over the journey I do not know, but in due time Dick found himself in the wonderful city which he had heard so much of and pictured to himself so grandly. But oh! how disappointed he was when he got there. How dirty it was! And the people, how unlike the gay company, with music and singing, that he had dreamt of! He wandered up and down the streets, one after another, until he was tired out, but not one did he find that was paved with gold. Dirt in plenty he could see, but none of the gold that he thought to have put in his pockets as fast as he chose to pick it up.

Little Dick ran about till he was tired and it was growing dark. And at last he sat himself down in a corner and fell asleep. When morning came he was very cold and hungry, and though he asked every one he met to help him, only one or two gave him a halfpenny to buy some bread. For two or three days he lived in the streets in this way, only just able to keep himself alive, when he managed to get some work to do in a hayfield, and that kept him for a short time longer, till the haymaking was over.

After this he was as badly off as ever, and did not know where to turn. One day in his wanderings he lay down to rest in the doorway of the house of a rich merchant whose name was Fitzwarren. But here he was soon seen by the cook-maid, who was an unkind, bad-tempered woman, and she cried out to him to be off. "Lazy rogue," she called him; and she said she'd precious quick throw some dirty dish-water over him, boiling hot, if he didn't go. However, just then Mr. Fitzwarren himself came home to dinner, and when he saw what was happening, he asked Dick why he was lying there. "You're old enough to be at work, my boy," he said. "I'm afraid you have a mind to be lazy."

"Indeed, sir," said Dick to him, "indeed that is not so"; and he told him how hard he had tried to get work to do, and how ill he was for want of food. Dick, poor fellow, was now so weak that though he tried to stand he had to lie down again, for it was more than three days since he had had anything to eat at all. The kind merchant gave orders for him to be taken into the house and gave him a good dinner, and then he said that he was to be kept, to do what work he could to help the cook.

And now Dick would have been happy enough in this good family if it had not been for the ill-natured cook, who did her best to make life a burden to him. Night and morning she was for ever scolding him. Nothing he did was good enough. It was "Look sharp here" and "Hurry up there," and there was no pleasing her. And many's the beating he had from the broomstick or the ladle, or whatever else she had in her hand.

At last it came to the ears of Miss Alice, Mr. Fitzwarren's daughter, how badly the cook was treating poor Dick. And she told the cook that she would quickly lose her place if she didn't treat him more kindly, for Dick had become quite a favorite with the family.

After that the cook's behavior was a little better, but Dick still had another hardship that he bore with difficulty. For he slept in a garret where were so many holes in the walls and the floor, that every night as he lay in bed the room was overrun with rats and mice, and sometimes he could hardly sleep a wink. One day when he had earned a penny for cleaning a gentleman's shoes, he met a little girl with a cat in her arms and asked whether she would not sell it to him. "Yes, she would," she said, though the cat was such a good mouser that she was sorry to part with her. This just suited Dick, who kept pussy up in his garret, feeding her on scraps of his own dinner that he saved for her every day. In a little while he had no more bother with the rats and mice. Puss soon saw to that, and he slept sound every night.

Soon after this Mr. Fitzwarren had a ship ready to sail; and as it was his custom that all his servants should be given a chance of good fortune as well as himself, he called them all into the counting-house and asked them what they would send out.

They all had something that they were willing to venture except poor Dick, who had neither money nor goods, and so could send nothing. For this reason he did not come into the room with the rest. But Miss Alice guessed what was the matter, and ordered him to be called in. She then said, "I will lay down some money for him out of my own purse"; but her father told her that would not do, for it must be something of his own.

When Dick heard this he said, "I have nothing whatever but a cat, which I bought for a penny some time ago."

"Go, my boy, fetch your cat then," said his master, "and let her go."

Dick went upstairs and fetched poor puss, but there were tears in his eyes when he gave her to the captain. "For," he said, "I shall now be kept awake all night by the rats and mice." All the company laughed at Dick's odd venture, and Miss Alice, who felt sorry for him, gave him some money to buy another cat.

Now this, and other marks of kindness shown him by Miss Alice, made the ill-tempered cook jealous of poor Dick, and she began to use him more cruelly than ever, and was always making game of him for sending his cat to sea. "What do you think your cat will sell for?" she'd ask. "As much money as would buy a stick to beat you with?"

At last poor Dick could not bear this usage any longer, and he thought he would run away. So he made a bundle of his things—he hadn't many—and started very early in the morning, on All Hallows' Day, the first of November. He walked as far as Holloway, and there he sat down to rest on a stone, which to this day, they say, is called "Whittington's Stone," and began to wonder to himself which road he should take.

While he was thinking what he should do the Bells of Bow Church in Cheapside began to chime, and as they rang he fancied that they were singing over and over again:

> "Turn again, Whittington,
> Lord Mayor of London."

"Lord Mayor of London!" said he to himself. "Why, to be sure, wouldn't I put up with almost anything now to be Lord Mayor of London, and ride in a fine coach, when I grow to be a man! Well, I'll go back, and think nothing of the cuffing and scolding of the cross old cook if I am to be Lord Mayor of London at last."

So back he went, and he was lucky enough to get into the house, and set about his work before the cook came down.

But now you must hear what befell Mrs. Puss all this while. The ship *Unicorn* that she was on was a long time at sea, and the cat made herself useful, as she would, among the unwelcome rats that lived on board too. At last the ship put into harbor on the coast of Barbary, where the only people are the Moors. They had never before seen a ship from England, and flocked in numbers to see the sailors, whose different color and foreign dress were a great wonder to them. They were soon eager to buy the goods with which the ship was laden, and patterns were sent ashore for the King to see. He was so much pleased with them that he sent for the captain to come to the palace, and honored him with an invitation to dinner. But no sooner were they seated, as is the custom there, on the fine rugs and carpets that covered the floor, than great numbers of rats and mice

Dick Whittington and His Cat

came scampering in, swarming over all the dishes, and helping themselves from all the good things there were to eat. The captain was amazed, and wondered whether they didn't find such a pest most unpleasant.

"Oh yes," said they, "it was so, and the King would give half his treasure to be freed of them, for they not only spoil his dinner, but they even attack him in his bed at night, so that a watch has to be kept while he is sleeping, for fear of them."

The captain was overjoyed; he thought at once of poor Dick Whittington and his cat, and said he had a creature on board ship that would soon do for all these vermin if she were there. Of course, when the King heard this he was eager to possess this wonderful animal.

"Bring it to me at once," he said; "for the vermin are dreadful, and if only it will do what you say, I will load your ship with gold and jewels in exchange for it."

The captain, who knew his business, took care not to underrate the value of Dick's cat. He told His Majesty how inconvenient it would be to part with her, as when she was gone the rats might destroy the goods in the ship; however, to oblige the King, he would fetch her.

"Oh, make haste, do!" cried the Queen, "I, too, am all impatience to see this dear creature."

Off went the captain, while another dinner was got ready. He took Puss under his arm and got back to the palace just in time to see the carpet covered with rats and mice once again. When Puss saw them, she didn't wait to be told, but jumped out of the captain's arms, and in no time almost all the rats and mice were dead at her feet, while the rest of them had scuttled off to their holes in fright.

The King was delighted to get rid so easily of such an intolerable plague, and the Queen desired that the animal who had done them such a service might be brought to her. Upon which the captain called out, "Puss, puss, puss," and she came running to him. Then he presented her to the Queen, who was rather afraid at first to touch a creature who had made such a havoc with her claws. However, when the captain called her, "Pussy, pussy," and began to stroke her, the Queen also ventured to touch her and cried, "Putty, putty," in imitation of the captain, for she hadn't learned to speak English. He then put her on to the Queen's lap, where she purred and played with Her Majesty's hand and was soon asleep.

The King having seen what Mrs. Puss could do, and learning that her kittens would soon stock the whole country, and keep it free from rats, after bargaining with the captain for the whole ship's cargo, then gave him ten times as much for the cat as all the rest amounted to.

The captain then said farewell to the court of Barbary, and after a fair voyage reached London again with his precious load of gold and jewels safe and sound.

One morning early Mr. Fitzwarren had just come to his counting-house and settled himself at the desk to count the cash, when there came a knock at the door. "Who's there?" said he. "A friend," replied a voice. "I come with good news of your ship the *Unicorn*." The merchant in haste opened the door, and who were there but the ship's captain and the mate, bearing a chest of jewels and a bill of lading. When he had looked this over he lifted his eyes and thanked heaven for sending him such a prosperous voyage.

The honest captain next told him all about the cat, and showed him the rich present the King had sent for her to poor Dick. Rejoicing on behalf of Dick as much as he had done over his own good fortune, he called out to his servants to come and to bring up Dick:

"Go fetch him, and we'll tell him of his fame;
 Pray call him Mr. Whittington by name."

The servants, some of them, hesitated at this, and said so great a treasure was too much for a lad like Dick; but Mr. Fitzwarren now showed himself the good man that he was and refused to deprive him of the value of a single penny. "God forbid!" he cried. "It's all his own, and he shall have it, to a farthing."

He then sent for Dick, who at the moment was scouring pots for the cook and was black with dirt. He tried to excuse himself from coming into the room in such a plight, but the merchant made him come, and had a chair set for him. And he then began to think they must be making game of him, so he begged them not to play tricks on a poor simple boy, but to let him go downstairs again back to his work in the scullery.

"Indeed, Mr. Whittington," said the merchant, "we are all quite in earnest with you, and I most heartily rejoice at the news that these gentlemen have brought. For the

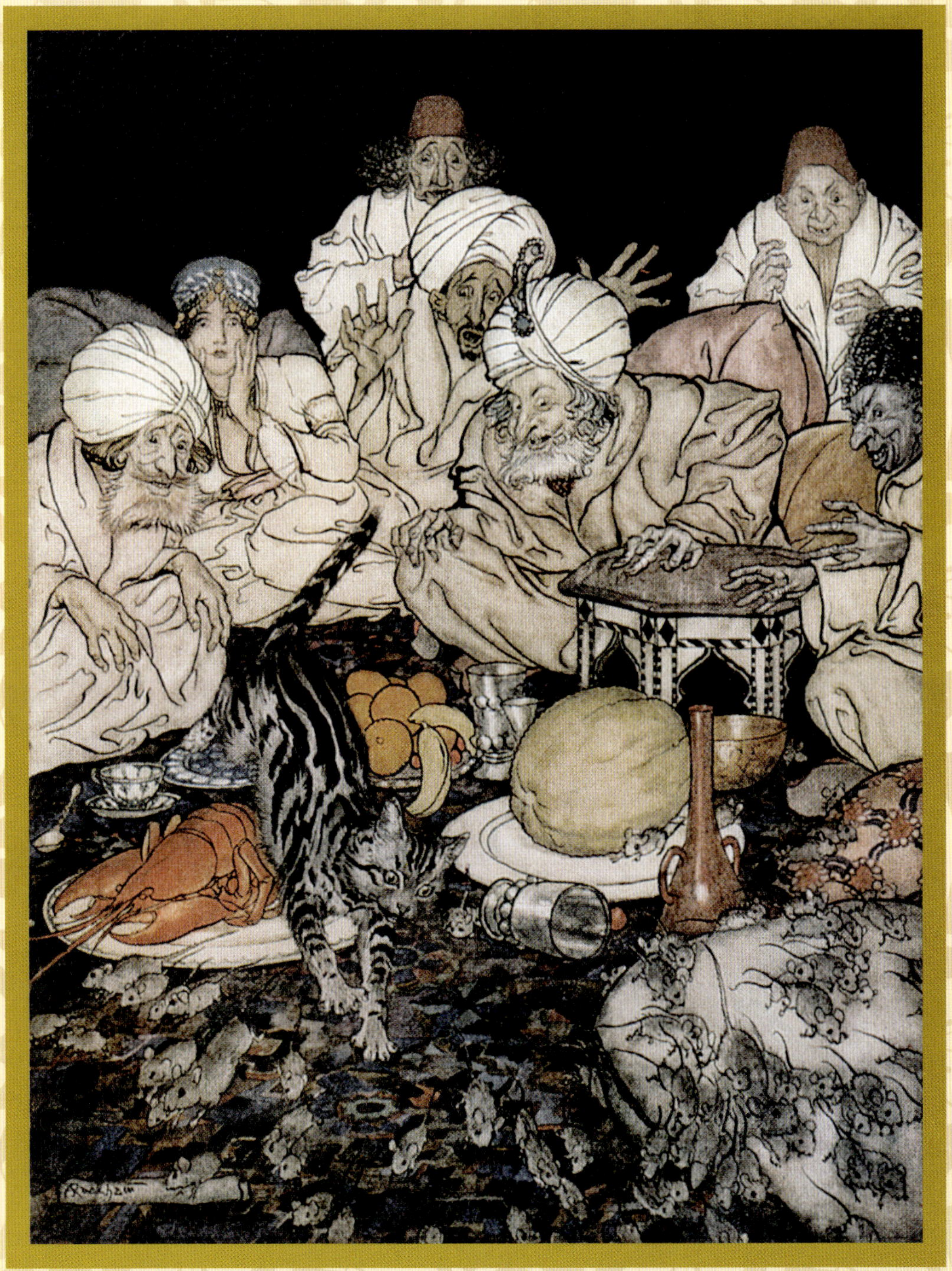

captain has sold your cat to the King of Barbary, and brings you in return for her more riches than I possess in the whole world; and may you long enjoy them!"

Mr. Fitzwarren then told the men to open the great treasure they had brought with them, saying, "There is nothing more now for Mr. Whittington to do but to put it in some place of safety."

Poor Dick hardly knew how to behave himself for joy. He begged his master to take what part of it he pleased, since he owed it all to his kindness. "No, no," answered Mr. Fitzwarren, "this all belongs to you; and I have no doubt that you will use it well."

Dick next begged his mistress, and then Miss Alice, to accept a part of his good fortune, but they would not, and at the same time told him what great joy they felt at his great success. But he was far too kind-hearted to keep it all to himself; so he made a present to the captain, the mate, and the rest of Mr. Fitzwarren's servants; and even to his old enemy, the cross cook.

After this Mr. Fitzwarren advised him to send for a tailor and get himself dressed like a gentleman, and told him he was welcome to live in his house till he could provide himself with a better.

When Whittington's face was washed, his hair curled, and he was dressed in a smart suit of clothes he was just as handsome and fine a young man as any who visited at Mr. Fitzwarren's, and so thought fair Alice Fitzwarren, who had once been so kind to him and looked upon him with pity. And now she felt he was quite fit to be her sweetheart, and none the less, no doubt, because Whittington was always thinking what he could do to please her, and making her the prettiest presents that could be.

Mr. Fitzwarren soon saw which way the wind blew, and ere long proposed to join them in marriage, and to this they both readily agreed. A day for the wedding was soon fixed; and they were attended to church by the Lord Mayor, the court of aldermen, the sheriffs, and a great number of the richest merchants in London, whom they afterward treated with a magnificent feast.

History tells us that Mr. Whittington and his lady lived in great splendor, and were very happy. They had several children. He was Sheriff, and thrice Lord Mayor of London, and received the honor of knighthood from Henry V.

After the King's conquest of France, Sir Richard Whittington entertained him and the Queen at dinner at the Mansion House in so sumptuous a manner that the King said, "Never had Prince such a subject!" To which Sir Richard replied, "Never had subject such a Prince."

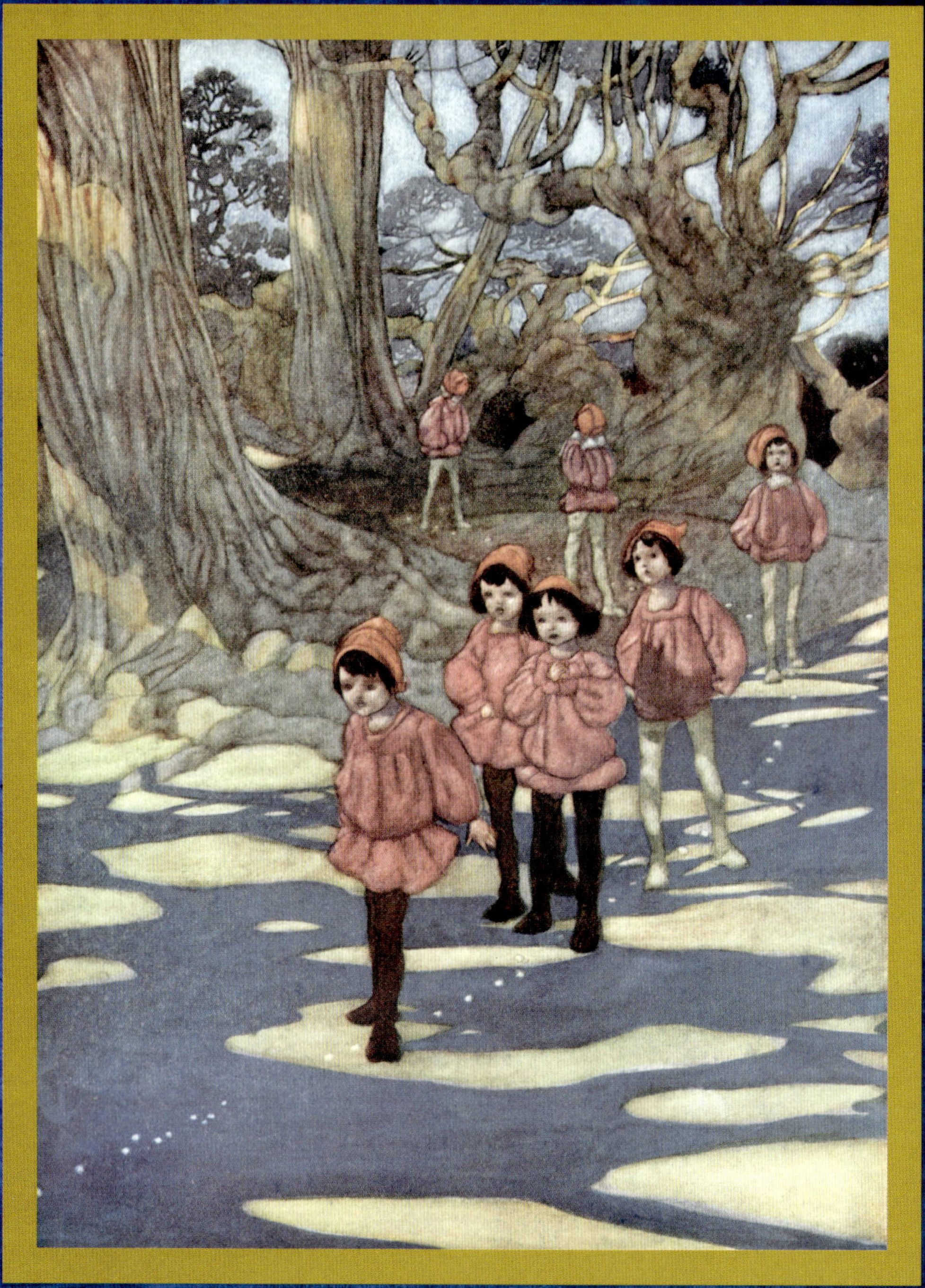

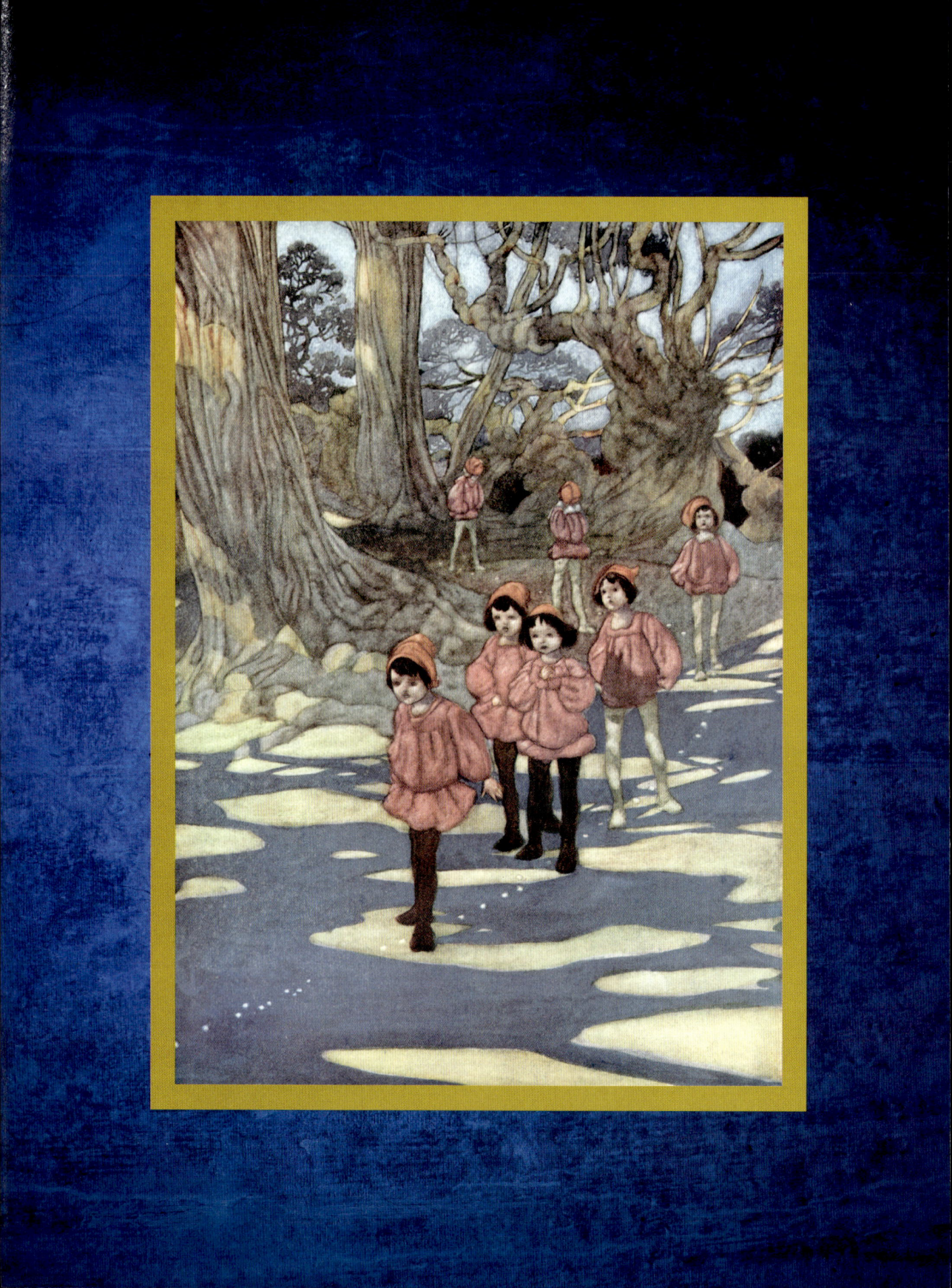

Hop o' My Thumb

Once upon a time there was a poor woodman who had seven children, all boys, the eldest no more than ten, the youngest only seven. The youngest was a puny little chap who rarely spoke a word; he was indeed the smallest person even seen, being when born no bigger than a thumb, and thus he got the name of Hop o' my Thumb. Still he was by far cleverer than any of his brothers, and though he spoke but little, he heard more than was imagined. The woodman and his wife at length became so poor that they could no longer give their children their usual food. One evening when the boys were in bed, the husband, sighing deeply, said:

"You see, dear wife, it is impossible for us to maintain our children any longer, and to see them die of hunger before my eyes is what I never could support. I am determined to take them to-morrow morning to the forest, and leave them in the thickest part of it, so that it will be impossible to find their way back."

"Ah!" cried the poor wife, "you cannot, consent to be the death of you own children!" but at length, considering how dreadful it would be to see them die of hunger before her eyes, she consented to her husband's proposal, and went sobbing to bed.

Hop o' my Thumb had been all the time awake; and hearing his father talk more earnestly than usual, he slipped away from his brothers' side, and crept under his father's bed to hear all he might say, without being seen. When his father and mother had left off talking, he got back to his own place, and passed the night in thinking what he should do the next morning.

He rose early and ran to the river's side, where he filled his pockets with small white pebbles, and then returned home.

All set out, as their father and mother had agreed on, and Hop o' my Thumb said not a word to his brothers of what he had discovered. They reached a forest that was so very thick, that at ten paces distant they could not see each other. The woodman set to work, cutting down wood, and the children began, to gather all the twigs, to make faggots of them. Then the father and mother, observing that they were all very busy, slipped away without being perceived by them, and getting into a by-path, they soon lost sight of the forest.

In a short time the children, finding themselves alone, began to cry as loud as they could. Hop o' my Thumb let them cry on; for he knew well enough how to conduct them safely home, having taken care to drop the white pebbles he had in his pocket the whole of the way by which they had come: he therefore only said:

"Never mind it, my lads: father and mother have left us here by ourselves; but only take care to follow me, and I will lead you back again."

They followed Hop o' my Thumb, who soon brought them to their father's house, by the very same path by which they had come. Just as the woodman and his wife had returned home without their children, a great gentleman of the village had sent to pay them two guineas, which had so long been owing for work they had done for him, that they never expected to receive it; this money quite rejoiced their hearts; for the poor creatures were exceedingly hungry, and had no means of getting anything to eat. The woodman sent his wife out immediately to buy some meat; and as it was a long time since she had made a hearty meal, she bought as much meat as would have been enough for six or eight persons: but it might be that she had not yet learned to leave out her children, when she was thinking of what would be enough for dinner. Indeed, she and her husband had no sooner eaten heartily, than she cried out:

"Alas! where are our poor children? How they would feast on what we have left! I told you over and over that we should repent the hour when we left them to starve in the forest! Oh, mercy! they may perhaps be already eaten up by the wolves!"

The woodman grew very angry with his wife, who repeated more than twenty times, that he would repent of what he had done, and that she had again and again told him so: he at last threatened to give her a good beating if she did not hold her tongue: not but that the woodman was quite as sorry as his wife for what had happened, but that her scolding teased him.

"Alas!" repeated she, "what is become of my dear children?" and once she said this so loud that the children, who were all listening at the door, cried out all together:

"Here we are, mother, here we are!"

She flew to let them in, and kissed every one of them.

"How glad I am to see you, you little rogues!" said she. "Are you not tired and hungry? Ah, poor little Bobby! why, thou art dirt all over, my child! come hither, and let me wash thy face."

Bobby was the youngest of the boys excepting Hop o' my Thumb; and had always been his mother's favorite. The children sat down to dinner, and ate quite heartily. The parents were quite delighted at having their children once again under their roof, and this continued till their money was all spent: then, finding themselves in the same condition as before, they, by degrees, again determined to leave them once more in the forest; and that they might not a second time be disappointed, they resolved to lead them to a much greater distance than they did at first. They could not, however, consult with each other on this business so secretly but Hop o' my Thumb found means to overhear all that passed. It gave him no uneasiness, for he thought nothing could be easier than to do exactly the same as he had done before: but though he rose very early to go to the river's side and get the pebbles, he could not get out, for the door was locked. Hop o' my Thumb was at a loss what to do; but his mother having given each of the children a piece of bread for breakfast, he thought he could make his share serve the same purpose as the pebbles. He accordingly put it carefully into his pocket.

It was not long before they all set out, and their parents took care to lead them into the very thickest and darkest part of the forest, and then slipped away by a by-path as before. This did not give Hop o' my Thumb any concern, for he thought himself quite sure of getting back by means of the crumbs he had strewed by the way; but what was his surprise at finding that not a single morsel was left! for the birds had eaten it all up!

The poor children were in a terrible plight; for the further they went, the more they found it difficult to get out of the forest. At length night came on, and they mistook the whistling of the wind among the trees for the howling of wolves, and every moment expected to be devoured.

When it began to grow light, Hop o' my Thumb climbed to the top of a tree, and looked on all sides, to discover, if possible, some means of assistance: he saw a small light like that of a candle, but it was at a great distance beyond the forest: he came down from the tree, thinking to find his way to it, but it had disappeared; and he was in perplexity what to do next. They continued walking in the direction in which he had seen the light, and at last, having reached the end of the forest, again got sight of it. They quickened their steps, and after great fatigue arrived at the house in which it was. They knocked at the door, which was opened by a very good-natured-looking lady, who asked what brought them thither? Hop o' my Thumb answered, that they were poor children, who had lost their way in the forest, and begged for charity's sake that she would give them a bed till morning.

The lady, seeing they had such pretty faces, began to shed tears, and said:

"Ah! poor children, whither are you come? Do you not know that this is the house of an Ogre who eats little boys and girls?"

Hop o' My Thumb

"Alas!" replied Hop o' my Thumb, "what shall we do? If we go back to the forest, it is certain that we shall be devoured by the wolves; we had rather, therefore, be eaten up by the gentleman; besides, when he sees us, he may perhaps pity our unhappy condition, and spare our lives."

The Ogre's wife, thinking she could contrive to hide them from her husband till the morning, let them go in, and made them warm themselves by a good fire, before which there was a whole sheep roasting for the Ogre's supper. When they had stood a short time by the fire, there came a loud knocking at the door. It was the Ogre! His wife hurried the children under the bed, telling them to lie still: she then let her husband in.

The Ogre immediately asked if the supper was ready, and if the wine was fetched from the cellar, and then sat down to table. Presently he began to snuff to his right and left, saying he smelled child's flesh.

"It must be this calf which has just been killed," answered his wife.

"I smell child's flesh," cried the Ogre. "I smell child's flesh; there is something going on that I do not understand."

Saying this, he rose and went straight to the bed.

"Ah! ah! deceitful creature, is it thus you think to cheat me? Wretch! but that thou art old and tough, I would eat thee too! But, come, what thou hast done is lucky enough, for the brats will make a nice dish for three Ogres, my particular friends, who are to dine with me to-morrow."

He drew them out one by one from under the bed. The poor children fell on their knees, begging his pardon as well as they could speak; but this Ogre was one of the cruelest of all the Ogres, and, far from feeling any pity, began to devour them already with his eyes, and told his wife "they would be delicious morsels if she served them up with a savory sauce." He then fetched a large knife, and began to sharpen it on a long whetstone which he held in his left hand, approaching all the time nearer and nearer to the bed. The Ogre took up one of the children, and was going to set about cutting him to pieces, when his wife said to him:

"What in the world makes you take the trouble of killing them to-night? Will it not be time enough to-morrow morning?"

"Hold your prating," replied the Ogre, "they will be the tenderer for keeping."

"But you have so much meat in the house already," answered his wife: "here is a calf, two sheep, and half of a pig."

"Right," said the Ogre; "give them therefore a good supper, that they may not lose their plumpness, and send them to bed."

The good creature was quite overjoyed at this, and accordingly gave them a plentiful supper: but the poor children were too much frightened to eat. As to the Ogre, he sat down to his wine extremely delighted with the thought of giving his friends so delicate a repast, and, drinking more than usual, found himself soon obliged to go to bed.

The Ogre had seven daughters, all very young. They had fair complexions, because they fed on raw meat like their father; but they had small gray eyes, quite round, and sunk in their heads, hooked noses, wide mouths, and very long sharp teeth standing at a great distance from each other. They were yet too young to have done a great deal of mischief; but they gave signs of being, when older, as cruel as their father, for they already delighted in biting young children, and sucking their blood. These Ogresses had been put to bed early, all in one very large bed, and each had a crown of gold on her head. There was in the same chamber another bed of equal size, and in this the Ogre's wife put the seven little boys.

Hop o' my Thumb, having observed that the Ogresses had all crowns of gold upon their heads, and fearing the Ogre might awake in the night and repent of not laving killed him and his brothers, got out of bed about midnight, as softly as he could, and, taking off their nightcaps and his own, crept with them to the Ogre's daughters, took off their crowns, and put the nightcaps on their heads instead of them; he then put the crowns on those of his brothers and his own, and again got into bed.

Hop o' My Thumb

Everything succeeded vastly well. The Ogre, having waked soon after midnight, was very sorry he had deferred till to-morrow what he could have done that very night. He therefore hurried out of bed, and, taking up his large knife—

"Let us see," said he, "what the young rogues are about, and do the job at once!" He stalked quietly to the room in which his daughters slept, and going up to the bed which held the boys, who, excepting Hop o' my Thumb, were all asleep, he felt their heads one by one.

The Ogre feeling the crowns of gold, said to himself:

"I had like to have made a pretty mistake!" He went next to the bed which held his daughters, and feeling the nightcaps: "Ah here you are my lads!" said he' and instantly cut the throats of all his daughters, one by one. Well satisfied, he returned to bed.

As soon as Hop o' my Thumb heard him snoring, he awoke his brothers, and told them to put on their clothes quickly, and follow him. They stole down softly to the garden, and then jumped from the walls into the road. They ran with all their strength the whole night, but were all the time so much terrified that they scarcely knew which way to take.

When the Ogre awoke in the morning, he said to his wife:

"Prythee go and dress the young rogues I saw last night."

The Ogress was quite surprised at her husband's kindness, not dreaming of the real meaning of his words. She went up stairs, and the first thing she beheld was her seven daughters killed. The Ogre, fearing his wife might spend too much time in what he had set her about, went himself to help her, and was not less surprised than she had been at the shocking spectacle.

"Ah! what have I done?" cried he; "but the little varlets shall pay for it, I warrant them!"

He threw some water on his wife's face; and as soon as she recovered he said to her:

"Bring me quickly my seven-league boots, that I may go and catch the little vipers."

The Ogre set out with all speed, and after striding over different parts of the country, at last turned into the very road in which the poor children were continuing their journey toward their father's house, which they had now nearly reached. They had seen the Ogre for some time striding from mountain to mountain at one step, and crossing rivers with the greatest ease. Hop o' my Thumb, after considering what was to be done, perceiving a hollow place under a large rock, made his brothers get into it, and then stepped in himself, keeping his eye fixed on the Ogre, to see what he would do next.

The Ogre, finding himself greatly tired with the journey he had made—for seven-league boots are very fatiguing to the person who wears them—began to think of resting himself, and happened to sit down on the very rock in which the poor children lay concealed. Being quite overcome with fatigue, he fell fast asleep, and soon began to snore so terribly that the little fellows were no less frightened than when the Ogre stood over them with a knife in his hand, intending to kill them. Hop o' my Thumb, seeing how much his brothers were terrified, said to them:

"Courage, my lads! never fear! You have nothing to do but to steal away and get home while the Ogre is fast asleep, and leave me to shift for myself."

The brothers followed this advice, and were very soon at their father's house. In the meantime, Hop o' my Thumb went softly up to the Ogre, and very gently pulled off his seven-league boots, and drew them on his own legs; for though the boots were very large, as they were fairies they could make themselves smaller and smaller, so as to fit any leg they pleased. Hop o' my Thumb had no sooner made sure of Ogre's seven-league boots, than he determined to go to the palace, and offer his services to carry orders from the King to his army, which was at a great distance, and bring His Majesty the earliest accounts of the battle they were just at that time engaged in with the enemy.

He had not proceeded many strides before he heard a voice which desired him to stop. Hop o' my Thumb looked about him to discover whence it came, and the same voice continued:

Hop o' My Thumb

"Listen, Hop o' my Thumb, to what I am about to say. Go not to the palace. Waste no time; the Ogre sleeps; he may awake. Know, Hop o' my Thumb, that the boots you took from the Ogre while asleep are two fairies; I am the eldest of them. We have observed the clever feats you have performed to keep your brothers from harm and have resolved to bestow upon you the gift of riches, if you will once more employ your wits to a good purpose, and be as brave as before. But fairies are not allowed to speak such matters as these. Break the shell of the largest nut you can find in your pocket, and in it is a paper which will tell you all that is necessary to be done."

Hop o' my Thumb, instead of wondering what had happened, instantly searched his pocket for the nut, and, having cracked it with his teeth, found in it a piece of paper, which he read as follows:

> Hie thee to the Ogre's door,
> These words speak, and no word more:
> Ogress, Ogre cannot come;
> Great key give to Hop o' my Thumb.

Hop o' my Thumb instantly began to say the two last lines over and over again, that he might not forget them; and when he thought he had learned them by heart, he made two or three of his largest strides, and reached the Ogre's door. He knocked loudly, and for the second time was received by the Ogre's wife, who at sight of Hop o' my Thumb started back, and looked as if she would have shut the door; but Hop o' my Thumb, knowing he had not a moment to lose, made as if he did not perceive how much she was afflicted at seeing the person who had caused her daughters to be killed by their own father.

Hop o' my Thumb accordingly began to talk as if he was in a great hurry, saying that matters were now changed; that the Ogre, having laid hold of him and his brothers as they were gathering nuts by the side of a hedge, was going to take them back to his house, when all at once the Ogre perceived a number of men who looked like lords, and were on the finest horses ever beheld, coming up to him full speed; that he soon found they were sent by the King with a message to borrow of the Ogre a large sum of money, the King believing him to be the richest of his subjects; that the lords finding themselves fatigued with the long journey they had made, the Ogre had desired them to proceed no farther, as he had with him a messenger who would not fail of doing cleverly whatever he was employed about: that the great lords had thanked the Ogre a thousand times, and, in the name of the King, had bestowed upon him the honorable title of Duke of Draggletail: that the Ogre had then taken off his boots, and helped to draw them on Hop o' my Thumb's legs; and charging him to make haste, gave him the following message:

Ogress, Ogre cannot come;
Great key give to Hop o' my Thumb.

The Ogress seeing her husband's boots, and being mightily delighted with the thoughts of becoming duchess of Draggletail, and living at Court, was very ready to believe all that was told her. She fetched the great key and gave it to Hop o' my Thumb, telling him, at the same time, where to find the chest of money and jewels to which it belonged. Hop o' my Thumb took as much of these treasures as he thought would be sufficient to maintain his father, mother, and brothers, without the fatigue of hard labor, saying to himself all the time, that it was better that an honest woodman should have a small part of such vast riches, than that an Ogre, who did nothing but eat children, should make no use of them whatever.

In a short time Hop o' my Thumb returned to his father's house, and was joyfully received by the whole family. The fame of his boots having been talked of at Court, the King sent for him, and, it is said, employed him frequently on the most important affairs of his Kingdom; so that he became one of the richest of his subjects.

Hop o' My Thumb

As for the Ogre, he fell in his sleep from the corner of the rock, from which Hop o' my Thumb and his brothers had escaped, to the ground, and bruised himself so much that he could not stir; he therefore stretched himself out at full length, and waited for some one to come by and assist him. But though several woodmen, passing near the place where the Ogre lay, and hearing him groan, went up to ask him what was the matter, yet the Ogre was so exceedingly big, that they could not have carried even one of his legs; so they were obliged to leave him; till at length the night came on, when a large serpent came out of a neighboring wood, and stung him so that he died miserably.

As soon as Hop o' my Thumb, who was become the King's favorite, heard the news of the Ogre's death, he informed his majesty of all that the good-natured Ogress had done to save the lives of him and his brothers. The King was so pleased that he asked Hop o' my Thumb if there was any favor he could bestow upon her.

Hop o' my Thumb thanked the King, and desired that the Ogress might obtain the honorable title of Duchess of Draggletail; which was no sooner asked than granted. The Ogress came to Court and lived very happy for many years, enjoying the vast fortune she found in the Ogre's coffers.

As for Hop o' my Thumb, he every day grew more witty and brave; till at last the King made him the greatest lord in the Kingdom, and put all affairs under his direction.

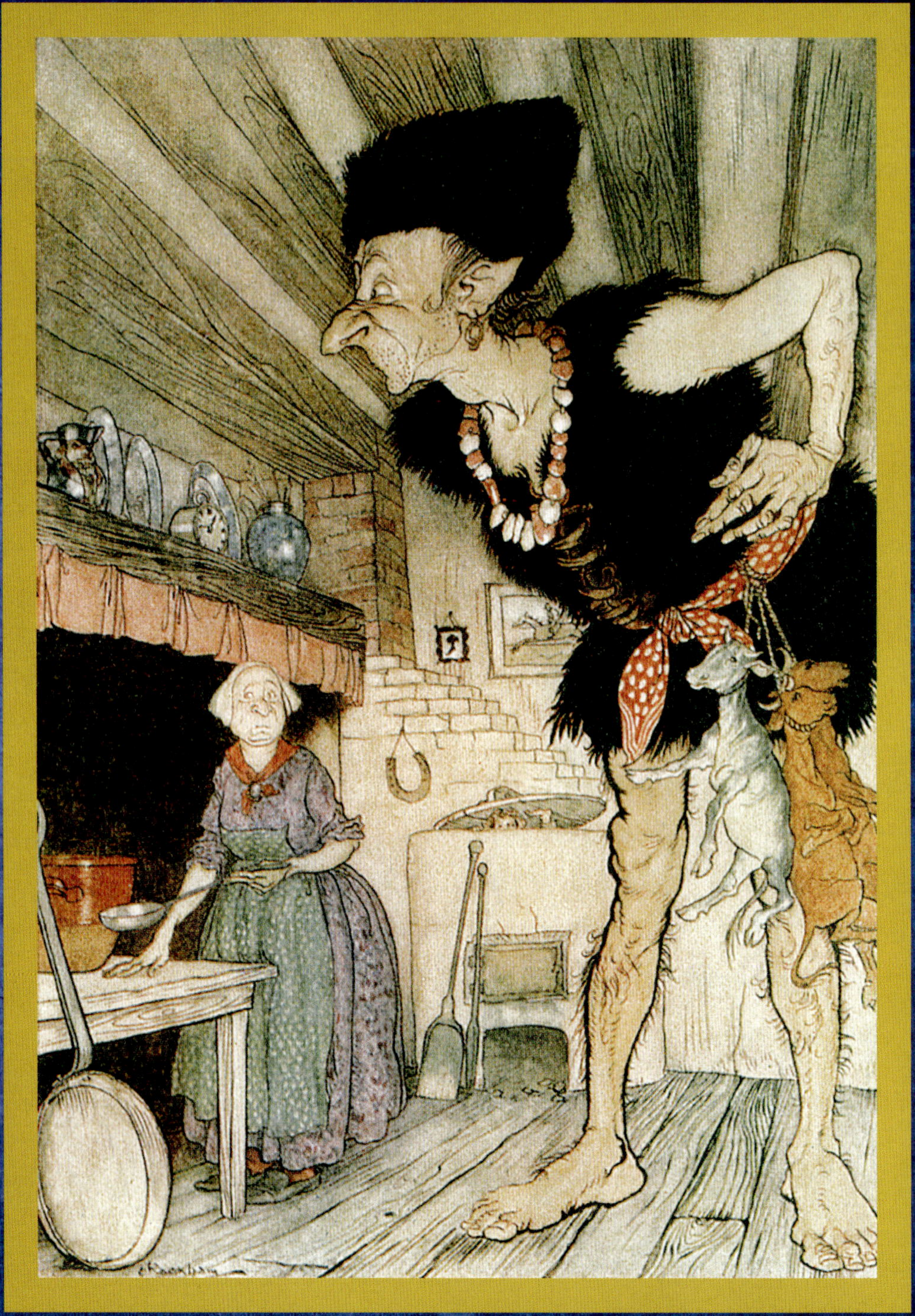

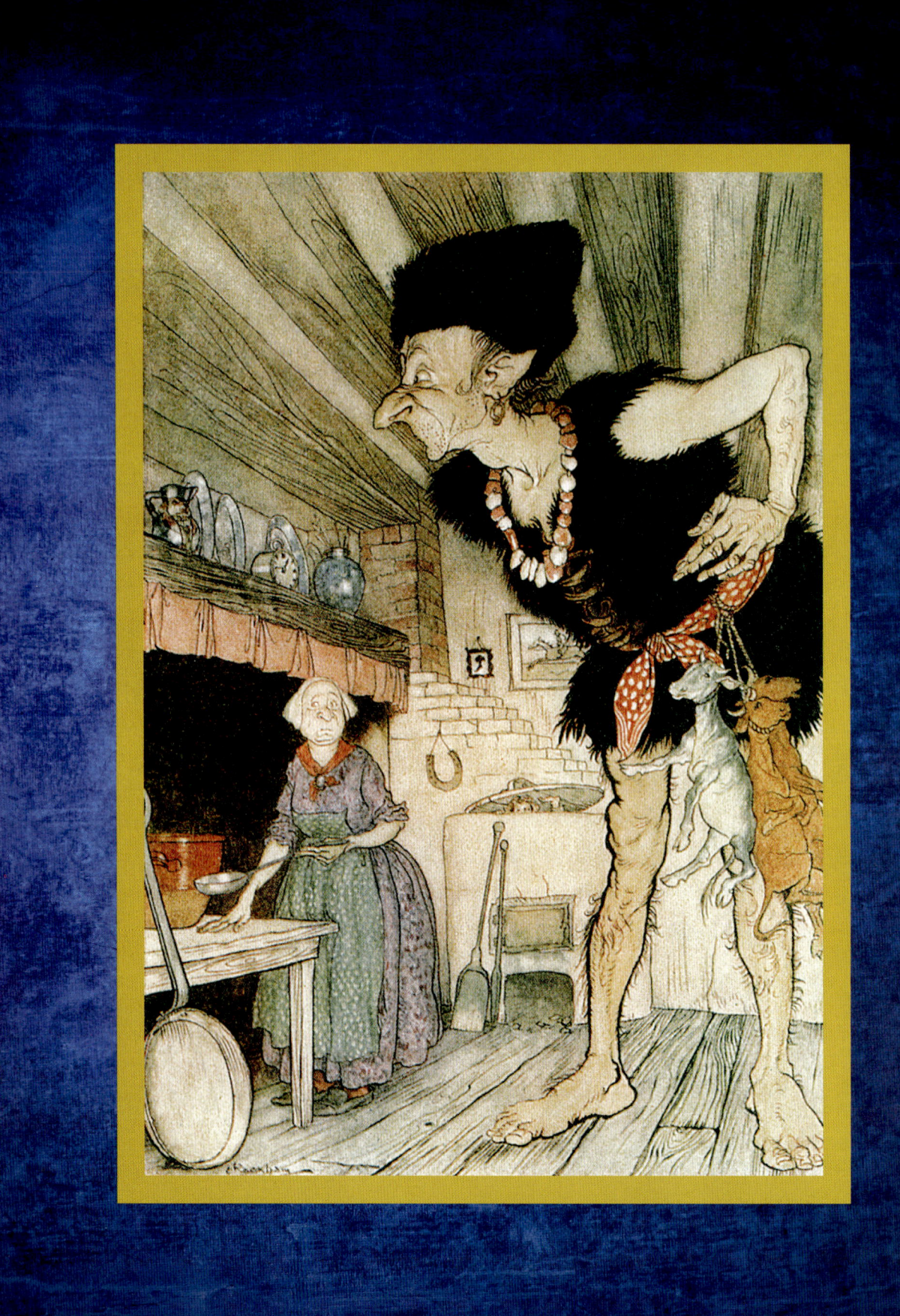

Jack and the Beanstalk

JACK SELLS THE COW

Once upon a time there was a poor widow who lived in a little cottage with her only son Jack.

Jack was a giddy, thoughtless boy, but very kind-hearted and affectionate. There had been a hard winter, and after it the poor woman had suffered from fever and ague. Jack did no work as yet, and by degrees they grew dreadfully poor. The widow saw that there was no means of keeping Jack and herself from starvation but by selling her cow; so one morning she said to her son, "I am too weak to go myself, Jack, so you must take the cow to market for me, and sell her."

Jack liked going to market to sell the cow very much; but as he was on the way, he met a butcher who had some beautiful beans in his hand. Jack stopped to look at them, and the butcher told the boy that they were of great value, and persuaded the silly lad to sell the cow for these beans.

When he brought them home to his mother instead of the money she expected for her nice cow, she was very vexed and shed many tears, scolding Jack for his folly. He was very sorry, and mother and son went to bed very sadly that night; their last hope seemed gone.

At daybreak Jack rose and went out into the garden.

"At least," he thought, "I will sow the wonderful beans. Mother says that they are just common scarlet-runners, and nothing else; but I may as well sow them."

So he took a piece of stick, and made some holes in the ground, and put in the beans.

That day they had very little dinner, and went sadly to bed, knowing that for the next day there would be none and Jack, unable to sleep from grief and vexation, got up at day-dawn and went out into the garden.

What was his amazement to find that the beans had grown up in the night, and climbed up and up till they covered the high cliff that sheltered the cottage, and disappeared above it! The stalks had twined and twisted themselves together till they formed quite a ladder.

"It would be easy to climb it," thought Jack.

And, having thought of the experiment, he at once resolved to carry it out, for Jack was a good climber. However, after his late mistake about the cow, he thought he had better consult his mother first.

WONDERFUL GROWTH OF THE BEANSTALK

So Jack called his mother, and they both gazed in silent wonder at the Beanstalk, which was not only of great height, but was thick enough to bear Jack's weight.

"I wonder where it ends," said Jack to his mother; "I think I will climb up and see."

His mother wished him not to venture up this strange ladder, but Jack coaxed her to give her consent to the attempt, for he was certain there must be something wonderful in the Beanstalk; so at last she yielded to his wishes.

Jack instantly began to climb, and went up and up on the ladder-like bean till everything he had left behind him—the cottage, the village, and even the tall church tower—looked quite little, and still he could not see the top of the Beanstalk.

Jack felt a little tired, and thought for a moment that he would go back again; but he was a very persevering boy, and he knew that the way to succeed in anything is not to give up. So after resting for a moment he went on.

Jack and the Beanstalk

After climbing higher and higher, till he grew afraid to look down for fear he should be giddy, Jack at last reached the top of the Beanstalk, and found himself in a beautiful country, finely wooded, with beautiful meadows covered with sheep. A crystal stream ran through the pastures; not far from the place where he had got off the Beanstalk stood a fine, strong castle.

Jack wondered very much that he had never heard of or seen this castle before; but when he reflected on the subject, he saw that it was as much separated from the village by the perpendicular rock on which it stood as if it were in another land.

While Jack was standing looking at the castle, a very strange-looking woman came out of the wood, and advanced toward him.

She wore a pointed cap of quilted red satin turned up with ermine, her hair streamed loose over her shoulders, and she walked with a staff. Jack took off his cap and made her a bow.

"If you please, ma'am," said he, "is this your house?"

"No," said the old lady. "Listen, and I will tell you the story of that castle.

"Once upon a time there was a noble knight, who lived in this castle, which is on the borders of Fairyland. He had a fair and beloved wife and several lovely children: and as his neighbors, the little people, were very friendly toward him, they bestowed on him many excellent and precious gifts.

"Rumor whispered of these treasures; and a monstrous giant, who lived at no great distance, and who was a very wicked being, resolved to obtain possession of them.

"So he bribed a false servant to let him inside the castle, when the knight was in bed and asleep, and he killed him as he lay. Then he went to the part of the castle which was the nursery, and also killed all the poor little ones he found there.

"Happily for her, the lady was not to be found. She had gone with her infant son, who was only two or three months old, to visit her old nurse, who lived in the valley; and she had been detained all night there by a storm.

"The next morning, as soon as it was light, one of the servants at the castle, who had managed to escape, came to tell the poor lady of the sad fate of her husband and her pretty babes. She could scarcely believe him at first, and was eager at once to go back and share the fate of her dear ones; but the old nurse, with many tears, besought her to remember that she had still a child, and that it was her duty to preserve her life for the sake of the poor innocent.

"The lady yielded to this reasoning, and consented to remain at her nurse's house as the best place of concealment; for the servant told her that the giant had vowed, if he could find her, he would kill both her and her baby. Years rolled on. The old nurse died, leaving her cottage and the few articles of furniture it contained to her poor lady, who dwelt in it, working as a peasant for her daily bread. Her spinning-wheel and the milk of a cow, which she had purchased with the little money she had with her, sufficed for the scanty subsistence of herself and her little son. There was a nice little garden attached to the cottage, in which they cultivated peas, beans, and cabbages, and the lady was not ashamed to go out at harvest time, and glean in the fields to supply her little son's wants.

"Jack, that poor lady is your mother. This castle was once your father's, and must again be yours."

Jack uttered a cry of surprise.

"My mother! oh, madam, what ought I to do? My poor father! My dear mother!"

"Your duty requires you to win it back for your mother. But the task is a very difficult one, and full of peril, Jack. Have you courage to undertake it?"

"I fear nothing when I am doing right," said Jack.

"Then," said the lady in the red cap, "you are one of those who slay giants. You must get into the castle, and if possible possess yourself of a hen that lays golden eggs, and a harp that talks. Remember, all the giant possesses is really yours." As she ceased speaking, the lady of the red hat suddenly disappeared, and of course Jack knew she was a fairy.

Jack determined at once to attempt the adventure; so he advanced, and blew the horn which hung at the castle portal. The door was opened in a minute or two by a frightful giantess, with one great eye in the middle of her forehead.

As soon as Jack saw her he turned to run away, but she caught him, and dragged him into the castle.

"Ho, ho!" she laughed terribly. "You didn't expect to see me here, that is clear! No, I shan't let you go again. I am weary of my life. I am so overworked, and I don't see why I should not have a page as well as other ladies. And you shall be my boy. You shall clean the knives, and black the boots, and make the fires, and help me generally when the giant is out. When he is at home I must hide you, for he has eaten up all my pages hitherto, and you would be a dainty morsel, my little lad."

While she spoke she dragged Jack right into the castle. The poor boy was very much frightened, as I am sure you and I would have been in his place. But he remembered that fear disgraces a man; so he struggled to be brave and make the best of things.

"I am quite ready to help you, and do all I can to serve you, madam," he said, "only I beg you will be good enough to hide me from your husband, for I should not like to be eaten at all."

"That's a good boy," said the Giantess, nodding her head; "it is lucky for you that you did not scream out when you saw me, as the other boys who have been here did, for if you had done so my husband would have awakened and have eaten you, as he did them, for breakfast. Come here, child; go into my wardrobe: he never ventures to open that; you will be safe there."

And she opened a huge wardrobe which stood in the great hall, and shut him into it. But the keyhole was so large that it admitted plenty of air, and he could see everything that took place through it. By-and-by he heard a heavy tramp on the stairs, like the lumbering along of a great cannon, and then a voice like thunder cried out:

> "Fe, fa, fi-fo-fum,
> I smell the breath of an Englishman.
> Let him be alive or let him be dead,
> I'll grind his bones to make my bread."

"Wife," cried the Giant, "there is a man in the castle. Let me have him for breakfast."

"You are grown old and stupid," cried the lady in her loud tones. "It is only a nice fresh steak off an elephant, that I have cooked for you, which you smell. There, sit down and make a good breakfast."

And she placed a huge dish before him of savory steaming meat, which greatly pleased him, and made him forget his idea of an Englishman being in the castle. When he had breakfasted he went out for a walk; and then the Giantess opened the door, and made Jack come out to help her. He helped her all day. She fed him well, and when evening came put him back in the wardrobe.

THE HEN THAT LAYS THE GOLDEN EGGS

The Giant came in to supper. Jack watched him through the keyhole, and was amazed to see him pick a wolf's bone, and put half a fowl at a time into his capacious mouth.

When the supper was ended he bade his wife bring him his hen that laid the golden eggs.

"It lays as well as it did when it belonged to that paltry knight," he said; "indeed I think the eggs are heavier than ever."

The Giantess went away, and soon returned with a little brown hen, which she placed on the table before her husband. "And now, my dear," she said, "I am going for a walk, if you don't want me any longer."

"Go," said the Giant; "I shall be glad to have a nap by-and-by."

Then he took up the brown hen and said to her:

"Lay!" And she instantly laid a golden egg.

"Lay!" said the Giant again. And she laid another.

"Lay!" he repeated the third time. And again a golden egg lay on the table.

Now Jack was sure this hen was that of which the fairy had spoken.

By-and-by the Giant put the hen down on the floor, and soon after went fast asleep, snoring so loud that it sounded like thunder.

Directly Jack perceived that the Giant was fast asleep, he pushed open the door of the wardrobe and crept out; very softly he stole across the room, and, picking up the hen, made haste to quit the apartment. He knew the way to the kitchen, the door of which he found was left ajar; he opened it, shut and locked it after him, and flew back to the Beanstalk, which he descended as fast as his feet would move.

When his mother saw him enter the house she wept for joy, for she had feared that the fairies had carried him away, or that the Giant had found him. But Jack put the brown hen down before her, and told her how he had been in the Giant's castle, and all his adventures. She was very glad to see the hen, which would make them rich once more.

THE MONEY BAGS

Jack made another journey up the Beanstalk to the Giant's castle one day while his mother had gone to market; but first he dyed his hair and disguised himself. The old woman did not know him again, and dragged him in as she had done before, to help her to do the work; but she heard her husband coming, and hid him in the wardrobe, not thinking that it was the same boy who had stolen the hen. She bade him stay quite still there, or the Giant would eat him.

Then the Giant came in saying:

> "Fe, fa, fi-fo-fum,
>   I smell the breath of an Englishman.
>   Let him be alive or let him be dead,
>   I'll grind his bones to make my bread."

"Nonsense!" said the wife, "it is only a roasted bullock that I thought would be a tit-bit for your supper; sit down and I will bring it up at once." The Giant sat down, and soon his wife brought up a roasted bullock on a large dish, and they began their supper. Jack was amazed to see them pick the bones of the bullock as if it had been a lark. As soon as they had finished their meal, the Giantess rose and said:

"Now, my dear, with your leave I am going up to my room to finish the story I am reading. If you want me call for me."

"First," answered the Giant, "bring me my money bags, that I may count my golden pieces before I sleep." The Giantess obeyed. She went and soon returned with two large bags over her shoulders, which she put down by her husband.

"There," she said; "that is all that is left of the knight's money. When you have spent it you must go and take another baron's castle."

"That he shan't, if I can help it," thought Jack.

The Giant, when his wife was gone, took out heaps and heaps of golden pieces, and counted them, and put them in piles, till he was tired of the amusement. Then he swept them all back into their bags, and leaning back in his chair fell fast asleep, snoring so loud that no other sound was audible.

Jack stole softly out of the wardrobe, and taking up the bags of money (which were his very own, because the Giant had stolen them from his father), he ran off, and with great difficulty descending the Beanstalk, laid the bags of gold on his mother's table. She had just returned from town, and was crying at not finding Jack.

"There, mother, I have brought you the gold that my father lost."

"Oh, Jack! you are a very good boy, but I wish you would not risk your precious life in the Giant's castle. Tell me how you came to go there again."

And Jack told her all about it.

Jack's mother was very glad to get the money, but she did not like him to run any risk for her.

But after a time Jack made up his mind to go again to the Giant's castle.

THE TALKING HARP

So he climbed the Beanstalk once more, and blew the horn at the Giant's gate. The Giantess soon opened the door; she was very stupid, and did not know him again, but she stopped a minute before she took him in. She feared another robbery; but Jack's fresh face looked so innocent that she could not resist him, and so she bade him come in, and again hid him away in the wardrobe.

By-and-by the Giant came home, and as soon as he had crossed the threshold he roared out:

> "Fe, fa, fi-fo-fum,
> I smell the breath of an Englishman.
> Let him be alive or let him be dead,
> I'll grind his bones to make my bread."

"You stupid old Giant," said his wife, "you only smell a nice sheep, which I have grilled for your dinner."

And the Giant sat down, and his wife brought up a whole sheep for his dinner. When he had eaten it all up, he said:

"Now bring me my harp, and I will have a little music while you take your walk."

The Giantess obeyed, and returned with a beautiful harp. The framework was all sparkling with diamonds and rubies, and the strings were all of gold.

"This is one of the nicest things I took from the knight," said the Giant. "I am very fond of music, and my harp is a faithful servant."

So he drew the harp toward him, and said:

"Play!"

And the harp played a very soft, sad air.

"Play something merrier!" said the Giant.

And the harp played a merry tune.

"Now play me a lullaby," roared the Giant; and the harp played a sweet lullaby, to the sound of which its master fell asleep.

Then Jack stole softly out of the wardrobe, and went into the huge kitchen to see if the Giantess had gone out; he found no one there, so he went to the door and opened it softly, for he thought he could not do so with the harp in his hand.

Then he entered the Giant's room and seized the harp and ran away with it; but as he jumped over the threshold the harp called out:

"Master! Master!"

And the Giant woke up.

With a tremendous roar he sprang from his seat, and in two strides had reached the door.

But Jack was very nimble. He fled like lightning with the harp, talking to it as he went (for he saw it was a fairy), and telling it he was the son of its old master, the knight.

Still the Giant came on so fast that he was quite close to poor Jack, and had stretched out his great hand to catch him. But, luckily, just at that moment he stepped upon a loose stone, stumbled, and fell flat on the ground, where he lay at his full length.

This accident gave Jack time to get on the Beanstalk and hasten down it; but just as he reached their own garden he beheld the Giant descending after him.

"Mother! mother!" cried Jack, "make haste and give me the axe."

His mother ran to him with a hatchet in her hand, and Jack with one tremendous blow cut through all the Beanstalks except one.

"Now, mother, stand out of the way!" said he.

THE GIANT BREAKS HIS NECK

Jack's mother shrank back, and it was well she did so, for just as the Giant took hold of the last branch of the Beanstalk, Jack cut the stem quite through and darted from the spot.

Down came the Giant with a terrible crash, and as he fell on his head, he broke his neck, and lay dead at the feet of the woman he had so much injured.

Before Jack and his mother had recovered from their alarm and agitation, a beautiful lady stood before them.

"Jack," said she, "you have acted like a brave knight's son, and deserve to have your inheritance restored to you. Dig a grave and bury the Giant, and then go and kill the Giantess."

"But," said Jack, "I could not kill anyone unless I were fighting with him; and I could not draw my sword upon a woman. Moreover, the Giantess was very kind to me."

The Fairy smiled on Jack.

"I am very much pleased with your generous feeling," she said. "Nevertheless, return to the castle, and act as you will find needful."

Jack asked the Fairy if she would show him the way to the castle, as the Beanstalk was now down. She told him that she would drive him there in her chariot, which was drawn by two peacocks. Jack thanked her, and sat down in the chariot with her.

JACK AND THE BEANSTALK

The Fairy drove him a long distance round, till they reached a village which lay at the bottom of the hill. Here they found a number of miserable-looking men assembled. The Fairy stopped her carriage and addressed them:

"My friends," said she, "the cruel giant who oppressed you and ate up all your flocks and herds is dead, and this young gentleman was the means of your being delivered from him, and is the son of your kind old master, the knight."

The men gave a loud cheer at these words, and pressed forward to say that they would serve Jack as faithfully as they had served his father. The Fairy bade them follow her to the castle, and they marched thither in a body, and Jack blew the horn and demanded admittance.

The old Giantess saw them coming from the turret loop-hole. She was very much frightened, for she guessed that something had happened to her husband; and as she came downstairs very fast she caught her foot in her dress, and fell from the top to the bottom and broke her neck.

When the people outside found that the door was not opened to them, they took crowbars and forced the portal. Nobody was to be seen, but on leaving the hall they found the body of the Giantess at the foot of the stairs.

Thus Jack took possession of the castle. The Fairy went and brought his mother to him, with the hen and the harp. He had the Giantess buried, and endeavored as much as lay in his power to do right to those whom the Giant had robbed.

Before her departure for fairyland, the Fairy explained to Jack that she had sent the butcher to meet him with the beans, in order to try what sort of lad he was.

"If you had looked at the gigantic Beanstalk and only stupidly wondered about it," she said, "I should have left you where misfortune had placed you, only restoring her cow to your mother. But you showed an inquiring mind, and great courage and enterprise, therefore you deserve to rise; and when you mounted the Beanstalk you climbed the Ladder of Fortune."

She then took her leave of Jack and his mother.

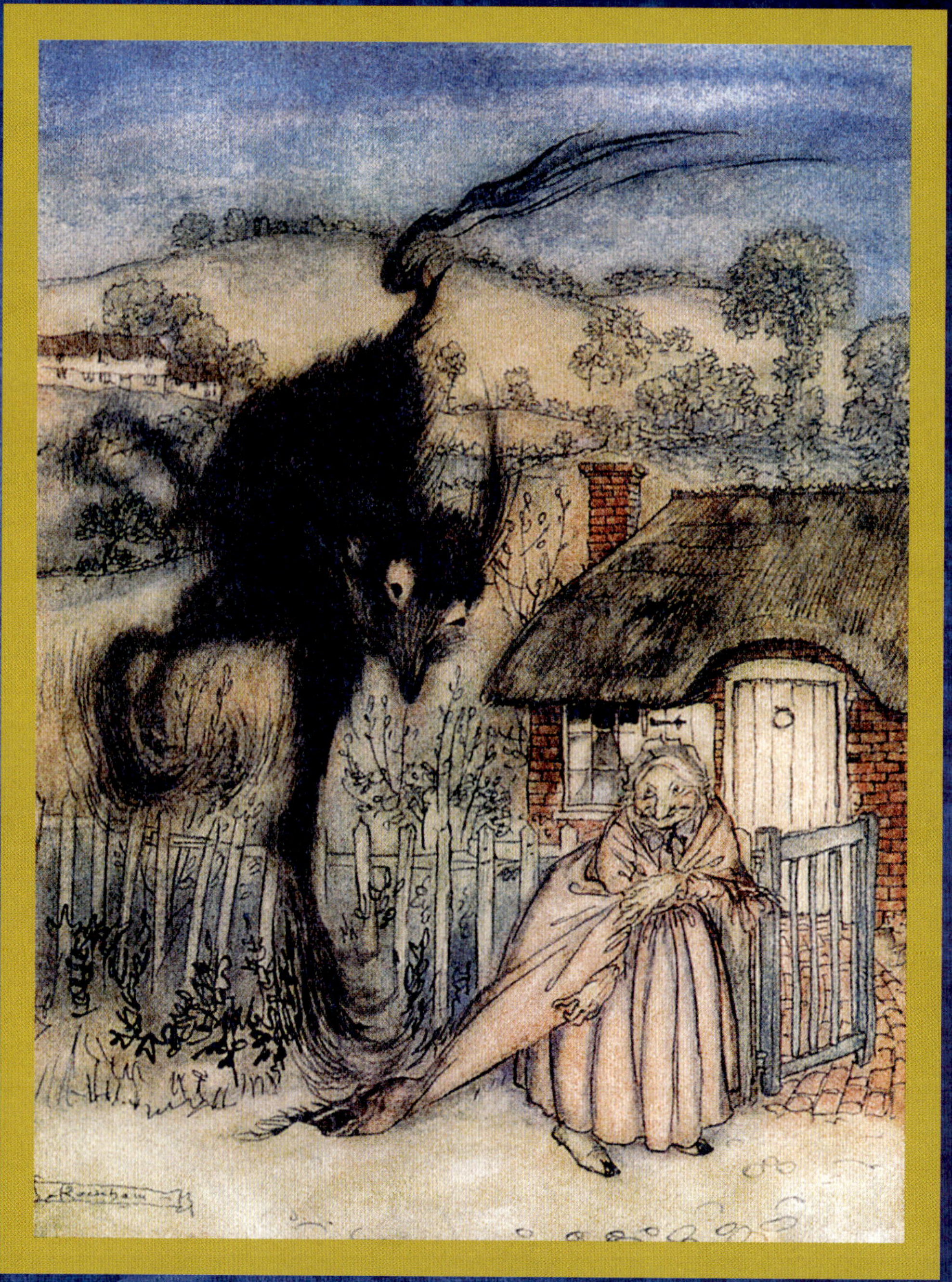

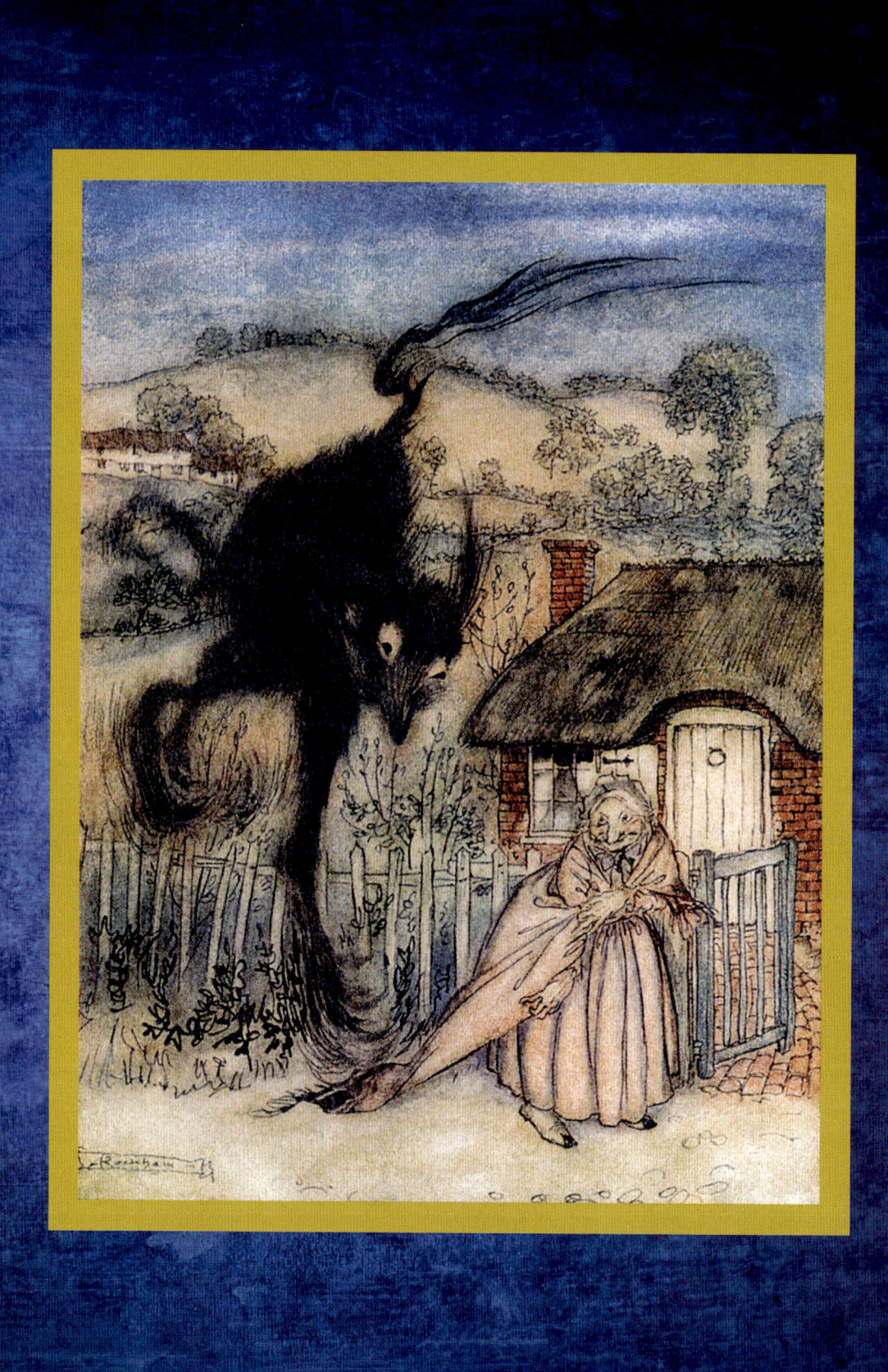

The Bogey-Beast

There was once a woman who was very, very cheerful, though she had little to make her so; for she was old, and poor, and lonely. She lived in a little bit of a cottage and earned a scant living by running errands for her neighbors, getting a bite here, a sup there, as reward for her services. So she made shift to get on, and always looked as spry and cheery as if she had not a want in the world.

Now one summer evening, as she was trotting, full of smiles as ever, along the high road to her hovel, what should she see but a big black pot lying in the ditch!

"Goodness me!" she cried, "that would be just the very thing for me if I only had something to put in it! But I haven't! Now who could have left it in the ditch?"

And she looked about her expecting the owner would not be far off; but she could see nobody.

"Maybe there is a hole in it," she went on, "and that's why it has been cast away. But it would do fine to put a flower in for my window; so I'll just take it home with me."

And with that she lifted the lid and looked inside.

"Mercy me!" she cried, fair amazed. "If it isn't full of gold pieces. Here's luck!"

And so it was, brimful of great gold coins. Well, at first she simply stood stock-still, wondering if she was standing on her head or her heels. Then she began saying:

"Lawks! But I do feel rich. I feel awful rich!"

After she had said this many times, she began to wonder how she was to get her treasure home. It was too heavy for her to carry, and she could see no better way than to tie the end of her shawl to it and drag it behind her like a go-cart.

"It will soon be dark," she said to herself as she trotted along. "So much the better! The neighbors will not see what I'm bringing home, and I shall have all the night to myself, and be able to think what I'll do! Mayhap I'll buy a grand house and just sit by the fire with a cup o' tea and do no work at all like a Queen. Or maybe I'll bury it at the garden-foot and just keep a bit in the old china teapot on the chimney-piece. Or maybe— Goody! Goody! I feel that grand I don't know myself."

By this time she was a bit tired of dragging such a heavy weight, and, stopping to rest a while, turned to look at her treasure.

And lo! it wasn't a pot of gold at all! It was nothing but a lump of silver.

She stared at it and rubbed her eyes and stared at it again.

"Well! I never," she said at last. "And me thinking it was a pot of gold! I must have been dreaming. But this is luck! Silver is far less trouble—easier to mind, and not so easy stolen. Them gold pieces would have been the death o' me, and with this great lump of silver—"

So she went off again planning what she would do, and feeling as rich as rich, until becoming a bit tired again she stopped to rest and gave a look round to see if her treasure was safe; and she saw nothing but a great lump of iron!

"Well! I never!" says she again. "And I mistaking it for silver! I must have been dreaming. But this is luck! It's real convenient. I can get penny pieces for old iron, and penny pieces are a deal handier for me than your gold and silver. Why! I should never have slept a wink for fear of being robbed. But a penny piece comes in useful, and I shall sell that iron for a lot and be real rich—rolling rich."

So on she trotted full of plans as to how she would spend her penny pieces, till once more she stopped to rest and looked round to see if her treasure was safe. And this time she saw nothing but a big stone.

"Well! I never!" she cried, full of smiles. "And to think I mistook it for iron. I must have been dreaming. But here's luck indeed, and me wanting a stone terrible bad to stick open the gate. Eh my! but it's a change for the better! It's a fine thing to have good luck."

So, all in a hurry to see how the stone would keep the gate open she trotted off down the hill till she came to her own cottage. She unlatched the gate and then turned to unfasten her shawl from the stone which lay on the path behind her. Aye! it was a stone sure enough. There was plenty light to see it lying there, douce and peaceable as a stone should.

So she bent over it to unfasten the shawl end, when—

"Oh my!"

All of a sudden it gave a jump, a squeal, and in one moment was as big as a haystack. Then it let down four great lanky legs and threw out two long ears, flourished a great long tail and romped off, kicking and squealing and whinnying and laughing like a naughty mischievous boy!

The old woman stared after it till it was fairly out of sight, then she burst out laughing too.

"Well!" she chuckled, "I am in luck! Quite the luckiest body hereabouts. Fancy my seeing the Bogey-Beast all to myself; and making myself so free with it too! My goodness! I do feel that uplifted—that GRAND!"—

So she went into her cottage and spent the evening chuckling over her good luck.

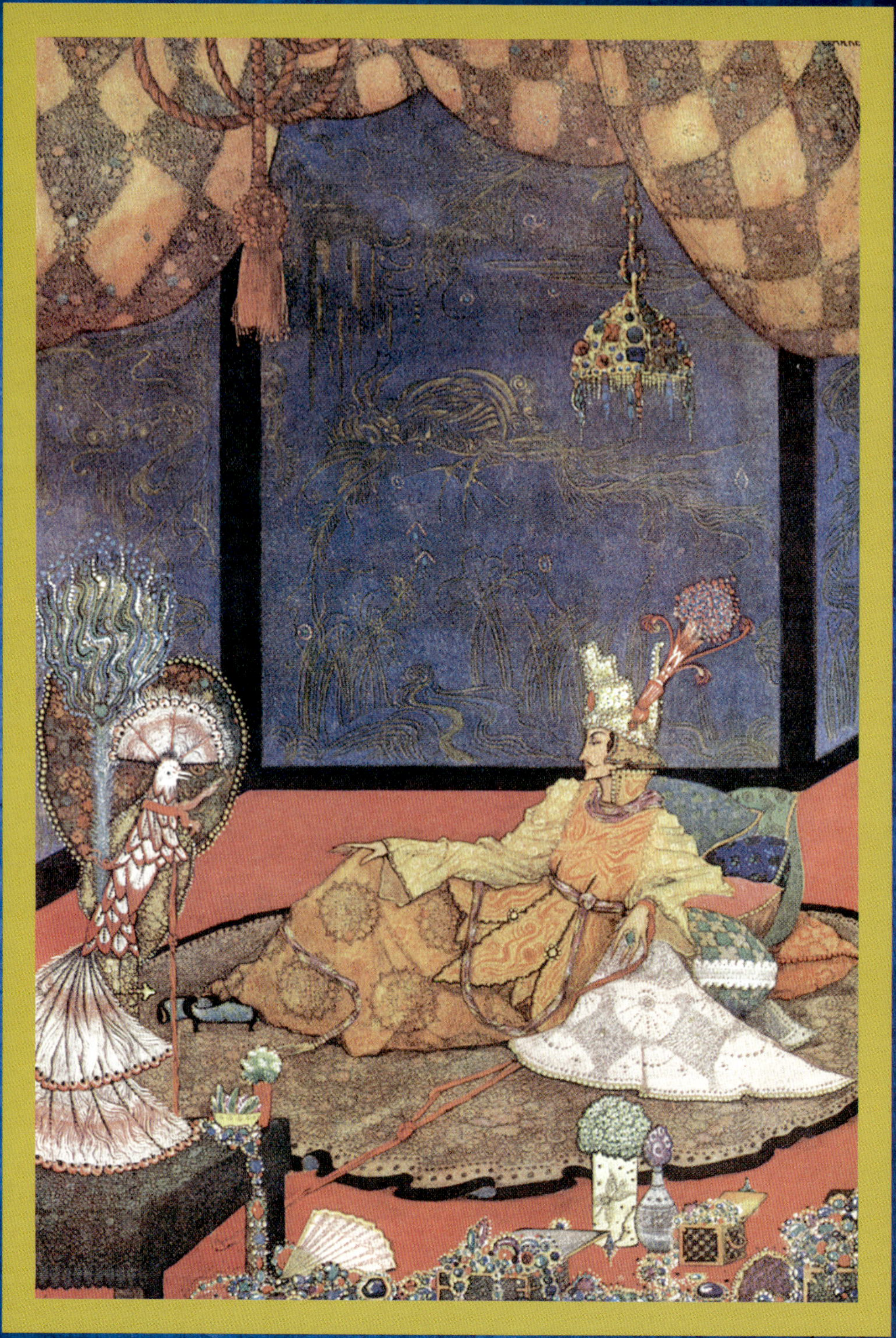

The Nightingale

In China, you must know, the Emperor is a Chinaman, and all whom he has about him are Chinamen too. It happened a good many years ago, but that's just why it's worth while to hear the story, before it is forgotten. The Emperor's palace was the most splendid in the world; it was made entirely of porcelain, very costly, but so delicate and brittle that one had to take care how one touched it. In the garden were to be seen the most wonderful flowers, and to the costliest of them silver bells were tied, which sounded, so that nobody should pass by without noticing the flowers. Yes, everything in the Emperor's garden was admirably arranged. And it extended so far that the gardener himself did not know where the end was. If a man went on and on, he came into a glorious forest with high trees and deep lakes. The wood extended straight down to the sea, which was blue and deep; great ships could sail, too, beneath the branches of the trees; and in the trees lived a Nightingale, which sang so splendidly that even the poor fisherman, who had many other things to do, stopped still and listened, when he had gone out at night to throw out his nets, and heard the Nightingale.

"How beautiful that is!" he said; but he was obliged to attend to his property, and thus forgot the bird. But when in the next night the bird sang again, and the fisherman heard it, he exclaimed again, "How beautiful that is!"

From all the countries of the world travelers came to the city of the Emperor and admired it, and the palace, and the garden, but when they heard the Nightingale, they said, "That is the best of all!"

And the travelers told of it when they came home; and the learned men wrote many books about the town, the palace, and the garden. But they did not forget the Nightingale; that was placed highest of all; and those who were poets wrote most magnificent poems about the Nightingale in the wood by the deep lake.

The books went through all the world, and a few of them once came to the Emperor. He sat in his golden chair, and read, and read: every moment he nodded his head, for it pleased him to peruse the masterly descriptions of the city, the palace, and the garden. "But the Nightingale is the best of all," it stood written there.

"What's that?" exclaimed the Emperor. "I don't know the Nightingale at all! Is there such a bird in my empire, and even in my garden? I've never heard of that. To think that I should have to learn such a thing for the first time from books!"

And hereupon he called his Cavalier. This Cavalier was so grand that if any one lower in rank than himself dared to speak to him, or to ask him any question, he answered nothing but "P!"—and that meant nothing.

"There is said to be a wonderful bird here called a Nightingale!" said the Emperor. "They say it is the best thing in all my great empire. Why have I never heard anything about it?"

"I have never heard him named," replied the Cavalier. "He has never been introduced at court."

"I command that he shall appear this evening, and sing before me," said the Emperor. "All the world knows what I possess, and I do not know it myself!"

"I have never heard him mentioned," said the Cavalier. "I will seek for him. I will find him."

But where was he to be found? The Cavalier ran up and down all the staircases, through halls and passages, but no one among all those whom he met had heard talk of the Nightingale. And the Cavalier ran back to the Emperor, and said that it must be a fable invented by the writers of books.

"Your Imperial Majesty cannot believe how much is written that is fiction, besides something that they call the black art."

"But the book in which I read this," said the Emperor, "was sent to me by the high and mighty Emperor of Japan, and therefore it cannot be a falsehood. I will hear the

The Nightingale

Nightingale! It must be here this evening! It has my imperial favor; and if it does not come, all the court shall be trampled upon after the court has supped!"

"Tsing-pe!" said the Cavalier; and again he ran up and down all the staircases, and through all the halls and corridors; and half the court ran with him, for the courtiers did not like being trampled upon.

Then there was a great inquiry after the wonderful Nightingale, which all the world knew excepting the people at court.

At last they met with a poor little girl in the kitchen, who said:

"The Nightingale? I know it well; yes, it can sing gloriously. Every evening I get leave to carry my poor sick mother the scraps from the table. She lives down by the strand, and when I get back and am tired, and rest in the wood, then I hear the Nightingale sing. And then the water comes into my eyes, and it is just as if my mother kissed me!"

"Little kitchen girl," said the Cavalier, "I will get you a place in the kitchen, with permission to see the Emperor dine, if you will lead us to the Nightingale, for it is announced for this evening."

So they all went out into the wood where the Nightingale was accustomed to sing; half the court went forth. When they were in the midst of their journey a cow began to low.

"Oh!" cried the court pages, "now we have it! That shows a wonderful power in so small a creature! I have certainly heard it before."

"No, those are cows lowing!" said the little kitchen girl. "We are a long way from the place yet."

Now the frogs began to croak in the marsh.

"Glorious!" said the Chinese court preacher. "Now I hear it—it sounds just like little church bells."

"No, those are frogs!" said the little kitchen maid. "But now I think we shall soon hear it."

And then the Nightingale began to sing. "That is it!" exclaimed the little girl. "Listen, listen! and yonder it sits."

And she pointed to a little gray bird up in the boughs.

"Is it possible?" cried the Cavalier. "I should never have thought it looked like that! How simple it looks! It must certainly have lost its color at seeing such grand people around."

"Little Nightingale!" called the little kitchen maid, quite loudly, "our gracious Emperor wishes you to sing before him."

"With the greatest pleasure!" replied the Nightingale, and began to sing most delightfully.

"It sounds just like glass bells!" said the Cavalier. "And look at its little throat, how it's working! It's wonderful that we should never have heard it before. That bird will be a great success at court."

"Shall I sing once more before the Emperor?" asked the Nightingale, for it thought the Emperor was present.

"My excellent little Nightingale," said the Cavalier, "I have great pleasure in inviting you to a court festival this evening, when you shall charm his Imperial Majesty with your beautiful singing."

"My song sounds best in the green wood!" replied the Nightingale; still it came willingly when it heard what the Emperor wished.

The palace was festively adorned. The walls and the flooring, which were of porcelain, gleamed in the rays of thousands of golden lamps. The most glorious flowers, which could ring clearly, had been placed in the passages. There was a running to and fro, and a thorough draught, and all the bells rang so loudly that one could not hear one's self speak.

In the midst of the great hall, where the Emperor sat, a golden perch had been placed, in which the Nightingale was to sit. The whole court was there, and the little cook-maid had got leave to stand behind the door, as she had now received the title of a real court cook. All were in full dress, and all looked at the little gray bird, to which the Emperor nodded.

And the Nightingale sang so gloriously that the tears came into the Emperor's eyes, and the tears ran down over his cheeks; and then the Nightingale sang still more sweetly, that went straight to the heart. The Emperor was so much pleased that he said the Nightingale should have his golden slipper to wear around its neck. But the Nightingale declined this with thanks, saying it had already received a sufficient reward.

"I have seen tears in the Emperor's eyes— that is the real treasure to me. An Emperor's tears have a peculiar power. I am rewarded enough!" And then it sang again with a sweet, glorious voice.

"That's the most amiable coquetry I ever saw!" said the ladies who stood round about, and then they took water in their mouths to gurgle when any one spoke to them. They thought they should be nightingales too. And the lackeys and chambermaids reported that they were satisfied too; and that was saying a good deal, for they are the most difficult to please. In short, the Nightingale achieved a real success.

It was now to remain at court, to have its own cage, with liberty to go out twice every day and once at night. Twelve servants were appointed when the Nightingale went out, each of whom had a silken string fastened to the bird's leg, and which they held very tight. There was really no pleasure in an excursion of that kind.

The whole city spoke of the wonderful bird, and when two people met, one said nothing but "Nightin," and the other said "gale"; and then they sighed, and understood each other. Eleven peddlers' children were named after the bird, but not one of them could sing a note.

One day the Emperor received a large parcel, on which was written "The Nightingale."

"There we have a new book about this celebrated bird," said the Emperor.

But it was not a book, but a little work of art contained in a box, an artificial nightingale, which was to sing like a natural one, and was brilliantly ornamented with diamonds, rubies, and sapphires. So soon as the artificial bird was wound up, he could sing one of the pieces that he really sang, and then his tail moved up and down, and shone with silver and gold. Round his neck hung a little ribbon, and on that was written, "The Emperor of China's Nightingale is poor compared to that of the Emperor of Japan."

"That is capital!" said they all, and he who had brought the artificial bird immediately received the title, Imperial Head-Nightingale-Bringer.

"Now they must sing together; what a duet that will be!"

And so they had to sing together; but it did not sound very well, for the real Nightingale sang in its own way, and the artificial bird sang waltzes.

"That's not its fault," said the playmaster; "its quite perfect, and very much in my style."

Now the artificial bird was to sing alone. It had just as much success as the real one, and then it was much handsomer to look at—it shone like bracelets and breast-pins.

Three and thirty times over did it sing the same piece, and yet was not tired. The people would gladly have heard it again, but the Emperor said that the living Nightingale ought to sing something now. But where was it? No one had noticed that it had flown away out of the open window, back to the green wood.

"But what of that?" said the Emperor.

And all the courtiers abused the Nightingale, and declared that it was a very ungrateful creature.

"We have the best bird, after all," said they.

And so the artificial bird had to sing again, and that was the thirty-fourth time that they listened to the same piece. For all that they did not know it quite by heart, for it was so very difficult. And the playmaster praised the bird particularly; yes, he declared that it was better than a nightingale, not only with regard to its plumage and the many beautiful diamonds, but inside as well.

"For you see, ladies and gentlemen, and above all, your Imperial Majesty, with a real nightingale one can never calculate what is coming, but in this artificial bird everything is settled. One can explain it; one can open it and make people understand where the waltzes come from, how they go, and how one follows up another."

"Those are quite our own ideas," they all said.

And the speaker received permission to show the bird to the people on the next Sunday. The people were to hear it sing too, the Emperor commanded; and they did hear it, and were as much pleased as if they had all got tipsy upon tea, for that's quite the Chinese fashion; and they all said "Oh!" and held up their forefingers and nodded. But the poor fisherman, who had heard the real Nightingale, said:

"It sounds pretty enough, and the melodies resemble each other, but there's something wanting, though I know not what!"

The real Nightingale was banished from the country and empire. The artificial bird had its place on a silken cushion close to the Emperor's bed; all the presents it had received, gold and precious stones, were ranged about it; in title it had advanced to be the High Imperial-After-Dinner-Singer, and in rank to number one on the left hand; for the Emperor considered that side the most important on which the heart is placed, and even in an Emperor the heart is on the left side; and the playmaster wrote a work of five and twenty volumes about the artificial bird; it was very learned and very long, full of the most difficult Chinese words; but yet all the people declared that they had read it and understood it, for fear of being considered stupid, and having their bodies trampled on.

So a whole year went by. The Emperor, the court, and all the other Chinese knew every little twitter in the artificial bird's song by heart. But just for that reason it pleased them best—they could sing with it themselves, and they did so. The street boys sang, "Tsi-tsi-tsi-glugglug!" and the Emperor himself sang it too. Yes, that was certainly famous.

But one evening, when the artificial bird was singing its best, and the Emperor lay in bed listening to it, something inside the bird said "Whizz!" Something cracked. "Whir-r-r!" All the wheels ran round, and then the music stopped.

The Emperor immediately sprang out of bed, and caused his body physician to be called; but what could he do? Then they sent for a watchmaker, and after a good deal of talking and investigation, the bird was put into something like order; but the watchmaker said that the bird must be carefully treated, for the barrels were worn, and it would be impossible to put new ones in in such a manner that the music would go. There was a great lamentation; only once in a year was it permitted to let the bird sing, and that was almost too much. But then the playmaster made a little speech, full of heavy words, and said this was just as good as before—and so of course it was as good as before.

Now five years had gone by, and a real grief came upon the whole nation. The Chinese were really fond of their Emperor, and now he was ill, and could not, it was said, live much longer. Already a new Emperor had been chosen, and the people stood out in the street and asked the Cavalier how their old Emperor did.

"P!" said he, and shook his head.

Cold and pale lay the Emperor in his great gorgeous bed; the whole court thought him dead, and each one ran to pay homage to the new ruler. The chamberlains ran out to talk it over, and the ladies' maids had a great coffee party. All about, in all the halls and passages, cloth had been laid down so that no footstep could be heard, and therefore it was quiet there, quite quiet. But the Emperor was not dead yet: stiff and pale he lay on the gorgeous bed, with the long velvet curtains and the heavy gold tassels; high up, a window stood open, and the moon shone in upon the Emperor and the artificial bird.

The poor Emperor could scarcely breathe; it was just as if something lay upon his chest: he opened his eyes, and then he saw that it was Death who sat upon his chest, and had put on his golden crown, and held in one hand the Emperor's sword, and in the other his beautiful banner. And all around, from among the folds of the splendid velvet curtains, strange heads peered forth; a few very ugly, the rest quite lovely and mild. These were all the Emperor's bad and good deeds, that stood before him now that Death sat upon his heart.

"Do you remember this?" whispered one to the other. "Do you remember that?" and then they told him so much that the perspiration ran from his forehead.

"I did not know that!" said the Emperor. "Music! music! the great Chinese drum!" he cried, "so that I need not hear all they say!"

And they continued speaking, and Death nodded like a Chinaman to all they said.

"Music! music!" cried the Emperor. "You little precious golden bird, sing, sing! I have given you gold and costly presents; I have even hung my golden slipper around your neck —sing now, sing!"

But the bird stood still; no one was there to wind him up, and he could not sing without that; but Death continued to stare at the Emperor with his great hollow eyes, and it was quiet, fearfully quiet.

Then there sounded from the window, suddenly, the most lovely song. It was the little live Nightingale, that sat outside on a spray. It had heard of the Emperor's sad plight, and had come to sing to him of comfort and hope. And as it sang the specters grew paler and paler; the blood ran quicker and more quickly through the Emperor's weak limbs; and even Death listened, and said:

"Go on, little Nightingale, go on!"

"But will you give me that splendid golden sword? Will you give me that rich banner? Will you give me the Emperor's crown?"

And Death gave up each of these treasures for a song. And the Nightingale sang on and on; and it sang of the quiet churchyard where the white roses grow, where the elder

The Nightingale

blossom smells sweet, and where the fresh grass is moistened by the tears of survivors. Then Death felt a longing to see his garden, and floated out at the window in the form of a cold white mist.

"Thanks! thanks!" said the Emperor. "You heavenly little bird! I know you well. I banished you from my country and empire, and yet you have charmed away the evil faces from my couch, and banished Death from my heart! How can I reward you?"

"You have rewarded me!" replied the Nightingale. "I have drawn tears from your eyes, when I sang the first time—I shall never forget that. Those are the jewels that rejoice a singer's heart. But now sleep and grow fresh and strong again. I will sing you something."

And it sang, and the Emperor fell into a sweet slumber. Ah! how mild and refreshing that sleep was! The sun shone upon him through the windows, when he awoke refreshed and restored; not one of his servants had yet returned, for they all thought he was dead; only the Nightingale still sat beside him and sang.

"You must always stay with me," said the Emperor. "You shall sing as you please; and I'll break the artificial bird into a thousand pieces."

"Not so," replied the Nightingale. "It did well as long as it could; keep it as you have done till now. I cannot build my nest in the palace to dwell in it, but let me come when I feel the wish; then I will sit in the evening on the spray yonder by the window, and sing you something, so that you may be glad and thoughtful at once. I will sing of those who are happy and of those who suffer. I will sing of good and of evil that remains hidden round about you. The little singing bird flies far around, to the poor fisherman, to the peasant's roof, to every one who dwells far away from you and from your court. I love your heart more than your crown, and yet the crown has an air of sanctity about it. I will come and sing to you—but one thing you must promise me."

"Everything!" said the Emperor; and he stood there in his imperial robes, which he had put on himself, and pressed the sword which was heavy with gold to his heart.

"One thing I beg of you: tell no one that you have a little bird who tells you everything. Then it will go all the better."

And the Nightingale flew away.

The servants came in to look to their dead Emperor, and—yes, there he stood, and the Emperor said, "Good-morning!"

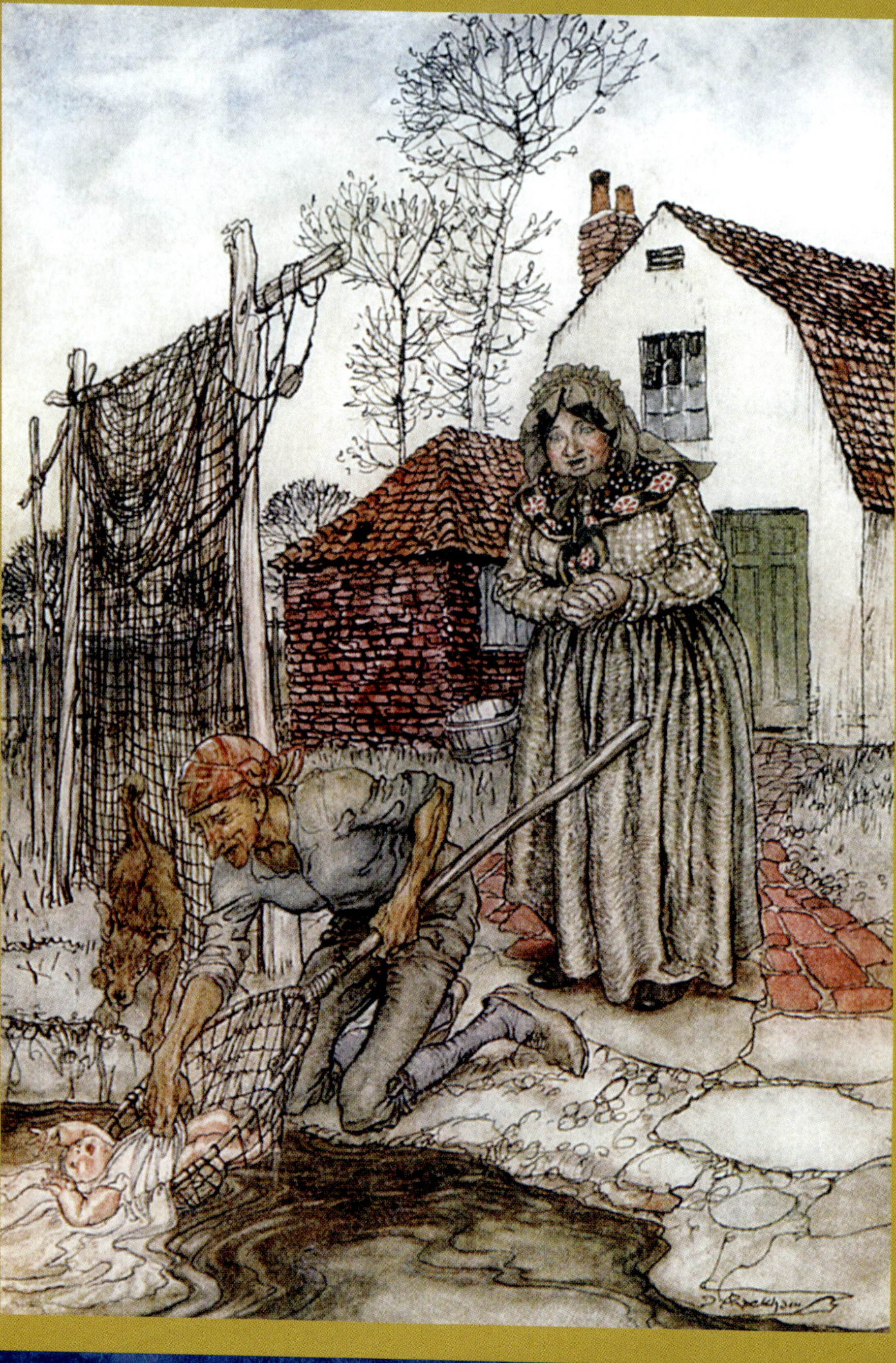

The Fish and the Ring

Once upon a time there lived a Baron who was a great magician, and could tell by his arts and charms everything that was going to happen at any time.

Now this great lord had a little son born to him as heir to all his castles and lands. So, when the little lad was about four years old, wishing to know what his fortune would be, the Baron looked in his Book of Fate to see what it foretold.

And lo and behold! it was written that this much-loved, much-prized heir to all the great lands and castles was to marry a low-born maiden. So the Baron was dismayed, and set to work by more arts and charms to discover if this maiden were already born, and if so, where she lived.

And he found out that she had just been born in a very poor house, where the poor parents were already burdened with five children.

So he called for his horse and rode away, and away, until he came to the poor man's house, and there he found the poor man sitting at his doorstep very sad and doleful.

"What is the matter, my friend?" asked he; and the poor man replied:

"May it please your honor, a little lass has just been born to our house; and we have five children already, and where the bread is to come from to fill the sixth mouth, we know not."

"If that be all your trouble," quoth the Baron readily, "mayhap I can help you: so don't be down-hearted. I am just looking for such a little lass to companion my son, so if you will, I will give you ten crowns for her."

Well! the man he nigh jumped for joy, since he was to get good money, and his daughter, so he thought, a good home. Therefore he brought out the child then and there, and the Baron, wrapping the babe in his cloak, rode away. But when he got to the river he flung the little thing into the swollen stream and said to himself as he galloped back to his castle:

"There goes Fate!"

But, you see, he was just sore mistaken. For the little lass didn't sink. The stream was very swift, and her long clothes kept her up till she caught in a snag just opposite a fisherman, who was mending his nets.

Now the fisherman and his wife had no children, and they were just longing for a baby; so when the good man saw the little lass he was overcome with joy, and took her home to his wife, who received her with open arms.

And there she grew up, the apple of their eyes, into the most beautiful maiden that ever was seen.

Now when she was about fifteen years of age it so happened that the Baron and his friends went a-hunting along the banks of the river and stopped to get a drink of water at the fisherman's hut. And who should bring the water out but, as they thought, the fisherman's daughter.

Now the young men of the party noticed her beauty, and one of them said to the Baron, "She should marry well; read us her fate since you are so learned in the art."

Then the Baron, scarce looking at her, said carelessly: "I could guess her fate! Some wretched yokel or other. But, to please you, I will cast her horoscope by the stars; so tell me, girl, what day you were born?"

"That I cannot tell, sir," replied the girl, "for I was picked up in the river about fifteen years ago."

Then the Baron grew pale, for he guessed at once that she was the little lass he had flung into the stream, and that Fate had been stronger than he was. But he kept his own counsel and said nothing at the time. Afterward, however, he thought out a plan, so he rode back and gave the girl a letter.

"See you!" he said. "I will make your fortune. Take this letter to my brother, who needs a good girl, and you will be settled for life."

Now the fisherman and his wife were growing old and needed help; so the girl said she would go, and took the letter.

And the Baron rode back to his castle saying to himself once more:

"There goes Fate!"

For what he had written in the letter was this:

Dear Brother,
    Take the bearer and put her to death immediately.

But once again he was sore mistaken; since on the way to the town where his brother lived, the girl had to stop the night in a little inn. And it so happened that that very night a gang of thieves broke into the inn, and not content with carrying off all that the innkeeper possessed, they searched the pockets of the guests, and found the letter which the girl carried. And when they read it, they agreed that it was a mean trick and a shame. So their captain sat down, and taking pen and paper wrote instead:

Dear Brother,
    Take the bearer and marry her to my son without delay.

Then, after putting the note into an envelope and sealing it up, they gave it to the girl and bade her go on her way. So when she arrived at the brother's castle, though rather surprised, he gave orders for a wedding feast to be prepared. And the Baron's son, who was staying with his uncle, seeing the girl's great beauty, was nothing loth, so they were fast wedded.

Well! when the news was brought to the Baron, he was nigh beside himself; but he was determined not to be done by Fate. So he rode post-haste to his brother's and pretended to be quite pleased. And then one day, when no one was nigh, he asked the young bride to come for a walk with him, and when they were close to some cliffs, seized hold of her, and was for throwing her over into the sea. But she begged hard for her life.

"It is not my fault," she said. "I have done nothing. It is Fate. But if you will spare my life I promise that I will fight against Fate also. I will never see you or your son again until you desire it. That will be safer for you; since, see you, the sea may preserve me, as the river did."

Well! the Baron agreed to this. So he took off his gold ring from his finger and flung it over the cliffs into the sea and said:

"Never dare to show me your face again till you can show me that ring likewise."

And with that he let her go.

Well! the girl wandered on, and she wandered on, until she came to a nobleman's castle; and there, as they needed a kitchen girl, she engaged as a scullion, since she had been used to such work in the fisherman's hut.

Now one day, as she was cleaning a big fish, she looked out of the kitchen window, and who should she see driving up to dinner but the Baron and his young son, her husband. At first, she thought that, to keep her promise, she must run away; but afterward she remembered they would not see her in the kitchen, so she went on with her cleaning of the big fish.

And lo and behold! she saw something shine in its inside, and there, sure enough, was the Baron's ring! She was glad enough to see it, I can tell you; so she slipped it on to her thumb. But she went on with her work, and dressed the fish as nicely as ever she could, and served it up as pretty as may be, with parsley sauce and butter.

Well! when it came to table the guests liked it so well that they asked the host who cooked it? And he called to his servants, "Send up the cook who cooked that fine fish, that she may get her reward."

Well! when the girl heard she was wanted she made herself ready, and with the gold ring on her thumb, went boldly into the dining-hall. And all the guests when they saw her were struck dumb by her wonderful beauty. And the young husband started up gladly; but the Baron, recognizing her, jumped up angrily and looked as if he would

The Fish and the Ring

kill her. So, without one word, the girl held up her hand before his face and the gold ring shone and glittered on it; and she went straight up to the Baron, and laid her hand with the ring on it before him on the table.

Then the Baron understood that Fate had been too strong for him; so he took her by the hand, and, placing her beside him, turned to the guests and said:

"This is my son's wife. Let us drink a toast in her honor."

And after dinner he took her and his son home to his castle, where they all lived as happy as could be for ever afterward.

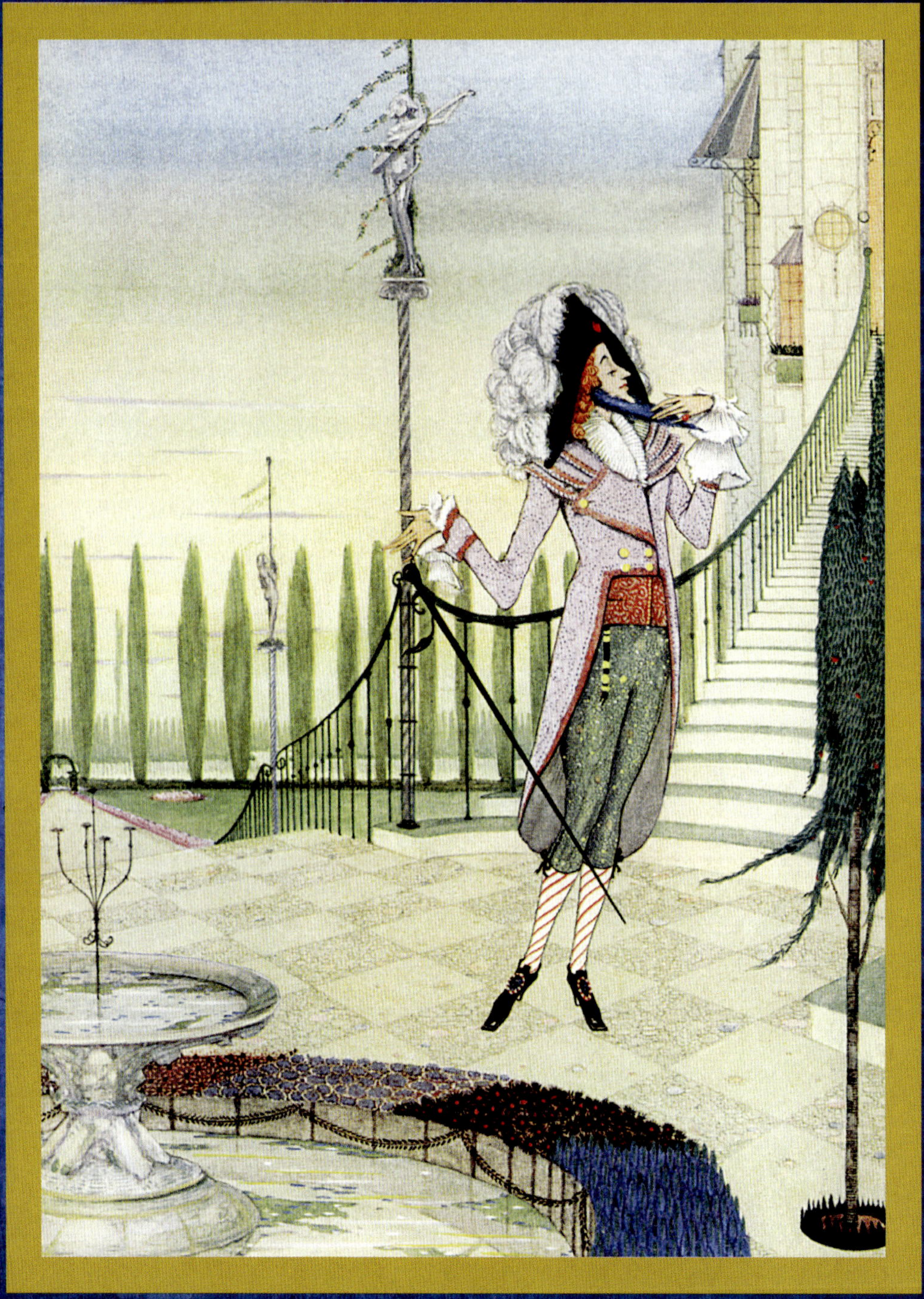

Blue Beard

There was a man who had fine houses, both in town and country, a deal of silver and gold plate, embroidered furniture, and coaches gilded all over with gold. But this man was so unlucky as to have a blue beard, which made him so frightfully ugly that all the women and girls ran away from him.

One of his neighbors, a lady of quality, had two daughters who were perfect beauties. He desired of her one of them in marriage, leaving to her choice which of the two she would bestow on him. They would neither of them have him, and sent him backward and forward from one another, not being able to bear the thoughts of marrying a man who had a blue beard, and what besides gave them disgust and aversion was his having already been married to several wives, and nobody ever knew what became of them.

Blue Beard, to engage their affection, took them, with the lady their mother and three or four ladies of their acquaintance, with other young people of the neighborhood, to one of his country seats, where they stayed a whole week.

There was nothing then to be seen but parties of pleasure, hunting, fishing, dancing, mirth, and feasting. Nobody went to bed, but all passed the night in rallying and joking with each other. In short, everything succeeded so well that the youngest daughter began to think the master of the house not to have a beard so very blue, and that he was a mighty civil gentleman.

As soon as they returned home, the marriage was concluded. About a month afterward, Blue Beard told his wife that he was obliged to take a country journey for six weeks at least, about affairs of very great consequence, desiring her to divert herself in his absence, to send for her friends and acquaintances, to carry them into the country, if she pleased, and to make good cheer wherever she was.

"Here," said he, "are the keys of the two great wardrobes, wherein I have my best furniture; these are of my silver and gold plate, which is not every day in use; these open my strong boxes, which hold my money, both gold and silver; these my caskets of jewels; and this is the master-key to all my apartments. But for this little one here, it is the key of the closet at the end of the great gallery on the ground floor. Open them all; go into all and every one of them, except that little closet, which I forbid you, and forbid it in such a manner that, if you happen to open it, there's nothing but what you may expect from my just anger and resentment."

She promised to observe, very exactly, whatever he had ordered; when he, after having embraced her, got into his coach and proceeded on his journey.

Her neighbors and good friends did not stay to be sent for by the new married lady, so great was their impatience to see all the rich furniture of her house, not daring to come while her husband was there, because of his blue beard, which frightened them. They ran through all the rooms, closets, and wardrobes, which were all so fine and rich that they seemed to surpass one another.

After that they went up into the two great rooms, where was the best and richest furniture; they could not sufficiently admire the number and beauty of the tapestry, beds, couches, cabinets, stands, tables, and looking-glasses, in which you might see yourself from head to foot; some of them were framed with glass, others with silver, plain and gilded, the finest and most magnificent ever were seen.

They ceased not to extol and envy the happiness of their friend, who in the meantime in no way diverted herself in looking upon all these rich things, because of the impatience she had to go and open the closet on the ground floor. She was so much pressed by her curiosity that, without considering that it was very uncivil to leave her company, she went down a little back staircase, and with such excessive haste that she had twice or thrice like to have broken her neck.

Coming to the closet-door, she made a stop for some time, thinking upon her husband's orders, and considering what unhappiness might attend her if she was disobedient; but the temptation was so strong she could not overcome it. She then took the little key, and opened it, trembling, but could not at first see anything plainly, because the windows were shut. After some moments she began to perceive that the floor was all covered over with clotted blood, on which lay the bodies of several dead women, ranged against the walls. (These were all the wives whom Blue Beard had married and murdered, one after another.) She thought she should have died for fear, and the key, which she pulled out of the lock, fell out of her hand.

After having somewhat recovered her surprise, she took up the key, locked the door, and went upstairs into her chamber to recover herself; but she could not, she was so much frightened. Having observed that the key of the closet was stained with blood, she tried two or three times to wipe it off, but the blood would not come out; in vain did she wash it, and even rub it with soap and sand; the blood still remained, for the key was magical and she could never make it quite clean; when the blood was gone off from one side, it came again on the other.

Blue Beard returned from his journey the same evening, and said he had received letters upon the road, informing him that the affair he went about was ended to his advantage. His wife did all she could to convince him she was extremely glad of his speedy return.

Next morning he asked her for the keys, which she gave him, but with such a trembling hand that he easily guessed what had happened.

"What!" said he, "is not the key of my closet among the rest?"

"I must certainly have left it above upon the table," said she.

"Fail not to bring it to me presently," said Blue Beard.

After several goings backward and forward she was forced to bring him the key. Blue Beard, having very attentively considered it, said to his wife,

"How comes this blood upon the key?"

"I do not know," cried the poor woman, paler than death.

"You do not know!" replied Blue Beard. "I very well know. You were resolved to go into the closet, were you not? Mighty well, madam; you shall go in, and take your place among the ladies you saw there."

Upon this she threw herself at her husband's feet, and begged his pardon with all the signs of true repentance, vowing that she would never more be disobedient. She would have melted a rock, so beautiful and sorrowful was she; but Blue Beard had a heart harder than any rock!

"You must die, madam," said he, "and that presently."

"Since I must die," answered she (looking upon him with her eyes all bathed in tears), "give me some little time to say my prayers."

"I give you," replied Blue Beard, "half a quarter of an hour, but not one moment more."

When she was alone she called out to her sister, and said to her:

"Sister Anne" (for that was her name), "go up, I beg you, upon the top of the tower, and look if my brothers are not coming over; they promised me that they would come to-day, and if you see them, give them a sign to make haste."

Her sister Anne went up upon the top of the tower, and the poor afflicted wife cried out from time to time:

"Anne, sister Anne, do you see anyone coming?"

And sister Anne said:

"I see nothing but the sun, which makes a dust, and the grass, which looks green."

In the meanwhile Blue Beard, holding a great saber in his hand, cried out as loud as he could bawl to his wife:

"Come down instantly, or I shall come up to you."

"One moment longer, if you please," said his wife, and then she cried out very softly, "Anne, sister Anne, dost thou see anybody coming?"

And sister Anne answered:

"I see nothing but the sun, which makes a dust, and the grass, which is green."

"Come down quickly," cried Blue Beard, "or I will come up to you."

"I am coming," answered his wife; and then she cried, "Anne, sister Anne, dost thou not see anyone coming?"

"I see," replied sister Anne, "a great dust, which comes on this side here."

"Are they my brothers?"

"Alas! no, my dear sister, I see a flock of sheep."

"Will you not come down?" cried Blue Beard

"One moment longer," said his wife, and then she cried out: "Anne, sister Anne, dost thou see nobody coming?"

"I see," said she, "two horsemen, but they are yet a great way off."

"God be praised," replied the poor wife joyfully; "they are my brothers; I will make them a sign, as well as I can, for them to make haste."

Then Blue Beard bawled out so loud that he made the whole house tremble. The distressed wife came down, and threw herself at his feet, all in tears, with her hair about her shoulders.

"This signifies nothing," says Blue Beard; "you must die"; then, taking hold of her hair with one hand, and lifting up the sword with the other, he was going to take off her head. The poor lady, turning about to him, and looking at him with dying eyes, desired him to afford her one little moment to recollect herself.

"No, no," said he, "recommend thyself to God," and was just ready to strike . . .

At this very instant there was such a loud knocking at the gate that Blue Beard made a sudden stop. The gate was opened, and presently entered two horsemen, who, drawing their swords, ran directly to Blue Beard. He knew them to be his wife's brothers, one a dragoon, the other a musketeer, so that he ran away immediately to save himself; but the two brothers pursued so close that they overtook him before he could get to the steps of the porch, when they ran their swords through his body and left him dead. The poor wife was almost as dead as her husband, and had not strength enough to rise and welcome her brothers.

Blue Beard had no heirs, and so his wife became mistress of all his estate. She made use of one part of it to marry her sister Anne to a young gentleman who had loved her a long while; another part to buy captains commissions for her brothers, and the rest to marry herself to a very worthy gentleman, who made her forget the ill time she had passed with Blue Beard.

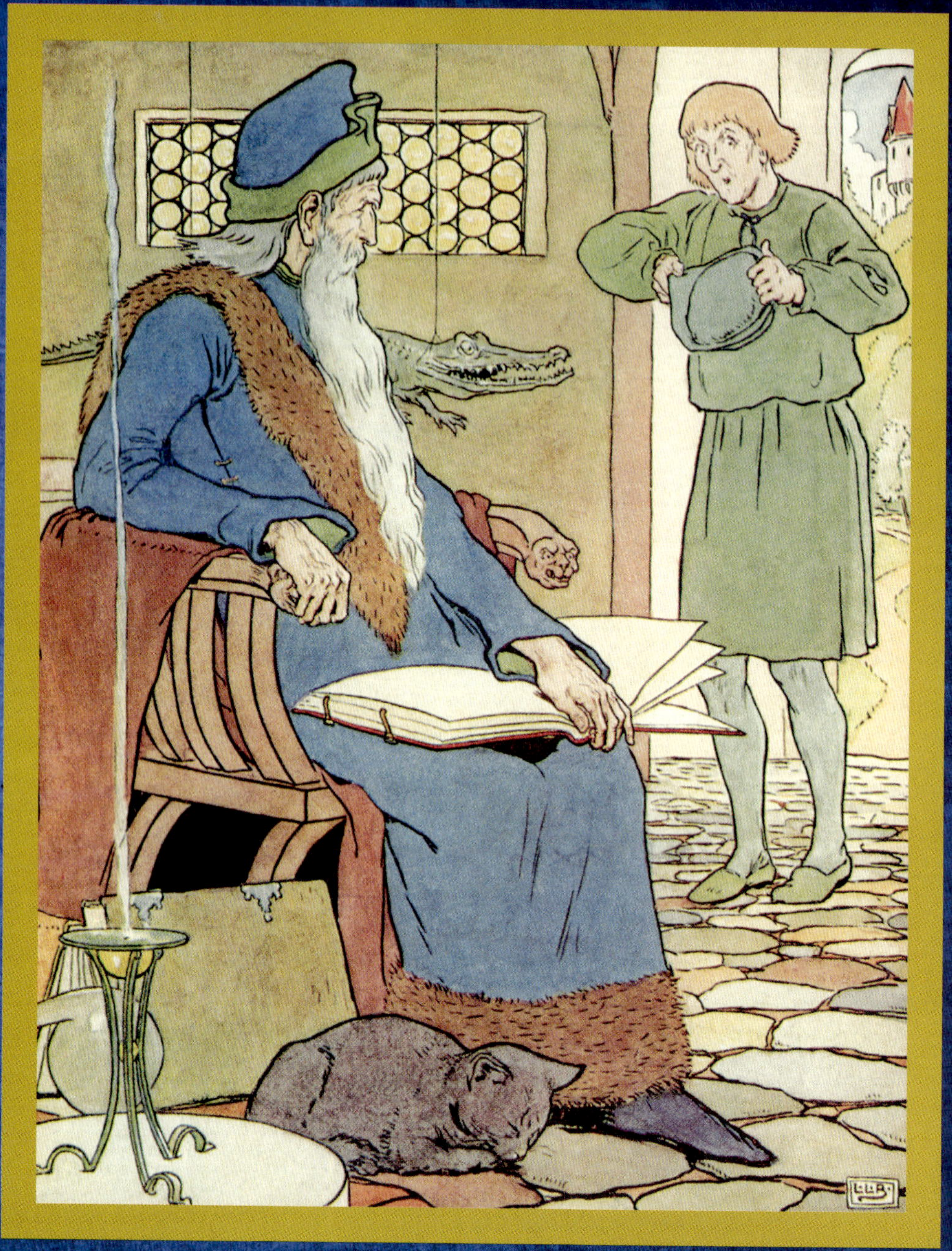

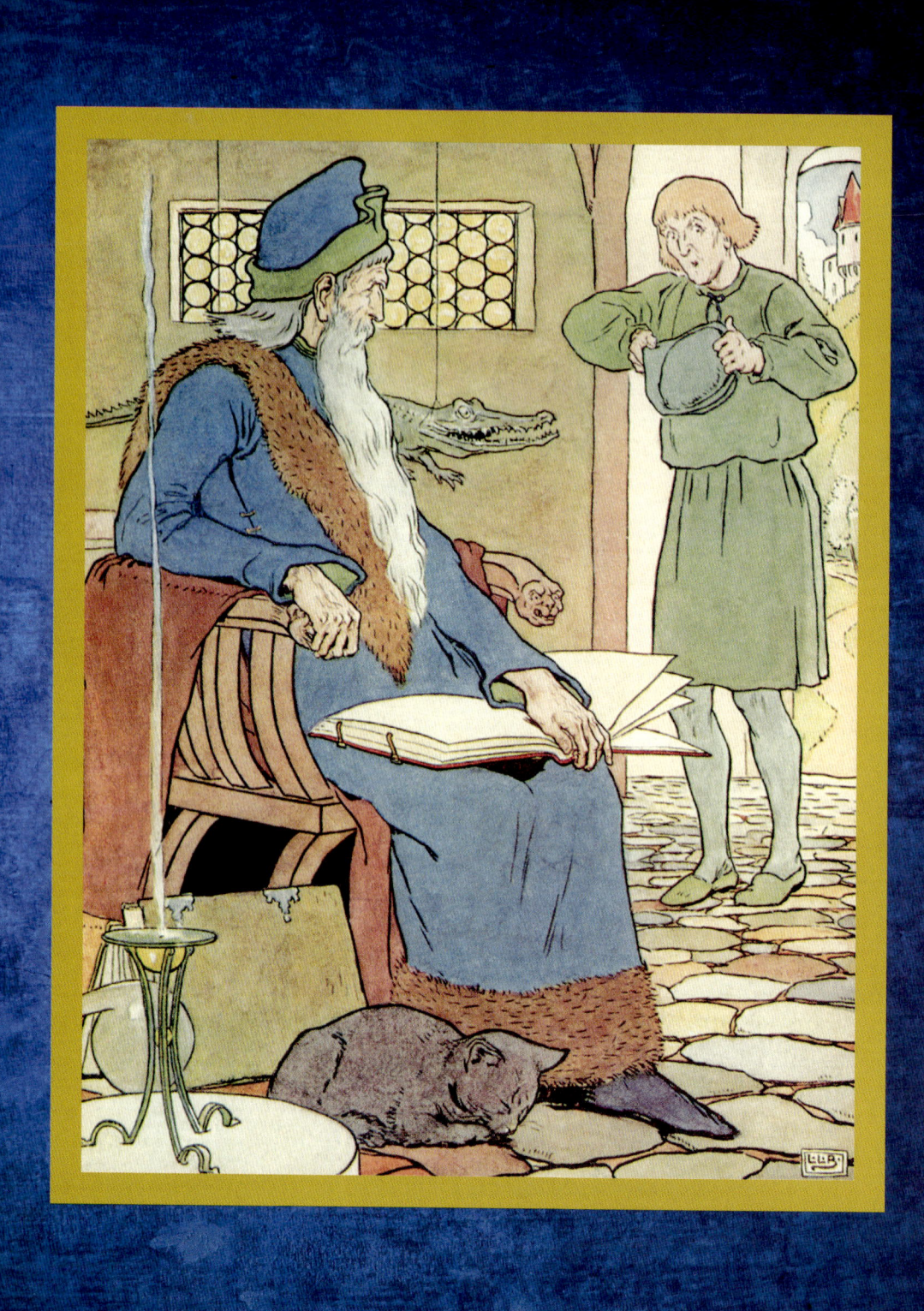

Tom Thumb

Long ago, in the merry days of good King Arthur, there lived a plowman and his wife. They were very poor, but would have been contented and happy if only they could have had a little child. One day, having heard of the great fame of the magician Merlin, who was living at the Court of King Arthur, the wife persuaded her husband to go and tell him of their trouble. Having arrived at the Court, the man besought Merlin with tears in his eyes to give them a child, saying that they would be quite content even though it should be no bigger than his thumb. Merlin determined to grant the request, and what was the countryman's astonishment to find when he reached home that his wife had a son, who, wonderful to relate, was no bigger than his father's thumb!

The parents were now very happy, and the christening of the little fellow took place with great ceremony. The Fairy Queen, attended by all her company of elves, was present at the feast. She kissed the little child, and, giving it the name of Tom Thumb, told her fairies to fetch the tailors of her Court, who dressed her little godson according to her orders. His hat was made of a beautiful oak leaf, his shirt of a fine spider's web, and his hose and doublet were of thistledown, his stockings were made with the rind of a delicate green apple, and the garters were two of the finest little hairs imaginable, plucked from his mother's eyebrows, while his shoes were made of the skin of a little mouse. When he was thus dressed, the Fairy Queen kissed him once more, and, wishing him all good luck, flew off with the fairies to her Court.

As Tom grew older, he became very amusing and full of tricks, so that his mother was afraid to let him out of her sight. One day, while she was making a batter pudding, Tom stood on the edge of the bowl, with a lighted candle in his hand, so that she might see that the pudding was made properly. Unfortunately, however, when her back was turned, Tom fell into the bowl, and his mother, not missing him, stirred him up in the pudding, tied it in a cloth, and put it into the pot. The batter filled Tom's mouth, and prevented him from calling out, but he had no sooner felt the hot water, than he kicked and struggled so much that the pudding jumped about in the pot, and his mother, thinking the pudding was bewitched, was nearly frightened out of her wits. Pulling it out of the pot, she ran with it to her door, and gave it to a tinker who was passing. He was very thankful for it, and looked forward to having a better dinner than he had enjoyed for many a long day. But his pleasure did not last long, for, as he was getting over a stile, he happened to sneeze very hard, and Tom, who had been quite quiet inside the pudding for some time, called out at the top of his little voice, "Hallo, Pickens!" This so terrified the tinker that he flung away the pudding, and ran off as fast as he could.

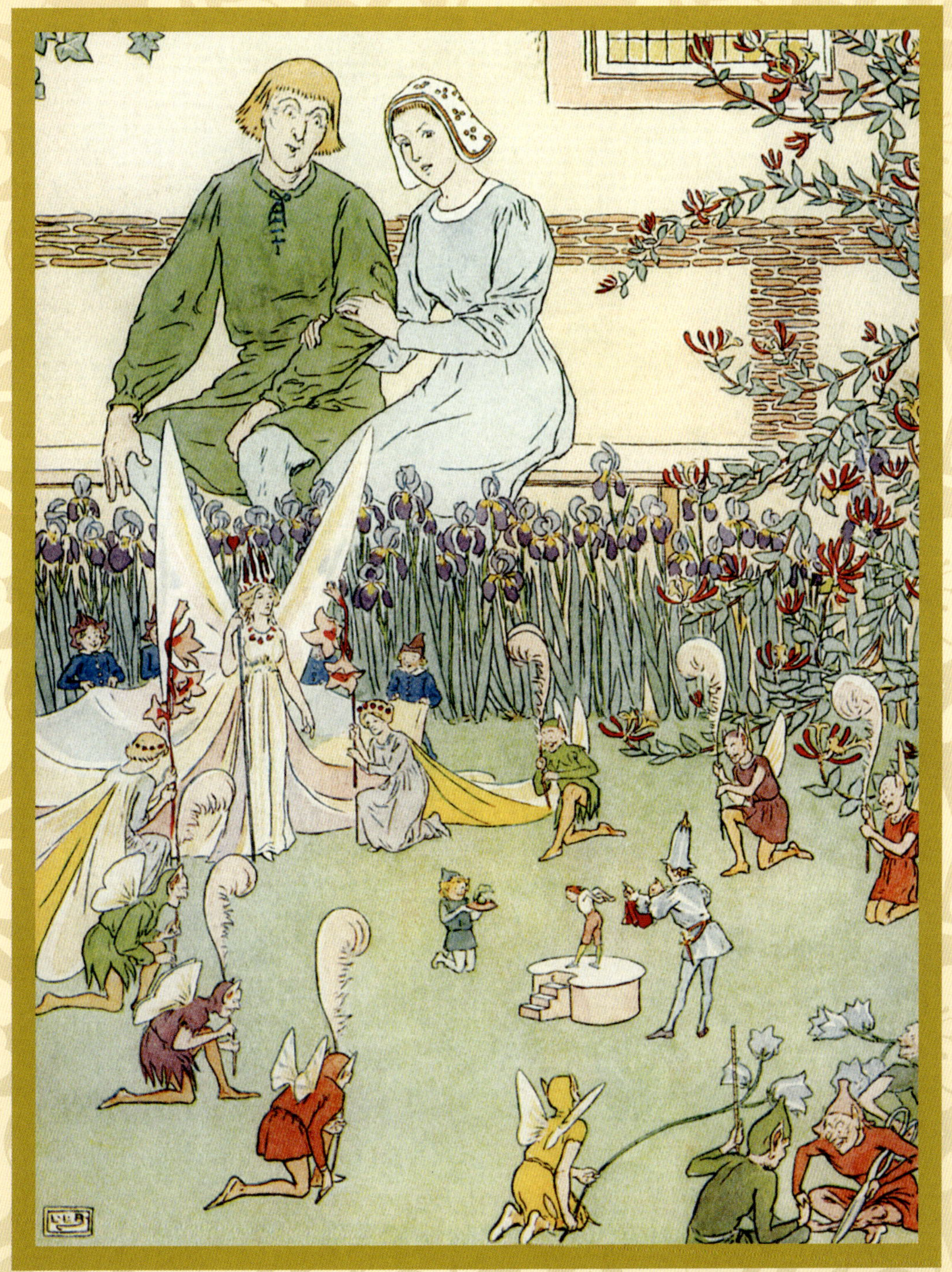

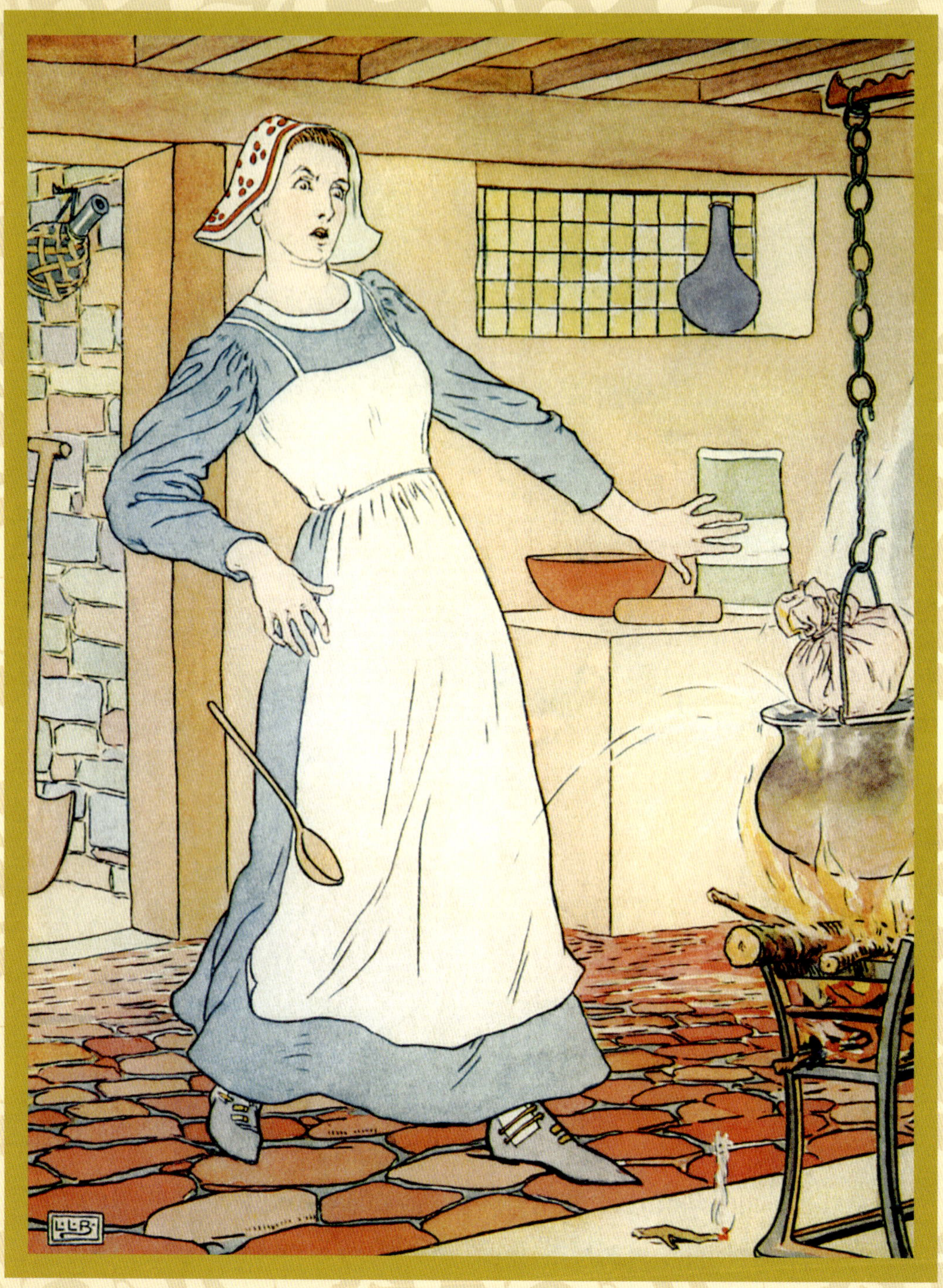

The pudding was all broken to pieces by the fall, and Tom crept out, covered with batter, and ran home to his mother, who had been looking everywhere for him, and was delighted to see him again. She gave him a bath in a cup, which soon washed off all the pudding, and he was none the worse for his adventure.

A few days after this, Tom accompanied his mother when she went into the fields to milk the cows, and, fearing he might be blown away by the wind, she tied him to a sow-thistle with a little piece of thread. While she was milking, a cow came by, bit off the thistle, and swallowed up Tom. Poor Tom did not like her big teeth, and called out loudly, "Mother, mother!" "But where are you, Tommy, my dear Tommy?" cried out his mother, wringing her hands. "Here, mother," he shouted, "inside the red cow's mouth!" And, saying that, he began to kick and scratch till the poor cow was nearly mad, and at length tumbled him out of her mouth. On seeing this, his mother rushed to him, caught him in her arms, and carried him safely home.

Some days after this, his father took him to the fields a-plowing, and gave him a whip, made of a barley straw, with which to drive the oxen; but little Tom was soon lost in a furrow. An eagle seeing him, picked him up and flew with him to the top of a hill where stood a giant's castle. The giant put him at once into his mouth, intending to swallow him up, but Tom made such a great disturbance when he got inside that the monster was soon glad to get rid of him, and threw him far away into the sea. But he was not drowned, for he had scarcely touched the water before he was swallowed by a large fish, which was shortly afterward captured and brought to King Arthur, as a present, by the fisherman. When the fish was opened, everyone was astonished at finding Tom inside. He was at once carried to the King, who made him his Court dwarf.

> Long time he lived in jollity,
> Beloved of the Court,
> And none like Tom was so esteemed
> Amongst the better sort.

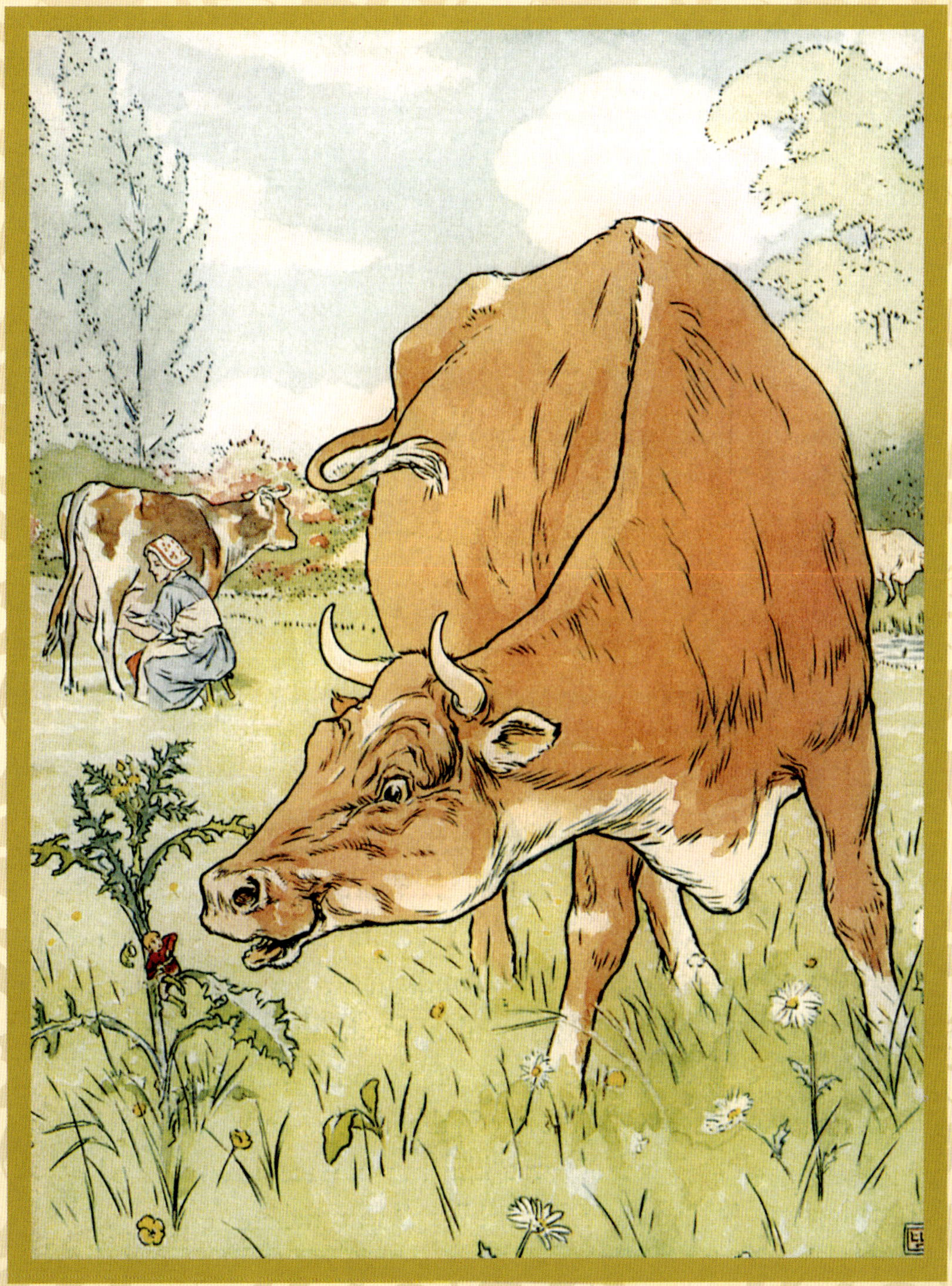

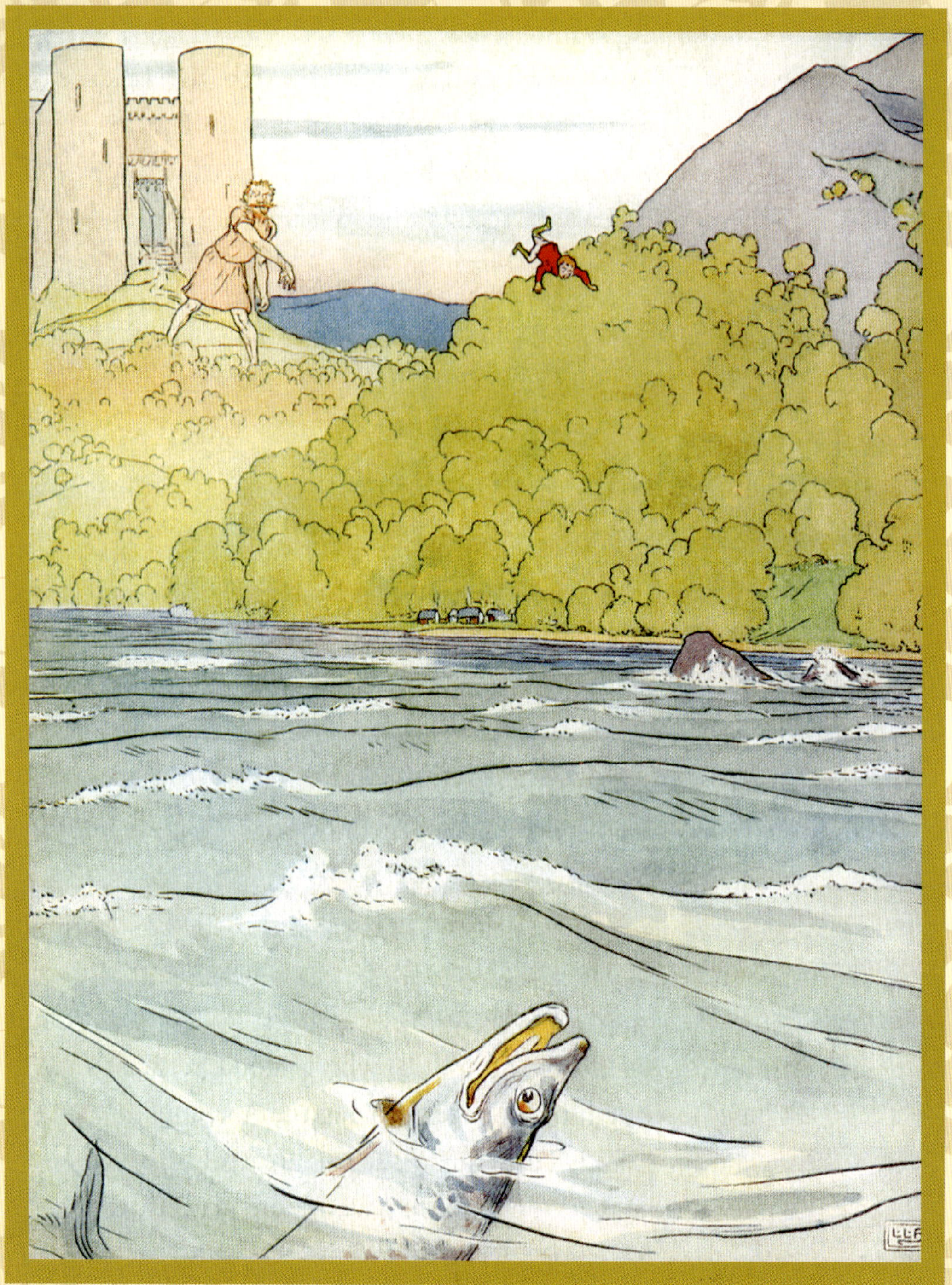

The Queen was delighted with the little boy, and made him dance a gaillard on her left hand. He danced so well that King Arthur gave him a ring, which he wore round his waist like a girdle.

Tom soon began to long to see his parents again, and begged the King to allow him to go home for a short time. This was readily permitted, and the King told him he might take with him as much money as he could carry.

> And so away goes lusty Tom,
> With three pence at his back—
> A heavy burthen which did make
> His very bones to crack.

He had to rest more than a hundred times by the way, but, after two days and two nights, he reached his father's house in safety. His mother saw him coming, and ran out to meet him, and there was great rejoicing at his arrival. He spent three happy days at home, and then set out for the Court once more.

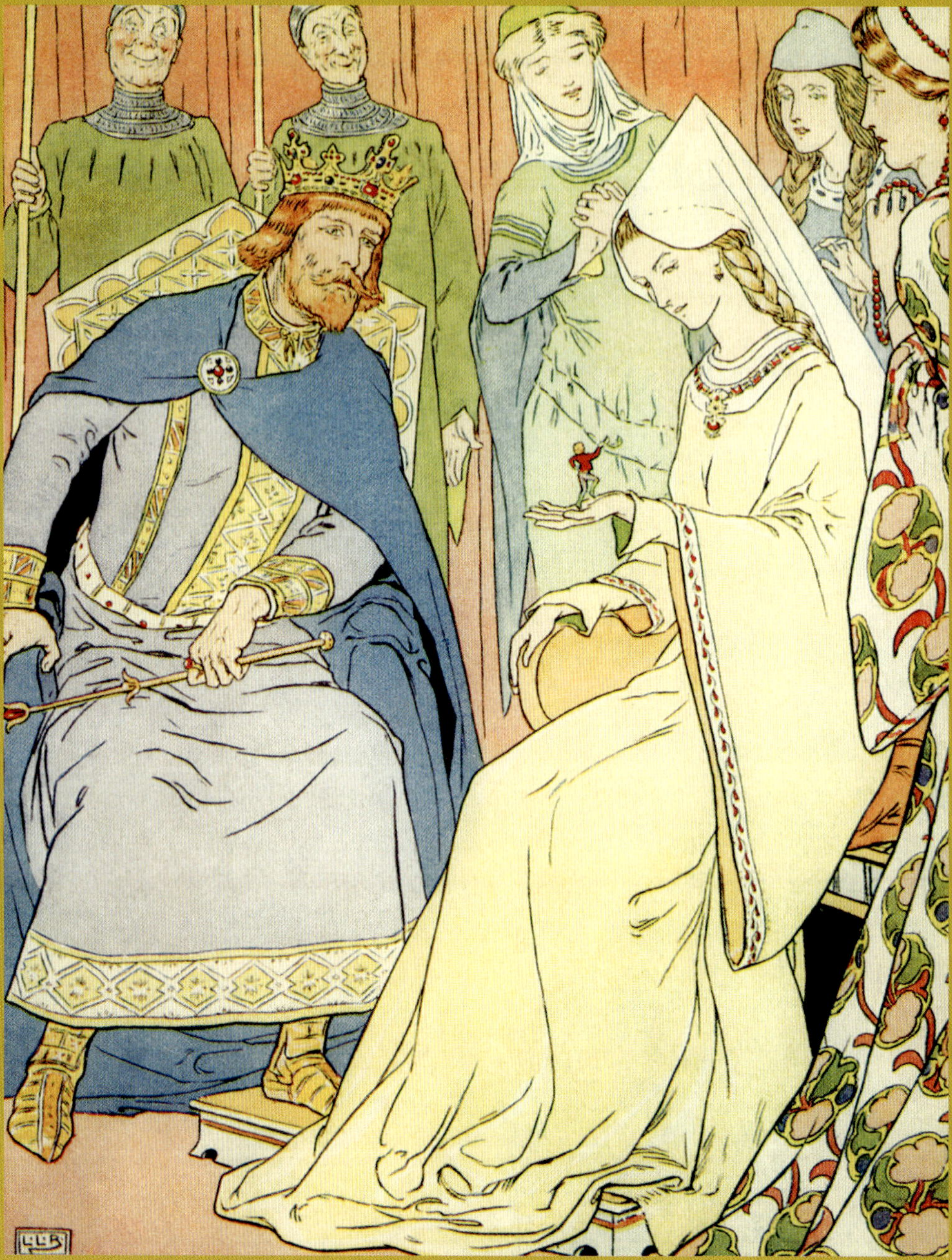

Shortly after his return, he one day displeased the King, so, fearing the royal anger, he crept into an empty flower-pot, where he lay for a long time. At last he ventured to peep out, and, seeing a fine large butterfly on the ground close by, he stole out of his hiding-place, jumped on its back, and was carried up into the air. The King and nobles all strove to catch him, but at last poor Tom fell from his seat into a watering-pot, in which he was almost drowned, only luckily the gardener's child saw him, and pulled him out. The King was so pleased to have him safe once more that he forgot to scold him, and made much of him instead.

Tom afterward lived many years at Court, one of the best beloved of King Arthur's knights.

> Thus he at tilt and tournament
> Was entertainèd so,
> That all the rest of Arthur's knights
> Did him much pleasure show.
> With good Sir Launcelot du Lake,
> Sir Tristram and Sir Guy,
> Yet none compared to brave Tom Thumb
> In acts of chivalry.

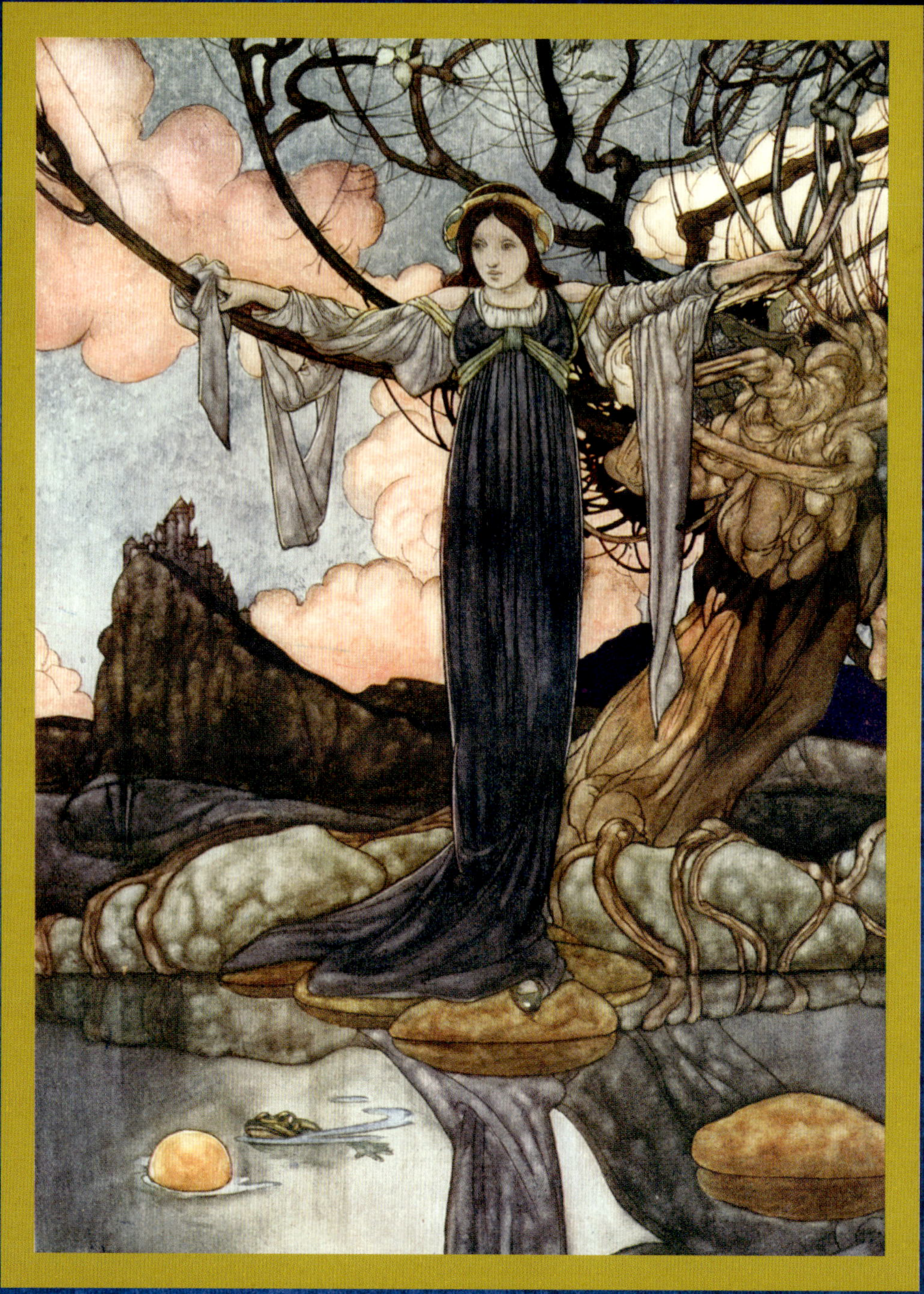

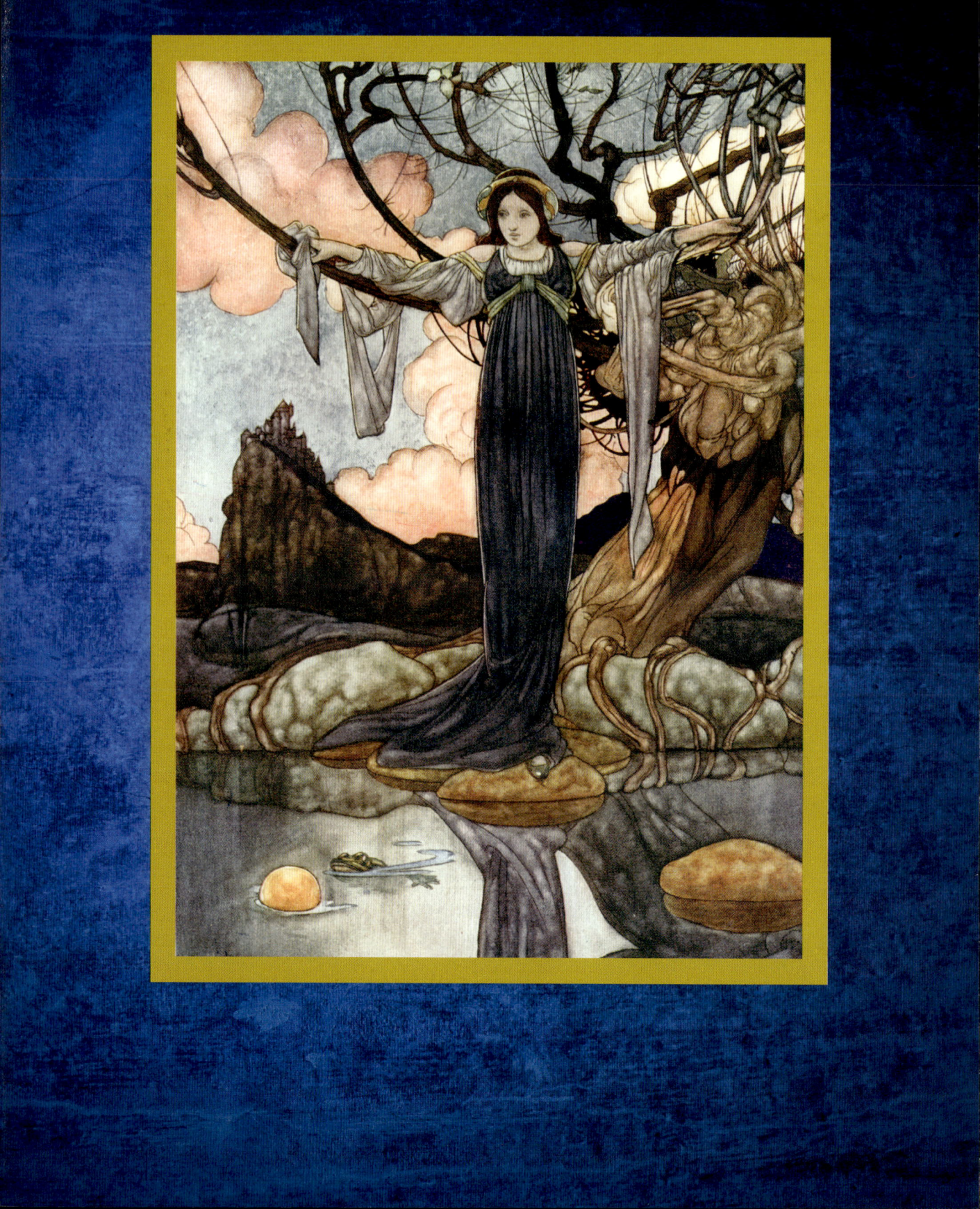

The Frog Prince

One fine evening a young Princess went into a wood, and sat down by the side of a cool spring of water. She had a golden ball in her hand, which was her favorite plaything, and she amused herself with tossing it into the air, and catching it again as it fell. After a time, she threw it up so high that, when she stretched out her hand to catch it, the ball bounded away and rolled along upon the ground, till, at last, it fell into the spring. The Princess looked into the spring after her ball, but it was very deep, so that she could not see the bottom of it. Then she began to bewail her loss, and said, "Alas! if I could only get my ball again, I would give all my fine clothes and jewels—everything that I have in the world." Whilst she was speaking, a frog appeared, and said, "Princess, why do you weep so bitterly?" "Alas!" said she, "what can you do for me, you nasty frog? My golden ball has fallen into the spring." The frog said, "I want not your pearls and jewels and fine clothes; but, if you will love me and let me live with you, I will bring you your ball again." "What nonsense," thought the Princess, "this silly frog is talking! He can never get out of the well: however, he may be able to get my ball for me; and therefore I will tell him he shall have what he asks." So she said to the frog, "Well, if you will bring me my ball, I will do all you require."

Then the frog put his head down, and dived deep under the water; and after a little while, he came up again with the ball in his mouth, and threw it on the ground. As soon as the young Princess saw her ball, she ran to pick it up, and was so overjoyed to have it in her hand again, that she never thought of the frog, but ran home with it as fast as she could. The frog called after her, "Stay, Princess, and take me with you, as you said"; but she did not stop to hear a word.

The next day, just after the Princess had sat down to dinner, she heard a strange noise, tap-tap, as if somebody was coming up the marble staircase; and, soon afterward, something knocked gently at the door, and said:

> "Open the door, my Princess dear,
> Open the door to thy true love here!
> And mind the words that thou and I said
> By the fountain cool in the greenwood shade."

Then the Princess ran to the door and opened it, and, behold! there was the frog, whom she had quite forgotten; she was sadly frightened, and, shutting the door as fast as she could, came back to her seat. The King her father asked her what had frightened her. "There is a nasty frog," said she, "at the door, who lifted my ball out of the spring last evening: I promised that he should live with me here, thinking that he could never get out of the spring; but there he is at the door, and wants to come in!" Whilst she was speaking, the frog knocked again at the door, and said—

> "Open the door, my Princess dear,
> Open the door to thy true love here!
> And mind the words that thou and I said
> By the fountain cool in the greenwood shade."

The King said to the young Princess, "As you made a promise, you must keep it, so go and let him in." She did so, and the frog hopped into the room, and came up close to the table. "Pray lift me upon a chair," said he to the Princess, "and let me sit next to you." As soon as she had done this, the frog said, "Put your plate nearer to me, that I may eat out of it." This she did, and, when he had eaten as much as he could, he said, "Now I am tired; carry me up stairs, and put me into your little bed." And the Princess took him up in her hand and put him upon the pillow of her own little bed, where he slept

The Frog Prince

all night long. As soon as it was light he jumped up, hopped downstairs, and went out of the house. "Now," thought the Princess, "he is gone, and I shall be troubled with him no more."

But she was mistaken; for, when night came again, she heard the same tapping at the door, and, when she opened it, the frog came in and remained all night as before, till the morning broke: and the third night he did the same; but, when the Princess awoke on the following morning, she was astonished to see, instead of the frog, a handsome Prince gazing on her with the most beautiful eyes that ever were seen, and standing at the head of her bed.

He then told her that he had been enchanted by a malicious fairy, who had changed him into the form of a frog, in which he was doomed to remain till a Princess should take pity on him, and let him sleep upon her bed for three nights. "You," said the Prince, "have broken this cruel charm, and now I have nothing to wish for but that you should go with me into my father's Kingdom, where I will marry you, and love you as long as you live."

The young Princess, you may be sure, was not long in giving her consent; and, as they spoke, a splendid carriage drove up with eight beautiful horses decked with plumes of feathers in golden harness, and behind rode the Prince's servant, who had bewailed the misfortune of his dear master so long and so bitterly. Then all set out full of joy for the Prince's Kingdom; where they arrived safely, and lived happily for a great many years.

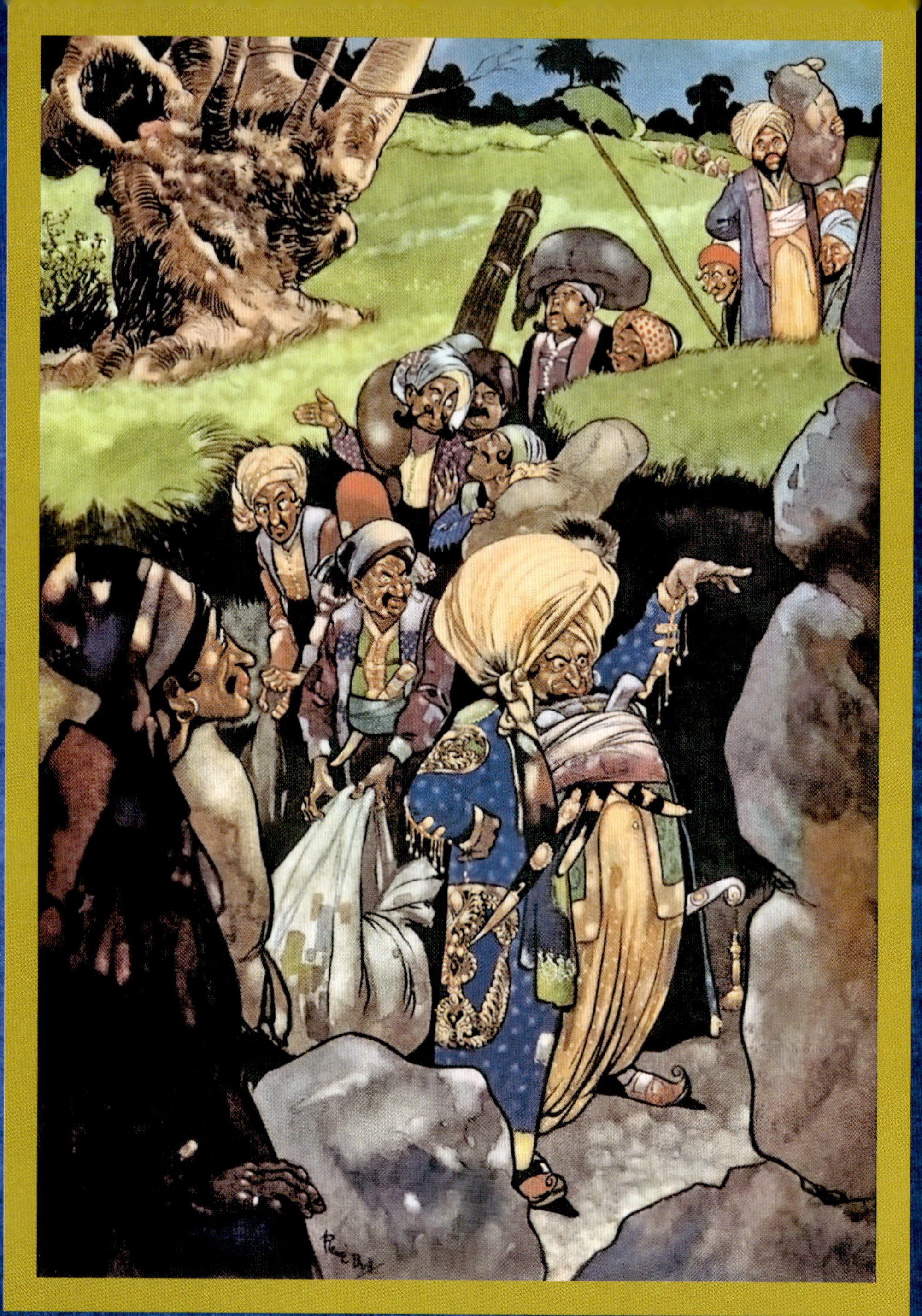

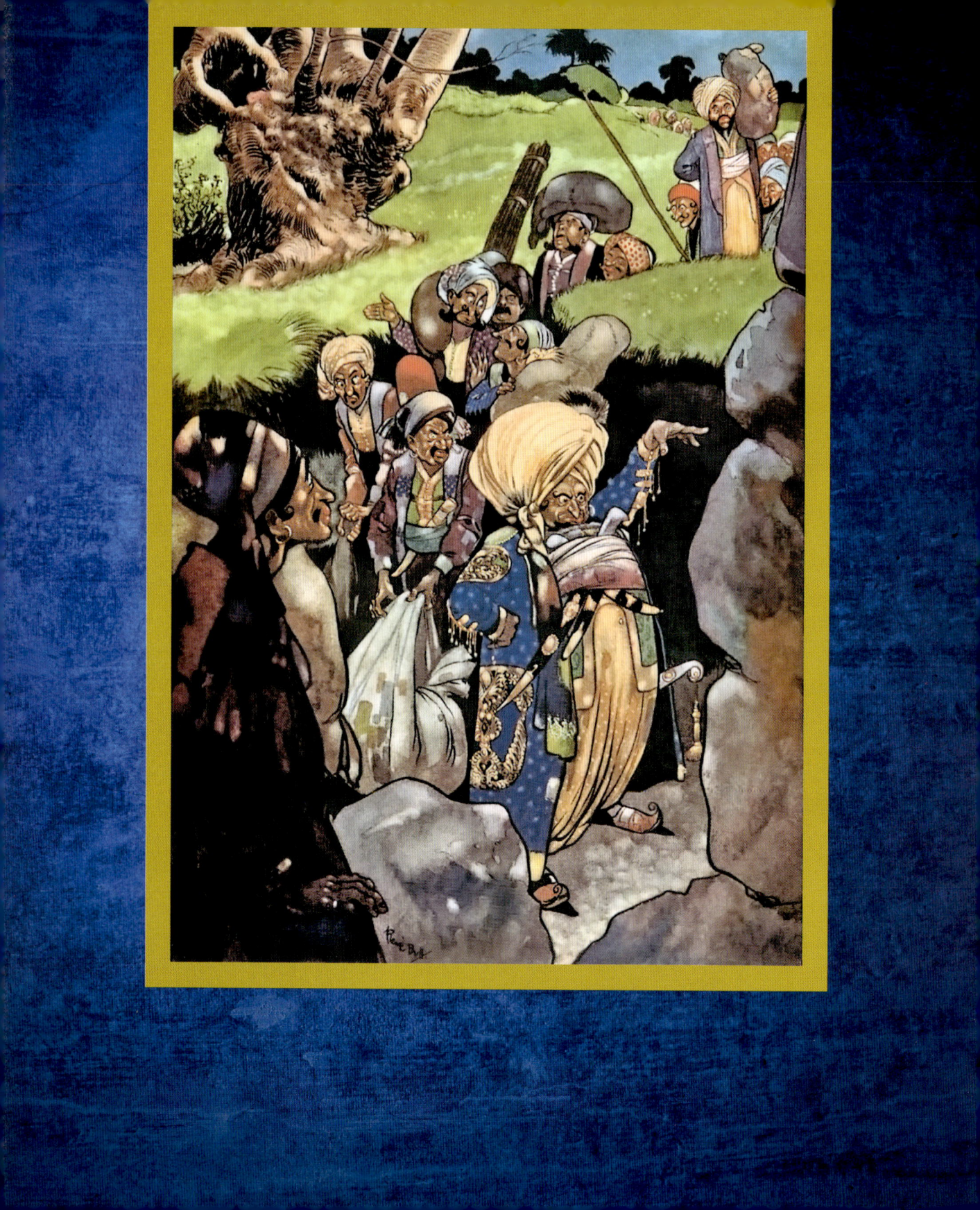

Ali Baba and the Forty Thieves

In a town in Persia, there lived two brothers, one named Cassim, the other Ali Baba. Their father left them scarcely anything; but Cassim married a wealthy wife and prospered in life, becoming a famous merchant. Ali Baba, on the other hand, married a woman as poor as himself, and lived by cutting wood, and bringing it upon three asses into the town to sell. One day, when Ali Baba was in the forest, he saw at a distance a great cloud of dust, which seemed to be approaching. He observed it very attentively, and distinguished a body of horse.

Fearing that they might be robbers, he left his asses and climbed into a tree, from which place of concealment he could watch all that passed in safety.

The troop consisted of forty men, all well mounted, who, when they arrived, dismounted and tied up their horses and fed them. They then removed their saddle-bags, which seemed heavy, and followed the captain, who approached a rock that stood near Ali Baba's hiding-place. When he was come to it, he said, in a loud voice: Open, Sesame! As soon as the captain had uttered these words, a door opened in the rock; and after he had made all his troop enter before him, he followed them, when the door shut again of itself.

Although the robbers remained some time in the rock, Ali Baba did not dare to move until after they had filed out again, and were out of sight. Then, when he thought that all was safe, he descended, and going up to the door, said: Open, Sesame! as the captain had done, and instantly the door flew open.

Ali Baba, who expected a dark dismal cavern, was surprised to see it well lighted and spacious, receiving light from an opening at the top of the rock. He saw all sorts of provisions, rich bales of silk, brocades, and valuable carpeting, piled upon one another; gold and silver ingots in great heaps, and money in bags. The sight of all these riches made him suppose that this cave must have been occupied for ages by robbers, who had succeeded one another.

Ali Baba loaded his asses with gold coin, and then covering the bags with sticks he returned home. Having secured the door of his house, he emptied out the gold before his wife, who was dazzled by its brightness, and told her all, urging upon her the necessity of keeping the secret.

The wife rejoiced at their good fortune, and would count all the gold, piece by piece. Wife, said Ali Baba, you do not know what you undertake, when you pretend to count the money; you will never have done. I will dig a hole, and bury it; there is no time to be lost. You are right, husband, replied she; but let us know, as nigh as possible, how much we have. I will borrow a small measure and measure it while you dig the hole.

Away the wife ran to her brother-in-law Cassim, who lived just by, and addressing herself to his wife, desired her to lend her a measure for a little while. The sister-in-law did so, but as she knew Ali Baba's poverty, she was curious to know what sort of grain his wife wanted to measure, and artfully putting some suet at the bottom of the measure, brought it to her with an excuse, that she was sorry that she had made her stay so long, but that she could not find it sooner.

Ali Baba's wife went home and continued to fill the measure from the heap of gold and empty it till she had done: when she was very well satisfied to find the number of measures amounted to so many as they did, and went to tell her husband, who had almost finished digging the hole. While Ali Baba was burying the gold, his wife, to show her exactness and diligence to her sister-in-law, carried the measure back again, but without taking notice that a piece of gold had stuck to the bottom. Sister, said she, giving it to her again, you see that I have not kept your measure long; I am obliged to you for it, and return it with thanks.

As soon as Ali Baba's wife was gone, Cassim's wife looked at the bottom of the measure, and was in inexpressible surprise to find a piece of gold stuck to it. Envy immediately possessed her breast. What! said she, has Ali Baba gold so plentiful as to measure it? When Cassim came home, his wife said to him, I know you think yourself rich, but you are much mistaken; Ali Baba is infinitely richer than you. He does not count his money, but measures it. Cassim desired her to explain the riddle, which she did, by telling him the stratagem she had used to make the discovery, and showed him the piece of money, which was so old that they could not tell in what Prince's reign it was coined.

Cassim was also envious when he heard this, and slept so badly, that he rose early and went to his brother.

Ali Baba, said he, you pretend to be miserably poor, and yet you measure gold. My wife found this at the bottom of the measure you borrowed yesterday.

Ali Baba perceived that Cassim and his wife, through his own wife's folly, knew what they had so much reason to conceal; but what was done could not be recalled; therefore, without showing the least surprise or trouble, he confessed all, and offered him part of his treasure to keep the secret. I expect as much, replied Cassim haughtily; but I must know exactly where this treasure is, and how I may visit it myself when I choose; otherwise I will go and inform against you, and then you will not only get no more, but will lose all you have, and I shall have a share for my information.

Ali Baba told him all he desired, and even the very words he was to use to gain admission into the cave.

Cassim rose the next morning, long before the sun, and set out for the forest with ten mules bearing great chests, which he designed to fill. He was not long before he reached the rock, and found out the place by the tree and other marks which his brother had given him. When he reached the entrance of the cavern, he pronounced the words, Open, Sesame! The door immediately opened, and when he was in, closed upon him. He quickly entered, and laid as many bags of gold as he could carry at the door of the cavern, but his thoughts were so full of the great riches he should possess, that he could not think of the necessary word to make it open, but instead of Sesame, said, Open, Barley! and was much amazed to find that the door remained fast shut. He named several sorts of grain, but still the door would not open.

Cassim had never expected such an incident, and was so alarmed at the danger he was in, that the more he endeavored to remember the word Sesame, the more his memory was confounded, and he had as much forgotten it as if he had never heard it mentioned. He threw down the bags he had loaded himself with, and walked distractedly up and down the cave, without having the least regard to the riches that were round him.

About noon the robbers chanced to visit their cave, and at some distance from it saw Cassim's mules straggling about the rock, with great chests on their backs. Alarmed at this novelty, they galloped full speed to the cave. Cassim, who heard the noise of the horses' feet from the middle of the cave, never doubted of the arrival of the robbers, and resolved to make one effort to escape from them. To this end he rushed to the door, and no sooner saw it open, than he ran out and threw the leader down, but could not escape the other robbers, who with their sabres soon deprived him of life.

The first care of the robbers after this was to examine the cave. They found all the bags which Cassim had brought to the door, to be ready to load his mules, and carried them again to their places, without missing what Ali Baba had taken away before. Then holding a council, they agreed to cut Cassim's body into four quarters, to hang two on one side and two on the other, within the door of the cave, to terrify any person who should attempt the same thing. This done, they mounted their horses, went to beat the roads again, and to attack the caravans they might meet.

In the meantime, Cassim's wife was very uneasy when night came, and her husband was not returned. She ran to Ali Baba in alarm, and said, I believe, brother-in-law, that you know Cassim, your brother, is gone to the forest, and upon what account; it is now night, and he is not returned; I am afraid some misfortune has happened to him. Ali Baba told her that she need not frighten herself, for that certainly Cassim would not think it proper to come into the town till the night should be pretty far advanced.

Ali Baba and the Forty Thieves

Cassim's wife passed a miserable night, and bitterly repented of her curiosity. As soon as daylight appeared, she went to Ali Baba, weeping profusely.

Ali Baba departed immediately with his three asses to seek for Cassim, begging of her first to moderate her affliction. He went to the forest, and when he came near the rock, having seen neither his brother nor the mules in his way, was seriously alarmed at finding some blood spilt near the door, which he took for an ill omen; but when he had pronounced the word, and the door had opened, he was struck with horror at the dismal sight of his brother's quarters. He loaded one of his asses with them, and covered them over with wood. The other two asses he loaded with bags of gold, covering them with wood also as before; and then bidding the door shut, came away; but was so cautious as to stop some time at the end of the forest, that he might not go into the town before night. When he came home, he drove the two asses loaded with gold into his little yard, and left the care of unloading them to his wife, while he led the other to his sister-in-law's house.

Ali Baba knocked at the door, which was opened by Morgiana, an intelligent slave, whose tact was to be relied upon. When he came into the court, he unloaded the ass, and taking Morgiana aside, said to her, Mention what I say to no one; your master's body is contained in these two bundles, and our business is, to bury him as if he had died a natural death. I can trust you to manage this for me.

Ali Baba consoled the widow as best he could, and having deposited the body in the house returned home.

Morgiana went out at the same time to an apothecary, and asked for a sort of lozenge very efficacious in the most dangerous disorders. The apothecary inquired who was ill. She replied with a sigh, My good master Cassim himself: he can neither eat nor speak. After these words Morgiana carried the lozenges home with her, and the next morning went to the same apothecary's again, and with tears in her eyes, asked for an essence which they used to give to sick people only when at the last extremity. Alas! said she, I am afraid that this remedy will have no better effect than the lozenges; and that I shall lose my good master.

On the other hand, as Ali Baba and his wife were often seen to go between Cassim's and their own house all that day, and to seem melancholy, nobody was surprised in the evening to hear the lamentable shrieks and cries of Cassim's wife and Morgiana, who gave out everywhere that her master was dead. The next morning Morgiana betook herself early to the stall of a cobbler named Mustapha, and bidding him good morrow, put a piece of gold into his hand, saying: Baba Mustapha, you must take your sewing tackle, and come with me; but I must tell you, I shall blindfold you when you come to such a place.

Baba Mustapha hesitated a little at these words. Oh! oh! replied he, you would have me do something against my conscience, or against my honor? God forbid! said Morgiana, putting another piece of gold into his hand, that I should ask anything that is contrary to your honor; only come along with me, and fear nothing.

Baba Mustapha went with Morgiana, who, after she had bound his eyes with a handkerchief, conveyed him to her deceased master's house, and never unloosed his eyes till he had entered the room, where she had put the corpse together. Baba Mustapha, said she, you must make haste and sew these quarters together; and when you have done, I will give you another piece of gold.

After Baba Mustapha had finished his task, she once more blindfolded him, gave him the third piece of gold as she had promised, and recommending secrecy to him, conducted bound his eyes, pulled off the bandage, and let him back again to the place where she first bound his eyes, pulled off the bandage, and let him go home, but watched him that he returned towards his stall, till he was quite out of sight, for fear he should have the curiosity to return and dodge her; she then went home.

The ceremony of washing and dressing the body was hastily performed by Morgiana and Ali Baba, after which it was sewn up ready to be placed in the mausoleum. While Ali Baba and other members of the household followed the body, the women of the neighborhood came, according to custom, and joined their mourning with that of the widow, so that the whole quarter was filled with the sound of their weeping. Thus was Cassim's horrible death successfully concealed.

Three or four days after the funeral, Ali Baba removed his goods openly to the widow's house; but the money he had taken from the robbers he conveyed thither by night. When at length the robbers came again to their retreat in the forest, great was their surprise to find Cassim's body taken away, with some of their bags of gold. We are certainly discovered, said the captain, and if we do not find and kill the man who knows our secret, we shall gradually lose all the riches.

The robbers unanimously approved of the captain's speech.

The only way in which this can be discovered, said the captain, is by spying in the town. And, lest any treachery may be practiced, I suggest that whoever undertakes the task shall pay dearly if he fails—even with his life.

One of the robbers immediately started up, and said, I submit to this condition, and think it an honor to expose my life to serve the troop.

The robber's courage was highly commended by the captain and his comrades, and when he had disguised himself so that nobody would know him, he went into the town and walked up and down, till accidentally he came to Baba Mustapha's stall.

Baba Mustapha was seated, with an awl beside him, on the bench, just going to work. The robber saluted him, and perceiving that he was old, said, Honest man, you begin to work very early: is it possible that one of your age can see so well? I question, even if it were somewhat lighter, whether you could see to stitch.

Why, replied Baba Mustapha, I sewed a dead body together in a place where I had not so much light as I have now.

A dead body! cried the robber, with affected amazement. It is so, replied Baba Mustapha; but I will tell you no more. Indeed, answered the robber, I do not want to learn your secret, but I would fain see the house in which this strange thing was done. To further impress the cobbler, he gave him a piece of gold.

If I were disposed to do you that favor, replied Baba Mustapha, I assure you I cannot, for I was led both to and from the house blindfolded.

Well, replied the robber, you may, however, remember a little of the way that you were led blindfolded. Come, let me bind your eyes at the same place. We will walk together; and as everybody ought to be paid for their trouble, there is another piece of gold for you; gratify me in what I ask you.

The two pieces of gold were too great a temptation to Baba Mustapha, who said: I am not sure that I remember the way exactly; but since you desire, I will try what I can do. At these words Baba Mustapha rose up, and led the robber to the place where Morgiana had bound his eyes. It was here, said Baba Mustapha, I was blindfolded; and I turned as you see me. The robber, who had his handkerchief ready, tied it over his eyes, walked by him till he stopped, partly leading, and partly guided by him. I think, said Baba Mustapha, I went no farther, and he had now stopped directly at Cassim's house, where Ali Baba then lived. The thief, before he pulled off the band, marked the door with a piece of chalk, which he had ready in his hand; and then asked him if he knew whose house that was, to which Baba Mustapha replied, that, as he did not live in that neighborhood, he could not tell.

The robber, finding he could discover no more from Baba Mustapha, thanked him for the trouble he had taken, and left him to go back to his stall, while he returned to the forest, persuaded that he should be very well received.

A little after the robber and Baba Mustapha had parted, Morgiana went out of Ali Baba's house upon some errand, and upon her return, seeing the mark the robber had made, stopped to observe it. What can be the meaning of this mark? said she to herself; somebody intends my master no good: however, with whatever intention it was done, it is advisable to guard against the worst. Accordingly, she fetched a piece of chalk, and marked two or three doors on each side, in the same manner, without saying a word to her master or mistress.

When the robber reached the camp, he reported the success of his expedition; and it was at once decided that they should very quietly enter the city and watch for an opportunity of slaying their enemy. To the utter confusion of the guide, several of the neighboring doors were found to be marked in a similar manner. Come, said the captain, this will not do; we must return, and you must die. They returned to the camp, and the false guide was promptly slain.

Then another volunteer came forward, and he in like manner was led by Baba Mustapha to the spot. He more cautiously marked the door with red chalk, in a place not likely to be seen. But the quick eye of Morgiana detected this likewise, and she repeated her previous action, with equal effectiveness, for when the robbers came they could not distinguish the house. Then the captain, in great anger, led his men back to the forest, when the second offender was immediately put to death.

The captain, dissatisfied by this waste of time and loss of men, decided to undertake the task himself. And so having been led to the spot by Baba Mustapha, he walked up and down before the house until it was impressed upon his mind. He then returned to the forest; and when he came into the cave, where the troop waited for him, said: Now, comrades, nothing can prevent our full revenge. He then told them his contrivance; and as they approved of it, ordered them to go into the villages about, and buy nineteen mules, with thirty-eight large leather jars, one full of oil, and the others empty.

In two days all preparations were made, and the nineteen mules were loaded with thirty-seven robbers in jars, and the jar of oil, the captain, as their driver, set out with them, and reached the town by the dusk of the evening, as he had intended. He led them through the streets till he came to Ali Baba's, at whose door he designed to have knocked; but was prevented, as Ali Baba was sitting there after supper to take a little fresh air. He stopped his mules, and said: I have brought some oil a great way, to sell at to-morrow's market; and it is now so late that I do not know where to lodge. Will you allow me to pass the night with you, and I shall be very much obliged by your hospitality.

Ali Baba, not recognizing the robber, bade him welcome, and gave directions for his entertainment, and after they had eaten he retired to rest.

The captain, pretending that he wished to see how his jars stood, slipped into the garden, and passing from one to the other he raised the lids of the jars and spoke: As soon as I throw some stones out of my window, do not fail to come out, and I will immediately join you. After this he retired to his chamber; and to avoid any suspicion, put the light out soon after, and laid himself down in his clothes, that he might be the more ready to rise.

While Morgiana was preparing the food for breakfast, the lamp went out, and there was no more oil in the house, nor any candles. What to do she did not know, for the broth must be made. Abdalla seeing her very uneasy, said: Do not fret, but go into the yard, and take some oil out of one of the jars.

Morgiana thanked Abdalla for his advice, took the oil-pot, and went into the yard; when as she came nigh the first jar, the robber within said softly: Is it time?

Morgiana naturally was much surprised at finding a man in a jar instead of the oil she wanted, but she at once made up her mind that no time was to be lost, if a great danger was to be averted, so she passed from jar to jar, answering at each: Not yet, but presently.

At last she came to the oil-jar, and made what haste she could to fill her oil-pot, and returned into her kitchen; where, as soon as she had lighted her lamp, she took a great kettle, went again to the oil-jar, filled the kettle, set it on a large wood-fire, and as soon as it boiled went and poured enough into every jar to stifle and destroy the robber within.

When this action, worthy of the courage of Morgiana, was executed without any noise, as she had projected, she returned to the kitchen with the empty kettle; and having put out the great fire she had made to boil the oil, and leaving just enough to make the broth, put out the lamp also, and remained silent; resolving not to go to rest till she had observed what might wfollow through a window of the kitchen, which opened into the yard.

She had not waited long before the captain gave his signal, by throwing the stones. Receiving no response, he repeated it several times, until becoming alarmed he descended into the yard and discovered that all the gang were dead; and by the oil he missed out of the last jar guessed the means and manner of their death. Enraged to despair at having failed in his design, he forced the lock of a door that led from the yard to the garden, and climbing over the walls, made his escape.

Morgiana then went to bed, feeling happy at the success of her design.

Ali Baba rose before day, and followed by his slave, went to the baths, entirely ignorant of the important event which had happened at home. When he returned from the baths, the sun was risen; he was very much surprised to see the oil-jars, and

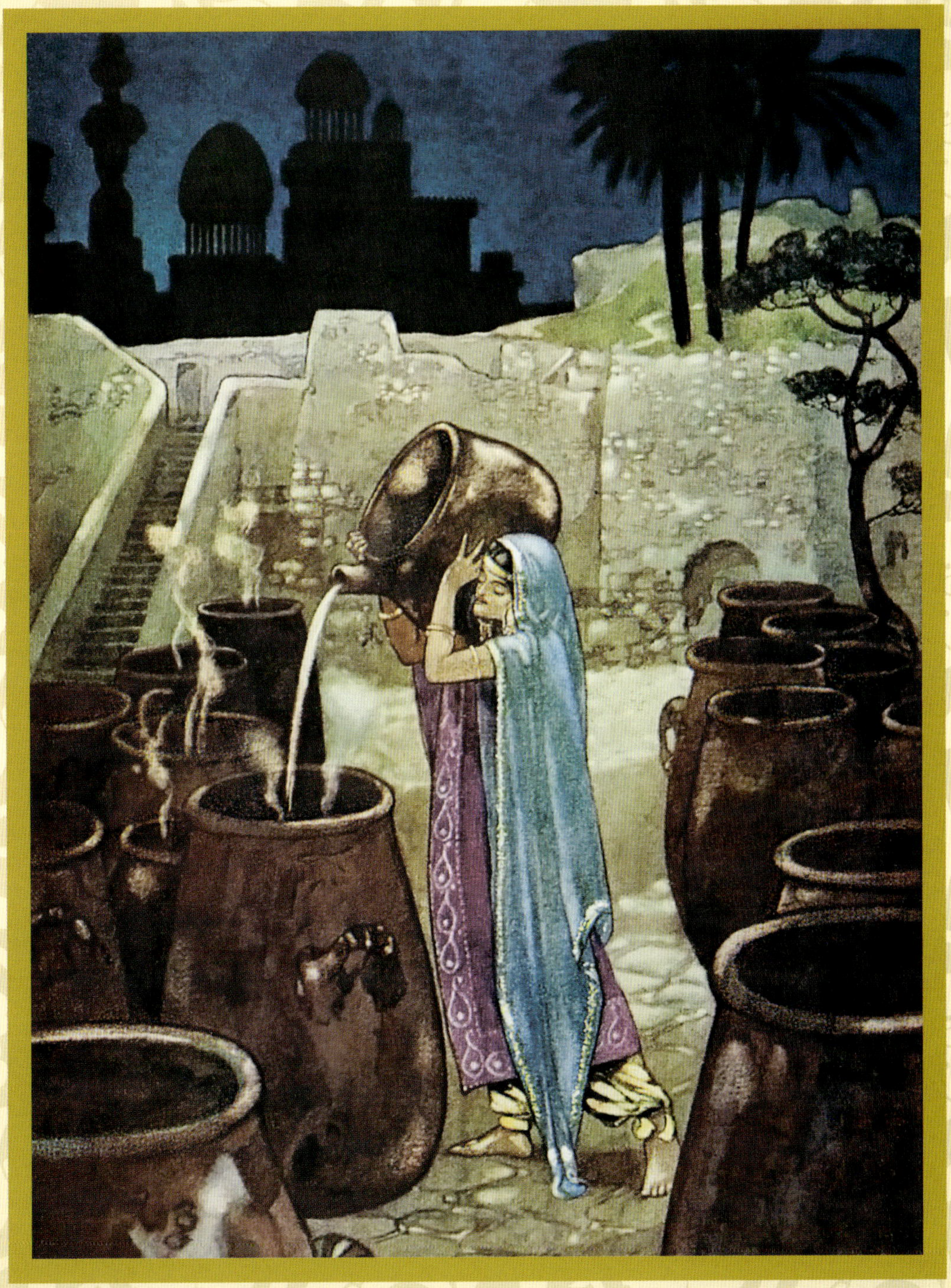

that the merchant was not gone with the mules. He asked Morgiana, who opened the door, the reason of it? My good master, answered she, God preserve you and all your family; you will be better informed of what you wish to know when you have seen what I have to show you, if you will but give yourself the trouble to follow me.

Ali Baba followed her, when she requested him to look into the first jar and see if there was any oil. Ali Baba did so, and seeing a man, started back in alarm, and cried out. Do not be afraid, said Morgiana, the man you see there can neither do you nor anybody else any harm. He is dead. Ah, Morgiana! said Ali Baba, what is it you show me? Explain yourself. I will, replied Morgiana; moderate your astonishment, and do not excite the curiosity of your neighbors; for it is of great importance to keep this affair secret. Look into all the other jars.

Ali Baba examined all the other jars, one after another: and when he came to that which had the oil in, found it prodigiously sunk, and stood for some time motionless, sometimes looking at the jars, and sometimes at Morgiana, without saying a word, so great was his surprise. At last, when he had recovered himself, he said, And what is become of the merchant?

Merchant! answered she, he is as much one as I am; I will tell you who he is, and what is become of him. She then told the whole story from beginning to end; from the marking of the house to the destruction of the robbers.

Ali Baba was overcome by this account, and he cried: You have saved my life, and in return I give you your liberty—but this shall not be all.

Ali Baba and his slave Abdalla then dug a long deep trench at the farther end of the garden, in which the robbers were buried. Afterwards the jars and weapons were hidden, and by degrees Ali Baba managed to sell the mules for which he had no use.

Meanwhile the captain, who had returned to the forest, found life very miserable; the cavern became too frightful to be endured. But, resolved to be revenged upon Ali Baba, he laid new plans, and having taken a shop which happened to be opposite Cassim's, where Ali Baba's son now lived, he transported many rich stuffs thither. And, disguised as a silk mercer, he set up in business, under the name of Cogia Houssain.

Having by chance discovered whose son his opposite neighbor was, he often made him presents and invited him to dinner, and did everything to win his good opinion.

Ali Baba's son, who did not like to be indebted to any man, told his father that he desired to ask him to dinner in return, and requested him to do so. Ali Baba readily complied with his wishes, and it was arranged that on the following day he should bring Cogia Houssain with him to dinner.

At the appointed time Ali Baba's son conducted Cogia Houssain to his father's house. And strange to say, when the robber found himself at the door, he would have liked to withdraw, though he had now gained access to the very man he wanted to kill. But at that moment Ali Baba came forward to receive him and thank him for his goodness to his son. And now, said Ali Baba, you will do me the honor of dining with me. Sir, replied Cogia Houssain, I would gladly, but that I have vowed to abstain from salt, and I scarcely like to sit at your table under such conditions. Trouble not yourself about that, answered Ali Baba. I will go and bid the cook put no salt in the food.

When Ali Baba went to the kitchen to give this order, Morgiana was much surprised, and desired to see this strange man. Therefore she helped Abdalla to carry up the dishes, and directly she saw Cogia Houssain, she recognized him as the captain of the robbers.

Morgiana at once decided to rescue Ali Baba from this fresh danger, and resolved upon a very daring expedient, by which to frustrate the robber's designs; for she guessed that he intended no good. In order to carry out her plan she went to her room and put on the garments of a dancer, hid her face under a mask and fastened a handsome girdle round her waist, from which hung a dagger. Then she said to Abdalla: Fetch your tabor, that we may divert our master and his guest.

Ali Baba bade her dance, and she commenced to move gracefully about, while Abdalla played on his tabor. Cogia Houssain watched, but feared that he would have no opportunity of executing his fell purpose.

After Morgiana had danced for some time, she seized the dagger in her right hand and danced wildly, pretending to stab herself the while. As she swept round, she buried the dagger deep in Cogia Houssain's breast and killed him.

Ali Baba and his son, shocked at this action, cried out aloud: Unhappy wretch! what have you done to ruin me and my family? It was to preserve, not to ruin you, answered Morgiana; for see here, continued she, opening the pretended Cogia Houssain's garment, and showing the dagger, what an enemy you had entertained! Look well at him, and you will find him to be both the fictitious oil-merchant and the captain of the gang of forty robbers. Remember, too, that he would eat no salt with you; and what would you have more to persuade you of his wicked design?

Ali Baba, who immediately felt the new obligation he had to Morgiana for saving his life a second time, embraced her: Morgiana, said he, I gave you your liberty, and then promised you that my gratitude should not stop there, but that I would soon give you higher proofs of its sincerity, which I now do by making you my daughter-in-law. Then addressing himself to his son, he said: I believe, son, that you will not refuse Morgiana for your wife. You see that Cogia Houssain sought your friendship with a treacherous design to take away my life; and, if he had succeeded, there is no doubt but he would have sacrificed you also to his revenge. Consider, that by marrying Morgiana you marry the preserver of my family and your own.

The son, far from showing any dislike, readily consented to the marriage; and a few days afterwards, Ali Baba celebrated the nuptials of his son and Morgiana with great solemnity, a sumptuous feast, and the usual dancing and spectacles.

Ali Baba, fearing that the other two robbers might be alive still, did not visit the cave for a whole year. Finding, however, that they did not seek to disturb him he then went to the cave, and, having pronounced the words, Open, Sesame, entered and saw that no one had been there recently. He then knew that he alone in the world knew the secret of the cave; and he rejoiced to think of his good fortune. When he returned to the city he took as much gold as his horse could carry from his inexhaustible storehouse.

Afterwards Ali Baba took his son to the cave, taught him the secret, which they handed down to their posterity, who, using their good fortune with moderation, lived in great honor and splendor.

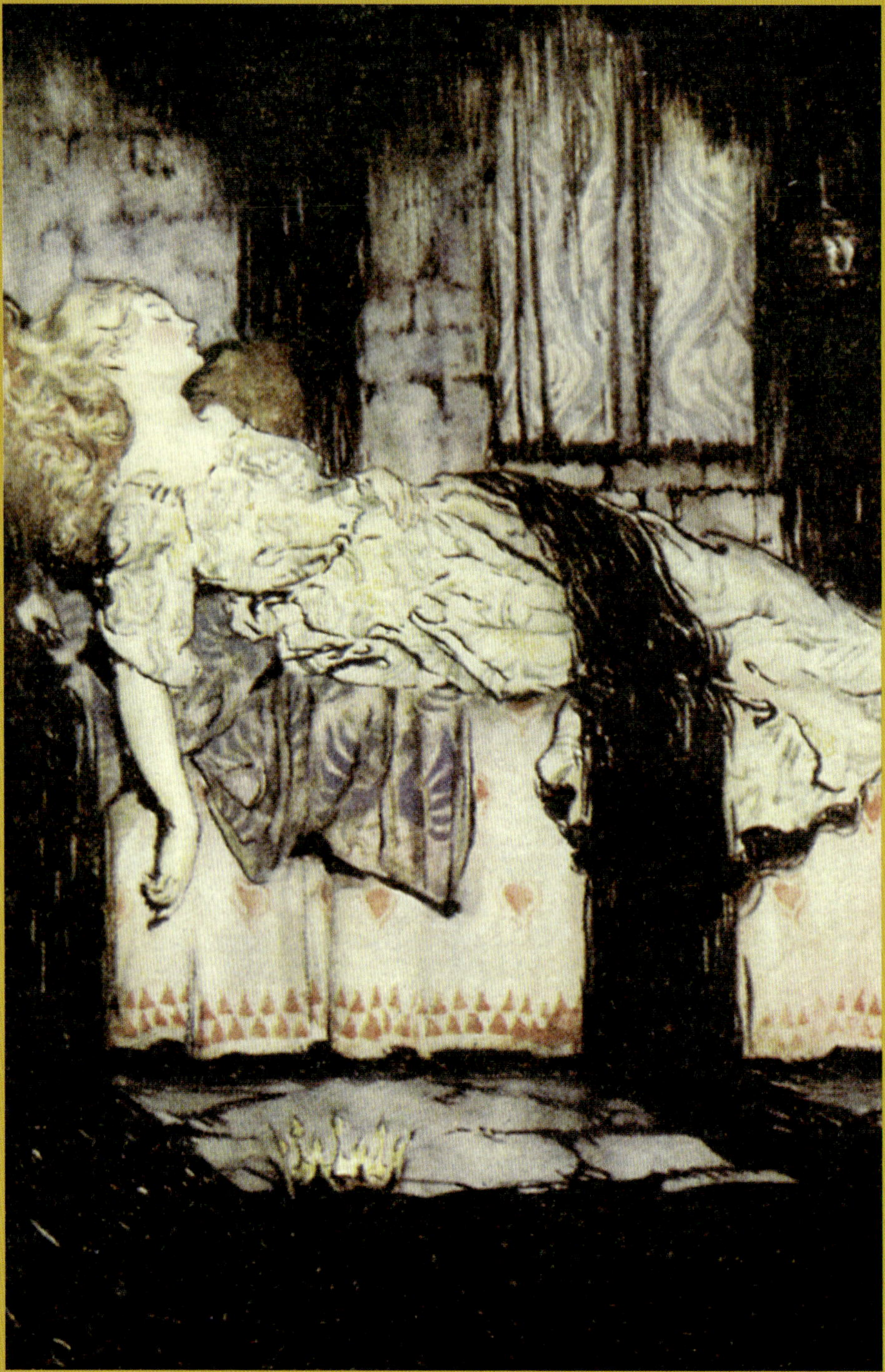

Sleeping Beauty

A LONG TIME AGO THERE WERE A KING AND QUEEN WHO SAID EVERY day, "Ah, if only we had a child!" but they never had one. But it happened that once when the Queen was bathing, a frog crept out of the water on to the land, and said to her, "Your wish shall be fulfilled; before a year has gone by, you shall have a daughter."

What the frog had said came true, and the Queen had a little girl who was so pretty that the King could not contain himself for joy, and ordered a great feast. He invited not only his kindred, friends and acquaintance, but also the Wise Women, in order that they might be kind and well-disposed towards the child. There were thirteen of them in his kingdom, but, as he had only twelve golden plates for them to eat out of, one of them had to be left at home.

The feast was held with all manner of splendor and when it came to an end the Wise Women bestowed their magic gifts upon the baby: one gave virtue, another beauty, a third riches, and so on with everything in the world that one can wish for.

When eleven of them had made their promises, suddenly the thirteenth came in. She wished to avenge herself for not having been invited, and without greeting, or even looking at any one, she cried with a loud voice, "The King's daughter shall in her fifteenth year prick herself with a spindle, and fall down dead." And, without saying a word more, she turned round and left the room.

They were all shocked; but the twelfth, whose good wish still remained unspoken, came forward, and as she could not undo the evil sentence, but only soften it, she said, "It shall not be death, but a deep sleep of a hundred years, into which the Princess shall fall."

The King, who would fain keep his dear child from the misfortune, gave orders that every spindle in the whole kingdom should be burnt. Meanwhile the gifts of the Wise Women were plenteously fulfilled on the young girl, for she was so beautiful, modest, good-natured, and wise, that everyone who saw her was bound to love her.

It happened that on the very day when she was fifteen years old, the King and Queen were not at home, and the maiden was left in the palace quite alone. So she went round into all sorts of places, looked into rooms and bed-chambers just as she liked, and at last came to an old tower. She climbed up the narrow winding-staircase, and reached a little door. A rusty key was in the lock, and when she turned it the door sprang open, and there in a little room sat an old woman with a spindle, busily spinning her flax.

"Good day, old dame," said the King's daughter; "what are you doing there?" "I am spinning," said the old woman, and nodded her head. "What sort of thing is that, that rattles round so merrily?" said the girl, and she took the spindle and wanted to spin too. But scarcely had she touched the spindle when the magic decree was fulfilled, and she pricked her finger with it.

And, in the very moment when she felt the prick, she fell down upon the bed that stood there, and lay in a deep sleep. And this sleep extended over the whole palace; the King and Queen who had just come home, and had entered the great hall, began to go to sleep, and the whole of the court with them. The horses, too, went to sleep in the stable, the dogs in the yard, the pigeons upon the roof, the flies on the wall; even the fire that was flaming on the hearth became quiet and slept, the roast meat left off frizzling, and the cook, who was just going to pull the hair of the scullery boy, because he had forgotten something, let him go, and went to sleep. And the wind fell, and on the trees before the castle not a leaf moved again.

But round about the castle there began to grow a hedge of thorns, which every year became higher, and at last grew close up round the castle and all over it, so that there was nothing of it to be seen, not even the flag upon the roof. But the story of the

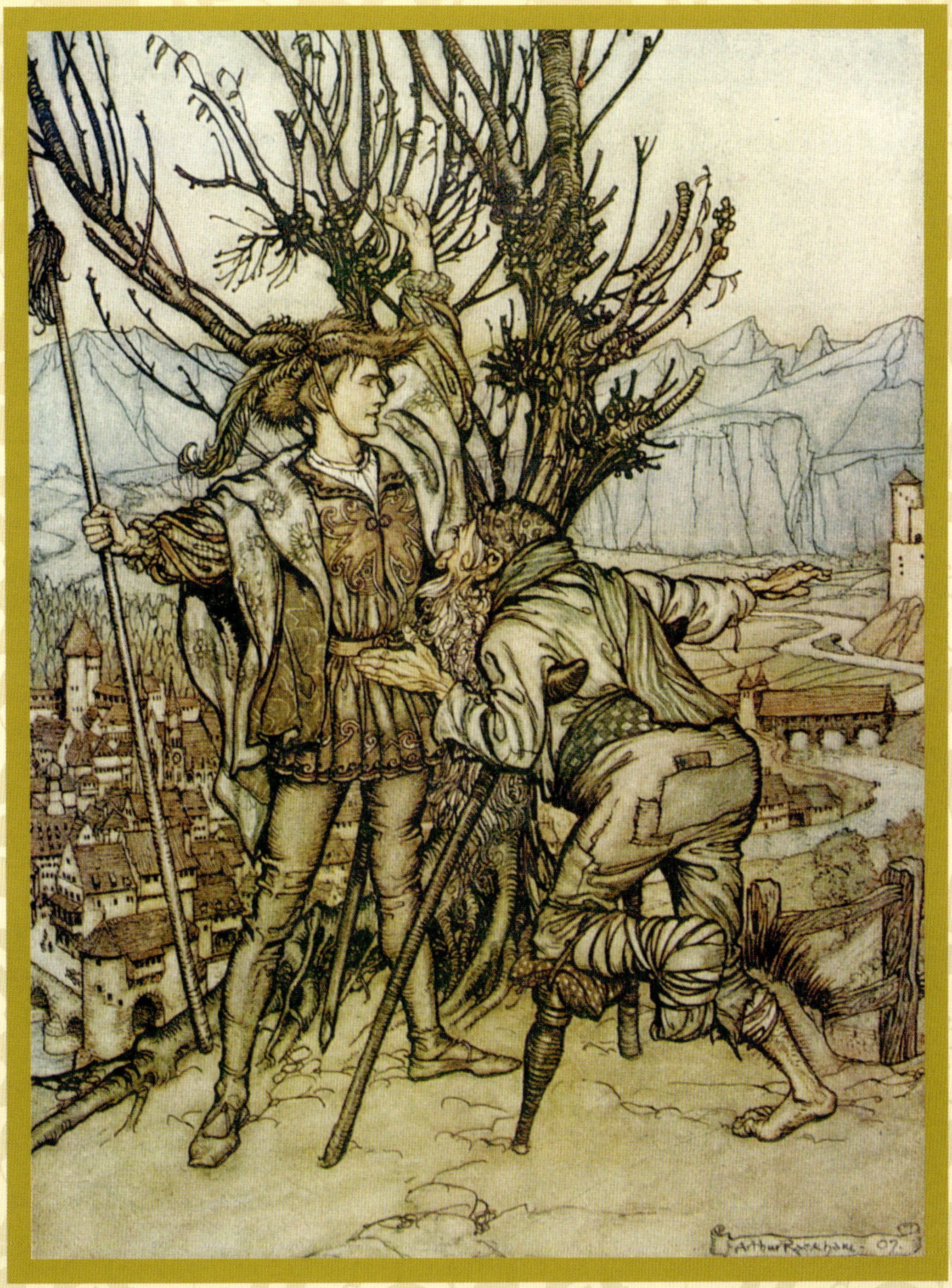
Arthur Rackham. 07.

beautiful sleeping "Briar-Rose," for so the Princess was named, went about the country, so that from time to time Kings' sons came and tried to get through the thorny hedge into the castle.

But they found it impossible, for the thorns held fast together, as if they had hands, and the youths were caught in them, could not get loose again, and died a miserable death.

After long, long years a King's son came again to that country, and heard an old man talking about the thorn-hedge, and that a castle was said to stand behind it in which a wonderfully beautiful Princess, named Briar-Rose, had been asleep for a hundred years; and that the King and Queen and the whole court were asleep likewise. He had heard, too, from his grandfather, that many Kings' sons had already come, and had tried to get through the thorny hedge, but they had remained sticking fast in it, and had died a pitiful death. Then the youth said, "I am not afraid, I will go and see the beautiful Briar-Rose." The good old man might dissuade him as he would, he did not listen to his words.

But by this time the hundred years had just passed, and the day had come when Briar-Rose was to awake again. When the King's son came near to the thorn-hedge, it was nothing but large and beautiful flowers, which parted from each other of their own accord, and let him pass unhurt, then they closed again behind him like a hedge. In the castle-yard he saw the horses and the spotted hounds lying asleep; on the roof sat the pigeons with their heads under their wings. And when he entered the house, the flies were asleep upon the wall, the cook in the kitchen was still holding out his hand to seize the boy, and the maid was sitting by the black hen which she was going to pluck.

He went on farther, and in the great hall he saw the whole of the court lying asleep, and up by the throne lay the King and Queen.

Then he went on still farther, and all was so quiet that a breath could be heard, and at last he came to the tower, and opened the door into the little room where Briar-Rose was sleeping. There she lay, so beautiful that he could not turn his eyes away; and he stooped down and gave her a kiss. But as soon as he kissed her, Briar-Rose opened her eyes and awoke, and looked at him quite sweetly.

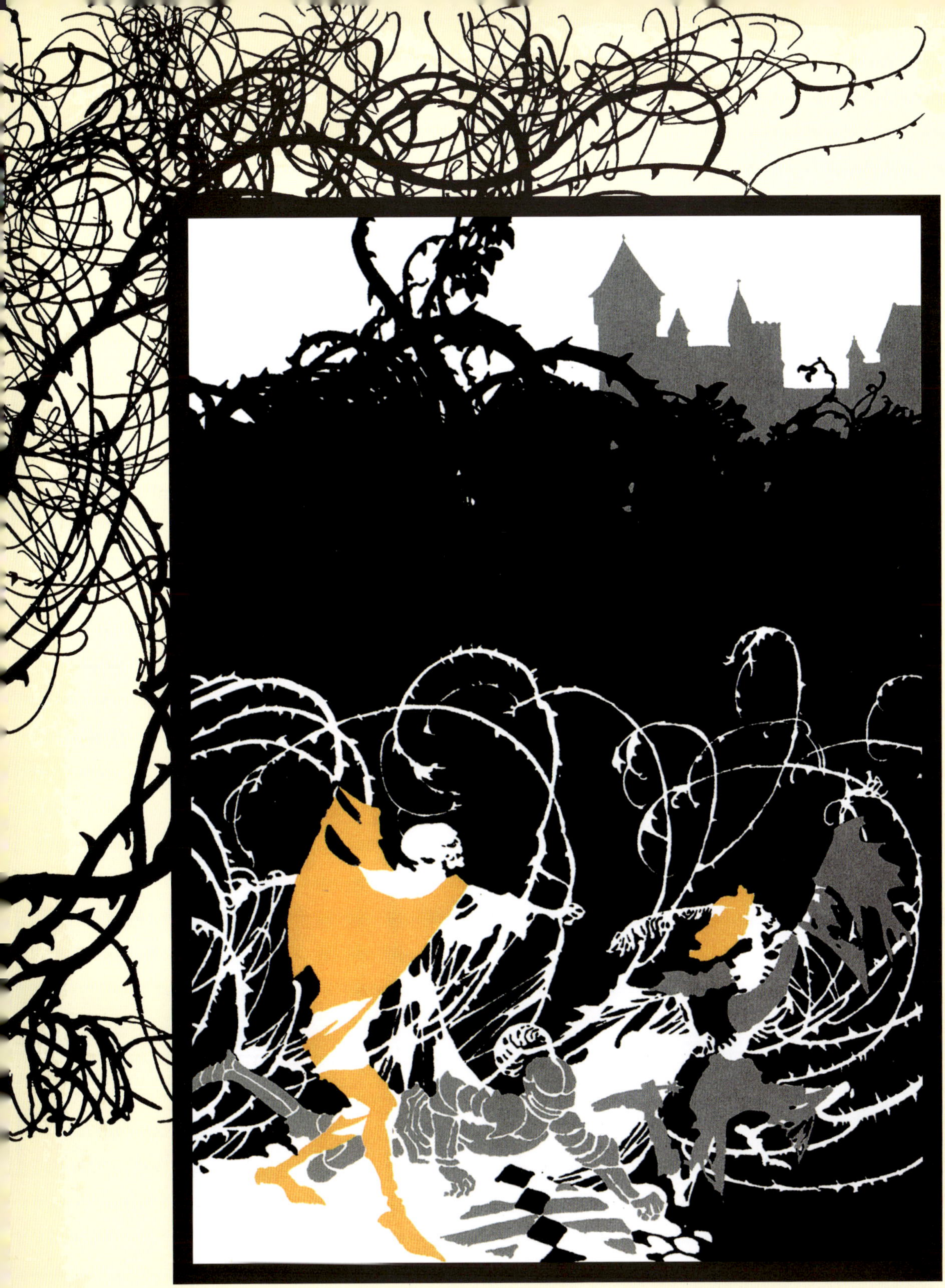